Jake Chapman

The Marriage of Reason & Squalor

FUEL

The Marriage of Reason & Squalor

First published in 2008

Murray & Sorrell FUEL ©
Design & Publishing
33 Fournier Street
London E1 6QE

www.fuel-design.com

All characters in this book are fictitious and resemblance to actual persons, living or dead, is purely coincidental.

A CIP catalogue record for this title is available from the British Library.

Designed by Murray and Sorrell FUEL
Printed in Hong Kong

Distributed by Thames & Hudson / D.A.P.
ISBN: 978-0-9558620-0-7

Chapter One

'A *whole* island?' an appetite for pathos twinkles in Chlamydia's eye like fossilised light flickering in a faraway galaxy.

'Don't fret – I can afford it,' boasts Algernon, mindful of his nebulous other half twisting the winking solitaire on her finger while gazing at him with a magnitude approaching cosmic awe.

'You'd squander your fortunes on me?' Tendered with faux timidity.

'Without a blink,' he declares, nun-the-wiser. 'The prospect of being sensible contradicts my nature – especially now I'm hopelessly in love...'

'*Sensible?*' The word cruelly tinged.

'Oh, but the island of Morass is truly sublime! I swear you'll die when you set eyes upon it...'

'*Sublime?*' The optic twinkle flares and somewhere a distant supernova incinerates.

'For God's sake! It's paradise on Earth!'

Reserved for this very moment, Chlamydia's booby-trapped anatomy belches into Algernon's arms with the violence of an overdue autopsy. 'Oh Doctor Hertz! I care for you with all my heart, lungs, pancreas and spleen!' she bleeds. 'It's the most amazing gift anyone could ever receive! But are you sure? Have you taken leave of your senses? What on Earth made you decide to do such a thing? Are you stark raving mad? When can we visit this paradise island of mine?'

Algernon plants a punctuating kiss on Chlamydia's furrowed stave – lifting her pounding torso from his chest, arms fully extended so as to read the ecstatic expression corrupting her face. In a display of obeisance behoven only to the altruistic mannerisms of those afflicted with faith, his mucous-grey eyeballs well-up and plead into hers with a confession –

'Well that's the thing… The thing is, I'd love to come with you, but I can't. As usual these accursed hands are well and truly tied…'

'Algernon!'

In severance to Chlamydia's barefaced disappointment Algernon sees fit to bait her with a thinly veiled provocation

'– unless you're prepared to delay the wedding?'

'Delay?' she barks. 'Over my dead carcass!' Her expression now contorted with incendiary rage, lengthy black mane flaring across the contours of a warped grimace. Only the most delicate surgical caress can tease static whiskers back behind fleshy lobes while Algernon's free hand locks her masticating trap shut.

'See for yourself – it's perfect – *like you,*' he says clutching at straws, 'I took the liberty of making arrangements. You depart tomorrow morning. Fly alone. Don't ask why…'

'Fly? Tomorrow? Alone? *What about the wedding preparations?*'

'One week in paradise… I beg of you, will you go?'

Feminine curiosity is pregnant enough to warrant a Caesarean, but womanly cunning is sharp enough to induce an efficient acquiescence, and so – 'If you must banish me to the ends of the Earth, I must pack, and so you, dearest Algernon, must leave…'

In the wake of her suitor's courteous retreat, Chlamydia vibrates with utter incredulity. Despite her best efforts to relinquish the conviction that only disastrous outcomes are to be expected of human interaction, this latest bombshell was far too good to be true. Algernon plainly relished startling his fiancée with impulsive projects and plans – proposing marriage before the heat of physical seduction had barely abated. Now, the gift of paradise was alloyed to the standing proposal of marriage, Chlamydia would need superhuman composure to avoid collapsing back into the doubt and despair where Algernon had found her. The prospect of aspiring to the post of *Mrs Consultant Surgeon Algernon Hertz* already caused imperilled nerves to wither and fray, and, despite Algernon's customary encouragements, his betrothed remained earnestly fearful of the social entanglements that would commence once they were legally spliced.

And yet, as the impending marital knot tightened, Chlamydia sensed Algernon's own conviction waver. He withdrew, became remote. While simple affairs and daily responsibilities were often lost in the contours of outlandish plans, improbable schemes were conjured into being as though to obscure the valence of his devotion to Chlamydia. Accordingly, feminine suspicion duly coagulated, and in her heart of hearts she speculated whether the family inheritance had quietly passed away in the night, leaving Algernon bankrupt – hopelessly destitute in the wake of financial ruin – perhaps regretting his knee-deep predicament…

When faith waned, grave questions clawed from the dank mausoleum of insomniac scepticism: *Could poor Algernon uphold his present lifestyle – could he finance the ostentatious wedding he was now committed to deliver, let alone obtain a tropical island wedding gift? Was he overextending the contractual requirements of marital gift-exchange on the false apprehension that his intended expected such material demonstrations of love? Why was he compelled by such desperate gestures?*

Suffice to say, however well the equitable forces of self-denial had implemented restraint inside Chlamydia's brittle psyche, she privately resented the idea of hiving off the evaporating fortunes of a downwardly immobile aristocrat – and in spite of her resolute fondness, she had absolutely no intention of joining the ranks of the nouveau bankrupt. Nonetheless, that evening, tainted with heart-aching uncertainty, tremulous preparations would begin in earnest for the mysterious journey into the sun.

• • • • •

Chlamydia's diaphragm remonstrates with pitiable wheezes, heaving the weathered Samsonite from the shadow beneath the chest of drawers, dragging it across the sheepskin to the queen-size futon holding court in the bedroom. Her holiday wardrobe executes its selection in accordance with the apparition of a sun-drenched tropical island found floating in the turbulent grey matter of Chlamydia's frontal lobe. Beneath the blistering apparition, epidermis breaks out in a phantom sweat, prompting the inclusion of a hypoallergenic sun cream scientifically designed to block delicate occidental pores from the indiscriminate radiation that mercilessly scorches the drought-ridden and sun-seeker alike. Distracted by the mindless task of packing possessions, Chlamydia's innermost thoughts soon belong to her fiancé – woeful that he must stay behind, sorrowful that he saw fit to send her alone and mournful that the Hippocratic oath obliged Consultant Hertz to the procession of patients queuing for the attention of his miraculous… scalpel.

Chlamydia arises sharply from customary nightmares, shallow slumber dissolved in meek anticipation of the forthcoming journey into the prenuptial abyss. Algernon, mysteriously agitated, anticipates dawn to deliver Chlamydia and her passport to the airport, and there, the voyager settles into the luxury of upper class, it being competently manned by a crew of tanned nomads whose sexual turbulence is held in check by the smooth-talking automatic pilot. The flight is pleasant and service congenial. Chlamydia clears customs and is duly escorted by security forces to a reputable western hotel where she remains holed up until the next morning. As dawn cracks its golden yolk, Chlamydia is snatched from her bed, taken by limo and hooded en route so as to avoid direct eye contact with blossoming decapitations planted on the streets by nocturnal death squads. At a secluded seaside quay she is transferred to a pretty naval vessel primed to navigate to the intermediary island resort of St Just. The voyage was pleasant – if a little choppy.

St Just is a far cry from London's defoliated sprawl. Lush tropical vegetation verges upon grinning Ivorine beaches, where festive souls gorge upon the solar tide such that they appear intoxicated by the sun's overwhelming charity. At the scurf edge of the island, nestled in Hotel Hachichin's high-class penthouse, the deepest cyanide-blue panorama robs Chlamydia's breath while the skeletal bellboy wrestles to unmanacle the bulging Samsonite. Hotel Hachichins's effusive decor oozes with buffered ambiance. The room hums with an inventive play of colours and a fearless juxtaposition of disparate elements – rattan and wicker furnishings bolstered by ample cushions, a cerise onyx bathroom, a generous four-poster bed swathed in a swollen snow-white duvet combining feather of bald eagle with feather of dove. If Algernon's promissory idyll is anything near as charming as St Just, Chlamydia will find no hesitation in snatching it up as the most perfect offering an ostensibly solvent man can give a dependably soluble woman.

So Algernon's absence was redeeming itself – steadily evolving up the cerated shores of Chlamydia's indubitable suspicion. Even so, an archaic inner doubt stirred its melodious ellipsis in a light-starved Scorpion mind – egoic pessimism revolving around saturnine cynicism – reactive forces stealing any semblance of optimism from escape velocity, until any vague trace of human positivity succumbed to the gravitational core of deep infernal loathing. In other words, *solar system Chlamydia* was a dependably cold, dark, hostile backwater of the universe, host to ill-fated entities, collectively doomed to a cataclysmic fate... Bolstered by ample cushions plus pockets of hot air trapped between eagle feather and flapping dove, Algernon swoops into mind with an untimely olive branch – reminding Chlamydia that an island's future lies in her gentle palm – and her feminine verdict, positive, negative or ambivalent is absolutely absolute.

In truth, Algernon's honorific sentiments existed in idea only. Bombing along en route to the airport in his Porsche 911 – the *Ground Zero* of all sports cars – Chlamydia felt obliged to block her ears when Algernon's motorway tête-à-tête had the temerity to veer and swerve as he made uncurbed hints to ensure his passenger was made acutely aware of the economic and personal sacrifices undertaken in the name of her flattery...

Hence, plummeting from the vertiginous heights of turbulent slumber down to sober sea level, Chlamydia boards a boat for the second leg of her epic voyage the very next morning. The boat is pretty. Made of wood and adorned with the name *The Amorous Peacock*. It has plump boat buoys strung around the hull that groan in the swell like camp guards barbed wired around the turret of a Russian T34. As the pretty wooden vessel sets sail, sharp palpitations begin to plague her pretty chest, and she blames their nagging insistence upon an unforeseen fear of the immensity of the ocean, cemented to the imminent encounter with unimaginable paradise. Thus, she yearns for Algernon to share the moment at which his magnificent gift will congeal from apparition into material being. So Chlamydia's dread lurches with the sea

– and to add insult to injury, naked irritation is added to personal discomfort when the passenger discovers the yacht is owned and skippered by a surgical client of Algernon's – Captain Oceanic – looming on the poop deck, overflowing with such a vile miasma that the imaginary rasp of a bilge pump accompanies the guttural drain of each and every soiled word spluttered from his foul plug hole…

'Doktor Hertz is ze numero-uno surgical genius! Ze patron saint of ze scalpel, ja? He save my life from death! Vas a miracle! Truly, I vas on ze vay out! Sick like ze gipsy, ja? Vas ready to swim vith ze fishes – but nein danke! No way José! Doktor Hertz rescue my sorry arse from ze cancer mass grave! Ja! For real!' He prods his elastic graft indelicately, the shrink-fit hide grinning taught over a death's-head skull. *'Ze tumour vas ze size of ze human fist! I have it – pickle in ze jar, ja? In ze cabin below… You vant to see my pickle tumour in ze jar in ze cabin below, ja? No? Vell, hell's-bells! I can tell you he save my life – I'm zo chilled unt zo happy I shit my own guts through my own arsehole unt skip – tra, la, la – like ze little child skips in ze long grass, ja?'*

Chlamydia nods in serene enjoyment of the apparition of the fool skipping with a length of his own bloody gristle. Undeterred, Oceanic claws inside his coat, flips open a wallet like an undercover vice cop.

'My wife! You dig chinky-chonks? Ja?' An inscrutable girly-boy squints laminated behind a grimy plastic window. *'Zo! Ze Doktor Hertz save your life too? It's maybe how you meet ze gut Doktor, Ja? Zo he help you – unt zo you help him, ja? – With ze little superdanke downstairs? Ja?'* Oceanic leers, as though his declaration of debt to Hertz entitles an unimpeachable feeling of pride, as though his surgical disfigurement would provoke envy in the malignant jealousy of others… *'Zo I think you must be lucky for ze special touch of Consultant Hertz too, Ja?'* He leers, unrequited.

'Yes I'm lucky,' stresses Chlamydia in his insinuating wake, *'but in an entirely different way.'* Facial dimples pitted in glowing hot cheeks, carbon black hair flaming furious in the salt breeze.

'Maybe our friend Monsieur Algernon is ze fortunate one, ja?' Maritime eyeballs swell beyond the threshold of courteous observation.

'We're *all* fortunate and we're *all* very lucky,' Chlamydia tenders a diplomatic tongue – fleshy glossa well accustomed to repelling unwanted attention, proving the aphorism that *gentlemen prefer blondes* was undoubtedly a falsehood in her particular case history. That the nest of crow-black hair crowning her head was patently irresistible for unsolicited admirers was as certain as the pull of gravity upon mortal objects. In the sign of her lunar ascendancy Chlamydia had been blessed with a paranormal facility for dealing with the impolite curiosity of others – and as she engaged her power, Captain Oceanic was so moved as to do nothing more than cast his seaman's eye while pursed leather lips warned his charge they were close to their destination, that the island would soon crystallise into view on the starboard bow.

On the starboard bow Chlamydia is seasick with anticipation, eyeballs swirling in a magnetic spin, keen to witness the first signs of landmass emerging on the skyline. Above the lick of jagged waves the vacant horizon betrays Morass, a grey amorphous volcanic form beginning to refract tropical colour as the wooden vessel carves closer in…

'All ze engines dead slow… like ze Slav! Ja?'

Chlamydia is lowered like thickened spittle into body-temperate shallows, knee-high in frothing waves. Oceanic lands her Samsonite while Chlamydia flounders in the breakers, a dripping organic vesicle defibrillated from the ocean – a lonely bundle of miniature seas held watertight inside a semi-permeable skin of bilayer membranes hung up on a calcium phosphate armature – even brittle bone formed from ancient sea salt precipitated from the ocean. Sheer relief sees fit to wave adieu to Algernon's medical miracle leering on the aft deck.

'I vill return in ze few days – if ze weather-bitch permits,' yells the rabid skipper above the clenched roar of the diesel engine. *'Mark my vords – you never vant to leave zis place... unt ven you do, you vish you never came, ja!'*

Chlamydia's sea legs stagger on shifting sand, sparing a moment for the waves lapping to and fro between her ears to calm their balance. In her mind's eye Morass was presumed to be one of those small generic desert islands, the kind seen in adverts, postcards, magazines, junk mail, airport posters, brochures, souvenir plates, holiday snaps, cartoons, films and atomic eruptions. But Morass far surpasses the off-the-peg prejudices she dragged with her, and, casting a wide-eyed glance around, she is interrupted by an abandoned conch washed up next to her own sunken footprints. As the breeze teases the conch's hole, an eerie howl pleads for an audience with Chlamydia's own shell-like. Ambivalence pays it a cursory glance. To stand in the magisterial presence of the immense ocean and slavishly harbour the mimetic whisperings of the conch is as farcical as pressing a dry rock to the ear to listen for the silence of the desert. And, as if by clockwork, the sound of scorched rocks begins ticking in the sun, one by one, tick... tock... the stones crack into pieces plus the pieces begin ticking plus cracking in turn. Chlamydia collapses to brittle knees and swipes the conch to hurl it into the sea. As the nagging hole drowns, the ripples of its sudden immersion are magnified a billion times, until an infinitely exaggerated wall of filthy water churns up the island until paradise resembles a burst sewer bobbing with tides of excrement – even the sea vomits its own species to bloat and explode on high ground under the murderous scrutiny of the sun. Chlamydia sees how the populations of sea and land are destined to a merciless exchange. She sees how the evil world is set against itself – earth, wind, fire and water – water against land, land against water – a pernicious marriage formed of elemental jeopardy. Chlamydia smiles. Only Nature's tendential violence gives rise to that opportune cheerfulness permitted by the noble precipitations of human struggle – *charity born of tragedy*. A mild shiver wriggles down Chlamydia's back as the oversized worm of human piety gorges on her spinal cord. She summons up thought of the burgeoning charity of her fiancé and her own passive financial disposition – struggles to shake off the nagging confession that her own happiness is a willing friend to wretchedness. To curb the tugging threads of masochism, Chlamydia turns to the clutch of ornamental secretions contributing a temporary respite from the involuntary momentum of her life – to home comforts like her house, her job, her car and cuddly pussycat Mr Lollipop – but most of all – she thinks of her forthcoming marriage *and like clockwork, cheerfulness slips like silt through fingers. She buckles in the imagination of destiny eagerly creeping to meet her in the form of maggots and the primitive guts of worms – gasps out loud in the realisation that time is little more than a sanitised abstraction of creeping ruination – groans out loud in the realisation that her mind is being stalked by the relentless nibble of the maggot jaws ticking away in the shadows of the grasping hands of the human clock... tick... tock...*

• • • • •

When Oceanic's vessel sinks out of sight, Chlamydia's sanity duly drowns. Leaden eyes tilt upwards into the mantle of a heavy brow, outsized hands reaching out to their centrifugal limit. She twists anticlockwise until fragments of semi-subconscious energy liberated by the annihilation of matter dislodge, flinging free to address Morass out loud –

'Is this to be my destiny? Is my fondness for Algernon to be tested by the gift of paradise? Oh how to confuse feelings! The foolish man has placed paradise between us – how can I be sure I am to marry Algernon and not Morass!'

Poor shambolic Chlamydia first committed her tumultuous inner-self to investigative therapy on the advice of friends and family who found her social interactions impractical. More than anything in the world she wished to be rid of the disease that freely vented through her mouth – implored her psyche to desist its perpetual hiss and pleaded her ears not to howl with the tinnitus reverb of mental isolation. On seeking the advice of a quack – was duly referred to a shrink.

Doctor Heimlich was an entity to be reckoned with – cartilaginous and implacable. The sum of her features hovered in holographic composition about her head, and if social pleasantries ever surfaced they came to fruition as though the owner was wracked with colic – hence smiles, if indeed they were smiles, were governed by the internal agony that makes an infant's grimace indefinite. Not that she was rude, just severe. Chlamydia took severity as a measure of brevity – took a shine to the good doctor – found comfort in honest harshness. Heimlich made assurances that her brand of neo-brutalist psychotherapy would substantially alleviate the burden of Chlamydia's insanity on account of its wisdom being gleaned from the empirical observation of symptoms collated over many, many, years – each mental corruption snowballing into an inventory of manifold sickness to which Chlamydia's own idiosyncrasies might first find a diagnostic home and then be coaxed to settle down.

Session one erupted with the promise of promises –

'I can't promise any miracle cure,' pledged the eminent therapist,

'but with honest hard work I swear we'll forge positive inroads into your mental confusion…'

Hence, any ludicrous dream of cure, miracle or not, gave way to the euphemistic promise of lasting employment – a candid enough disclosure on the part of Ms Heimlich – who celebrated the opinion that neurosis was an occupational hazard of the modern age. So she frothed – *'Social obesity, reward indifference, and a workshy labour force are the unequivocal causes of today's sick-minded evil. Only hard work and earnest sublimation can produce healthy subjects with healthy ontologies, and when personal rectitude falls by the wayside, the sick must be dealt with in accordance to the rules of an industrial dispute. Only then can the infirm be returned to good working order…'* Cast iron conditions of engagement as follows: *'Time is money. Flunk an appointment – pay double. Flunk consecutive sessions – you're fired!'* she yelled. *'Charity breeds emotional dependence. I shall not indulge your psychological bullshit without prompt and proper payment. If the tenth-floor window ledge beckons and I'm required to talk you down by way of the stairs, you'll be charged triple time for the inconvenience. If you jump – I'll invoice your next of kin. Inconclusive overdose, slashing of wrists, hanging or any such self-harming bullshit necessitating my presence (postmortem or ex nihil), will incur severe and punitive costs – if you waste my time I'll make you pay through the nose. Accept my conditions or accept the door – you will not confuse me with Mummy or Daddy. I say again – you will not fuck me over to get back at them.* All rates exclusive of VAT. There is no guaranteed cure and customers reap whatever psychological rewards they sow regardless of the claimed effectivity of treatments on offer. Terms and conditions apply, details available on written request.'

'And direct debit?' says Chlamydia with a daughter's unrequited love twinkling in her eye.

' – Are you nuts? CASH IS KING…'

Chlamydia promised to undertake Heimlich's offer of hard labour with unerring conviction and was promptly enrolled into group therapy. Her spirit was buoyant. Being mad amongst lunatics would make her own disturbances seem mundane when compared to the damaged specimens she might encounter, and to her pleasant surprise, was received into the bosom of the group's collective psychosis with unwarranted enthusiasm. Heimlich ran the sessions – the damaged souls cowering in turn like delicate insects performing an inverse Mexican wave as the shrink's cast-iron finger haunted the circle of shame to settle upon her prey with an unspoken demand that they shed light on the darker aspects of their ill-being. Ritually disrobed and reduced to an excoriated mess of naked nerves – wise words were prompted from the supplicant's unstable colleagues, who, gushing like bedwetting infants desperate to impress their paternal overseer, poured with Pavlovian common sense. If at any time the ensuing psycho-babble dared to dry out midstream, Heimlich would goad beyond the zoo of humble stutters and tics, making reference to intimate details of sex crimes, violence and other confidential matters, by way of subauditional suggestion, whispers and flashes of the all-seeing eye. Chlamydia, for her sins, took to group therapy like a duck to water, shrugged off the therapeutic mind games like water from a duck's back. Before she knew it, a confessional stream cascaded from every entry and exit port on her beset corpus until her pathologised factory was riddled with herniated lacerations, buboes and weeping wounds, on which the elated shrink set to work, tapping the crazed discharge – much the same as an opium grower might scrape a leaking poppy bulb. Despite her notoriously stringent work ethic, Chlamydia observed that quite often her mentor became visibly feverish – much the same as a religious prophet is made delirious by the promissory apparition of God, Heimlich was at times ecstatic, fevered by the manifestation of psychic sickness deluging from her beaming patients. Hence Chlamydia learned to be symptomatically prolific, and while Heimlich was tenacious like a dog with a bone, Chlamydia was Pavlov's puppy, digging and digging, yapping and barking and howling plus scratching away at the back door of sanity. She learned to indulge capricious memories of the past and regard the odd bout of acute melancholia as an essential component to the therapist's archaeology of blame. In short, the trick was to remain unwell *in the past* in order to be positively well adjusted *in the future*.

And so, brushing sand from the dunes caught in the digression of inner-thought, giddiness applies its attention inland. Curiosity narrows along a small road scything into the latticed mesh of variegated trees, ferns, and palms. Above the withering passage a bleached-white house balances in the sky like a piece of delicate origami, crowning the grey volcano with a presiding view over the lurid intensity of the jungle below. The house winks in the sun with arrogant crystalline surfaces overlapping geometric planes, its *moderne* form and function an indelible sign of occidental algorithms. Beneath the ostentatious structure the naive green tangle sways idiotically in the breeze – *Mother Nature's* fiscal potential awaiting liberation from the chaos... *fiscal potential* – perhaps this was the key to Algernon's anthropomorphic ambition for Morass – the subtle force motivating his generosity... Chlamydia slaps her hand fully in the face.

'Vile pessimism,' she spits.

'I'm sorry.'

'You should be.'

'*We are...*'

An ox cart materialises in the distance, crawls on all fours from the jungle, enduring a lifetime to draw alongside before the native driver slides from wooden seat to hot sand. He approaches brandishing a joyful smile while presenting a laminated card with Chlamydia's very own surname in bold Helvetica. He has a sooty face that sweeps long and equine like an ass, and a nibbled straw hat. He wears a moth-eaten string vest and cotton-picking slacks shy of solid ankles and raw feet.

'*Miss Love?*'

Good manners offers its hand to be met by a weathered palm, resonant with toil, gripping and shaking her own dainty paw with potlatch enthusiasm.

'Yes that's me – I'm *Miss Love!* Chlamydia Love… Lydia for short. I had absolutely no idea I was to be met in such a romantic manner – how exciting! I've been sent quite blindfolded by my fiancé – it's a magical mystery tour! – We're thinking of buying the island. I was beginning to wonder what to do next – feeling a little marooned. Are you my main-Man Friday?'

'I am Isaiah…'

Grimacing without reserve, native Isaiah easily manhandles the bulging Samsonite into the rear of the cart and heaves Chlamydia up onto the seat ditto. Next to Chlamydia's pale thigh a paperback declaring the oddest of titles – *Explaining Christians to Dinosaurs*. The driver snatches it from sight, applies a lacerating whip to a bovine groan and the cart is coaxed into excruciating motion.

In Chlamydia's fertile mind, the vehicle travels backwards in time into a past age where progress stands still. Thus for ever, Isaiah and Chlamydia lurch along lanes shaded by giant palms until eventually lumbering into the secluded grounds of Hotel Krauss, a colonial plantation set into a leaf-green cavern carved into solid forest. Serenity bleaches the hotel grounds with the purest oxygen that only comas are made of. Fruit trees suffuse fecund smells into the heavy saccharine air, muscular branches drape with ripe flesh ready to drip to the ground where rotten seeds await distribution through the manifold guts of foraging beasts.

Krauss's central hub is single storey, orbited by a loose cosmology of small chalets tangled into the surrounding vegetation. Roofs are thatched and stone walls whitewashed. *Chlamydia Love* enrols on the register and is summarily escorted to her quarters by the effusive duty manager (whose face is a coagulant smear stippled with a spirited bloom of angry crimson vessels shimmering around the base of a single eye-stalk, teased into extension by the lurid brass keyholes which are his duty to attend). He is ladled into a double-breasted suit over shirt and tie, topped off with a pillbox hat jauntily tilted towards the authority that imposes such humiliating attire.

'*Congratulations for choosing to experience the opulence of the colonial world...*' he recites. '*Welcome to the unhurried rhythm of Hotel Krauss – tropical oasis for connoisseurs of fine living and good health. You will no doubt notice that the Hotel has been stunningly restored from its late-nineteenth-century omission – and wherever you cast your inscrutable eye you will witness the finest of rich fabrics and meticulous furnishings that form the backdrop to a worldwide anthology of fine art and finest antiques. Our elegant volcanic spa is inspired by the meditative cultures of the ancient Orient – in fact, we boast over seventy-three personally tailored cures for whatever ailment may have delivered you to our healing shores, whether it's the big C, ME, HIV – or if you're just plain old seasonally maladjusted. Our indigenous health technicians provide the full gamut of hands-on treatment – for purists or tourists. Swedish or Shiatsu, reflexology, ultrasonics, hydro and abreactives, new-age Ayurvedics, aromatherapy, Vichy shower or Pompeian ash bath, Tsunami whirlwind, Ecuadorian mud bath, primal algae bath, yoga, Pilates, indoor and outdoor resistance pools, gym and whirlpool, cosmetic, facial, colonic or zyklonic, dilapitory, bio-cleansing or life stress recovery. If these foolproof pampers fail to get your blood boiling we can even arrange dolphin therapy – the sea's the limit!'*

'And the telephone?' Said with Algernon in mind.

'Tut-tut! Mais non, non, non! Pas de telephones on Morass at all – anywhere. No cell coverage at all! Strictly off limits! Verboten! Communiqué severance is de rigueur! The dependable Captain Oceanic takes all correspondence to the mainland office to be passed on from there – you can try popping a message in a bottle if you like, post it in the sea – it's as reliable as the Captain!'

'Thank you,' says Chlamydia. 'You've been… painstaking.'

The gelatinous *suck* of a bulging eyeball relaxed from female flesh follows on the Cuban heels of the duty manager's exit. Nonetheless, she is thankful for the sumptuous colonial bungalow, it being eerily deceptive in scale, yet light, airy and unnaturally cool. The suite is steeped in the luxury of plush comforters, Frette linen, Hermès bath amenities, an elegantly draped canopy bed with plump goose down pillows and handmade exotic fabrics woven together from all around the whole.wide.world.com. Charm and authenticity congeal in the form of antique trunks, endangered species salvaged from extinction in the form of hunting trophies, original indigenous handicraft, handmade potato-print wallpaper, period stained ornaments and a detonation of fresh flowers breathtaking enough to invoke atypical pollinosis in healthy lungs. A wrought-iron coffee table also presents an overbearing stock of reading material with titles worthy of a cure for insomnia, plus lithe sliding doors divide inside from outside where a modest maple terrace is well hung with tangles of poinsettias, lewd orchids and industrious insect reproductive organs hovering in tremulous attendance. It is all so uncannily sympathetic to her personal taste that Chlamydia wonders why her fiancé failed to elect the Krauss for their forthcoming honeymoon…

Out of the hydrocyanic blue Algernon's absence avalanches.
Chlamydia's heart feels vagrant. So alone, morose…
'Buck up bu-tt-er-cup!' she quivers.
'*Don't be soft…*' she barks.

• • • • •

Once more unpacked, another outfit selected, Chlamydia's weary soul presents itself to the hotel's spa lodge where the resident triage nurse takes pity and implements an urgent Thalassotherapy bath with underwater jets designed to invigorate her patently fading aura and revitalise her fuzzy-wuzzy metabolism. A gentle stream of tepid herbal infused oils are dripped drip by drop onto Chlamydia's pineal gland to distillate the sleepy inner-eye into activity. She settles under duress to the pleasant torture, maddened by the endless crescendo of easy listening weaving in and out of tangled dolphin/seagull lament. As vitality slips away to within a millimetre of its miserable existence, Chlamydia watches her own self languish in the gritty saline shallows from the fishy-eyed perspective of an out-of-body experience bobbing on the sunken ceiling above. From up here vertigo is sincerely anxious about the hapless state of the listless husk wallowing down below. The leaden drip-drip-drip-drip-drip-drip-drip-drip-drip echoes in the dark dank cavern of her imagination where rancour resides in exile, plus, the evil pantomime cast of Chlamydia's recurrent nightmares are soon disturbed from temporary slumber: *the illustrious maggots and dreaded worms who are, at this very instant, as we speak, blindly inching their way through their own generational continuum towards a future reconciliation with Chlamydia's livid meat*. Locked inside such degrading thoughts, morbid self-indulgence summons an impression of the rotten morsels and titbits being feasted upon by her primordial ancestors right now, at this very instant, as we speak – Chlamydia forgiven for imagining hungry maggot jaws nibbling on her own spoiled flesh, even forgiven for conjuring into mind a schematic maggot family tree where she visualises herself impaled on the loftiest branch. A mortified mouth pronounces an elastic apology around the shouting fountain of rainbow-coloured bile belching all over the panic-stricken nurse who fumbles to administer the tourniquet, syringe and adrenaline…

• • • • •

Chlamydia reels from the spa, holistically rejuvenated and emotionally replete, fighting fit, fit as a fiddle, tiptop, top-notch… all in all, able and willing to undertake an island exploration with calm repose. From the comfort of the recovery position she is able to fathom that the pretty island of Morass is nucleated by a volcanic peak with an accessible slope on one side and a near-vertical escarpment on the other. She appreciates the obscene protuberance might offer a perfect aspect to survey her prenuptial domain, and in weighing up the looming mass, elects to wait until early evening when the spiteful sun is less hostile. To pass the time of day she chooses to render Morass in watercolour or gauche – *souvenirs for Algernon perhaps*.

With artist's palette, paint and sketch pad quashed under sweltering armpit the untimely watercolourist takes shade under a kindly palm found stranded on the poisonous beach. At first, sheer unadulterated beauty stays the artist's hand, during which time the faintest flicker of a damaged fluorescent tube commences to blink inside a derelict head before a whiplash lunge forward with ECG conviction puts hand into motion. Pencil lead is brought to bear upon paper to hatch a feathered outline, the fuzzy graphite conjuring up magic shapes and divining the suggestible volumes of sea, sand, jungle, the dominating volcano, the crowning house and the over-arching sun. The artist's head nods in silent conversation with hand as pencil is cast aside in favour of sable brush dipped in water and twisted on colour block to tint sea blue, then yellow for the sand, green for jungle, black for the volcano, white for the house and orange for the sun. She switches to medium flat hoghair, dipping and dragging cobalt sea to wash into sulphate sky. She drains the brush in clear seawater to burst a deep cerulean bloom. Like this the humming proboscis sets to work tickling petals of colour and light one after another until the simmering sand is littered with the steaming fruits of Chlamydia's artistic toil – each study saturated with the indelible history of its struggle; dappled light striated by refracted haze, silhouettes and washes tantalised between illusion and chaos – each stroke precariously balanced on the edge of emotional transition while betraying the disquieting morphologies that haunt the artist's inner-self…

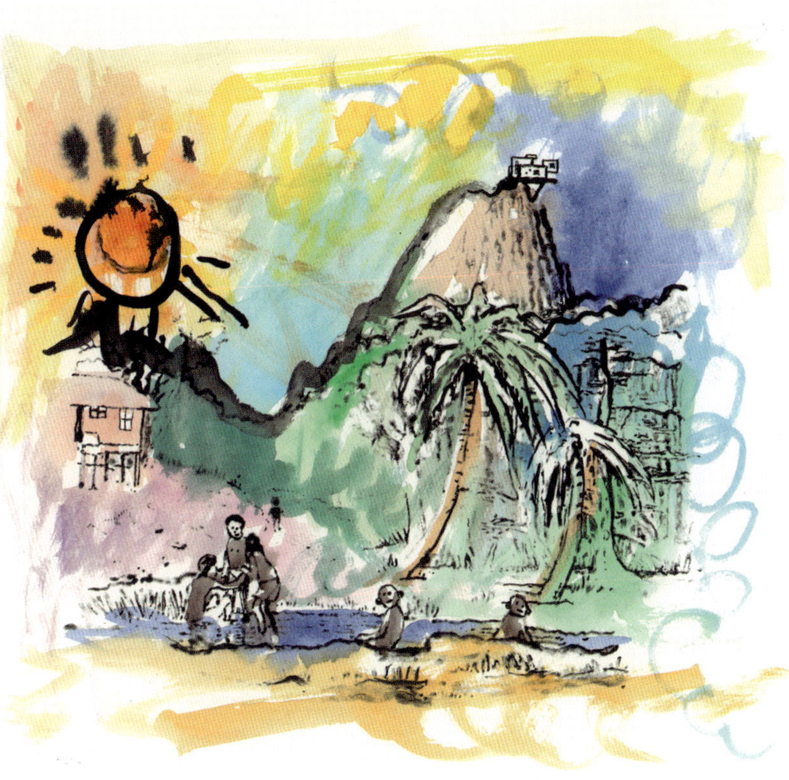

Visions of Morass

Part I

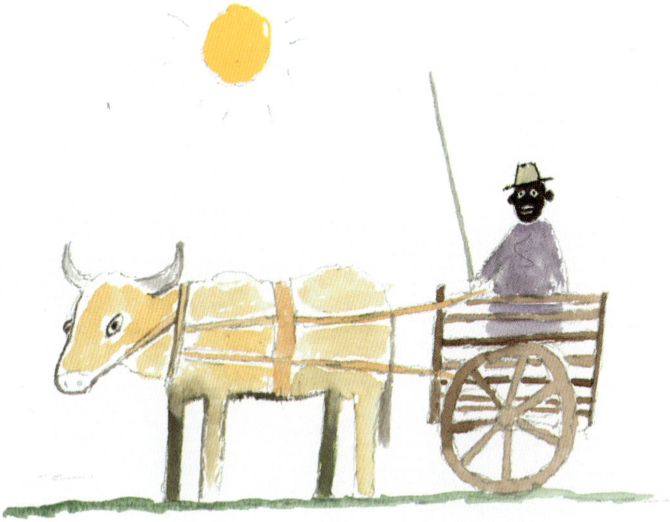

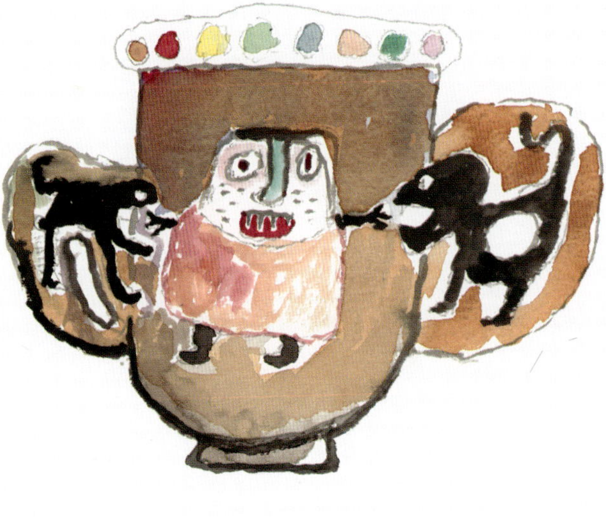

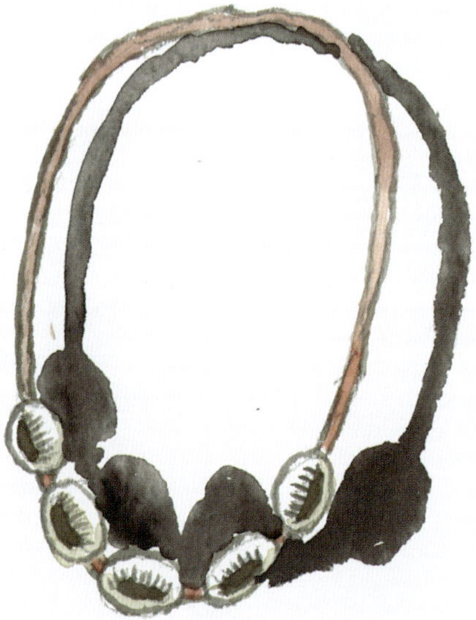

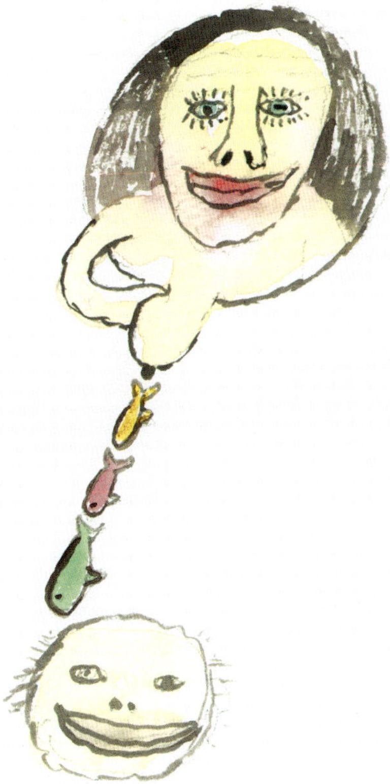

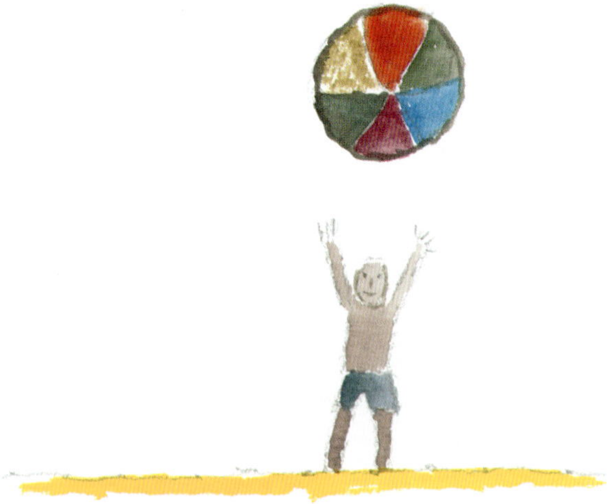

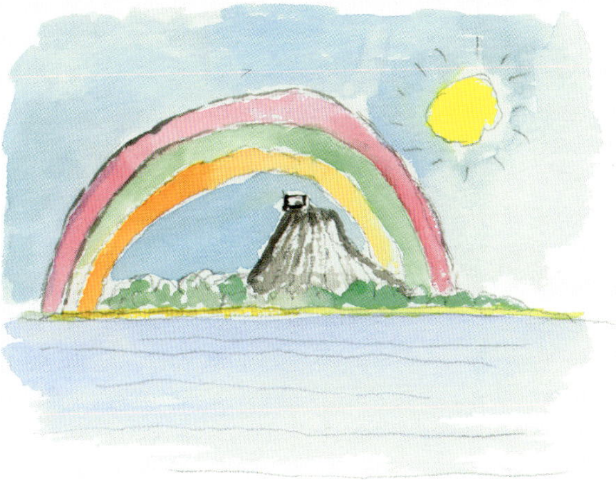

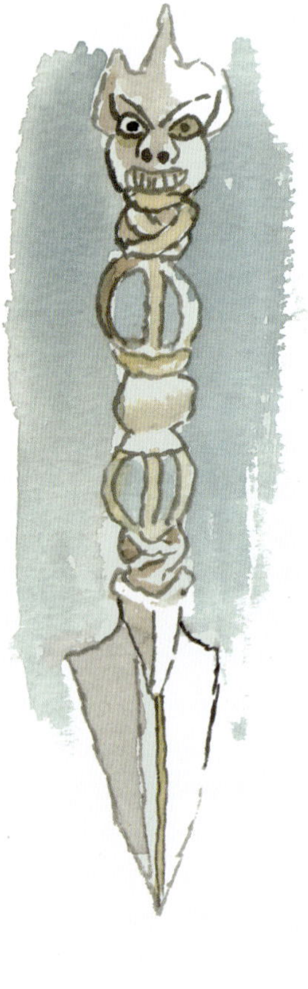

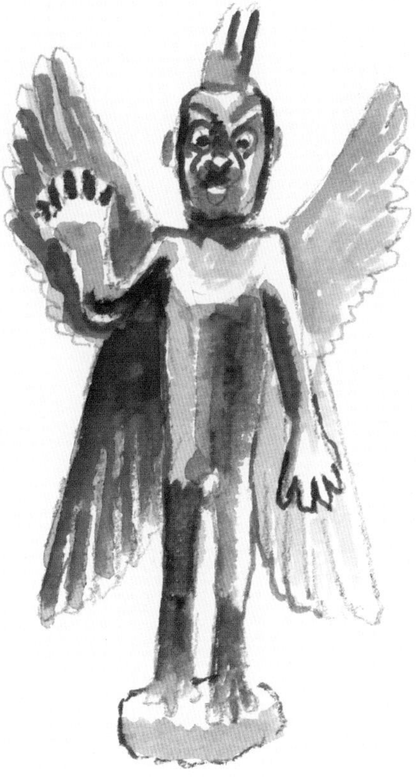

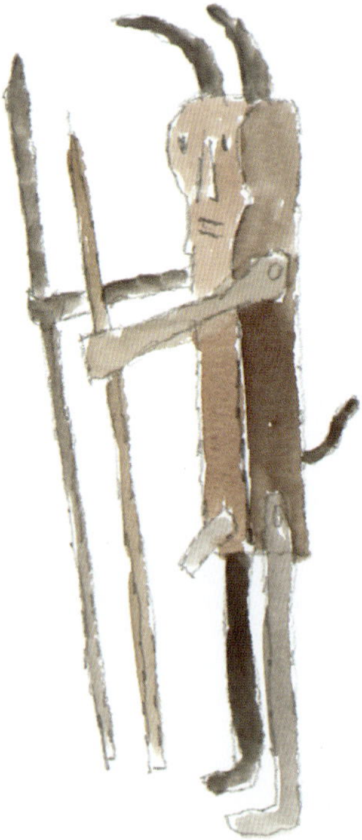

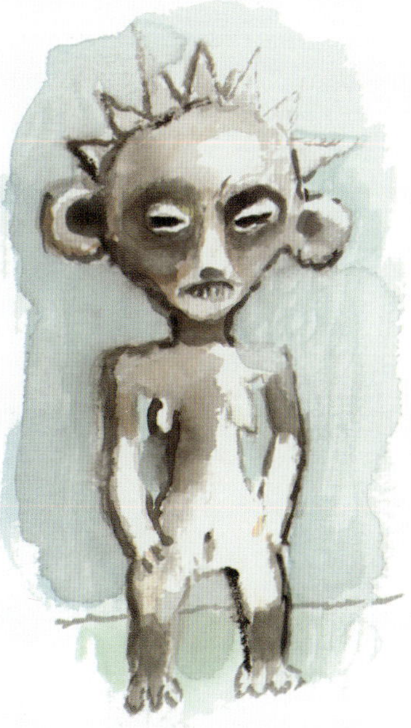

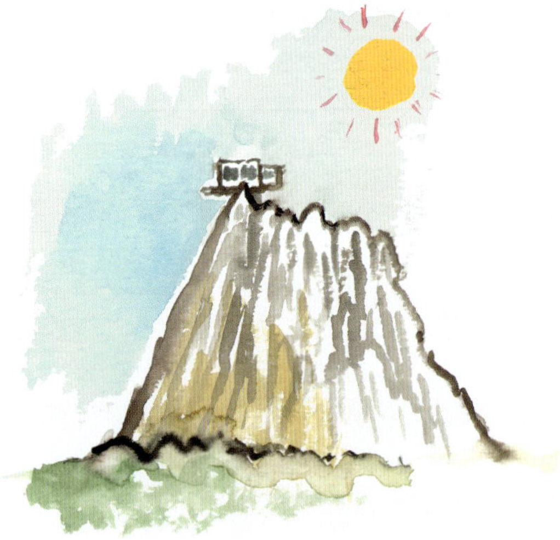

Chlamydia's curiosity commences its ascent as the sun's incendiary wrath softens its daily punishment upon the few subjects toiling below its rage – but not before good sense sees fit to urge a film of sunblock upon sallow skin. Paranormal compounds applied in a gentle anticlockwise motion to congest the epidermis, refusing entry to photon particles, plus active in stemming the spread of abnormal pigmentation before it forms ugly rogue maps across the unchartered membrane. At the foot of the volcano Chlamydia approaches a small wooden lean-to and recognises the forlorn ox shackled outside. The pitiful creature bellows out loud, alerting Isaiah to appear in the rustic windowpane to wave as if he is on fire. Chlamydia returns the gesture, then continues on her way. The rise is steep but the narrow track zigzags politely to accommodate the fierce gradient. Onwards and upwards she rises, closer and closer to the looming sun. The boiling volcano draws pearls of sweat that pause long enough to evaporate a little and cool the raging pellicle before cascading erratically around the contortions of face, neck, breast and thoracic cavity. Soon enough the climber is filled with doom, found scaling an impossible beanstalk only for a gigantic thirst waiting at the top to choke her.

'Of course you've forgotten water!' she croaks.

'Typical!

'Never mind! – we can always ask at the house,' she says all cheery-pops.

'– Well let's hope there's someone in – for your sake!'

• • • • •

Atop the vile volcanic rim, Chlamydia's eyestalks soak up the just rewards withering in the deteriorating beams of the sun; the charcoal shoreline marking the ruptured tear between land and water, the island's cerated bite bleeding into the sea;

irrigating the polished molar roots that recede beyond the hydraulic fault line where land is a dissolving clot. In the dusk, the luminous water edge ebbs away from the forest line – the jungle tamed by a poisonous band of golden-grey pumice sand strangling paradise. Below, the hotel complex nestles against the solidified volcanic buttress, and straining up into the dwindling sunlight yet laden by the overwhelming force of gravity, the upper canopy clenches into a defeated porous tangle of phototropic matter – the jungle seething with reflex organisms held in mutual competition for sustenance or annihilation. Everywhere, death stalks life – or its premature dismemberment – entropy snatching unkindly at the double-edged gift of life. Even in the dusk, nature flares up as a lurid scorch mark, a peculiar magnification of intense energy on a stochastic conduit, localised to the point of combustion; a relentless emerald incandescence, where leaves puff, mushrooms cloud, bushes bustle – billowing with bright green chlorophyll released in a slow-motion celluloid explosion, smouldering with an inferno of energy held hostage before being sporadically disgorged into the atmosphere, as the protuberant vent once belched superheated magma in its original moment of thermospasmic climax, the violent event of baby-Morass's vertical birth.

Rising up from the jungle's embryonic eruption, Chlamydia's shell-like eavesdrops a clearing withdraw around the shrill protest of a lone bird found struggling against asphyxiation – the shriek of death demanding the forest holds its breath, a sympathetic hush heeding the sound of feathers flapping against criminal incisors clamped on splintering bone. When sound gushes back into the vacuum, the memorial hush shatters into a cacophonous howl erupting all around in sudden licentious disdain. Nature respires once again in all its manifest glory. To this trivial event Chlamydia's crow's feet crack a wry smile. Her flesh well appreciates that organic vitality is matter-energy tortured – consciousness, a dyspeptic ulcer vigilantly cradling the substance of its own necrotic irritation – as though only pain sufficiently acquaints being with the realm of the apperceptual. The sheer audacity of life is its suicidal tendency, flaring up as a temporary incandescence, a deviation of energy – a solar reciprocity and abstraction of incendiary stimulation. Sovereign matter is indolent of the compositions of human anxiety, its petty cultivations – the religious accretions and the immodest perspectives of those captured in the merciless reflection of their own cosmo-theological insignificance. And why oh why did vile *Mother Nature* ever conceive *Homo sapiens* – only to handicap the Earth's *self-appointed* species with an injured solipsism? Teasing each and every human voyager as they teeter, orphaned, at the incomprehensible brink of finitude?...boo, hoo, who.

From the dank sanctuary of the convent latrines, scratched into ancient brick, the words of the heretic Martin Luther return to Chlamydia, strained through gritted teeth like filthy plankton:

'I am the turd that is ready
and the world is the wide open anus.'

Chlamydia's sanity is hanging on by a threadworm.
Nature is a circus and humanity its clown.
Thank God for Nature and Mankind for tragedy...

Shooing her morbidly infected thoughts away with a surprise eruption of laughter, tossing raven hair as though a flock of birds had taken fright, Chlamydia's toes tip closer to the volcano's edge, black bile vacillating loudly around the mad cow's arterial transport system. Suffice to say, rudimentary ox carts provide the only form of wheel-driven transfer on the island, and from this superior vantage point, Chlamydia's squint can just about witness their agonising weave along the network of sandy roads latticing the earth like razor welts in the dwindling light. Where are they going? Where have they come from? *Why are we here?*

Peculiar as a polished tooth in an irritated gum, the arrogant white house is set into the volcano rim and is, close up, evidently larger than binoculars could glean from ground level. It perches over and cuts into rock – a cantilevered structure hung indolently over the precipice, harsh geometric forms cradled by volcanic rock, the ancient spur now truncated by a high-modernist temple oozing with stratified taste. Steel storm shutters are pinned back to expose floor-to-ceiling glazing, dormant lava lamps and petrified lost-wax bronzes situated as sentinel beings presiding over the pernicious mangle below. The balcony deck is broad, ornamented with Ivorine garden furniture blooming immense red parasols, furled and pointing to the sky like intercontinental ballistic missiles ready to ejaculate into the sun. The severe minimal form is counterbalanced by investigative strings of exotic plants anarchically intertwined with the anodised balustrade leading up to the main portal. Such a soulless dwelling might suggest it was derelict, unloved – but rustic tastes are by no means universal and wide open glass portals gape for air, hinting to Chlamydia that this new-fangled structure is, on the contrary, occupied, breathing…

Led by a parched tongue dryly goading her upwards, thirst hankers at the door all timid like a mouse, keen not to disturb anyone at all – so she taps with a little more conviction – mightier than a mouse but nevertheless verminous, pounding up the food chain until feminine knuckles hammer on the portal like a disturbed vivisection primate. Yet without reply, self-entitled zeal takes the handle in its opposable grip and the door falls open unlocked. Chlamydia enters with humble ergonomics – cowering and bowing – deferential movements meek enough to make trespass appear pious even to a transgressed owner.

'Trespass not against those who trespass against you,' she whispers.

'*The meek shall inherit a drink*,' she replies.

A long white uterus blinks before shrinking pupils. Framed at the far end of the hallway a weathered Eames chair sits at rest with attendant footstool, above, an immodest painting of naked Adam and stripped-bare Eve spread-eagle across a jagged surface of broken crockery.

'Anyone home? Hello? Anyone? Anybody? Home?'

Good manners would always avoid entering a European household without an owner's permission, yet, here in paradise, thirst felt justified in crossing the threshold since malicious or criminal intent belonged a multi-million miles away. To wit, a bone-dry tongue is crumbling in fast-evaporating lather, rehydration fast becoming a matter of physiological necessity if called upon to beg apology – let alone pant back down the volcano to the hotel mini-bar. Under such circumstances it was absurd to imagine a humane objection to an honest body entering a house for need of a simple sip. In its defence, etiquette had endeavoured to make its intrusion known – could only give fair account of its imposition if the owner appeared forthwith. Hence the owner would understand their own part in the paradox; in a way, it was partially their fault – if Chlamydia was guilty of thirst, the owner proved guilty of placing their hospitality beyond reach.

Evaporating fast, thirst sips along the hallway to reach the kitchen only to catch its stomach retching in the doorway. The room is bubonic – steadily eating its insides out.

Nonetheless, human consumption is not the subject of the feast; a mist of intoxicated fruit flies gorged on fermenting fructose are hovering above a green haze describing the collapsed outline of rotten food. On the kitchen table spoiled plant stems sip on heavy water sagging in the seat of a decorative vase, stench diffused up through the crown of lifeless flowers. Naked animal bones litter the kitchen floor, circled by the stained forensic eluvium that describes the intimate process of their dismemberment. Key to the digestion process, fetid maggots link the kitchen's industrious decay in chain gangs of invaginating guts, pulsing with the selfless hard labour purposeful in returning vagrant matter back into the continuum of resurrected life. Deposited over work surface and kitchen table, bottles of rank milk reek with autopoietic potential – lipids and enzymes catalyse and emulsify with dynamic morphological transfer. Chlamydia witnesses vile biology truly expressing its multiple personality, such that the clots of matter straining to emerge from each strangled bottleneck rasps in a chorus of emphysemic tracheotomies. Added to this mess, a multifarious array of visible insectoid life forms active in pollinating the synchronised transversal bloom – massaging the involuting scullery-organ to breathe *in and out* – gasping *in and out*… In the midst of all this wheezing matter, an aluminium stepladder straddles etched black scribble where its own four feet have been dragged screaming and kicking about the kitchen tiles. Ever so faintly audible above the respiration, mocking fridge magnets whisper '*Eat me! Eat me!*' but anorexia resists, standing firm – Chlamydia's self-loathing is so famished that it is already happily cannibalising her mind. So she urgently searches for a glass, well aware that the brazen hide-and-seek could be easily misconstrued. And so she excuses herself with the invention of a pleasant handwritten note to accept the owner's charity by way of proxy. Common sense would prevail. Nonetheless, she would prepare the note in such a way as to cajole the owner's innate moral imperatives politely into partisan response. While mentally composing the note in the safety of her own mind she outwardly opens a cupboard to find precision-cut Royal Doulton glasses stacked in haphazard order inside. Gaucherie reaches for a single glass but disturbs the eccentric balance of the whole and one by one the vessels leap from the ledge to crash, bang, wallop. Frozen stiff by this disastrous turn, Chlamydia is rendered deaf to the sound of disturbed footsteps getting bigger and BIGGER. Concentrating on the amended wording of her memorandum, she is aware of nothing else before a vehement male tone booms into her paralysis –

'Fee fie fo fum,
I smell the blood of a menstrual woman,
be she alive or be she dead,
I'll crush her bones to make my b-b-bread!'

Turning to take delivery of the giant's wrath, Chlamydia's fear is met by an extremely petite figure with an oversized head and compressed ferocity tightly knotted into two gristling fists. Transfixed in the instant of her seizure, Chlamydia yearns for the dormant volcano to open up and swallow her hole. Held rigid by the helter-skelter stare and shrink-wrapped by humiliation, Chlamydia's zealous masochism sees fit to conjure a mental recollection of her shrink's headquarters back home where the tidy desk sits in mockery of her messy head, and the pink alabaster pen pot bristles with eternally whittled pencils, and a cheerless watercolour frames a forlorn figure pacing a nameless beach with dissolved reflection drowning in a grey sea, while the bookshelf burgeons with a host of psychoanalytic luminaries looming over her tortured denials with the embryonic menace of *unheimlichkeit* henchmen – this luscious mental picture summoned from the horizontal perspective of the eminent Dr Dora Heimlich's professional leatherette recliner that persists in obliging Chlamydia's skin to wring wet with pre-emptive guilt… For once in her life, Chlamydia is abandoned of anything that might effectively counter-transfer her to this livid man and him to her – and so she proffers an unfussy apology…

'I can't tell you how truly mortified I am about the tumblers – *tumblers!* Ha ha! In all honesty my physical clumsiness is tantamount to a mental handicap! Of course I'll cough up every single penny for their replacement. The awful truth is, I climbed the volcano today all by myself and forgot to bring water – silly me! I was sooooooooooooo thirsty and saw your house and naturally I knocked. Well, no one answered, but the door was open so I entered. I was gasping for a little *aqua minerale*. Then I was going to leave a note to say thank you – and then *another*, apologising for the damage. I hope you don't mind.'

'Do you know who I am?' The voice is shallow, evidently latent. Carbon-black dots scan her wilting form with ancient menace. Chlamydia's deferential vision seeks refuge below her fringe, defensive grimace expressing private health crenulations, so she withers to the floor, bending on all fours in a passive genuflection, trembling paws nervously rake at glass shards probing for a small-time injury to introduce a little human empathy into the animal encounter.

'No –' she says. 'I have absolutely no idea who you are. Should I?' she says. 'Besides, I *did* knock for ages and the door *did* swing open and I was genuinely really very thirsty. Parched. It's an extremely long hike up the volcano, and a very long way down… if that makes any sense…'

'I'm not interested in your personal dehydration. My home

isn't predisposed to the incompetence of tourists. Thirst doesn't provide permission to barge into my house.'

'Well that's an exceedingly un-Christian sentiment.'

'Privacy isn't a sentiment it's a law.'

'And the law would begrudge me a glass of water?'

'No one can begrudge you what you were prepared to steal. Now get out,' he says, gesturing to the door and stepping aside to make way for the eviction.

'What about this mess?' she points, marking the distinction between *his 'n' hers*.

He disturbs her, this windswept man with petrified enmity written on his face. He is arresting in a distressing kind of way – also oddly familiar. Such a man would be difficult for such a woman to forget. Sensing the inscrutable feminine gaze, male eyes narrow to take aim along the barrel of an imaginary gun.

'Oh please!' he snipes. *'I'd sincerely appreciate you taking the trouble.'*

'And a glass of water?' Chlamydia blinks and ice-blue eyes visibly thaw.

'Oh that too!' he nods emphatically. 'But be quick about it. You've interrupted my work, and my work can't stand being interrupted.'

'Well lead me to the Hoover and I'll begin sucking.'

'Find it yourself,' he says flatly. 'You've cut your finger,' he adds matter-of-factly, pointing to pretty red petals pitter-pattering on the ceramic floor below her left hand shaking like a leaf. He takes her paw. It lacks sensation in the extremity. A phantom limb or numb prosthetic – detached from Chlamydia's body. A triangular shard of glass projects from the engaged ring finger like a light beam throbbing from a crimson lighthouse. Holding her hand over the sink he wrings the lighthouse of signal red. So it throbs even more.

'Accident prone?' he says blankly.

She shrugs. 'Not especially.'

Enmity drags the screeching stepladder across the floor to the chipped lip of the enamel sink, climbs up to snatch a first aid box from the very cupboard where the tumblers are now badly stacked no more. Tin box clenched beneath wing, the mini-mountaineer levers the lid open with broken teeth to find a piece of dusty cotton gauze and a single loose plaster. Midway down the steps he pauses to moisten the mildew under the tap, then descends to ground floor, passing the tin to Chlamydia's good hand to hold while he takes her bad hand in his own claw and attends to the wound. Chlamydia might prefer to halt this abrupt display of remedial concern, might prefer to notify him in no uncertain terms that, in point of fact, the injury was self-inflicted and intended to mollify his anger, and under the circumstances, such a minor injury did not give permission to assume major intimacy... But Chlamydia's tongue is tied-up bound and gagged – especially manacled when the jaundiced grip tightens upon her feminine wrist, him dabbing the gash in her swollen finger. His touch is anything but gentle, but Chlamydia suppresses the protest, maintains mute composure until pink elastic waterproof stretches around her finger's diameter, until adhesive is firmly stuck one end to the other. She exchanges her limp paw for an expression of abject disgust before allowing the sneer to fissure neatly into a *trompe-l'œil* smile and a faux,

'Thank you!'

The first aid kit is returned where it lives upstairs, and while peering up at the paranoid Samaritan proudly crowning the waist-high summit of the stepladder, Chlamydia is made aware of two aqueous orbs bulging down at her seeming to suffer an unnatural gravity – she is accordingly conscious of her immaculate white Lacoste tennis shorts and green polka dot Miu Miu halter top revealing a partial account of her upper anatomy. To wit, her hair had been tied back prim and proper that very morning, but in the bustle of her encounter has slipped loose from its rein and now hangs in a silken black whip across red-raw cheeks. Her fringe, thickened and heavy with mountain dew, curtains her brow of any manifest sign of expression.

Evidently their bout of *doctors and nurses* is over since his eagerness to be rid of her has abated.

'You have a timeless beauty,' he announces, out of the blue and all at sea. 'If I were prone to the witless mysticism of the common *untermensch* I would claim you were the reincarnation of the goddess *C-C-Cytherea*...'

It is not the first nor last time Chlamydia Love has/will be sold cheap compliments. Once upon a time a two-bit mystic told how – in a former life (during the Roman occupation), Chlamydia was a lowly lavatorium attendant – an uncharacteristic occupation (conceded the mystic), especially since the gamut of clients were more typically found to be oracles, sages, soothsayers, gladiators or high priestesses (*– and so it follows that in the olden days divine beings and deities were as common as muck, whereas common muckrakes were as rare as rocking-horse shit*).

And so, here and now, self-assurance tosses its head scornfully as though to chemically peel the creamy remark from her face, neck and especially breasts. The slur was evidently elliptical – nonetheless, Chlamydia's heart is pounding on account of her own endogenous wares freely flowing, especially now the vascular ante of their intimate tête-à-tête is eagerly raised. The pendular mood has swung – now he prefers to impede her departure with cloying observations designed to congeal her to his withering sight. He drags the screeching stepladder to the utility cupboard, mounts the apparatus to manhandle the anodised latch and free the melamine door. The kitchen squalor palpably flinches in the face of the chemical nemesis stockpiled in the gloomy cupboard – power sprays, multi-purpose surfactants, thickest-ever bleach fatal to all known germs, anti-bacterial cleansers deadly lethal to E. coli, salmonella, listeria, campylobacter and rotavirus: a cocktail of domestic toxins boasting benzisothiazolinone, methylisothiazolinone, glutaral, hexyl cinnamal, butylphenyl methylpropional, hydrochloric acid, non-ionic and anionic surfactants for bathroom, kitchen and baby too... The sneer derides down the ladder, drags the shrieking apparatus to its home then takes tactical position next to the cupboard, leaning indolently – small arms pretending to fold across chest, audacious eyes welded to her especial physique.

'Feel free,' he says nodding sideways at the cleaning products, but the pronunciation is all maleficent and *feel free* sounds like '*filthy*'.

Chlamydia is awestruck by the shabby-chic stone-washed jeans and matching blue singlet seeming in patent contradiction of his claimed tenure over the property. Mere scrutiny of his material appearance spurs doubt to freely articulate from Chlamydia's cocky mouth thus:

'*Exactly who are you?*' she teases, tone tinged with superiority. 'Exactly what right do you have to order me from this unhygienic abode? You've the poise of a circus freak – and from the squalor that surrounds you I'd hazard a bet that you're nothing more than an itinerant squatter taking mendacious gain from the owner's absence.'

'*Squalor? Squatter? MENDACIOUS GAIN?*' Flung headlong into a premature spin-cycle, fury begins to froth. '*You best clean up the m-m-mess then make yourself very, very s-s-scarce!*' He jerks a wooden broom from its diagonal buttress in the utility cupboard, thrusts it at Chlamydia violently enough for her to stumble backwards in anticipation – not quite saving her balance by grasping the flimsy cupboard door before it unhinges apropos her weight, both flapping to stagnant tiles. Outraged by the cascading damage, male wrath storms for the exit to direct female calamity into the corridor and on its merry way. But as fury turns to inflict its finger of scorn, a bottle of bleach reputedly fatal to all known germs rotates on its trajectory to strike the Messianic buffoon square in the chops. The chucker is transfixed by her miraculous accuracy – yet torn between tears of mirth or empathy, she sooner senses it is merely male pride that is mortally scathed and so permits guttural amusement to billow out through feminine lips. Stationed head to head, *his* sorely wounded expression is symmetrically distorted by *hers* – sorely pained by laughter. The injured party makes a sudden grab for Chlamydia's funny bone, shaking her by the elbow, so violently in her pretty shoes that expensive ivories rattle in a costly surgical gum. Chlamydia looks the pitcher of innocence, but the injured party is having none of it.

'I'm s-s-s-so s-s-s-sorry,' she judders, pleasantly surprised by his hidden muscle. 'I honestly d-d-d-didn't intend for it to actually hit you! It was a lucky shot – that's all… *or unlucky – depending on your point of view*…' Chlamydia's sexy squint oozes unconscious yearning.

'I should punch yer' flamin' face in!' The threat snags over broken teeth but soldiers on regardless: 'Not bloody well content with wrecking my h-h-house you assault my person!

Go! Before I do something *you'll* regret!'

He pushes at Chlamydia with all the repellent force little hands can muster then turns away to seize his fury in a conscientious display of anger management and self-composure. The upshot is that his small body heaves on the spot. During physical contact Chlamydia had been touched by something supernatural, nay paranormal – stirred by something other than the agent of her discomfort, but surrendering any option of flight, she remains fixed by her own stare boring deep into the very small of his back, tempted to risk another verbal apology if only to incite further incendiary reaction from the apoplectic frame convulsing before her. When he is good and ready, he faces Chlamydia with fossilised enmity and angered eyes flecked with petrified contempt. His eyes grip like annealed barbs tugging her pale white skin with raised Braille malice – or on the other hand, his eyes are like Taser barbs repelling her with fifty-thousand volts of electronic hatred. Hypnotised by fiery eyes, Chlamydia's elastic flesh creeps loose of its skull with the yearning to be excused of the duty of face to face expression. But she is unable to animate pore nor bone nor limb – confronted by the searing spectre of distilled loathing, a curious urge rises up to contest this murderous immunity to her unanimous appeal – in Chlamydia's book, *all men are immune deficient – and she is not prepared to accept any exception to this rule…*

Being Chlamydia, feline curiosity moistens its cutaneous fun-hole with the prehensile tip of her glossa – which is all she can do under the circumstances of her general paralysis. Her coquettish epidermis blushes in reciprocation of the biological potential parading its fitness before her – suffice to say, engorged capillaries on Chlamydia's reddened face match distended vessels in his cock… and in the sudden sobering prick of a child's balloon a ballast rush of over-zealous conscience delivers Algernon to the fore of Chlamydia Love's mind's eye. But Consultant Hertz's gossamer apparition is too late – tenacious mitts pull roughly at Chlamydia's moribund corpse, burying her in his shallow chest, his busy mouth nibbles, bites, licks and scratches selfishly, as though burying a bone – a grubby paw slips inside her halter-top to snatch at loose flesh sagging from her empty udder. Elsewhere, dignity struggles beneath the urgent pressure of sneering lips and snapping teeth, yet, inside the violently conjoined embrace Chlamydia's mouth suckles like a newborn baby tugging at mother's angry teat. Hence respiration for both parties is understandably ragged, tidal saliva sluices to and fro between his 'n' her gum disease while the communal lust ignites a funeral pyorrhoea. Chlamydia's self-restraint merrily dilapidates to make way for the cannibalistic advance of lust-driven flesh, and as the carnivorous communion is set to go all the way to the marrow, the capricious El Niño thrusts its rag doll from the cot to invent its own local tragedy:

'*Well, well, well! How opportune! You and me, mouth to mouth… How very p-p-predictable!*'

'You don't like how I kissssssssssssssssssssssss…?' Chlamydia bleats.

'*Au contraire*! You're clearly a seasoned professional! However – *you've been rumbled!*'

'*Rumbled?* Oh! Less of the boring old chitchat – *more kisssssssssssssssssssing*…' Chlamydia's eyelids tip and gob puckers shut in a passive invitation.

'*Kissing? Sorry, but I wouldn't touch you with yours*…' he rasps, with unnatural disaster pictured in cyclonic eyes. '*Tell me who put you up to it! Who's hired out your wares this week – who's pimping you out – kiss 'n' tell whore! And where's the camera, eh? Eh? EH? WHERE'S THE CAMERA?*'

'*Camera?* I get it! You're under the impression I'm being paid… to *seduce* you? – *You're having a laugh!* Ha, ha, ha…!' Female conceit thrusts its left hand in a horizontal salute and the brilliant solitaire winks with Algernon's symbolic reservation. '*I'M ENGAGED TO BE HAPPILY MARRIED!*' she declares, but the bright words no sooner ring out than sound tarnished, dull, lacklustre, jaded, or weary even. She can even see her own misgivings in his eyes – the reflected spectre of a life form less than subhuman.

'*Engaged?* Well, the poor sap has my deepest sympathy. So if you're not seducing me for financial reward, what exactly are you after?'

'Oh you're surely barking up the wrong tree stump! A simple glass of water is all this girl desires!' her rebuttal nevertheless offends vanity, leaving wounded pride to eclipse modesty:

'Well you can have your precious glass of water! I'll even fetch it all by myself!'

She watches, stunned by the unfolding scene – the tortured stepladder dragged screaming and kicking to the chipped sink once more, him scramble up to the cupboard once more, snatch a glass, descend halfway, lean over the enamel sink for the tap, fill a glass, descend to the floor, address Chlamydia with a full glass before slinging it in her cold… wet… face.

'*There… rehydration, the last surviving glass worth.*' he says, dropping the glass to the floor. 'Now clear the mess and disappear from sight!'

Chlamydia's rubber jaw clenches into alginate overbite.

'What if I don't?'

'You'd better.'

'*Really?* What'll you do if I don't?' she says all coquettish and insolent.

'Try me and find out…' he says, *cuntish*.

Dripping wet sagacity bows to its knees to sweep glass shards into the belching pedal bin. Chlamydia seeks intermittent approval from her tormentor who stands guard in the lower third of the door.

'I'm done,' simpers poor little Cinders. 'I'll leave you alone with your chronic paranoia – I imagine it's stimulating company.

I'm sure you prefer the voices in your head to *real* people.'

'*Bravo!*' he says, barely clapping. '*Very good! Very impressive*… Since my work has been well and truly interrupted there's little chance of carrying on where I left off – and since you entertain propositions favourably, I *propose* you join me for a proper drink…'

Feminine disbelief gapes spread-eagled, tempting Chlamydia to fling the roguish offer back in his face. But thirst wins over the superficial triumph of a rhetorical reprisal, and a counterfeit nod spasms reluctantly as a subordinate 'yes' falls from grace.

'Glorious… Then we'll sit out on the terrace, its pleasant *plein air*. We'll assume you're familiar with the layout of the house. Go ahead – relax, take the burden off your legs, I'll join you in a jiffy.'

Cantilevered over thin air Chlamydia takes time to condense first impressions into everlasting generalisations. She surmises that her host is an acutely embryonic specimen – deduces that his chronic deviousness is born of an articulation of the *survival of the weakest* – and yet, as if in confirmation of the mollifying effect of such a cunning trait upon others – her character assassination falls short of condemning the vile specimen out of hand, she fails to come to her senses and part his company without delay for fear of blemish or personal injury. In fact, *his survival through weakness* is triumphant in cancelling out her *self-preservation instinct*… Furthermore, she makes no hesitation in drawing her own fiancé into cold comparison – even eclipsing the good doctor's countless acts of wanton compassion (ie: urging his gym to host a sponsored Stairmaster© climb for the victims of 9/11 – promoting a three-legged race in aid of the amputees of Afghanistan – staging a sodden wet T-shirt contest for the drought-ridden of Darfur). In light of Chlamydia's present fixation, the good doctor's reputation unjustly tarnishes in the polluted light of her present company. But who is this oxidising enigma? A celebrity of some sort? A psychic or religious teacher? A guru? Actor? Director? Recluse? Who the hell knows? One hundred watt charisma radiates brightly from the twinkling eyes (until blackest crude oil swells the retinas when enraged), and even his unforgivable dress sense has its charm, and his tiny gammon hands enjoy an oddly erotic quality even though they clawed at her with tireless conviction. Chlamydia trembles at the selfish gammon hands snatching at loose flesh with tireless conviction, her own palm involuntarily drawn to the place where ham-fists had been. A leaden ache settles in her tripe... *Why do I allow this creature to cause me such unwarranted disturbance when I possess a perfectly credit healthy fiancé waiting patiently for my return?*

Algernon deteriorates in the dusk altogether, and as if chewing gossip with a porous girlfriend, Chlamydia tells herself she is only having a bit of harmless fun – but as her chatty friend is keen to point out, if Algernon acquires the island, what then? – It would be absurd to imagine Algernon never bumping into this larger than life persona.

And what then Chlamydia?

The chink of cut-price Chinese plastic shatters Chlamydia's reverie, now cow-eyed mooning up at her knee-high host as he fumbles the laden tray onto the table top. He is sporting toy sunglasses, a dilapidated off-white dressing gown with woolly gold lamé embroidery with capitalised *h* and capitalised *m*. The game has shifted shape and now they are to play best friends enjoying an innocent drink perched up on the edge of the dormant volcano waiting for a gout of superheated magma to engulf them.

Chlamydia smiles like a good sport. 'Aren't you afraid it

might erupt one day?' she quips, frivolously.

'It lay spent aeons before mankind was ever a twinkle in the Creator's eye...'

In failing light he cranks the table's parasol until fully unfurled and sinks below its unnecessary gloom. 'Shall I be mummy?' Chlamydia offers with conviction aborted.

He nods back into the ample lap of his seat, observing dainty fingers quench the plastic beakers with crushed ice before dousing the cracking rock with premium quality vodka and a slash of medicinal quinine laced with Paki tonic. Politeness offers the first beaker to the eager digits that sweep hers in a creepy exchange, triggering a neuronic fuse to fizz all the way up her arm. She sips, paying no heed to the cheap sunglasses hellbent on absorbing her mannerisms into greedy black holes.

'I can see you needed that. All better now?' he says.

'Oh well that's just a little audacious in light of your recent behaviour – but I doubt we're very big on apologies.'

'Really? Oh do tell me more. I *adore* hearing about myself.'

Chlamydia cocks her lollypop head to one side and feigns thinking aloud:

'*Mmmmm... He strikes me as a man with amorphous qualities... the epitome of the diminutive Lilliputian, found perched on a big, big volcano... a man afflicted by a gargantuan perspective born of an unresolved inferiority complex... a man who mistakes the diurnal elongation of his own shadow for a measure of priapic prowess.*'

Chlamydia forecasts ill-tempered weather, told by the sight of demented brows gathering their storm above the rim of toy sunglasses – beyond the childish shade, angry eyeballs melt and burn like blobs of fat pirouetting in a frying pan.

'Well, what an unpleasant mouthful of words...' he says, adding sternly: '*Now tell me what I am...*'

'You've the stomach for it?'

'*NEVER YOU FRET!*' he yelps, goading her invective as an excuse to proffer his own rage. '*I can stomach your bellyache all day long! THIS HERE BELLY IS BULLETPROOF! You'll never penetrate me with your cheap shots! NEVER!*'

Chlamydia is no less guilty of enjoying her own subconscious motivations:

'It intrigues me that you pose as the respectable owner of this ostentatious house and yet air the personal demeanour of a common pig – you're pig-ignorant and prone to porky pies…' Arrogance punctuates with a pause, yet receives nothing for its courage. So she continues: 'Added to pig-headedness, you're a vain man – and vanity is surely the most hideous of male vices. You place yourself head and shoulders above all others – and the prize of your fascination is *you* – a plain narcissist – unable to afford others the respect you insist for yourself…'

In the distance the sea rolls onto the beach and the early evening breeze tangles with limp leaves. Chlamydia expires as though the respiratory exhaust of her very being is being drawn from her lungs by the tidal swell clawing the shoreline. She feels the Earth gasp – expelling saturated heat back into the twilight.

'And you,' he begins, 'I suspect… that the insinuating web you endearingly regard as your *engagement* has merely rewarded your efforts with an archetypal male specimen willing for the perverse comfort of capture. I suspect this man of yours is willingly oblivious of the fact that you've absolutely no love for him whatsoever, and while coalescence is a sure sign of utter surrender, in the thrill of triumph you fail to see that the superiority you've gained is mutually dependent upon his wilful degradation. It is power and not true love that drives you – and all that drives him is male gratitude mesmerised by female ambivalence…'

Chlamydia's resentment is obligatory: 'You don't know me

well enough to psychoanalyse my relationship!'

'If the heart is content, why come here – *why come to me?*'

'You're deaf and dumb as well as blind Mr Magoo! GOODNIGHT!' Chlamydia springs to attention, swings an open hand at her tormentor, but is caught in an underdeveloped grip, yanking her down on cooperative knees as best he can given his challenged physiognomy.

'*NOBODY WALKS OUT ON ME MIDSTREAM!*' sounds the blowhole as though set to blubber, '...why travel all the way to Morass alone other than for a chance dalliance before slithering home to put this lame pet out of *your* misery? Or perhaps you've chosen to escape the clamming clutches of your deluded lover, to escape the fawning dependence of that nibbling domestic wretch with the doe eyes and baby drool who nags how he needs you *sooooo* much? Or perhaps you descended on paradise to decide if emotional suicide is worth it – *whether this conjugal coma rather than any other will be rewarding once you've flogged the doting sap into the filthy soil and reaped your widow's rewards?*'

'Oh how wrong can one man be! Well, I've got good *and* bad news... The *good news* is that I've been sent to decide whether paradise is a fitting enough wedding gift from my filthy rich fiancé Algernon. *The bad news* is that I'm going to be your landlord!' – The fatal blow delivered all metallic and cruel, as though programmed like an inhuman robot.

Moved first to silence, then to whisper,

'*Algernon?*' softly – the last gasp of a dying man squandered on the name of his assassin... '*Algernon?*' Now a little louder, '*Algernon?*' Louder still, '*Algernon?*' The dying man, feeling better... '*ALGERNON? ALGERNON HERTZ? "DOCTOR" ALGERNON HERTZ!*' Toy sunglasses tip from his face misshapen by the mental spasms wrenching the nucleated knot that is his central nervous system, flinching from contact with the outside world, his hands clenched, drawn into his ribcage, tight fists set to lash out. There is insignificant latency in the white knuckles but Chlamydia thinks it best to act afraid.

'You *know* Algernon?' she stutters biting her nails. 'H-h-h-how?'

'KNOW HIM? ARE YOU MAD?' The cascade of unmentionable insults wane only when a malignant realisation dawns inside the thunder. *'HE SENT YOU HERE ON PURPOSE!'*

'Yes, like I said – to decide if I like the island.'

'HE SENT HIS PRETTY FIANCÉE TO DO HIS DIRTY WORK – I get it – you worm your way inside, screw me over while Hertz shaves another millimetre closer to stealing my property.'

'Steal your property? How can he *steal* your property?'

'He didn't happen to mention that he's been trying to buy me out?'

'Buy your house?' she says.

'Buy Morass,' he says.

'You own Morass – to sell?'

Chapter Two

'I own Morass, but not to sell – *NEVER!* I'd spoil it with plague, pestilence, famine, AIDS – I'd dig a hole with these very hands and push Morass in before I sold out to that cretin.'

It is an unforeseen revelation – it tips Chlamydia from her chair – a whimper tumbles with her:

'My wedding present…'

'Wedding present! *The nerve! – BASTARD!'* A tiny morsel of male pity hauls Chlamydia back up onto her seat. 'How long have you known Hertz?' he says.

'Ages…'

'I think not. He was here last summer skulking around with a repulsive blonde. *Were you platinum last season?'*

'We weren't engaged then…' she says, faltering at the offence like a young foal. 'I've known Algernon long enough to trust him. Anyway, if he wanted me to influence you he would have mentioned you so as to ensure I made contact. And what if you *were* won over by my feminine charm – what possible good could it do him?'

'He covets what he can't have – and he can't have Morass. He's fixated to the point of self ruin. He'll do anything and use anyone to get it.'

'He loves me unconditionally,' says Chlamydia, 'like a puppy dog loves a slipper.'

'You're mistaken. You're a cog, a fan belt, a spark plug, a windscreen wiper – you're an unwitting mechanical component in a larger mechanical mechanism. But his mechanical plan is flawed – foiled by one simple oversight.' His gaze roams freely across the reciprocating contours of Chlamydia's body like a deodoriser ball lapping up body odour.

'Why,' asks the lump in Chlamydia's throat. 'Because I'm

not your type?'

'Because my need for a simple life is far greater than my desire for the prittle-prattle of human intimacy.'

'Solipsism,' she says, nodding, '*– how quaint* – presumably you can afford to turn down a fortune?' Disdain casts a flaring glance over the worn textures of the dressing gown.

'I live according to my needs – I have little need for anything nor *anyone*.'

'You're a recluse? A loner? The world has spurned a wish and driven you to reproach it by withdrawing into obscurity – an immodest sentiment indeed!' Said lasciviously, refilling her glass indolently without asking or offering. 'Anyway,' she adds, 'I don't see where we're going with this conversation.'

'For dinner –' he says '*– you're going to join me for dinner.*'

Eyes frost-bitten onto his, Chlamydia places her glass on the table and extends her cold hand outstretched and diffuses her precious name into thin air. He inhales as though the sound were perfume, takes her paw firmly and kisses it hard.

'Delighted to meet you *Chlamydia Love*. What a beautiful name...'

'It's Greek for *contagiously popular*.'

'How delightful – *Helmut Mandragorass at your service...*'

'Helmet...' she says, rolling it around in her mouth. 'Mysterious name,' she says. 'Where is it from, what does it mean?'

'*Helmut* means "*hell hound*". *Mandragorass* derives from a shamanic shrub known as the mandragora or mandrake – a rootstock believed by the ancients to thrive from the sperm-soiled earth found beneath the feet of men who met their fate hung by the neck.'

'Charming. And what's for dinner Mr Helmut

Mandragorass?'

'You are...'

'I'm hardly dressed for dinner...' Chlamydia's confession is proud to observe her host's mouth softening in acknowledegment of the backhanded reference to his own ramshackle appearance.

'Oh let's not allow petty social protocols to spoil our evening – and anyway, I've been swept off my feet by the *contagiously popular* Chlamydia Love...'

Chlamydia smiles. Mandragorass has a tendency for baroque ornamentation, a penchant for self-satisfied pleonasms, for pure and simple *pig-headedness*... Perhaps Helmut is a forlorn poet soured by some such tragedy that put him all out to sea and then washed his sodden husk ashore Morass... Chlamydia enjoys her mental crucifixion.

'If you'll permit my abandoning you out here in the twilight,' he says at length, 'I'll go see about din-dins. I do apologise if it's a paltry offering – my dear old housekeeper prepared something earlier before I knew I was to have *a guest.*'

Being momentarily governed by politeness, Chlamydia offers to help.

'*How kind!*' he says, with sarcasm expanding into the open gesture surrendered to his disposal.

'Don't be insulting Mr Mandragorass, I may leave if you insist on being insulting.'

'Poor Chlamydia – first you were thirsty... now you're hungry. If you wish to stay, stay.' And gesturing towards the volcanic slope – 'If you wish to go, you'll find gravity in your favour...'

Chlamydia's eyes sting, anger wanes but then dimples sweetly.

'Forgive me for saying,' she says, 'but your need for solitude is symptomatic of an unhealthy loathing of women...'

Symptomatic is a truly superior adjective. To repudiate its accusation is merely to add to the density of self-incrimination. Heimlich told Chlamydia so – didn't so much tell her than demonstrated the fine art of symptomatology upon her own damaged being. Heimlich was a *shrink's shrink*, and to substantiate her indubitable powers of animism, the good doctor owned a shrunken ethnographic head displayed on a sinister black spigot standing guard over her desk in her office-cum-clinic. Chlamydia's encounter with psychic health care blew her mind so much that when released from its mental incarceration, her bloated brain spilled out into the atmosphere – a hyperaesthetic tangle of psychic ectoplasm warranting the craft of a shrink's shrink to contain its chaotic expansion, to wrestle and compress its madness back inside Chlamydia's empty skull (and this, presumably, is why shrinks are called shrinks).

'*– to escape from mankind*,' mutters Helmut to himself.

'Pardon?'

'– that's why I spend so much of my precious time here on Morass... *My need for solitude* – you accused me of shrinking from the female of the species – but it's not just the company of women I shrink from.'

'You find *Homo sapiens* so wretched?'

'You misunderstand me...' he says. 'But it doesn't really matter –' Melancholy rises to its miserable height to go fetch dinner as promised, but progress is stunted by a sudden glitch that paralyses motion. Chlamydia witnesses determination doomed by physiognomy, half expects his conniving flesh to dematerialise and pass unhindered between the gaps in the atomic fabric of the solid kitchen wall. Rash-red tingles around marbled fatty deposits, innards bulge, cruelly dislocated as clustering organs jostle towards the strange attractor whirring before her. Streams of male orgones are flooding her phase space, his necromantic gland now tuned to seductive overkill. Chlamydia's pride considers throwing itself from the terrace. Then wrenched from Helmut's paranormal spell: '...I don't live here all of the time,' he says, 'but for the periods that I do, simple peace and quiet is all I seek.'

'Where do you live the rest of the time?' she says politely, encouraging...

sliding back in her seat,
scouring the host for a clue, or simple hint
as to why the cloud of hydrocarbon molecules
loitering before her stay loyal to such an abysmal formation.

It would be a wanton act of kindness to free his blood from the purgatory of endless circulation –

'I have other houses dotted around. I love to visit them, but I tend to travel by necessity rather than choice. Morass is my home – headquarters for inner contemplation.'

'It's an exquisite island. The fauna and flora compliment each other perfectly. The sea is a delightful asset to the island and the volcano is a wonderful attraction. Your house is very impressive. *Tres moderne,*' she says, graciously,

and stirring beneath superficial pleasantries,
a mind clouds with premonitions
of a marionette being wrenched asunder,
livid meat thrown to the frothing jaws of starving half-human pigs,
who mangle flesh trodden undertrotter –
Mandragorass's soul fused with inchoate matter –

'I was born here on the island. I have a strong bond. The Morasseans have a unique spirit.'

'Yes, they seem ever so friendly,' says Chlamydia, amiably,

inner eye flaming wide angry as the sun,
a blast hole coronated by flaring lashes;
in her mind's eye she is blinded
by the image of white ribs

peeling from the gaping chasm of wrenched thorax.

Pure white daisies push up through the factory of rotten minerals draping in trapeze webs from the bleached ribs of a shivering carcass, and through the heady haze of imaginary murder she comes to realise that Helmut Mandragorass is alive and kicking and scrutinising her goosebumps in fine detail –

'You seem preoccupied,' he says.

'No,' she says, dimpling sweetly. 'Not at all…'

They gobble on the wooden terrace cantilevered over the depthless drop. Chlamydia's elastic conscience dangles her other-half into mind intermittently. But each time, helpless Hertz wafts away into the twilight air, relinquished like a cheap balloon from a sickly child's clasp. Chlamydia's anorexia picks at the housekeeper's avocado and tiger prawns drowned in clotted cream – nibbles at mixed leaf salad, plucks at plump chicken hearts and sluices with razor bone-dry Rhodesian Chablis. Chlamydia picks and Helmut devours. Conversation is cursory, light and uncomplicated. Mandragorass manages to lock away any pejorative thoughts from the proven articulation of a foul mouth, and when Chlamydia announces she is delightfully replete and Helmut stuffed, Chlamydia is governed by good manners and begins to tidy prawn tails and chicken gristle.

'Leave it. My housekeeper will see to it in the morning.'

'But I can do it now,' said gaily, 'it's the least I can do after this evening's misunderstanding.'

'In lieu of payment for breakages?' he mocks, '*Oh I'm sure I can think of a more sympathetic way.*'

'I'm *sure* you're sure Mr Mandragorass, but if it's all right with you, I prefer to tidy.'

Chlamydia makes excuses to abandon Helmut all amused by himself, slumping deep into the seat of his yawning chair.

In the kitchen squalor Chlamydia finds light relief in the asthmatic chaos – until hydrochloric misgivings in her gastric pit foam up to breach her esophageal hiatus and force Helmut's sour inseminations into her squalid imagination by way of a bitter mouth… *Why would Algernon send her* (belch) *alone? Why did Algernon* (belch) *neglect to mention Helmut? What special* (belch) *interest did Algernon have in* (belch) *Morass beyond the* (belch) *pretence that it was a* (belch) *wedding gift? Who was the repulsive blonde?* (belch).

From the kitchen, Chlamydia discovers the terrace vacant. She waits, naturally perplexed, ploughing an irritable scalp until desiccated eczema weeps for attention. Caught in the cooling airstream trapped high above sea level, her loitering conscience is popped by the vindictive beak of a wheeling vulture. Helmut appears over her shoulder like bird shit.

'May I use your telephone (belch)?' she says.

'*Tut-tut! Mais non, non, non! Pas de telephones on Morass at all – anywhere. No cell coverage at all! Strictly off limits! Verboten! Communiqué severance is de rigueur! The dependable Captain Oceanic takes all correspondence to the mainland office to be passed on from there – you can try popping a message in a bottle, post it in the sea – it's as reliable as the Captain*… I've put music on – join me inside.'

Helmut leads Chlamydia by hand through the house to the lounge. The lounge is sunk deep in crimson carpet, walls stained flesh pink, pocked by a holocaust of maleficent etchings and tearful watercolours wrapping around the room in an endless hellscape – images of vulnerable human forms decapitated and crowned with ambivalent clown heads – stick figures haunted by evanescent dreams, hellish depictions conjured into being by rampant paranoia; allegorical apparitions fuelled by fevered imagination, walls distempered with compassion fatigue and the four corners of the room dominated by sculpture; *here,* a hanged man's jaw lies cracked open and an anorexic woman reaches up to filch his teeth – *there,* naked bodies hang from a barren tree rendered derelict of dignity and sagging with mortal gravity – *everywhere,* mouths leer, grin, gape and hanker for crime. The inhuman alimentary system linking these mouths to their vomit belches out the sole truth that binds life to an inexorable and filthy soil; it bemoans: '*your flesh is born to Rot Into Pieces!*' The sadistic portals wink out from the wall where each is hung by nail, tooth and wire; infantile images proud of their adult lacerations – a lithe and unrepentant festival of transversality where conjoined figures of undeniably inhuman form tease at sane anthropoid shapes. Chlamydia makes out a figure with an erect male member for a pointed nose and a shady opening for a mouth.

'Pinocchio is a story about a little boy who learns about honesty *the hard way*...' Chlamydia cries, '...not a lurid metaphor for *sex!*'

'But children are unable to tell complex lies. Lies and duplicitous behaviour come with adolescence, and so does Pinocchio's physical ability to enlarge his *nose!*' says Helmut, all engorged.

Nonetheless, Chlamydia's sense of self-ridicule panics in the face of the sculptural conundrum, such that she had never felt so confused about the correct placement of anatomical parts since participating in pin the tail on the donkey at Dr Barnardo's kindergarten. Who would sink so low? – Devise such diabolical forms to confuse good taste? For whom are these creations intended? Such merciless expressions could only emerge from a cruelly adulterated childhood, and if Chlamydia were ever certain about witnessing subconscious yearning it is right now in this very instant – the hotchpotch clutter of symptoms crying out in this agonised room are nauseous enough to send even a shrink's shrink plummeting into the murky depths of madness and despair.

'Can we *never* learn?' she howls into the icy womb of an apathetic universe.

'*Impossible!*' – a solemn tone – '*Man is condemned to the crimes that define his elevation from the petty and uninspired violence of mere beasts! Ha, ha, ha, ha, ha, ha, ha...! Life – pain – d-d-death!*'

Suddenly a shard of mental lightning sparks Chlamydia's imagination alive as though she were electronically resuscitated from a drab thousand-year slumber.

'*Yes! I understand!*' she shrieks. '*I was blind! Now I can see!*'

In a single blink, Modern Art opens Chlamydia's eyes to its power to redeem the ugliness of the world, to its power to compensate the terminal illness of life, to its power to ornament the wretched gap between life and death. Chlamydia sees how Modern Art rescues humanity from the mortal disappointment that gives rise to an extinction of the spirit...

'*Oh the marriage of reason and squalor!*' she weeps.

In the face of the legion of winking ulcers and vile mouths hungrily sucking the empathy from her body, Chlamydia understands how even the very cruelest of images can brighten up what might at first seem a pointless humiliation of flesh – likening it to excruciating medical vivisection – each experimental atrocity added to the endless anatomy of pain composing the highest of principled traits – *human guilt augmented by elaborate contrition*. Chlamydia sees the architecture of human penitence gape wide like the ribbed vaults of a great cathedral – and as she wrenches eyelids apart yet even further, forcing naked eyeball to gape without a flinch or flicker at the bulging faces of death congealing before her like shivering brawn – her flaming guilt complex is moved to weep pearls of mirth – *and because she now wept like a baby she knew all was right with the murderous shitty world*. Truer still, the creator of this art was unquestionably a genius – but what of the absorbent enigma who freely chose to adorn his quarters with such taxing ornamentations?

Helmut, now a sentinel being, lurks amongst a dark forest of animistic wood carvings from Ekoc, Camgib and Seirf – each embellished with potlatch forms that resonate in the heavy pit of Chlamydia's empty stomach. Helmut is placed poised on hand, waiting for Chlamydia to snap out of her good/evil epiphany. Even though she is now well and truly replete after expelling her dinner anticlockwise into Helmut's water closet, the oddly familiar votive carvings make her yearn for fast food, a hamburger, some fries and even a chocolate milkshake.

Soft music suffuses into the atmosphere – a sad song about cosmic insignificance and the tragedy of small-time hope drifts out through large sliding doors gaping with a view drowned in twilight:

Sittin' on top of the vol-cano
rimming the abyss of dooooom
Only the threat of erup-tion
Can uplift these feel-ings of glooooom

So just take a look down – my friend
Take a look at the ground – dearest fool
Just take a look at God's little crea-tures
Cos' life is just plain cruel

Plant life twists over the window's balustrade from the infinite outside to overflowing into the room. A small area corralled by deep-set armchairs upholstered in big game fur is set aside for wild dancing. It is a dark place designed to trap daylight – a place where an individual might lounge in sunlight and contemplate self-harm as night falls and hearts sink... Yet Mandragorass failed to strike Chlamydia as a restful soul – she imagines him pacing the chamber as a tiger languishing in captivity, tortured by the imprudent attentions of human captors. Even his passive deportment suggests something of an energy-cell ready to blister with volcanic episodes, such that his body exists at arrested velocity, head bound to shoulder by taut sinew, craning his face towards the next imminent spasm. The very idea that Helmut Mandragorass took to Morass for peace and quiet blatantly contradicted the latent menace of his neuro-physiognomy. He made mention of work, but what form of employment could a man of such untrustworthy mannerism undertake on the island of Morass? Curiosity could not fail to intrigue Chlamydia – now foraging across carpet in search of clues, she settles, swallowed whole by a hungry armchair. Helmut tracks her scent and pauses ready to pounce. He studies Chlamydia, lust jeering, twisting close enough to contempt for Chlamydia's core temperature to rise. Likewise her eyes are all over Helmut like hives and the more his skin pustulates with prickling feminine attention the more she appreciates what her squint sees. Chlamydia sees honesty in his pandemonium.

'How d'you know him?' she says, at last, 'Algernon, I mean. How d'you know Algernon?'

'We were at college together,' he says, registering her angst.

'You studied medicine too?'

'Medicine? No, no, no... We were good friends once, but after university we went our separate ways... Hertz was ambitious...'

'He's not using me,' says Chlamydia firmly, 'if that's what you're implying.'

'I wasn't – but in point of fact he *is* using you – whether you choose to recognise it or not. Those promissory sunbeams he emits are not what they seem. I fear your petty engagement is nothing but a humiliating sham... My advice is to shake off any promise you've made to that man before it's set in stone.'

'How can you be so cocksure,' Chlamydia fingering her ring.

'Because I know your beloved Algernon Hertz very well – and better still, *I study human behaviour* – it's what I do – you could say it's my calling...'

'Your calling? What *is* your job for God's sake?'

A brand new smile tangles across Mandragorass's complex face.

'I'm surprised it hasn't twigged. I find I'm usually recognised on sight'.

'Are you disappointed you weren't recognised on sight?' This is not to say Mandragorass is unfamiliar – Chlamydia is positive she has witnessed his face condensed in glossy reproduction somewhere or other. 'So who are you?' she says – '*Mandragorass the murderer or Mandragorass the arsonist? Let me guess – Mandragorass the paedophile or Mandragorass the big fish in a little pond?*'

The sweetly efferent melody lamenting the nature of Creation withers to a close as though sucked back into the big bang from whence it came. Chlamydia's predatory eye stalks Helmut's progress across the room as Mandragorass-the-host flips vinyl. He is an obstinate character, more so than any male specimen she had teased before. Even with all his financial vigour, Algernon Hertz was weak, and so she looked upon little Helmut with rising admiration. And so it was time to go.

'It's late and I've interrupted your work...' she disgorges

her comfy carcass from the lazy mouth of the seat. Helmut intercepts with his meagre trunk, eyes mooning up at her, taking her fleshy hands in his own meathooks.

'Chlamydia! Dearest Chlamydia! Have you bitten off more than you can chew, *chew, choooo?*' Now Mandragorass is a steaming engine with furious pistons battering Chlamydia's jelly.

'Thank you Mr Mandragorass, for the delightful supper! But "*no thank you*" to desert! I want my bed.' She tugs her marigolds half-heartedly from his lame grip, and they easily snap to her sides. She feels bereft, dropped from a great height by the hands that should have held for ever.

'But the night-mare is still young!' Helmut winces in strangled falsetto.

'And I'm engaged!' she bemoans defensively.

'Engaged yes! But have I made any improper advances? No! I've only menaced you ever so lightly... We've done nothing to offend dearly departed Hertz – nothing at all to compare to the magnitude of *his* deceptions – I ask you! – ushering you off to Morass under the pretext he was buying it for you as a wedding present! Really! The cheek! *What a rotten porky pie!*'

Chlamydia's eyes liquefy beyond the rims of sustainable containment.

'Oh what now!' he chides. 'What further injustice?'

'I need a drink...'

'Whatever you wish! – A drink, some food, *an island...*' He pours a glass of amber liquid tasting foul but pleasantly medicinal. She sips.

'To an interesting evening!' he says.

'You're not drinking?'

'Oh, your need is far greater than mine – drink up!' By force of habit Mandragorass's voice mocks, and lowly

Chlamydia feels customarily insulted.

'I came to this god forsaken paradise for one simple reason,' she says. 'The last thing I expected was to encounter a *complication* like you. I don't think I deserve your endless insinuations, not least because I believe you're being deceitful. I want you to stop. I insist!'

'You're right. I've upset you. I've been unfair and mean…'

'I'm no pushover, despite your attempts to haggle with my self-worth. I see through your bigwig persona – you're nothing more than a highly-wrought digestion tract designed for the passage of excrement. I see right through you Mr Mandragorass – I see the true light of day. I know where the drink, soft music and fine words lead!' She swigs the amber drink defiantly, and winces. Mandragorass's impervious smile leers into Chlamydia's personal space. Fingers dab over stiffened shoulder blades, slip beneath lumbering hair, wither down the spastic column where Chlamydia is found shuddering at the bottom. Arousal has never been so agitated. Even Consultant Hertz's miraculous surgical gloves paled into insignificance – even when the anaesthetic waned. The good doctor did shower Chlamydia with material incarnations of affection, precious matter dangled on endless chains – but failed to get her body to feel quite so light-headed, quite so porous and spongiform as her glutinous tissue feels now. Plus Chlamydia is also beginning to feel quite odd upstairs.

Her nose beginning to twitch.

Sobriety senses insurrection in its pretty capitulum – head feels all fuzzy-wuzzy, like it's twisting out of shape.

Now Helmut is beginning to change. His face is bulging, visibly transforming into a pig right in front of Chlamydia's very own eyes. His snout even snorts at her. 'Ha!' Chlamydia squeaks in sincere amazement, '*HELMUT, YOU'RE A BLOODY PIG!*'

But Helmut-pig looms over shrinking Chlamydia, pig mouth leering with ill intent and crackling capillaries engorged with blood. His snout is dripping with pork dew and piggy eyes narrow. His ham-fisted trotters snatch at her and he grunts, snatches busily, snatches grunting plus snatching. Poor Chlamydia tries to lodge a verbal interjection but finds her gob obstructed, and in the muffled tangle she manages to paw her maw but finds two outsized front teeth biting down into her bottom lip. Now the coarse pig has hold of her floppsy ears, holding her head still against her will, the pig struggling to get its wicked way.

'What's up doc?' Chlamydia muffles, but Porky Pig is already hard at work threading his corkscrew sausage into Bunnywabbit's pussy. Bunnywabbit tries to resist, goddamit, but Porky Pig is too big and fat to shove off – squealing like a rubber tyre taking a bend way too tight. Bunnywabbit wriggles, writhes plus kicks like a fucking donkey. All around the violent struggle, ornamental voodoo masks plus clown-heads leer and groan, benign carvings plus malignant etchings plus tearful watercolours come alive, dripping, swirling plus crosshatching around the turbulent room – the womb coils back into itself then spwings out, expands then contwacts plus even bweaks up into slashing machetes plus rwandom tribal pixilations. Chlamydia subsides beneath volleys of proxy spasms, P-P-P-P-Porky Pig clings on to the white-knuckle ride for dear life:

'NOW WE'RE MAKIN' BACON! Uh… uh… uh… uh… I'm coming! Uh… uh… uh…' and then, with an ear-splitting invocation of the all-powerful, Porky Pig's genetic compliment thermospasms out loud:

'OH GOD………!'

Deep downstairs
a factory farm of microscopic piglets
herd from corkscrew
to funhole…

When Porky Pig eventually stirs from post-coital slumber, he finds Bunnywabbit's breath a shallow purr, her limbs lifeless and dreadful eyes pinned to infinity. A timid pulse tells Porky that Bunnywabbit is on her way out, flesh and blood surrendering to the stagnant pool of energy from which life emerged…

'*Chlamydia! CHLAMYDIA!*' huffs Porky Pig. 'Come on! Wake up! Shake a leg! Get busy! Don't make a fucking meal of it!' Earnest grunts complement the cardiopulmonary resuscitation procedure being entertained on Bunnywabbit's flat-lined chest. '*OPEN YOUR EYES!*' it says inbetween snorting '*ONE*' plus '*TWO*' plus '*THREE*' plus '*FOUR*' plus '*FIVE*'. Porky's rhythmic shunts echo in the abstract abyss rumoured to have once been occupied by a 'Miss Chlamydia Love', plus somewhere in the tangled warren of Chlamydia's memory a downtrodden identity begins to stir plus claw its way back to the surface.

'*SIP SOME WATER!*' Porky's panic gushes into Bunny's hallucination and overflows her plughole. All of a sudden, rudely expelled from her submissive languor, Chlamydia Love belches awake in a frothing fountain of liquid, and in a flutter of energetic spunk, catapults Helmut from her convulsive frame. From her goofy gob there escapes an absolutely unconditional shriek:

'*WHERE AM I? WHAT ARE YOU DOING TO ME?… I'M NOT A HAPPY BUNNY! NOT A HAPPY BUNNY AT ALL!*'

The wailing carcass embraces rebirth with a chorus of

screaming epidermal pores resurrected into an inheritance of unbound pain – the injurious skin leaps to its feet, its dreadful shriek swallows up the corridor plus gasps out into the night. Lagging behind, Mandragorass's dwarfish legs are no match for Chlamydia's primal scream, which has taken flight down the volcano before his warning wafts feebly into her sonic wake... 'Come back! It's not safe for you to leave! The night belongs to them! *IT BELONGS TO THEM I TELL YOU!*'

On that dark metholated night, screaming jungle Bunnywabbit hared her way down the volcano slope, blindly ran the gauntlet of werewolves, vampire bats and rabid dogs that snatched and snapped at her fun-fur. Poor Bunny even continued to squeal down the invaginated folds of her soiled burrow until her terror was snug as a bug between Hermès linen. She was petrified sheet-white and pink eyes wept just like a Lethal Dose vivisection experiment, aaah, cute.

• • • • •

In the first light of day, Chlamydia's respiratory system gasps awake with the conviction that it is the last ever lungful of air left in the hole-wide-world. Unmitigated terror shatters the dreamer into brittle consciousness and finds a corpse sweating like a sow tethered on Old Macdonald's insemination rape bar. When reason comes to realise this is not the case, Chlamydia calms and a convenient morning-after-amnesia sweeps over. Added to this selective loss of memory, her mouth is dry as pig parchment – memory and parchment both blank. After teasing breakfast in bed, migraine decides to detox under the sun. Short-term memory is eclipsed and suits Chlamydia's dim suspicions fine. The sun, on the other hand, is faithfully remorseless, tendering maledictive blindness, execration and madness – a reliable penitence for Chlamydia's presumed nocturnal transgressions.

Her finger throbs beneath the pink plastic plaster with which it is mysteriously adorned – yet pain fails to cough up the truth of its injury. This morning's tightly sprung mortal coil is extra wound with general foreboding – and in the absence of lucid recollection, conscience is keen to nag about guilt, shame and remorse. In her mind's eye the omnipotent power of guilt is akin to the flagellating sun strung up above the Earth – remorse is a malevolent presence accepted by mankind as an almighty sublimation and corollary of intense solar power. So the sun inflicts its scalding authority over those convicted subjects found terminally indebted to its sacred phosphorescence, and so, under duress of this cosmically automated life–death mechanism, Chlamydia obediently sinks to the heated sand to lie flat and gather her corrupt flesh, laying prostrate beneath the relentless radiation. She'll gladly burn with remorse, will doze, drenched in the harsh photon wave attack while dark psychic forces trepan their way deep into her boiling mental core.

Soon she wakes inside a dream, alone in a dark suburban cul-de-sac, poised staring at Sunbelle Old Folk's Home, rendered nice and homely for the shamefaced retreat after visiting hour. Inside, godly cleanliness is plagued by the everlasting stench of weary human life. Gouged from the intravenous track-marks of ancient vinyl a feint easy-listening melody pipes Chlamydia along the corridor to a smoke-choked communal room where armchairs huddle in familial groups – backs broken by the relentless burden of tea-time reminiscences. A varicose chain of elderly folk executing the conga distends into the room to loop around Chlamydia, dentures cackling without reserve, skin and bone vying for the visitor's fresh-faced participation. Weary hydrocarbon is circling in a holding pattern, planning escape from the bodies that hold it hostage. But the shuffling chain passes and transforms into a procession of slaves linked by blasphemous carnal connections, the old man heading the invertebrate tailback is baby Jesus Christ, likewise, behind him Gandhi – but Gandhi is fused to our Lord from the rear in sinful fashion, plus, behind Gandhi, Mary Magdalene, likewise shafted by Jehovah-licked-by-Brahma-blown-by-Mother-Teresa-tossed-off-by-the-King-Chimp-of-plastic-surgery-cum-patron-saint-of-child-abuse(you-know-who)-shafted-by-Nostradamus-hand-in-hand-with-Bhudda-shafted-by-Sigmund-fucking-Freud-shafted-by-Adolf-fucking-Hitler-shafted-by-mean-Mother-fucking-Nature-while-Matthew-fucked-Mark-fucked-Luke-fucked-John-fucked-Peter (the prophet Muhammad was absolutely nowhere to be seen...) – the blind-leading-the-blind through the eye-stinging miasma of their own decay – the queue of spineless Old Aged Pariahs shambling by, each convict linked to the next by the incriminating scorn of their very own children who line the path of shame, openly baying plus jeering...

'CORRUPTORS! IMPOSTORS! FRAUDS!'

Dappled in gangrene fluorescence, a lone figure lies restrained to a bed frame by impenitent Velcro ties. In the half-light, Chlamydia observes the silhouette of the Holy Ghost looming over the girl Mary while she sleeps or is abnormally somnolent. But it occurs to the witness that the Holy Ghost is not watching over the girl at all but looming in such a manner that Mary is *virgin* no more...

'Immaculate?' says Chlamydia, *'not very immaculate at all...'*

The looming Spirit acknowledges Chlamydia's revulsion.

'You know me – and you know me too well –' he says. 'I am the comet yearning for collision, the mushroom in the cloud, the impetuous itch in the trigger finger, the unexploded tick tock; I am death warmed up – architect of doom and designer of mud slides – I am the tightrope and the tempest, I am the oil slick choking the sea, I am the overhanging avalanche, the severed cable, the frayed parachute, the icy road, the kitchen knife and the prescription overdose… I am the tarnish to all things bright; I am the hollow sound in the question: '*why am I here?*' I am the lead weight to nimbleness, the immense void crushing down on the obedient prayers of the meek, I'm the smotherer of babies – slayer of Santa Claus, stubber of toes, slipper of discs – I am the bringer of light but brandisher of blindness, I am the giver of life but the subtractor of its worth. You know me well, for I am also the light at the end of the tunnel, the answer to all your prayers, light of your life, reason for being, the candle in the wind, the pot of gold at the end of the rainbow, your salvation, benevolent Redeemer and in-flight Host – I am key to eternal life and Landlord of the hereafter. And what are you? Mere mortal – nothing but the cause of the tinnitus that nowadays haunts these waxen ears. The yobbish infiltration of my peace and quiet – the endless *sweet nothings* whispered into the stratosphere, breathless incantation of my good Name taken in vain simply to add fervour to human coitus – "*uh… uh… uh… uh… I'm coming! Uh… uh… uh… oh my GOD!*" – is this all that I've become to you… this "*uh… uh… uh? MY GOD?*" Does only orgasm invoke the name *GOD* with any conviction? From the darkness of shame, this noise pollution deafens me! *Wretched humanity!*' – and before this pointless digression can meander any further, Chlamydia comes to in the realisation that her pale skin has baked, burned and peeled for the nocturnal sins she assumes to be hers. She has implicit understanding for what it is for heretic flesh to become charcoal – barbequed by the sun – simmering and sagging into indented sand. To add insult to injury, insect life is swarming upon Chlamydia's dopey mass, attracted to the organic capital held captive inside the semi-permeable membrane that defines sloppy insides from arid outside.

On this very morning, beaten by sun and intravenously poisoned by insect anti-coagulants and human pharmaceuticals, dying God did whisper in sweet Chlamydia's shell-like that she no longer – perhaps never did – love her true love Algernon Hertz.

So vindicated by diligent sun worship and punitive dreamtime, Chlamydia crawls to her room to find well earned respite in afterburn lotion and shade. Only now did it impress upon slow burn logic that the heap of hardbacks arranged more or less casually upon the coffee table were boasting a singular moniker on each spine that, only now, begged full attention – only now the mugshot defiling the inside fold of one of the dust jackets confirmed acquaintance with the implacable entity tangled with in real life the night before.

So the bad penny dropped.

Of all possible germinal points on the planet, blessed Morass is the chosen sanctuary of celebrated writer and literary genius Helmut Mandragorass. Of all possible hidey-holes on planet Earth, this is where the legendary enigma settles down to *work*.

Furthermore, it dawns upon dullard Chlamydia that she is the only island visitor blissfully unaware of her proximity to a source of dazzling brilliance other than the sun. In addition, the fact that a selection of celebrated works adorn the table in an unauthorised tribute to his local prominence attests to the legitimacy of his suspicious nature. Such a bestselling voice would surely need to protect its privacy once the sanctity of the creator's lair had been breached and subjected to a prying world. No wonder Helmut had acted all furious when his precious flow was disturbed, no wonder he had thrown her from his house – *but what was she doing up there in the first place?*

Chlamydia mouthed Mandragorass's auspicious titles out loud just to savour their pretentiousness in the open air:

Insult to Injury
Some of My Best Friends Are Geniuses
Unholy Libel
The Involution
My Poetry
Meatphysics
Explaining Christians to Dinosaurs
If looks could kill, you'd be fucking mincemeat – a vegetarian cookbook.

The modest portrait on the dust jacket proves Helmut's head once sprouted hair and it was once ginger. In the portrait, carrot coils coronate the very expression of pure astonishment that Chlamydia recognises as the spastic rage lying latent in Helmut's physiognomy.

'So my little secret's out…' A big headed tone tightly framed in the narrow doorway.

'That you once had hair?'

'No… that I'm *a writer.*'

'Why didn't you say?' Dangling *Explaining Christians to Dinosaurs* by its dog-ear as proof of his shameless deception.

'Because I reserve the right for me to be me – to be more than just a public persona. And I was a little curious to know whether you knew – whether you were toying with me.'

'I have a bad feeling about you – can't quite put my finger on it.' Chlamydia's finger throbs, but the hurt is all abstract and lacking lucid memory of its cause. 'What happened last night? *What did you do to me?*'

'*You can't remember?*' deceitful piggy eyes shift to the book hanging in the balance by a taut page. 'Well… For a start you walked home alone in the dark – I told you it's not safe.'

'Really? Why?'

'You can't wander around after dark on your own.' And nodding to the book. 'So you'll read it?'

'It's unlikely...'

'Why?'

'Because it doesn't want to be read – none of your scribble does. It's mostly unreadable. To be honest, I can't fathom out why you bother to write.'

'I don't *bother* to write, I'm compelled. Compulsion has little regard of consequence.'

In deadpan reply, Chlamydia allows the book to drop. The corner dents cruelly, pages flutter over the broken spine with a feint gasp.

'Quite.' He nods, injured.

'Why aren't you writing today? I thought you were terribly busy.'

'I was, but you disturbed me – now I'm terribly disturbed.'

'And you just happened to be in the neighbourhood?'

'I was just mooching around my island...'

'Gosh, yes – *your* island. I remember... last night...'

'Anything else?'

'No. The odd snippet. Why? Was it so memorable? Did you confess your undying love for me or are you here to confess some dark secret... Why *are* you here?'

'A mental block. A rock solid mental block. I hoped you might help me unblock myself...'

'I'm to be a petty distraction to Mr Mandragorass's mental obstruction? A human purgative? How sweet of you to think of me at such a time. Should I be flattered Mr Mandragorass?'

'Who knows... I merely thought you might want to experience something of the island before rushing home to your pressing wedding preparations.'

Chlamydia glints, sharp as the bright rock being manipulated in full view of Helmut's fascinated, captive eye. She must have blabbed the night before – let the cat out of the bag concerning her misgivings about her engagement to Algernon Hertz.

'Besides,' he says, 'I know Morass like the back of your pretty paw... Please, your carriage awaits...'

Outside, ox shackled to wooden cart, burdened under the delirious sun, spittle-strung muzzle pulled to the soil, weary eyes rolling. The pie bald hide sags from sharp blades of bovine armature as though the creature is impaled upon its own skeleton. The ox is possessed *by an expression of misery* – an anthropomorphic judgement, Chlamydia concedes, unfairly applied to a reflex organism... and yet... while human creatures vomit, curse, shit and howl beyond the sufficient bestiality of animals, they also parade ignobility, filth, and an elegant capacity for torture and dissection. An honourable aim for the vivisectors would be to teach an animal to feel *disgust*. Only then could it be truly civilised... Chlamydia nods up at Isaiah gaily. Sunny Isaiah smiles down with savage gravity. Isaiah remains fixed upon his seat, considerate of Helmut's opportunity to show chivalrous. Helmut ladders up the wheel spokes onto the wooden bench barely to reach down for dainty Chlamydia waiting all prim and proper on the whiter than white grey sand.

'Your hand...'

Isaiah thrashes the beast. Pain shoves forward in the vain hope of escaping further strikes of Isaiah's evil stick. Such is the nature of forward motion on the wheel-shaped island of Morass.

'Isaiah, dear friend, did you find the book I left for you at your house?' and to Chlamydia: 'Isaiah is my most vociferous critic!' Helmut's voice cloys above noisy wooden wheels rasping over dirt and bone. The casual query is designed to draw credulous Isaiah into ironing out the damaged integrity of the very same book abandoned on Chlamydia's chalet floor – although this is a *symptomatic* evaluation, Chlamydia is quite sure that Helmut's manipulation is *at the very least* subconsciously motivated.

'Me tink dat book is a work of genius – as sure as de sea is blue, Boss!' says Isaiah, and, to add gravitas to his answer, whips the ox. 'Explaining Christians to *de* Dinosaurs *is a very fine ting, Boss. Tis sure as de sea is blue dat dem unholy dinosaur fossils id a grave matter t' Genesis, a grave matter t' Creation indeed! – But t' what end Boss? T'what end? Me tink you be scourged wid de idea o' truth Mr Mandragorass – bu' nobody seh blind Faith was anyting to do wit de truth. Ah say de world turn wit' no need o' proof! Truth be a matter fo' de white folk Boss!'* Isaiah teases the beast once more.

'Indeed Isaiah, *indeed… indeed…*' Helmut's petering out speaks volumes nonetheless. Chlamydia's joy leers heavy on Helmut's dented composure while he sheds symptoms profusely for Chlamydia to collect up like sea shells telling tales on de blue, blue sea, Boss.

Mandragorass's ox-drawn tour of picturesque Morass massages its way from Krauss to ocean, picks up the wide coralline road orbiting the island to mimic the rolling shoreline clockwise. Threading from the sea, small dust tributaries work back into the jungle, acting as spokes seeking out the central hub of the volcano. Distributed in clusters along the orbital are traditional buildings built by fisher folk constructed above sea level that now subside into ruin. Lifeless tenants remain, long since surrendering their temperamental living from the undiluted chaos of the ocean. Morass's fishing tradition died exactly where the long charcoal boats lay discarded on the sinister afternoon of their final foray, now broken memorials clogged and sunk by grey sand. All around, endless shrills and catcalls link exotic birds to the licentious attention of intimate predators – animal emissions snake and rasp deep inside the knotted jungle, tangling time and space with the surfeit of life forms that weave and petrify inside the jungle's twisting vortices.

Grazing the sea route Isaiah's ox cart pronounces its graceless arrival before entering occupied territory, and each time the ox cart lumbers into view the few visible islanders cease languid goings-on to diligently return the greedy scrutiny of the passing passengers. Those savages found sitting, stand up, those standing – stand upright. Mandragorass obliges such gestures with a barely detectable nod. Suffice to say, Chlamydia clocks his reciprocation, but abstains from comment. Condemned to thunderous forewarning, Chlamydia concedes that the tour is to be governed by glimpses of the population of Morass represented by a sequence of static vignettes in which an unashamedly indifferent cast hover with hapless wooden poses in stilted sets. Despite this unforeseen anthropological disappointment, Morass possesses a charm far exceeding Algernon's faded presentiments of paradise, and however persistently he manages to nag into mind, Chlamydia refuses to regard him as anything other than an encumbrance to her present adventure – and rather than galvanising Hertz's appeal, her first-hand experience of Morass was beginning to crystallise a fresh view of her fiancé *– she now regarded her fiancé's earnest recommendation of Morass as nothing more than a manipulation of her powerless love of nature – binding her to a suffocating matrimonial contract*… On the other handy-pandy she knew it would be silly to dispense with the good doctor prematurely for fear of unleashing Helmut Mandragorass into the predatory breach… so far, she thought, Mr Mandragorass had been the perfect gentleman…

Eventually, Morass's central village-proper is a lacklustre huddle of whitewashed grey cabins laying siege to a small rectangular square, where open-fronted shops prolapse slag heaps of pewter trinkets out into the molten sun and a café leaks lazy atonal song punctuated by the crisp fizz of the island's sole Insect-o-cutor™. Occupying the marketplace an alfresco bazaar brims with pre-colonial curiosities and evil tribal antiques far exceeding the productive capacity of the Morassean sun-bleached ennui. Only great white hunter-gatherers enjoying day release from Hotel Krauss move with premeditated urgency in the midday sun, smoking out counterfeit holiday bargains, expediting an economic privilege that permits them to haggle the indigenes into submission while competing with other like-minded first-world folk in a frenzy of tightfisted frugality:

'Oh Marcel! This beautiful Dahomean fertility stool was an absolute steal! I managed to haggle the poor soul down to next to nothing! NEXT TO NOTHING MARCEL, D' YOU HEAR! NEXT TO NOTHING I TELL YOU!'

In the exotic ulcer wrenched between the *diseased life* and *economic death* of those unfortunate souls rendered vacant to touristic trysts, the visitor dutifully acknowledges his own providential fortune by sprinkling a little trickle-down economics into the pain, if only to animate the spell of wretched indebtedness that gives guilt its tangible rate of exchange...

...because
at the saline lakes of pure misfortune
the persistent flies congregate,
sipping at the bone-dry tear ducts
of poor little babies too frail
to wave them away...

...oh too ready for the death that stalks short-lived lives...

With a half-hearted shrug, charity utters its magic spell in the jingle-jangle of loose change:

'Well, it's better than nothing!'

In the marketplace a shop-soiled minor is ordered from the business side of a busy stall making a massacre in ethnographic reliquaries and shrunken heads, assorted cursed totems, obsidian skulls, mummified hands, human ears, human noses, human teeth, human soap, fangs of slain prey, sacrificial animal bones hand-carved into magical cattle prods by deft artisans, shell-decorated petroglyphs, plastinated foetal charms, ancestral figurines carved from bonsai wood, blood-stained terracotta earthenware, flagellated skins scarred with the suture marks of ritual dissection with stonewashed serial numbers, and zodiacal plans salvaged from crashed UFOs.

Now the little naked feet tiptoeing on boiling sand, fleeing the red sun, into a ramshackle hut set back from the hustle-bustle, where, dappled in palm leaf shade, the child, boy or girl, it matters little, wrestles the pinewood lid from one of a stack of tea crates stencilled *Made in China* – leaning all the way into the box, lifting out a clump of straw, fingers with a starving bird's beak, plucking straw onto the floor until the floor is matted with straw and the wild-eyed child stands bewitched by the ominous black relic plucked from the UPS lottery box.

Such is the promiscuous nature of exchange, where *Made in China* designates the class of surfeit voodoo commodities cursed with the supernatural power to cost *even less* than *next to nothing...*

Helmut and Chlamydia pass by the village square, orbit the

communal satellite dish portending the heavens as though it were a votive bowl awaiting visitations from insane and mangled gods. Isaiah's painful wand speeds them quickly past old planters' houses, past introverted dwellings perched on paranoid wooden pillars wincing above an imaginary carpet of insects. Derelict for years, the dilapidated shade now hosts the activities of verminous orphans who interrupt their precocious games to chase after the cart and beg for humane debris. But Isaiah's evil stick slashes left and right, opening up juvenile flesh to weep and wail into the maternal shadows. Soon Helmut and Chlamydia draw near to the leering clapperboard church – pure crystallisation of the starched fantasies of early nineteenth-century missionaries; broken envoys of the Faith exiled into the heart of darkness – abandoned in paradise profane; where theological convictions wane in the *schrecklich* heat, malaria and protozoan delirium procuring relief from scepticism, and only the Holy Spirit 'alcohol' can assuage the pagan excesses delivered by midnight mosquito. So the soused heretics were left to grapple with the sickened visitations of an archaic Divinity already murdered by pious minds back home – God dispatched by doubt, paranormal superstition exorcised in favour of secular reason. Nonetheless, the feverish hallucinations of the ritually oppressed lie dormant right here below the extinct volcano, pushing up daisies in regimental succession around the powder-white church – hence, Morass's well tended cemetery accommodates its generations with sun-burnished headstones, choked with fresh flower – albeit garish in modesty, nevertheless indicative of a healthy collective memory of the dearly departed in the zealous Christian minds of the barely living.

Foaming at the beach Chlamydia and Helmut slip into swimwear. Chlamydia wears a two-piece peach Agent

Provocateur bikini set and Helmut strips down to unnameable off-white Y-fronts. They bathe in clear blue water, laughing and screaming, breaststroke and doggy-paddle, splashing and playing like young lovers. To dry off they lie on bone-dry sand and soak up the midday sun. Isaiah conjures a sixteen-litre Thermos Lifestyle Cooler Bag from nowhere, from which Helmut magics edibles for him and her to feast like famished young lovers. Lying on the sand replete, Chlamydia permits Helmut's thigh to brush hers, a forked electric current hisses from the slimy eel, triggering ladylike reflexes to spring uptight.

'It's time you returned me to where you found me,' she hisses.

Isaiah stirs and the ox shuffles.

'Lie back Chlamydia. Relax with me – you're on holiday.'

Isaiah shuffles and the ox stirs.

'I must get back now. My finger hurts. I've had enough fun for today.'

'Enough of *my fun* for today?'

More than is healthy, she thought. Mandragorass's attentions threaten to cleave Chlamydia's immunity wide open and ruin the island of paradise Morass might have been had his libido been marooned elsewhere. Regretful of divulging the slightest of misgivings about Algernon, Chlamydia is now beset by endless defamations – the customary manipulation of the fairer sex by the unfair sex. And while female decorum might prefer to fall out of love gracefully, male eagerness urges its prey over the edge with the ignoble purpose of catching her as she plummets to sentimental obliteration.

If in Chlamydia's mind's eye Algernon might be described as handsome, Helmut is kind on the eye, yet a compost of protean features tangled up in soiled union – eyes, brow, nose, lips, cheeks – each rudimentary feature at loggerheads with the manifest expressions mutually intended to form – in total, an anomalous entity animated by the metabolic spasms that ripple through the bacterial eruptions conscripted into the rank of Helmut's epileptic body, itself an ill-contented population of captive biological souls – from maternal mitochondria to paternal organelle – in short, a wretched hive of discomfort – nonetheless, a *being* of infinitely more celebration to Chlamydia's newborn eye than her faraway suitor Algernon Hertz.

Hotel Krauss eventually in sight, Isaiah thrashing pain-driven ox gasping in forward motion, Chlamydia composed, Helmut dares:

'Will you join me for dinner tonight?'

'Only if you let me rustle something up,' she says.

'Rustle?' says Helmut.

The ox gulps.

Chapter Three

As agreed, Isaiah returns to Hotel Krauss with a freshened ox fit enough to plough Chlamydia up the hill to the white blemish on the harelip of the extinct volcano. There, the visitor is directed to the scullery where a voluminous apron awaits her, mapping the obese abdominal geography of Helmut's discharged housekeeper; and amongst the squalor prepares a simple feast from ingredients judged by eye, touch and tongue to be relatively safe for human consumption.

Helmut displays effort in the alteration of his attire. He wears a bluebottle chemise with ample sleeves rolled up to allow his hands, a linen shirt and fetching ochre tie, moleskin slacks and ebony non-slip pumps. In short, Helmut Mandragorass is magnificent. Only the calloused tips of his digits advertise the wear and tear of a prolific writer, and Chlamydia duly indulges an image of Helmut pounding at the qwerty keys then slips unpunctuated into the fantasy of prolific digits fingering prolific dabs on her taught skin, his tap-tap-tap spelling out b-l-i-s-s...

For their entrée, Helmut enjoys honey melon slices, progresses to meat and two veg in the form of fish fingers, beef steak, courgettes and boiled potatoes. For desert Helmut has stewed plums and stewed banana overcome with mushroom tinted crème fresh. Helmut pours wine – a full-bodied blood-red Austrian with peppery flavour that stings Chlamydia's palate and makes her head feel pleasantly packed with gauze in lieu of attending to an oral abscess. Chlamydia's host manages to lock away any pejorative thoughts and is even complementary about the cooking – in point of fact it is a lifetime since Chlamydia spent such a pleasant evening. When they are done and dusted, Helmut is momentarily governed by good manners and begins to tidy.

'Leave it,' chides Chlamydia, 'can't your imaginary housekeeper see to the mess in the morning?'

'Touché. I'll put some music on in the lounge – join me.'

Helmut leads Chlamydia to a gorgeous room doused in sumptuous crimson carpet, lush pink walls decorated with pretty watercolours and drawings. Very curious free-standing ethnographic sculptures and statuettes dominate the floor space, attesting to Helmut's passion for art and all things sublime. The entire end wall of the room is glazed with sliding doors drawn wide open, the sublime view suffused with milky twilight. Helmut mans the Ferguson high-fidelity, elegantly guiding the stylus to a sad ballad drumming-in hopelessness and human insignificance.

I spy free 'n' easy dol-phins
Breakin' surf in the settin' sun
I'd maim for such meek sim-plicity
Cos' I really dig friendly fun

Now just take a look up-wards – my friend
Just take a sim-ple look – dear fool
Take a look right up into the sky
Cos' one day it's all gonna' fall

'I l-l-love this song,' says Helmut breaking out in broken karaoke, a glimmer of heartfelt grief fissuring the atonal accompaniment whilst whimsical words dissipate into asphyxiating twilight. As if in sarcastic exchange, beautiful wild flowers with perfumed holes blossom into the room – winking around the window's anodised balustrade where Chlamydia settles. Helmut joins her. Chlamydia regards Helmut with satisfaction, likewise Helmut regards Chlamydia with stiffening happiness.

'So, tell me, how do you know my fiancé Dr Algernon Hertz?'

Helmut's impulsive grin capsizes below an ensuing frown, the sodden grin now a wet grimace registering the sincerity of Chlamydia's iceberg query, realising she does not at all recall having made the very same inquiry the night before.

'We were at university, together. We were friends... We lost touch... We had nothing in common...'

'You think he's using me,' says Chlamydia, cutting to the chase.

'Yes I do – I *know* he's using you.' Helmut, ditto.

'How can you be so sure. So adamant?' Chlamydia anxiously fingering her sore ring finger.

'I just am...' Mandragorass's déjà vu tangles uncomfortably across his face. 'I need a slash,' he winces midstream, disappearing into the corridor sharpish.

In Helmut's absence Chlamydia explores the mumbo-jumbled room. It is an eclectic cacophony of objects, objets d'art and objects devoid of reasonable explanation – loosely juxtaposed to form a haphazard synthesis – a three-dimensional incarnation of Helmut's acrazed subconscious coated with the undisturbed dusts of time. Adorning the mantlepiece a papier-mâché effigy of Louis X hung on a miniature wooden gibbet, a luminous obsidian Luger pistol dedicated to Huitzilopochtli studded with pearls and precious stones set snug in its skin holster, a symbol of the animistic objective behind ritual holocaust and expressing the belief that those powers having left the dead will come to inhabit the body of the executant – all seven million of them. A plastic bejewelled sugar skull originating from Mexico's feast of the dead accompanies a forged iron statuette heralding from Fedhala, in Morocco, which depicts a man in an attitude of obeisance but who also appears to be urinating; a gourd in the coincidental shape of a bird, a Congolese tribal adversary represented in mummified wood and racked with tetanus-tipped rusty nails, a fine engraving executed by John Martin depicting Satan flying over the river of Hell… Permeating the musty miasma, Chlamydia is drawn to the row of dust-free books betraying Helmut's transparent pride and joy. Helmut Mandragorass's most prized possessions bark aloud in trained sequential order. Chlamydia slips an early volume out from the shelf, flicking through clogged black pages, pausing here and there to scan the stoned-dead prose, the leaden poetics and Messianic transmission – twisted prattle wrought in a metallic timbre peculiar only to Helmut's tin-pan voice. Such was the bittersweet triumph of his creative genius: selfless artistic experimentation undertaken to satisfy ambitions far exceeding the prejudicial demands of mortal entertainment. But the cherry on the cake is the incriminating portrait planted on the back cover of the book Chlamydia is holding – the book's encephalitic author possessed by an expression of pure astonishment, crowned by a ginger wisp combed from ear to there. Chlamydia's eye follows the publisher's caption sunk beneath the erstwhile likeness:

Bestselling author Helmut Mandragorass lives and works on the island of Morass with his wife and child…

In a molten rage, female anger slides down the mountain into the steaming cold shower, necking an icy vodka tonic snatched en route from minibar to marble bathroom. Chlamydia's heart weighs heavy as igneous rock – white-hot pyroclastic emotions now become granite cold, solidified by the cruelty of a sadist's ice-cool manipulation. She senses love's demon seed unfairly germinate deep inside her, the mandragora taproot, its supple shoots searching out every love-tangled branch of her arterial wound – now irreversibly pollinated, shedding floods of tears, wailing for her own desperate plight, wishing to prune the villainous deceiver from the vulnerable blossom of her senses. Inconsolable self-pity sobs its listless husk into the soothing suffocation of bed – the luminous apparition of Morass for ever tarnished.

• • • • •

Morning no sooner yawns wide awake without reward after a night of sleepless slumber. Chlamydia comes to under the weather, below par, off-colour, poorly and down in the dumps. The injured soul steals from its crib bright and early, skips breakfast for fear of her tormentor swooping down from the volcano to reclaim her attention after she absconded without word the nightmare before. She is resigned to endure another bleak day in paradise profaned, before the boat returns the next day to rescue her – suffice to say, there is no way of drawing the errant skipper to bring his boat any earlier and Chlamydia elects to occupy herself with a stroll through the warped landscape of her tortured mind. Hence vascularised by hate, torment paces. It tramples on the conjured visage of Helmut's wife, and inside the privacy of her own imagination stalks with murderous intent for Mr and Mrs Mandragorass's criminal offspring. Like this, inner-rage circles the volcanic hub with the sun beating progress from behind; raw determination is doomed to the direction filth drains, and now the volcano is a wide open anus, and Chlamydia drains anticlockwise.

Soon enough Chlamydia slumps to dirt when limp legs can

carry dishevelled body no further. She pauses under leafy shade, sits lifeless, waiting for any residual energy to show itself and be sequestered into the forced march. Like this, she walks, crawls and collapses – in this manner she makes progress around Morass, but as the vicious journey persists, the evil twins *hunger* and *thirst* petition with insipid demands. Choosing to avoid the potlatch generosity of islanders and the cloying attention of sun-frenzied tourists, Chlamydia investigates the ragged forest edge for the luck of complimentary sustenance. Fortune finds fresh bananas fallen on the ground, the sugary laevulose tastes so sweet she gorges herself on their soft flesh until her punishing hunger is satiated, then she punishes her hunger by forcing her tripe to vomit the sweet pulp back up. She follows tainted thirst venture into the jungle, pursuing a native path leading to a small glade with a stream teasing worn banks, divulging its regular use for laundry, swimming and washing. Kneeling to sip from the flowing miracle, all around exotic birds link in chains of interweaving contrapuntal, cool air suffuses with the catcalls of invisible life forms co-existing in mutual balance – the gift of life teetering on the edge of its violent subtraction. Emerging from shaded forest, compulsed by the magnetic swell of the shore, Chlamydia submits to the invitation of the sun to lie on heated sand and be luxuriously radiated. She does her best to dispel Helmut from her mind's eye, staring up at the luminous pink fury through clenched tight eyelids.

Superheated gases owing nothing to the temperature of the sun belch violently from the bilious aperture of the volcano with black ash plus pumice mixed with the bright efflorescence of sulphur. Turbulent clouds coil with the cumulative insistence of a morbid nightmare – curling plus entwining with puffs of mephitic vapour winking indolently from the Earth's gigantic blowhole. Poisonous fumes choke the air, black soot plus incinerated basaltic rock propelled by the vertical pressure of seawater gushing into the white-hot magma chamber fuelling the obese paroxysm from deep inside. The heat ripples the purple sea, the sum fury of every single lightning strike to have hailed from sky to Earth, now polarity reversed, after a million years of accumulated wrath – thus, the tectonic holocaust rages from Earth's monstrous bowels, a corpse-grinder's revenge thrust upwards into a mortally wounded heaven. Chlamydia witnesses the planet's subductive power erupt through Morass's volcanic aperture. As the sky absorbs the onslaught, water surrounding the island draws back as though aghast, peeling back from the obscene protuberance to reveal in the vacated abyss many legions of sea creatures stuck fast in slime, vast mountains plus deep valleys hidden in unplumbed depths. The sea rises in its turn, dashes mightily against Morass. It overwhelms the shoreline easily levelling the frail white church plus brittle fishermen's abodes, engorging the populations of animal plus man in sickening affray. Soon the sun is dimmed by a dark mass so dense the cloud begins to collapse under its own weight, a black avalanche raining down from a ruined sky. The horrible cloud begins to sprout filaments that twist plus turn, twisting inside and out of Moebian convection currents, twisting and turning as though a cognisant swarm is moving en masse with nucleated aim. As the air thickens, singular elements begin dropping from the cloud one-by-one-by-one to combine a living, breeding carpet on the ground, plus swathing the earth with the noise of industrious insect jaws. The gluttonous locusts attack everything, distributing systematic genocide to every particle of matter prone to destruction by relentless mandible gnaw. Plus before Chlamydia's very eyes, matter is tortured and transformed, matter replaced *kind* for *unkind*, until locust excrement tints the blue sea dark brown plus green land black. Like clockwork, Chlamydia is drawn into a giddy spin, slowly at first – hollowing out a vacuum inside the locust swarm. From the spindle of her accelerating turbine, mental matter springs from her inner core, centrifugally expelled from a disordered mouth that is no longer hers to monitor. K…O… U… R… U… K… O… R… U… O… K… over plus over… K… O… R… U… Chlamydia spinning in a trance… K… O… R… U… now a man's voice… *R… U… O… K…*

'Pardon?' says Chlamydia politely bewildered by the sudden invasion of coherence.

'*R U O K?*' it says again.

'Who are you?'

'Günter,' it says.

'Who?'

'*Günter*… my name is Günter – are you OK? You've fallen asleep in the sun – I'm afraid you're quite sunburnt.' The soft voice floats down from the brightly crowned silhouette kindly blotting out the scalding sun.

'A white angel – an elderly white angel!' she says.

'*Nein! I'm a retired doctor!*' says the old man. 'Come! Come with me – my wife's got healing cream. She used to be a nurse. My dear wife and I are surely qualified enough between us to attend to a spot of female sunstroke!'

Chlamydia struggles to weary feet.

'That's funny, my fiancé's a surgeon too,' she winces, 'I've got special cream back at the hotel.'

'You mean Hotel Krauss? It's the only hotel on the island. It's an hour's forced march from here – two hours in your barbequed state. Your blood will congeal, stiffen in the vessels like black pudding – you'll risk an embolism. I suggest you come with me. We live just around the other side of those palm trees. I insist…'

Günter takes Chlamydia's hand, leads the trusting child. She follows because the old man has kindness in his manner and Chlamydia is sorely needy. Arriving at the bijou bungalow suffused with an atmosphere of retirement and sporting a healthy kidney-shaped swimming pool, the old man formally introduces Chlamydia to his dear old rubber-gloved wife attending to the kidney.

'This is Brunhilde – my sweetheart Brunhilde! This is our house – our humble abode, our little ghetto in paradise!'

'Very pleased to make your acquaintance, my name is called Chlamydia,' she slurs onto the glacial terrazzo, out cold…

• • • • •

'Christ! It's as hot as a flaming crematorium in here!' shrieks Chlamydia in the kitchen.

'Poor Cinders!' the woman coos as bingo wings lap cool air over exotherming skin. 'Why on earth did you sleep in the sun, silly child!' says the old elderly woman.

'I had nightmares last night. Couldn't sleep. I was so tired…'

'There, there,' Brunhilde soothes, applying soothing cream onto Chlamydia's crust as old hubby Günter cranes nearby adding his oar in.

'A young girl with bad dreams? Can only be b-o-o-o-y trouble!' chuckles Brunhilde.

'B-o-o-o-o-o-y trouble!' chuckles Günter.

Chlamydia shakes her head in denial, but merely augments the feverish shiver already articulating her frame. Branded onto her blistering side a warning: *Caution, filling may be hot*. Skin textured like Pop Tart, brain puréed into delirium, kind Brunhilde pats Chlamydia's insane forehead with a cold wet cloth and whispers encouragement for the sonic reverb to ring off and let her sleep, *sleeep*, *sleeeeep*…

Chlamydia wakes to a glass of ice-cold milk and a warm proposal of dinner. Nurse Brunhilde tells her the fever has safely subsided.

'It's not often that my dear wife and I have such delightful company,' wisps the old crane. Brunhilde endorses Hubby's earnest inflection with a diagonal smile slicing a rueful expression with one of medicated euphoria. Chlamydia instantly warms to companions Brunhilde and Günter. She tells how as an infant she was orphaned in tragic circumstances and so relishes the opportunity for the mature affection of an elderly couple. They are down-to-earth folk, Günter and Brunhilde, and to their invitation of dinner Chlamydia replies she could eat a horse – and to her offer of help, is politely banished from kitchen to lounge.

Chlamydia finds the lounge languishing with the poignant refrains of Richard Strauss's *Metamorphosen*. It is a nice room, ample in size – not especially comfy – sparse but not Spartan. An ornamental duelling sabre is slung above the door, crossed with a brutalised riding crop. An antique glass cabinet guards the inside wall, containing obsolete medical instruments and war medals placed with their red, white and black ribbons draped proudly. A battered Stradivarius is hung by a thread of rustic barbed wire next to a sacred Hindu motif perching atop a Gothic revival bookshelf with volumes dedicated to the first, second, third, fourth, and fifth Reich. The room is gently illuminated by a pink lampshade, the pretty shade striated with tiny ochre veins like pressed leaves held up to a sunny window. In the corner, an upright Steinway hums along with the more strident moments of *Metamorphosen* – accompanied by the odd shiver of the violin's archaic gut.

Dominating the room is a large open fireplace with a heavy wood railway sleeper acting as the impressive mantle. On the mantle a guilt-framed sepia photograph captures the marriage of young Brunhilde to Günter, newly wedded, set in a bleak landscape. Bleak but beautiful like Machu Picchu. The happy bride and groom are posed amongst uniformed friends – all raising a single arm up to shield their pale sepia-blue eyes from the sun. Next to the picture, a fine example of domestic needlepoint modestly framed. Gilded silk lilies ornament an idyllic text by the poet Heinrich Heine:

Mine is a most peaceable disposition.
My wishes are: a humble cottage with a thatched roof,
but a good bed, good food, the freshest milk and butter,
flowers before my window, and a few fine trees before my door;
and if God wants to make my happiness complete,
he will grant me the joy of seeing some six or seven of my enemies hanging from those trees.
Before their death I shall, moved in my heart, forgive them all the wrong they did me in their lifetime.
One must, it is true, forgive one's enemies – but not before they have been hanged.

'Dinner is served!' hails steel-eyed Brunhilde, synchronised with the wall-mounted cuckoo clock expelling its stripy inmate from dogmatic slumber. Dinner is incinerated sauerkraut, hot onion rings, lukewarm chicken drumsticks, cool bratwurst and cold kidney beans. After resolving Chlamydia's alimentary congestion the threesome chitchat long into the early evening. Her immediate preoccupations simply dissolve in Brunhilde and Günter's verdant reminiscences.

'*Oh boo-boo!*' Günter intermittently sopped when his captive sweetheart touched upon a memorable nerve. '*Oh stop it bright-eyes!*' Brunhilde would giggle all coquettish and dilapidated.

'So Günter, tell me how you came to be a doctor,' says

Chlamydia.

'My dear, if you're interested I'll tell you... I studied precociously at school and was admitted to study medicine at the University of Munich and then Vienna. I worked as a medical assistant at the Medical University Clinic in Leipzig and graduated to Frankfurt where I was appointed head experimental physician at the University Institute for Genetics and Eugenics. In the early thirties – *the good old bad old days* – I joined the Stahlhelm, and later the ranks of the Sturmabteilung. After that I made candidate for membership in the party...'

'Party?' says Chlamydia. '*I love parties!*'

'*Günter! Hush!* You're boring our guest...' Brunhilde scolds the old fool with looks that could exterminate, and as the evening drags on Chlamydia comes to appreciate Brunhilde and Günter more and more. In her heart of hearts she hoped one day she too would find similar companionship to share her twilight years. She certainly enjoyed their company, although Brunhilde seemed especially tenacious in her curiosity of Chlamydia's visit to Morass. Shy of admitting the purpose of her journey, she tells how she is on holiday – simply utilising the infamous spa services at Hotel Krauss. She tells them about her Thalassotherapy bath with underwater jets designed to invigorate her fading aura and revitalise her fuzzy-wuzzy metabolism. She tells them about the tepid herbal-infused oils dripped drip by drop onto her pineal gland to distillate the sleepy inner eye into activity. She tells how she submitted to the pleasant torture but was maddened by the endless crescendo of easy-listening music weaving in and out of tangled dolphin/seagull lament. She tells how she was a millimetre away from death, and how she watched her own self languish from the harrowing perspective of an out of body experience bobbing on the sunken ceiling.

Brunhilde dilates a cavernous yawn, and Chlamydia rises to leave for the hotel. She is met with die-hard resistance – both Brunhilde and Günter insisting she remain – Poor Günter is unable to walk the whole distance to Hotel Krauss and back again, so Chlamydia must stay the night and leave in the morning. Short of being detained by force, Chlamydia overwhelms their protests with an eagerness imbibed by their own spirited hospitality. Returning to Hotel Krauss is a *cathartic* necessity, she explains, leaving them unimpressed by her Jew psycho-semantics. Worse, Brunhilde and Günter's anxiety intensifies tenfold when she drops the doodlebug that she is to leave Morass the very next day. Although Chlamydia swears on her dead mother's life to return in the morning to bid farewell before undertaking her long voyage, Brunhilde nonetheless fills the doorway with fading petitions.

Poor Günter perseveres in escorting her as far as senile ailments allow, but his delicate luminous outline eventually fades and shrivels in the moonlight as vivacious Chlamydia trots on:

'Chlamydia be careful! Keep to the shore road... Chlamydia! Please stay! Don't go!'

Beneath the star-pricked blackness the silver beach tempts Chlamydia around the volcanic hub. Blinded by the tarry darkness and compressed by crushing inconsequentiality, she harkens to the night as it is sucked into the black hole of the inhaling volcano. Companion to her side, the shore unfolds a cool sea breeze sweeping inland. All seems well with the dying world – the Earth is scorched pitch black for nightmares to rage, the night is pH7 22° centigrade – ideal incubation temperature for soil to reek with effervescent eukaryotic cells and plant life to breeze carbon dioxide – venting the night with sufficient morbid gas to resuscitate somnolent anoxic vampires... Brisk-paced Chlamydia is struck by the idea that the Earth's atmosphere may only contain a finite number of breaths. She belches stringent exhaust, paces and respires in the knowledge that her industrious lungs are busy depleting the dying world's diminishing oxygen volume. She might try minimising her aerobic intake, but no sooner collapses into energetic panting. The embryonic jungle shivers thin air in her asphyxiated wake... Shadow meshes of variegated vein lattice with thorn or nettle stem; tiered leaves wave at the Moon's deflected sunlight, anamorphic foam structures ushered by the surf tumble up the shore, cross her path to gently collide into weed trip-wires that trigger delicate frames that collapse and liquefy. Mother Nature's power cell is bursting with alkaloid sap, verdant surfaces herniating with anti-personnel bulbs itching to explode radon mushroom clouds, phosphor needles laced with nerve toxin, ricin, opium, C13HN2O3P2, happy-triptomines, parasitic ergot – the sun's refracted delirium held captive inside photosynthetic plant life: psychotropic seedlings clenched inside time-release kernels, napalm snares and tuborescent grasses primed to scatter their innards outwards into the dying atmosphere. Above the necrotic svelte, cellular cloud swarms hang, circulating turbulently with contagious intent, puppet colonies formed of weightless microbes trapping moonlight like frozen breath vapour leaking from an invisible organism...

Marching anticlockwise in the vain hope that time might be reversed – Chlamydia heads home – unwinding the beach parallel to the coralline road, ignoring the peculiar white-hot star hung above the cloaked black shape of Morass's volcanic hub. She ignores the sixty watt supernova burning with incandescent rage in the window of the injurious house up high... Then soft music floats down, trembling delicately upon the breeze. So she pauses to gather the sweet and unmistakable melody, but an inharmonious male tone cleaves through an angel's voice like axe splitting bone…

Sittin' on top of the vol-cano
rimming the abyss of dooooom
Only the threat of erup-tion
Can uplift these feel-ings of glooooom
So just take a look down – my friend
Take a look at the ground – dearest fool
Just take a look at God's little crea-tures
Cos' life is just plain cruel

I spy free 'n' easy dol-phins
Breakin' surf in the settin' sun
I'd maim for such meek sim-plicity
Cos' I really dig friendly fun
Now just take a look up-wards – my friend
Just take a sim-ple look – dear fool
Take a look right up into the sky
Cos' one day it's all gonna' fall

Time waits for no man
To decipher the riddles of chance
The blind are leadin' the blind
In a deaf 'n' dumb barn dance
So take a peek inside yourself
Take a look – dearest fool
Take a peek inside your human soul
Cos' pride is vanity's mule

When Mother Nature finally rag-es
And the cradle blooooows its top
All the world's child-ren

Will be turned to vol-can-ic rock
S-s-so look downwards – my d-d-dearest friend
P-P-PEEK RIGHT INSIDE – DEAREST F-F-FOOL
LOOK AROUND AT YOUR FELLOW CREATURES
COS' GOD IS COLD AND C-C-CRUEL

As the prescription dirge fades to the sound of the blunt needle scuffing dust, a lone voice wails deep into the night…

Tomorrow Chlamydia Love will leave Morass for ever. Never to return.

She will initiate the disavowal of her own innermost feelings for Helmut-the-unattainable.

She will bid farewell to dear Günter and Brunhilde in the morning.

She will return home to face fiancé Consultant Surgeon Algernon Hertz once and for all.

She will take responsibility for her life.

She will make a mental note.

A psychological list.

Glancing up at the human lightbulb waning amongst the stars, Chlamydia wonders what exact earthly distance will permit her to forget Helmut. She concludes: *half the circumference of the world plus the height of the highest mountain*… A rabid howl carries on the wind beyond the domain of the beast's territorial influence. The forest shivers. The ocean's ragged edge splinters into the infinite fractals that make up its fluid motion. The world worlds and the demented moon moons…

The missionary church is crystallised in Morassean moonlight, luminous white, serene and pious – too late for the dead God it was dedicated to. Cemetery flowers reek in the night, blossoming above the subterranean souls laid to rest beneath the soiled fears of the living. In the dead of night, devoid of daytime hue, stagnant perfume stenches the air, choking the atmosphere with the odour of morbid excrescence. The moonlit picket fence wrenches upright from consecrated soil in the manner of a cheap fluoridian smile shielding the dilapidated gravestone molars relegated to buckle in the yawning darkness behind. As Chlamydia crosses the lifeless church without due attention to its foreboding ordinance, she is swiftly vigilant of drums and human chants dampened by the sound of lashing waves. She draws closer to the uncanny hint of fire flickering beyond the furthest row of moonlit gravestones. Compelled by natural curiosity (compacted under jurisdiction of a moral obligation), nosiness deviates from its route to enter the wooden gate, sneaks along the gravel path grovelling up to the church door – now goodie-two-shoes genuflects cowardly – passes onto the cemetery lawn, crawls on all fours until crouching behind a small headstone. Illuminated shapes are animated by raking light, jagged profiles tangled by silhouetted layer of plant, tree, vine and bush. Further enflamed, curiosity stalks closer to the inferno, delivering prying eyes behind a large memorial, still nearer to the scene. Clinging to the stone, peering above its chipped top edge, a tender finger digs into the stone's chiselled inscription…

FAMILY MANDRAGORASS

Of course. Poetic injustice. *Here rests Chlamydia* – embracing Mandragorass on all fours, knees pressed in mandrake sod. Yet from this unholy position she can make out anamorphic silhouettes chasing dancers plus animals around an excited fire. The illegitimate blaze stokes out of control, encouraged by the presiding spectre of obese proportion who delegates incomprehensible orders to the participants who respond in kind with delirious enthusiasm. Some such resonant order issues – the dancing alters configuration, shapes twisting and turning and latticing with the twisting turning pattern of the drums. Emerging from the deepest shadow a limp body fetched on a bamboo stretcher to be placed next to the fire. Firelight recognises the lifeless body of Isaiah the ox cart driver. The high priestess lumbers forward to perform intimate rituals with Isaiah's lifeless body before the profaned corpse is tipped unceremoniously into a shallow grave beyond the pyre. Ecstatic dancers jostle at the filthy precipice of the hole taking turns to leap across as though it were an abysmal chasm reaching down to Hell itself. A nubile savage girl ushers forward with the purpose of lifting her grass skirt to gush urine into the hole. A shackled goat plus clenched chickens twitch while orders bark. Now the figures halt, the drumming stops, the rigid goat is drawn to the flames, the plump chicken bodies attached by elongated necks. The totemic figure tips into the firelight, flames lick her big fat whitened black face pink. Menace forms its malevolent smile, has evil in mind, and from the tangle of charred trees, a host of glazed red eyes open wide and stare from the abysmal shadows of powdered pale black flesh in the sudden direction of Chlamydia's shallow grave.

'*You!*' she points. '*You mus' ged away from dis place! Ged away! Ged away while yo' can! Ged away before de demon seed begin growin' in yo' sof' belly! Ged away! FLEE! LEAVE MORASSSSSSSSSSSS!*'

The obese spectre's gimlet eyes are all aflame. She is delirious. Chlamydia is petrified.

The chilling forewarning twists through quaking trees and shivering leaves, the bird necks are wrenched, plus the goat loses its head. The quaking, shivering body of goat plus chickens are thrown into the fire – a comet of red embers spray into the carbonised trees plus the dancers go berserk, the drumming now ragged, superhuman leaps being performed plus the berserkers shrieking as if their raw flesh is burning with fizzing leopard spots or napalm. Chlamydia rises slowly from the Mandragorass family grave, blindly stepping backwards keeping one eye trained on the volatile countenance of her accuser – a petrified exodus stiffly controlled by ribs of rigid muscles plus gritted nerve; after a short and stilted distance she turns to escape – her method sheepish at first – then hoofing it like a donkey, head locked forward by the thought of what noumenal phantasm might be tailing behind. Behind, a cacophony of noise urges her flight. Chlamydia ushered from church by her own vile imagination – sprinting across the sand, desperate for the safety of Hotel Krauss *with its unhurried rhythm and fine living*…

• • • • •

Morning yawns wide without reward after a night of sleepless slumber. Chlamydia is markedly under the weather, below par, off-colour, poorly and down in the dumps. So the injured soul steals from its crib dull and early, skips breakfast, packs the hideous Samsonite and dumps it on the windswept porch in readiness for escape. Outside, chalk storm clouds scrape across slate sky, wind rakes the shore and sea raises to a boil. She will wait until lunchtime when the boat is due to come rescue her from Hell's island. Suffice to say, politeness had sufficient time to visit good friends Günter and Brunhilde.

'We're so glad you came –' sing Günter and Brunhilde above the squall, '– we were *so* concerned about you walking home alone like that last night – really!' They greet Chlamydia into their abode with offers of a tepid bratwurst breakfast.

'Well 'tis odd you should say…' says Chlamydia, feeding the

intrigue. 'On my way home last night I came across a real life voodoo ceremony in the grounds of the little white church – of all places, the cheek! I saw them bury poor Isaiah the ox cart driver, they danced over flames and slaughtered animals. I saw it all with my own eyes! The high priestess even warned me to leave Morass!'

'Mumbo jumbo!' mocks Brunhilde, nervously.

'Jumbo mumbo!' mocks Günter, fretfully. 'Isaiah'll be fine,' he says. 'He's been lightly paralysed with blowfish poison. When the drug wears off, he'll climb out of his grave as though he's returned from the dead! But I promise you, old Isaiah's alive and kicking!'

'– His head will be thumping! To be sure, a real life zombie…!' Brunhilde takes up hubby's slack but changes tack: 'Yes! We hoped you hadn't forgotten your promise to visit us in your eagerness to leave last night – *and how is your nasty sunburn and nasty finger?*'

'I wouldn't have missed saying adieu to my old friends Günter and Brunhilde – not for the whole wide world!'

'Say *goodbye?*' quizzes Günter.

'*Goodbye?* I don't think so,' adds Brunhilde. 'Can't you feel it? Shhhh! Listen. There's a mean old storm brewing. The *Amorous Peacock* won't be going anywhere today!'

'*But it must come! I must go!*' cries Chlamydia.

'There, there,' soothes the old woman sagely, 'you're missing your young man…' Taking Chlamydia's hand in her own to study the swollen finger, now smooth impersonal skin, Chlamydia's fingerprint erased by swelling. 'Well that's no good,' she says ushering hubby. '*Come and see,* bright eyes! Doctor Günter! Examine poor Chlamydia's finger!'

Günter arrives with disinfectant and swab.

'*I must leave this place! The boat must come!*'

'The storm is dangerous,' says Brunhilde, and looking at the ring disappearing on Chlamydia's big fat finger adds: 'Anyway, I can't imagine why your young man even let you come here all by your own.'

'*Nonetheless*...' shouts Chlamydia waving goodbye, disappearing into the meteorological turmoil determined to meet the imaginary boat.

Chlamydia sat on the shore clutching her Samsonite. The mocking sea danced wildly before bobbing eyes and the wind whistled in and out of her ears, nose and throat. Iron cast in foetal position she waited nearly all day for the vessel to break the horizon, watched the storm rise as the likelihood of escape sank from sight. Chlamydia wept floods as evening dawned and light failed. She returned to smug Hotel Krauss *with its unhurried rhythm and fine living*, only to find her chalet reallocated to a hysterical French couple with a newborn *enfant terrible* whose own residence had become infested with sheltering insects, rats and snakes and crocodiles and bugs...

'*No Miss Love... there's no mistake. If you recall, your original booking (made with our office on the mainland) was for three nights only...*'

• • • • •

It is dark by the time Chlamydia billows onto Günter and Brunhilde's doorstep. She hesitates before knocking on account of eavesdropping the sound of animal pain howling inside. Outside the storm rages and Chlamydia knocks hard enough to distinguish herself from the tyranny of the weather. Red-faced Brunhilde opens up and ushers Chlamydia in.

Wincing Günter takes time to materialise.

'Come in, come in!' sings Brunhilde above the thunderstorm, welcoming the windswept orphan into the house. 'What's happened? Didn't you return to the hotel?'

'There's no room at the inn!' she wails. 'They reallocated my room to someone else because I was supposed to have left Morass already and the storm has already damaged some of the rooms and they don't have anywhere for me to stay tonight, I mean, can you actually believe that? The boat didn't come – perhaps it sank – there's no way to contact the mainland and the supply boat doesn't come for days! I'm stuck fast – going nowhere at a rate of nots – *oh! And I'm supposed to be getting married!*'

Brunhilde and Günter pity the crestfallen specimen, usher her tears to the sofabed on account of their house only having a master bedroom and no designated guest room. Günter fetches stripy pyjamas reeking of stale mothballs – 'From the Sudetenland,' he says, with sentimental gravity pulling sad old eyes downwards. 'Sleep now, dear child, and in the morning we'll attend to your tragedy.'

Chlamydia fell asleep exhausted, haunted by vindictive elements swirling inside plus out. In her sleep she is whisked away on Captain Oceanic's boat, bobbing violently on the waves, as though the vessel is a toy in the hands of a God-sized delinquent child playing in the bath. Oceanic is all fingers plus thumbs plus even speaking in tongues. Chlamydia is trying to escape Morass by boat, but also trying to escape the filthy clutches of the captain of the boat she is trying to escape Morass on. Before she can resolve her tangled flight, a huge unfriendly wave swallows the boat hole and Chlamydia, sucked under by the swell, sinks, down and down and down to the bottom of the deep blue sea sea sea. And all that she can see see see is licentious sea life clenched around a phosphorous fire waving twigs of seaweed, chanting at the spray of red embers sparking up into the inhaling current. Evil in itself appears in a fancy-dress pig suit, holding a torch that casts bright disco light onto the seething burlesque for wild go-go dancers convulsing as though their scaly skin is being burned by napalm. Although Chlamydia is happily amphibious she is still compelled by the shore. Invaginated rings appear around her blubber and pulse along her length in turn, allowing her to crawl from the shallows. But no sooner has she escaped the rasping sea than she becomes driven sick for fear of the future maggots gnawing their way through endless unmitigated muck towards a time in the near future when they must gnaw at her unadulterated filth. As her invaginated body worms up the beach she realises that she has become a big fat amphibious maggot…

• • • • •

Morning brought obscene calm and the evidential remains of the proceeding violence. Chlamydia felt sick as a dog and the ransacked shore was littered with pretty patterns of waterlogged debris and sand exchanged and fought over by sea and land. At breakfast Günter and Brunhilde told Chlamydia this: 'Chlamydia, we have a solution. We shall ask our son if you can stay with him until the boat comes.'

'You've a son? *Here? On Morass?*'

'Yes!' Günter and Brunhilde sing. 'Yes we do! A son!' sings Brunhilde. 'Günter can take an ox cart to see him – soon as greedy Günter finishes his breakfast, won't you piggy-wiggy-woo?'

'It'll be a pleasure,' says Günter's snap, crackle and pop.

In Günter's absence Chlamydia and Brunhilde sip Earl Grey and chew the fat and sift through the night's flotsam and jetsam. Günter returns with happy news:

'He's glad to help, but wonders if you might assist him with some work.'

Brunhilde's steel-blue eyes stab at the old man.

'*WORK!*' she says. 'Work? Trust him to find something practical in a charitable gesture! He'll work himself into an early mass grave.'

'Please Brunhilde – don't chafe! It'll give me something to do,' says Chlamydia. 'I'd be grateful to do *something* for my keep! It'll keep me occupied! Anyway, what does he do – this mysterious son of yours?'

'I write... *I'm a writer...*'

Chapter Four

Isaiah, devoid of his usual potlatch smile and reeking of soiled earth, tortures the emaciated ox forward with a relentless stick while uptight Helmut torments passenger Chlamydia with downright silence. The ox heaves above Helmut's hush while Chlamydia ponders her fate, which, given this new turn of events, seems especially spiteful – since Günter and Brunhilde's act of paternal beneficence has played their newly adopted daughter into the tiny gammon hands of their son – Chlamydia's erstwhile tormentor. And what of this oddity? Observing Helmut, who betrays little hereditary likeness to Brunhilde or Günter save for his diminutive stature, sits rigid with a hideous and vengeful profile. Chlamydia expects Mummy and Daddy Mandragorass are unconditionally proud of this malignant primordial dwarf, who, against all odds, has eked out singular success from a full-sized world.

The tumultuous sky looms above the humbled volcanic morass which looms, in turn, over the swaying emerald jungle – everything looms, woven into the very fabric of Chlamydia's anxiety as she weaves towards the luminous house. Today the house seems altogether different on account of a strange fate laying in wait for Chlamydia indoors. Reluctance climbs the steps and Helmut struggles with the luggage behind. The front door swings open wide unannounced, and an obese black spectre spills from the gaping frame like a sickly tongue, gimlet eyes freely bulge at poor Chlamydia with savage disapprobation. Fear wilts down the balustrade, deferring to Helmut in the assumption that he fully appreciates that the unwelcome visitor is not only a thief disgorging from the house with stolen goods but *the high priestess of local voodoo*…

'We have a guest…' says Helmut addressing the spectre,

pleasant as his present bitterness permits.

'Yes Massa…'

The housekeeper's attention weighs heavy on Chlamydia such that Chlamydia well appreciates that the insinuating high priestess has recognised her from their midnight encounter in the church cemetery. Helmut manhandles the Samsonite into the hallway tenacious like a dung beetle.

'*Maman Terreblanche* will show you to your room.'

Maman Terreblanche, the human boulder, thunders down the hallway with Chlamydia in gravitational tow. In stark contrast to the splendour of the rest of the house the room set aside for Chlamydia is Spartan – less a guest room than a *gemütlich* staff quarter. The bare boards pine out in neglect of carpet and the walls are scrubbed a perfunctory brilliant white. A solitary bed with a white cotton throwover speckled with embroidered fragments of broken glass sits uncomfortably to one side of the chamber, while a petite dresser stands ornamented with a pink lampshade, the pretty shade striated with tiny varicose veins – like pressed leaves held up to a sunny window. Above the table a narrow portal squints out over the angry jungle swirling below.

Maman Terreblanche heaves Chlamydia's case onto the bed and withdraws to observe the unwelcome guest digest the composition of her simple abode.

'Its… cute! Cosy! Homely! I'll surely be snug-as-a-bug-in-a-rug here!' humble pie turns with a home-made smile crafted for Maman Terreblanche's benefit, but the obese carbon spectre is nowhere to be seen. Chlamydia's internal monologue freely admits she is fortunate to have a roof over her head and the opportunity to work to repay the privilege. She wishes for no further entanglement with the author of her heartache, since there can be no satisfying conclusion to such a relationship and the wisest course is to scupper any still buoyant feelings and sink with the doomed vessel. She will keep herself to herself and await news of Captain Oceanic. Two or three weeks wait for the supply ship is a fate worse than death… But touch driftwood, the Captain will come sooner.

While unpacking her Samsonite Chlamydia's thoughts settle upon her fiancé – now bound by disappointment, she sorely begrudges his two-facedness, and now even doubts the existence of those poor unfortunates queuing for the attention of his doubtful scalpel. Nevertheless, Chlamydia is quietly confident that once the wedding preparations grind to a thankless halt, her absence will be noted – at least by those expecting to be paid for their labour. Then, Algernon will come find her. And perhaps poor Captain Oceanic *has* been swallowed by the storm. Perhaps someone has already been dispatched to fetch her. Perhaps she best leave a note at Hotel Krauss advising any would-be rescuer where to find her. Perhaps not. Perhaps Algernon can simmer in his own panic, suffer for his deception – *alleged or not*.

By way of pressing an ear to each successive door along the corridor downstairs, Chlamydia finds Helmut's study by the sound of A4 being mistreated by typewriter. She taps at the door without hope of being heard, yet it swings open with an uncanny perception of her presence.

'What do *you* want?'

'To work – as agreed…'

'Well, try knocking with a little vigour! – Next time refrain from loitering around my keyhole like some tremulous chambermaid!'

• • • • •

So Helmut is nice no more. No more Mr Nice Guy is now the ill-mannered boar that Chlamydia loves and loathes helplessly

– the unwholesome *Schweinhund* she is now doomed to muck in with each and every working day. On the other trotter, resolute abhorrence is preferable if Chlamydia is to toil in such close proximity to this pig, otherwise she has little hope of avoiding lapsing back into the self-doubt and despair where Algernon found her…

He steps aside, inviting Chlamydia's eye inside.

'This is *the* study. This is where I *write*…'

Chlamydia beholds a forest of pulp teetering beyond its plausible balance – loose leaves already toppled from the upper canopy littering the clearing where Helmut's wooden desk and manual typewriter sit huddled in volcanic conspiracy, an island of tranquillity surrounded by towers of babble – *a holocaust of words chattering with profligate prose*… Books lay open everywhere – spines broken and hearts plagiarised. The filing cabinet is weighed down by reams of paper, drawers retch half-open and box files dented on the floor where content cascades from disorder to chaos. Bookshelves bulge with essential existentials like: *Kane and Abel, The Prodigal Daughter, First Among Equals, A Matter Of Honour, As The Crow Flies, Honour Among Thieves, The Fourth Estate, Twelve Red Herrings, The Eleventh Commandment, To Cut A Long Story Short, Sons Of Fortune, A Prison Diary (I-III), False Impression, The Gospel According To Judas, A Prisoner Of Birth, Overcoming Low Self-Esteem: Self-Help Guide Using Cognitive Behavioural Techniques*… The floor is strewn with yellowing newspaper cuttings curling like autumn leaves and tight-fisted pages shaped like dirty snowballs; an archaic Dictaphone rests broken on the floor where impatience hurled it – analogue tape spews from the magnetic head with Helmut's precious words indolently rejected. It is plain to see that Helmut's literary world is in sore need of feminine attention! Incriminated by the chaos, Helmut stands uncomfortably accused by Chlamydia's presence.

'I need these papers tidied – pronto!' he says, pointing all about the room, rendering the specificity of the task and the authority of the taskmaster ludicrous.

'*My God!* How can anyone function in such an adolescent mess?'

'*Mess?* One man's mess is another man's method...'

'Indeed, indeed... *Indeed.*'

'The research notes from my last bestseller *Meatphysics* need collating. The British Library archivist is harassing me endlessly, but I don't have time to do it myself – I'm knee-deep into the next project. And this is it...' He pats the manuscript on his desk like a father bestows a son his hands-on praise. 'You keep your grubby mitts off!' he snaps. 'And no peeking! No one but Maman Terreblanche handles my work before it's handed to the publisher. Read me?'

'*LOUD AND CLEAR!* Actually I'm quite au fait with the art of publishing – my dear Aunt Shigella is senior editor at—'

'*Oh spare me the tyranny of Aunty Shigella's expertise!*'

With a demonstrative surrender, Chlamydia concedes to humble knees to begin gathering Helmut's sedimentary litter. Helmut is greatly pleased by Chlamydia's submission, but from the deliberate humility of the floor, crafty Chlamydia freely examines the mollified oddity square up to the modified typewriter whose qwerty keys are greatly enlarged (like an infant's toy) to accommodate the author's especial needs. She watches Helmut linger before the mocking machine, teetering before the rewardless banalities that lie in wait. With a metallic clutter Helmut hurls everything into the next sentence with ferocious fingers thrust forward in an irreversible kamikaze dive. Chlamydia can only imagine: '*The night descended like a slab of dead black meat...*' or: '*His black heart sank as darkness fell like a slab of dead meat...*' or: '*The slab of black night fell dark like meat...*' despite the ergonomic crudity of the machine, Helmut types like the wind.

'Anyway...' yells Helmut, thinking aloud above the mechanical chatter – *'If I want to read a bestseller, I'll b-b-bloody well write one...'* Each staccato volley pounded into the machine culminates in a climactic clot of keys tangled together on the page. The foul-mouthed wordsmith unpicks the clogged-up mechanism, rips paper from machine, screws it into a ball and flings it at the autographed mugshot of Jeffrey Archer, guilt-framed and banged up on the facing wall. From the floor Chlamydia ascertains her task is a lifetime's work, and will receive minuscule praise for her labour in relation to the accolade the author has already deserved for his. So she pursues the paper chase across the room, inventing a path that winds to the writer's desk where she hopes that, one day – if tidiness proves its worth – she might even earn the right to take dictation; wishing to forge a way into Helmut's latest work and thus into Helmut's mind, considering that it would be nigh impossible for an author to write a book without a significant compliment of his aboriginal inner-self making the transversal leap from imagination to blotted blank page.

Where Chlamydia finds evidence of an earlier stab at filing – presumably by some other lackey press-ganged into similar contract – subjects have been arranged A–Z but without proper sub-indices or general categories. Arthropod, aeroplane, antelope, anaemia, anaerobiosis, autopoeisis and army ants are all filed under A without care for their evident heterogeneity. Hence it is a mammoth task with a capital *m*. Nonetheless, Chlamydia is determined to apply herself without discouragement, sorting and stacking, collecting and collating while Helmut savages his machine with furious digits hammering injurious thoughts onto page after page after page after page page after page after page after page page after page after page after page page after page after page after page page after page after page after page violently torn from the typewriter, screwed into tight balls and chucked at Jeff.

So the room bristles with static energy such that the loose pages Chlamydia endeavours to tame tend to stick to her body as though she is covered in glue. Helmut hammers on relentless while Chlamydia claws the floor, gathering paper to her magnetic body as best she can, but here and there the odd word begins to leap out from the errant debris of Helmut's *Meatphysics*... odd words like 'tyranny'... 'membranous'... 'despotic'... 'crack-baby'. She pretends to ignore them and persist with the alphabetical task, but soon whole sentences begin to appeal to her attention such that a deranged monologue begins to accompany her labour... 'Stimulated cellular orgies coagulate and unclench... in rupturous movement...' the voice becoming deafening... 'Junkie tracks crushing bodies into ulcerated crater plague pits serving to gestate future fuel for future war machines to jack-up and jack-boot...' Chlamydia is compelled... 'The magnetic form of the predicate jerks you back into the terminal clot of dominant significations...' Now a complete page reads itself aloud without reserve... 'The sun deluges its chemical holocaust to the earth with blinding indifference... Oncogenic mutations distribute the embalmed solar energy, happily expediting their planetary obligation in the diffusion of their inherited share... The oceanic scaling device vomits on the shore like a doG disgorging bloody chicken bones stolen from its master's drain... Convulsed bulimic tides spit out burdened skeletal detritus... Tearing out the impersonal fossil scars and perjurious bone matter betraying its atheism by outliving ragged flesh... The lipid husk found clinging to armature for drearest life... Bone is the crucified memory of a goD whose perdulant ruins fuse the collective un-body... The crustaceous exoskeletal silica and de-fleshed calcium phosphate forming the ossuary reef...

Wrenched from the sea the fusion-nucleated atoll is a vast alien formation… A trans-taxonomic ferment and mass grave of compound organic and inorganic trash washed-up the selection gradient of Darwin's beach… ˝dO‹È?!dM]«A°¨S o&R?& à?|© ±&??5û <…?Q?≠ »O!?Ébe"ui…/V]Qöèëî ï+‹;©¡» 8ù,=√$DÒ%g§°Ìa?√a"⁄t• ÓW?? °P a g e N u m b e rOJ QJ mH%^$ü†çÇ< A@Úˇ° <%4 Z@ Ú 4 P l a i n]G êT®````…`°```¬`∫` Ta n 5 ê Ë¨çu¢››fi·° »Ä S y m b o l 3 êƒÎÙ¨ ·ªª(‹›°WÂÊÁÏÌÔ¨hëA r i a l 3 ê ~uüµ¬%… ?/+_@ [ªºº ê 7 ê ub Ëø ˘¬¬¬¬HG— — — C o u r i e rÚ˜lä ±Æ2 T *•¶‡flfi i™⁄— , @Òˇ , —Ò˜˜Ó©ÁN o r m a l †Êøù~Ú?fÅ '?À!È).oMX?FAk ·§•??öˇ?ûY?±P?]5P?? ;r≠ S!áäàeTÌ´©]3?"ë~µ·ï=±©õ?+·'| ßl ????ô÷ ~?ªqöqpn?›^É=âJ ´msDå·J?ù%?¯,yÁÍ5JQ¶ rU'ãÿiù??Õ9àÍ¡Ú HÖ&Á‡Y\~1}®?°1†SÉµ KóI d"- A THRESHOLD?A?â»¨,? ??Ò'+±JWHERE ¥‹@° & Cursed by diseased articulation, negotiating humane essence out of informatic loss – howling at evolution's horizon, which shimmers in the promissory future&Ì?4 aÔë] ë?È™GôúAÈ? 2·q∆∆è›åâ?A |mÒ ô·@?? %E5ÆyÌ"ï VbùQ<Waterlogged souls drag themselves over the *Homo sapiens'* shoreline,UBà∂iC ÆÕ? gÌ¡(êßÖ9°î'ÿÂ∑ç9;•ü›*bU|áç†"1Å kxE?∆b9nù?eZ— ª ˇ'_Ó—È?¿≠M >DA?e :∂??]å©??& %± ?Ò59Jô…=(≠£ àthe elevation of filth gives birth to the atheology of the biological continuum… The vagrant threshold marking the inhuman manifold from which mammalian patri-linearity evolves…

'"*Inhuman manifold*"?' whines Chlamydia, spiritedly tinged with sarcasm and vitriol – '"*Mammalian patri-linearity*"? *Bloody Hell!* You're so immersed in the theology of self-interest you can't even smell your own bullshit! And what's all the scribble? – all the "ù~Ú?fÅ™#fl—°…°ÏÎÍÂ‰'?À!È) .oMX?FAk ·§•??öˇ ûY?ÈÔÔÔªº¨fi›##‰±P?]5P?? ;rS!áäàeT?" Why abuse your reader? They're prepared to do you the favour of reading your worthless drivel! A mess! Pure gobbledygook!' She throws the papers into the air and crumples to the floor. 'I… I… I just find it so… *claustrophobic, impenetrable, pessimistic and utterly, utterly pointless*… it has nothing to do with what's important in life…'

The airborne pages smile, with mocking arcs down to the floor.

Chlamydia sobs deep into her diaphragm while Helmut looks on genuinely astonished.

'*Massa Mandragorass, 'tis time to eat. I bring soul food for de brain*…'

Helmut punctuates the intervention with a deliberately pointed full stop, abandons his desk to relieve the tray of food from Maman Terreblanche.

'Considerate beyond the call of duty. I take my hat off to you dear lady and friend!' The obese soul casts Chlamydia a disparaging gimlet eye and reverses from the room. Helmut decants a plate of tepid braunschweiger and glass of Lucozade and returns to his clearing to devour the spicy liver and aid his recovery. He gestures to the second plate and snorts:

'*Mange! Mange*…'

So the day drags with nauseous reluctance – time's gentle tick tock harassed by the storm that rages and wanes petulantly outside. At seven on the dot Helmut's hammering grinds to an exacting full stop. Chlamydia's knees are worn, and hands, arms and face lacerated with paper cuts. Her finger hurts so it weeps, sniffles and stinks. Helmut stretches to full gauge, yawns open wide, muscles to the edge of his chair and slips off onto the floor beaming with self-satisfaction.

'That's enough for today. I'm done. You're excused…'

In the kitchen Chlamydia picks at titbits then resolves to inch her way down the volcano to visit her dear old friends

Brunhilde and Günter. At Günter and Brunhilde's, Chlamydia finds difficulty in attracting their attention over the noise of the angry sea. When she applies added vigour to the door it swings open on its hinges. She enters, shouting her dear old friends' names out loud in the assumption of Brunhilde and Günter's weak hearing. Chlamydia's own youthful ears pick up vibrations from the bathroom, and through a serendipitous gap between door and frame, witnesses Brunhilde holding Günter's old head firmly underwater in the bath, him thrashing like a baby, the choppy water boiling over the enamel rim, until Brunhilde's hubby is let up to break the surface in a brief respite, spluttering and gasping for the air deprived him while submerged. Günter moans like Isaiah's ox. Sodden Günter is wearing striped pjs. Brunhilde is wearing a jet-black uniform truncated with leather belts and outlined with striking white piping. She wears an officer's hat with a stiff rim shielding her eyes from contact with Günter. Worn on her arm a red, black and white band with the Hindu symbol for *have a nice day*. Brunhilde is rasping commands in an exotic foreign tongue. Chlamydia beats a stealthy retreat, leaving them to the privacy of their game of doctors and nurses – exits the house with a gratifying sense of fondness and affection – as an innocent child might witness the parents she never had in a tender act of love...

• • • • •

Darkness dims an extra notch by the time Chlamydia arrives back at the ominous white house. There she finds Helmut waiting, albeit casually lounging on the leather Eames, rigid tiptoes resting on the footstool below the craggy crockery oil painting of naked Adam and stripped-bare Eve.

'And what time do you call this?'

'I don't know Helmut, *bedtime?* What time do *you* call this?'

'I told you, Morass is unsafe after dark…'

'Why? – Are there poisonous snakes that come out at night? Or wild beasts? Hyenas? Wolves? Vampire bats? Or might you be referring to the fact that voodoo is openly practised here on Morass? *THAT'S RIGHT! VOODOO! I SAW IT WITH MY OWN EYES! IN THE CEMETERY, NEXT TO THE CHURCH – OF ALL PLACES ON EARTH!* So, Mr Mandragorass, if, as you say, you're only concerned with my safety, wouldn't you say that I'm already at risk staying under the same roof as your "*housekeeper*" – *if that's what you insist on calling her…*'

Helmut dims like the storm and circles Chlamydia like a coy dogfish.

'No, Chlamydia… No snakes… No wild beasts… No hyenas…' Helmut circling, circling… 'No wolves, vampire bats, venomous spiders nor deadly scorpions here on Morass… *I'm afraid its only you who's poisonousssssssssssssssss…*' out of nowhere, from behind, Helmut lunges at Chlamydia like a hissing cobra. She sees fit to struggle dutifully before succumbing to the incongruous physical outburst – even rotates in his undersized hug to seek out an imaginary kiss. But in its tender place, Chlamydia is roughly ejected from his hold, and staggering backwards witnesses Helmut exorcising his primal desire with a condescending sneer.

'*Snake in the grassssss…!*' he hisses, then slithers off to his study – the big door slamming in the miniature wake, agitated sounds numbed by the door, the qwerty absorbing Helmut's fury into its analogue mechanism – elegant phrases tinged with real life venom. '*Let him work all night long,*' thinks Chlamydia. '*Let him type himself into an early grave – and maybe Maman Terreblanche can bring him back to life…*'

The very next morning Chlamydia wakes with a sudden start. Helmut is on top of her, straddling her chest and pinning her arms. His face is painted just like a circus clown and he is pointing rudely in her face while digits are pounding out the letters: *W-A-K-E-U-P-Y-O-U-I-N-C-O-M-P-E-T-E-N-T-B-I-T-C-H* on her forehead. She wakes with a genuine start and a thumping headache pounding from the inside out. It is ten o'clock – later than she needs it to be if she is to evade the insinuating inflection of her employer. She throws herself from bed, selects an outfit at breakneck speed, hurls from the room, down the corridor, no time to be sick, into the study… to find Helmut, crumpled at his desk all lifeless and limp.

The scene implores a forensic examination – a kitchen knife stuck in his back. Time of death captured in the weave of the victim's shirt, the absorbent grid marking the rate at which the flow congealed. She examines the manuscript – taking page after page, reading through the beautiful prose to discover that it is a romance set in an austere house on a volcanic atoll… She clears her throat of wishful thinking, coughing loud to announce her presence. Helmut's dead face frowns on the manuscript, his skin furrows and wrinkles the page his cumbersome bonce weighs upon. An eye opens, sees Chlamydia. The upper body suddenly springs upwards and hands fumble for the machine's keys, depressing them in a panic…

'*MORNING!*' he shouts over the cacophonous clatter as the keys clench into a knot.

'*Sleep well?*'

• • • • •

By mid-morning Chlamydia's gag reflex is gagging for food to chew on, masticate and expel. She is hungry, and without daring to derail Helmut's train of thought slips from the room with the earnest intention of the toilet via the kitchen. There she finds Maman Terreblanche creating lunch on the large tray. Diplomacy notices an opportunity to endear itself to the caustic rustic soul, and offers to deliver the heavy tray to Master Mandragorass in the study.

'Back off motherfucker – 'fo' I busta' cap in yo' ass! Anyways, yo' better take it easy girl, in yo' condition an' al...' she winks and sucks her teeth.

Chlamydia is honestly perplexed – dares to tiptoe behind Maman Terreblanche at a safe distance to the study. Helmut arrests his literary purge, leaping up to retrieve the tray from his struggling housekeeper.

'Oh Maman! *You read a writer's mind!* God bless you!'

'Massa Mandragorass, yo' lookin' tin, poor boy! Gotta fat yo' up befo' yo' go back to de city!'

'Oh you spoil me! Maman – where would I be without you?'

Maman Terreblanche and Helmut cast Chlamydia a combined gimlet eye before the housekeeper reverses and Helmut stuffs his turkey with a chicken sandwich. Chlamydia sheepishly plucks the remaining sandwich, shamefaced, as though pilfering vital sustenance from the mouth of a genius, hence jeopardising the future of literary history.

'How late did you write?'

'Until the energy drained from my fingers and I could depress the keys no more...' he sobs.

'You must be exhausted. You should rest.'

'I appreciate your concern but I'm not soliciting for advice on writing methods from *you*.'

'I'm not giving advice, I just think you should take care of yourself.'

'What's it to you anyway? Concerned because I didn't sleep in my bed – or because you expected me to creep into yours when you were asleep? Have my wicked way with your sleepy hollow and permit you to use slumber as a subterfuge for your smutty desires.'

'Let's get it straight – if I'd known Brunhilde and Günter were your parents I'd never have accepted the kind offer from their *perfect* son to stay in his house. I was obliged out of respect for *their* feelings, not *yours* – in fact, it was *you* who couldn't resist manipulating your own parents' kindliness in order to extort further revenge on me… But don't you worry your little big head, when the first seaworthy vessel arrives I'll be clinging to it like a barnacle. I'll leave you to the indignant selfishness you call personality. You can forget that you're precious paradise was ever contaminated by my unwelcome presence.'

'You're quite fond of them – my parents…'

'Yes… Yes I am. I think they're wonderful. *But how you fit in – I've no idea…*'

Helmut's hard shell cracks half a smile. He turns in his seat to tease the writing machine with the remotest sign of brilliance.

The next few days passed without significant incident inside and rained continuously out. In the kitchen Chlamydia found a small cloth doll on the floor – aged, loosely sewn and patched together. Beneath the aura of sewing pins covering it, the doll bares an uncanny resemblance to its finder. When curiosity extracts one of the rusty steel pins, poor Chlamydia suffers the sensation of a dagger being plucked from her own darling body. She then suspects the doll to be the cause of her sickness and so confiscates it from you-know-who to hide it under her mattress you-know-where.

Helmut and Chlamydia settle down to work each day in the study, rarely speaking, unless courteous interaction cascades into boorish tit for tat. In the evenings Helmut usually leaves the house and returns around twelve. By that ungodly hour,

Chlamydia has retired – frustrated by her own nagging company. In Helmut's absence, Chlamydia has taken to reading his published works and now secretly considers herself an avid fan. Her superior filing system has acquired its momentum and is steamrollering through the alphabet at breakneck speed, adding sub-indices and appendices to the cosmology of Helmut's shambolic parts. The more Chlamydia becomes drawn into Helmut's hostile solar system the more her scorched heart burns – Chlamydia's Eros fast conceding to Helmut's Thanatos. And labouring each day in his company and lying in bed to shelter under the same infernal roof contrives a miserable existence. The nights are terrible. Long lonely nights in a narrow single bed, the rain driving her insane as sorrow lies waterlogged on the mattress, weeping, forlorn – hopeless and wet.

On Wednesday morning the rain ceases and the jungle begins to steam. Chlamydia finds Helmut in the study, looming all over the filing cabinet, green like the jungle and steaming with rage, waiting for the author of his inchoate anger, papers already scattered all over the shop.

'Where in Hell's name have you hidden my notes on *the synthesis of alchemical operations and the conjunction of primordial forces associated with the experimental investigations of Paracelsus?* I can't find them anywhere.'

'Paracelsus' experimental investigations would be filed under *p for Paracelsus* – if I'd reached *p*. I assume your notes were in my "to be filed" stack – before you saw fit to scatter them over the floor. I should remind you that I'm working as efficiently as I can, and still you haven't managed to utter the words *thank you*.'

'If it's praise you want you're messing in the wrong pigsty. I'll remind you of our little agreement – you earn your keep –

nothing more, nothing less.'

'Am I nothing to you? Would you prefer I leave?'

'Poor Chlamydia, first you were thirsty and now you choose to be homeless...' Helmut levers one eyebrow diagonally, efficiently emphasising the point that, until there is another sea vessel – a ferry, yacht, boat, schooner or supply ship – , there is no way to flee the island, plus, there is no room at Hotel Krauss on account of storm damage, plus his own mother and father have insufficient space for her to stay any length of time.

'What if someone gets ill? What then? What if *I* get ill? *Seriously – ill. What then Helmut?'* Chlamydia is screaming. '*What if my finger turns gangrenous and my eyes swell and turn beetroot red? What if my tongue blackens and my teeth crumble? What then Helmut? What will you do then – eh?'*

'There's a d-d-doctor on the island...' Helmut's glitch is showing, 'and a small i-i-infirmary of sorts...' Chlamydia has an affection for Helmut's glitch.

While Helmut draws sinews into repose, Chlamydia gathers her own composure. In her mind's eye she is unable to imagine this uptight soul allowing his own comings and goings to be dictated by the erratic behaviour of capricious sea vessels. She visualises a helicopter lurking somewhere in the jungle, primed to scramble at a moment's notice and rush the author to his next international book signing...

'I'll wager you have a helicopter on standby in a clearing somewhere nearby...'

'Buffoon!'

An empty box file bounces off Helmut's crown onto his desk, toppling his tidy manuscript onto the floor. He rounds on Chlamydia in a roar, hands outstretched as though set to strangle the drear life out of the poor wretch.

'You'd better stop chucking things at my head or you'll be

out on your ear!'

'Golly – gosh! I'm sorry... I don't know what came over me.'

Chlamydia abseils to her knees to gather up the spilt manuscript, but Helmut beats her to the floor, hands down, to snatch pages from Chlamydia before Chlamydia can read anything. She braves his snatch regardless, gently gathering, and he seems to soften – allowing her to gather gently without him snatching, snatching, snatching...

'What's that awful stench?' he says.

'It's my finger. I'll gather but I promise not to read.'

'Fine. Gather away. Ask Maman Terreblanche to dress the wound. Gather, but don't read.'

'I promise. I'll go to the Infirmary for antibiotics –'

'*Infirmary? F-f-forget the Infirmary! Never go there... it's... unhygienic*. Ask Maman Terreblanche for medicine... *NOW GATHER!*'

Agitation urges Chlamydia's pulse to boom like voodoo jungle drums pounding in her ear. She fears the percussion is escaping her tympanic snare – the bloody flush staining her cheeks and screaming for attention. She wonders whether her host feels anything at all visceral for her.

'*Helmut* –' she says tenderly, 'let me put the pages back in order – to make up for my tantrum...'

Suspicion relinquishes its hold on the precious papers. Placing the pages into numeric order, Chlamydia is respectful of his privacy, endeavouring to turn a blind eye but finds the odd word and sentence too eager to be ignored. Moments of high stimulation are indicated by erratic staccato, incoherent jumbles of letter and word – Chlamydia imagines Helmut desperately unclogging typewriter keys from their over-excited snarl. And without ruining it for you, Helmut's new work speaks with an entirely new voice. Foremost, it is a novel, and gushes with pathos – it howls without reserve into an ocean of profligate introspection, sentiment unbound; all in all it is a love-death triangle that juxtaposes the Sisyphean with the Herculean – and now Chlamydia far better appreciates the author's sensitivity to his destined magnum opus being read before the author achieves emotional closure. Once the papers are properly collated she returns them to the desk. Helmut gives an absent-minded nod, without faltering at the oversized keys of his virulent machine. In stark contrast, Chlamydia looms… fruitless.

• • • • •

So it came as a sincere surprise when Helmut announced that he would not be leaving the house, and that his house guest would have the pleasure of his company during dinner.

Upstairs Chlamydia hums as she pupates from slave to butterfly, transformed into a flesh-pink evening number with glittered fairy wings. Downstairs Helmut greets his guest wearing a cream evening suit and Ivorine smile. He has never looked so fetching. The underlying spasmodic frown has flown and a tranquil countenance has come home to roost. They settle to eat with compliments fairly traded. During their meal Chlamydia turns on Helmut's writing. She favourably critiques the several books she has skimmed and, without a second thought, enquires on the progress of Helmut's latest struggle.

'*Taboo!*' he yells, slamming his little paw on the table. 'The subject is taboo! I won't permit questions about my book until it's in the hand of my publisher! You should know better! I won't be derailed by your big nose!'

'I was only asking…'

'Well desist… Desist!'

'Suit yourself.'

'Oh, you think I'm being *unreasonable?* You feel unfairly

scorned?'

'As a matter of fact I do. I'm trapped here on Morass flogging myself to the bone in return for a roof over my head and food in my gut. Yet again, you lull me into a false sense of security by allowing me to break bread with the great genius. I unwittingly violate one of your piteous prohibitions and the evening is ruled, once again, by your witless impatience. Considering my apparent plight, I think you're being unnecessarily cruel and antisocial.'

Helmut's nostrils flare wide as tunnels and knuckles gleam white as sausage fingers tighten over knife and fork. Chlamydia has the feeling that Helmut would like nothing better than to stab her in the face. Helmut has the look of murder in his eyes while Chlamydia has the demeanour of a victim to reciprocate. It is far beyond Chlamydia's imagination why Helmut is so zealous about his new project. Without ruining it for you – Helmut's novel is a very moving story and from the little she managed to digest Chlamydia can tell it is written with great feeling – each word torn from ragged experience.

'Perhaps it would be better,' he says at length, 'if you and I work in separate rooms.'

'Why? I don't inhibit your work at all. You seem to be working very well – hammering at your little typewriter like there's no tomorrow. You don't stop – tap, tap, tap, tap, tap – I don't know how you do it. At this rate you'll have finished your little story in a week – I'm sure.'

'Now you're an authority on writing? You wouldn't know the first thing. Every word I've written since you invaded my island has been utter rubbish. A mockery of effort itself. I told you, *you disturb me!*'

Helmut disturbs Chlamydia but not in the manner Chlamydia wishes to be disturbed. She pushes her plate away, sickened by this bittersweet interlude – yearning to be released from torment.

'Where d'you think you're going?' Helmut demands savagely.

'Suddenly I'm not hungry.' Bile bites up her oesophagus as her acerbic host rises to his feet.

'Damn the food! This is the sustenance you're after!' He snatches at her hair, lifting himself on tiptoe to obtain a proper handful. He smothers her neck with rough kisses, pulling at hair to reach face, and smother it with kisses too. She bends to accommodate – her mouth docking with his mouth in a harsh meeting of mind, body and tongue.

Chapter Five

Chlamydia relaxes backwards onto the carpet, inviting Helmut who looms like a distant giant threatening to cleave her asunder. It is the oddest time for Chlamydia's dubious sanity to sequester reminiscence of her out of sight and out of mind fiancé Algernon – and while her sanctimonious scruples see fit to indulge this inopportune mental visitation, her right hand takes subconsciously to massage her empty *digitus medicinalis*, or *digitus annularis*, or *digitus quartus*, or *digitus IV* – the digit on the left hand reserved for the task of indicating the matrimonial status of any given body. Hence Helmut, captivated in mid-descent, notices the auspicious vacancy and allows dull eyes to duly flare –

'The ring!' he exclaims out loud, '... tis gone!?' Is Algernon's odious reservation annulled? By its absence rendered null and void? Simply cancelled? And intonates melodramatically '*– tell me it's all over between you and h-h-him! Oh Chlamydia, dear Chlamydia, tell me you've come to your senses at last!*'

'Not at all!' she contends, wary of the knee-jerk ridicule that lurks around the bend. 'My finger swelled like a Cumberland sausage. It smelled pungent, porky, meaty – humming with rot. I thought it best at least to remove Algernon's ring before the blood supply was restricted – I certainly didn't want my wedding ring finger to drop off... Not before my wedding...'

'*Sssssssstrangulation!*' hisses Helmut to the sausage analogy. 'You're dead right! Chronic sssssstrangulation! That menace to all-things-bright-and-beautiful began sucking the vitality out of you when you permitted him to jam the abysmal thing on your finger!' Helmut bunny hops to his feet, clutches his own underarms like a triumphant athlete.

Chlamydia remains flat on her back, lost for words. She

considers sitting up to pound out an injurious retort on Helmut's chest, but sinks further into despair on account of the fact that she wants to be Helmut's lover, to marry him, to bear Helmut's progeny, to share her entire life with Helmut and even die in Helmut's miniature arms. In her mind's eye she knows only too well that her emotional yearning enjoys no reciprocation with the object of her devotion. *His* desire is carnal, carnivorous, cannibalistic, crude – filed under capital *c* for charlatan.

'Don't do this Helmut, please, I beg you…' she says, choked with hidden heartfelt emotion, the cartilaginous box-shaped part of the respiratory tract between the level of the root of the tongue and the top of the trachea barely able to muster up a simple phonic rejoinder to his malicious accusation: 'Listen here yo-yo!' she says. 'You're up and down like a whore's knickers! Half the time I don't know whether I'm coming or going and the other half I don't know whether I'm going or coming. I don't appreciate you off-loading all this tit for tat bullshit on me! It takes two to tango, and ever since I arrived you've been stamping all over me like Christopher Reeve on a hot plate. One day it's all Barbie and Crystal Ken, the next it's all Klaus Barbie and *Kristallnacht*!'

Helmut's eyes bulge, big, wet and almost believable.

'Oh but you relish my unerring attention – like an exquisite flower, relentlessly absorbent – an emotional panty pad – regardless of the withering victims that fall prone to your toxic beauty – you've sucked the last beams of energy from my bloody soul…'

'*Spare me the poetry – I already made the mistake of reading your gut-wrenching witterings:*

I've given up trying
It's too tiring
I'm retiring
I prefer dying… *RUBBISH!*

If I'm a flower you're a penis flytrap. Come clean Helmut, drop the pose, you're just trying to invade my knickers…'

'Despite what that house-trained conscience nags inside your cul-de-sac skull,' he says, prodding her on the forehead with his finger, 'Hertz has you pegged – worse still does your analyst – you're buggered before you're fucked –' He struts to the Regency drinks cabinet, pours himself a whole miniature whisky, downs it and casts a huge distorted gimlet eye through the bottom of his cut-crystal tumbler. Chlamydia feels a leaden tear load into the breach of her stinging squint that tempts her to flood from the scene, but she tempers herself as any emotionally damaged girl would when a man as vile as Helmut tries to assault them.

'I'd like a drink too,' she says.

'Well you're a big girl now – get it yourself…'

Propped at the drinks cabinet Chlamydia discovers a chance insult; '*Napoleon Brandy?*' she howls. 'Oh how very appropriate!' She pours it neat and necks the short in one and slams the little glass down.

Accompanied by a temporary smile rendered sinister by the sinews that contort it: 'So what'll you tell darling Hertz when you get back? If you're telling me the truth about your reasons for being here, won't your true love deserve a blow-by-blow account of our ins-and-outs – an explication of our more intimate moments? Will you come clean about your indiscretion? Or will you be reporting back on the murky details of a botched plan? *Which is it?*'

'*The truth* – facts will suffice,' Chlamydia retorts. 'I don't want your island, nor anything remotely associated with you, and what I mention to my fiancé is none of your business!'

'And you still believe Hertz intends to buy *my* island for *you?* You haven't yet twigged he wants it for himself – that his big boy plans don't involve you beyond your immediate purpose.

Aren't you at all curious to find out where it all leads? Doesn't the thought that he might reimburse you for your initiative even tempt you to cut your emotional losses and try to persuade me to sell?'

'The day I'm compelled to do anything with you is the day I'll happily commit to a straightjacket,' she says. Helmut presses his face to hers. Her heart flutters in its rusting cage.

'Tell me you don't find the challenge exciting? Tell me it wouldn't give you at least a frisson of revenge on Algernon to twist me around your finger? Try it – let's see if you can. Go on, flutter those tarantula lashes and spin your web. You were sooooo willing a moment ago. What happened? Did an ungracious apparition of Doctor Hertz cramp your style?'

Chlamydia shakes. 'You sad, sad, specimen! If Algernon is as you say, then he can do his own dirty work – if you're right, you fucking well deserve each other!'

'Oh! Sweet sewer mouth!' Helmut howls, hollow like a tin machine and moves forward, harsh like a robot. He takes Chlamydia with stainless claws nipping tight on human love handle. She raises hands to fend him off, but he laughs, advances his impassive robot face into hers, industrial kissing without tenderness, now harsh and brutal like a man, her grimace pressed back onto receding gums. The iron tongue invades the moist inner-membrane cavity with savage strength, such that she feels as though the last ebb of her absolutely sovereign being is being drained from her body, and if the robot lets go she will fall into a mess of quivering human nerves. The robotic kisses relentlessly mock her *Homo sapien* weakness, teasing the reflex pleasure mechanism that goads her forward for more – *like a machine, only soft*.

'Oh Helmut!' she gasps, all transparent.

Helmut shoves her away forcefully and she carelessly loses her balance and collapses back to the ground.

'It's no good throwing yourself at me!' He cackles, all digital and subzero.

'Village idiot!' she rasps at the robot.

'Better to be a village idiot than the city idiot!'

'Nincompoop! Twit! Rascal! Low-life! *MAGGOT!*'

'I've done nothing any full-blooded grown alfalfa-male-of-the-species wouldn't do when it's handed out on a platter!'

Chlamydia scrapes herself from the floor once more, wrestles the pink evening dress into order and marches away across the room with her wire-frame glitter wings bent out of shape. Taunts escort her to the door: 'Fly away home sweet fairy! Perhaps you'll have second thoughts before running to my mummy with porky-pies that I abuse you. Ha!'

'Goodnight,' says Chlamydia, 'thank you so much for an unpleasant evening.'

• • • • •

Chlamydia tips Algernon's diamond ring from the little green porcelain milk jug on her dressing table and bravely squeezes it over her enlarged finger. The ring is stubborn on account of the infected tissue, but as she twists, glutinous pus weeps from the cut and lubricates the jewel's downward motion to the base of the finger. Although the ring is now tarnished by Chlamydia's own duplicity she decides to reinstate it to act as a symbolic barrier between Helmut and herself – even though she intends to return the luxury item to her would-be fiancé when she returns to the United Kingdom.

And so another black-hearted slab of dead black meat night weighs heavy beneath Chlamydia's mooning eyes. She arrives in the author's study in advance of her employer, unusually, and so speculates whether the exchange of unpleasantries the preceding night may have played a part in Helmut's auspicious absence. It would be nice to think so. It might at least betray a small chink in his amour… But it dawns upon Chlamydia that Helmut may have slept soundly, *as soundly as a baby,* so deeply in fact that he has overslept, in which case, his apathetic indifference to their state of war weighs as heavily as Helmut's deep sleep on Chlamydia's feelings – and so Chlamydia feels aptly slighted. She at least might wish for a cot death.

An hour later Helmut drags in with pinpricks in a nightmarish sky. He skulks, wordless, to his desk, seats himself, clears sputum and begins his day's toil. But today's tap, tap, tap lacks the usual unmitigated stream of consciousness that poor Chlamydia experiences day after day. Today Helmut's lacklustre creation comes in fits and bursts punctuated by blasphemous curses and paper snatched from machine, screwed into balls and hurled at Jeff's guiltless grin.

When Maman Terreblanche reverses into the room arse first with a tray loaded with barely edibles, Helmut pounces on the aromatic instant coffee and pours himself a cup, downs it in one, and, howling through the third degree, pours another. Beneath Chlamydia's sardonic gaze, he snatches what he wants like a grimy feral child and retreats to the safety of his desk. Aware of Chlamydia's derisive scrutiny, his guilty conscience snarls on the attack:

'What's bugging you, *eh?*'

'I was just thinking how tired you looked when you shambled in,' she says.

'Well you're no fucking oil painting, *eh?*' he snaps.

Chlamydia's graciousness persists,

'You didn't sleep well?'

'No… not much. What of it *Miss Marple, eh?*'

'Because of our lovers' tiff – last night?' tendered with wasted sincerity since Helmut resumes his broken mechanical flow without sacrificing a single itty-bitty answer. So Chlamydia goes for the jugular: 'Are you having trouble with your writing?'

'Am I having trouble with my…?' The chair slides backwards violently as Helmut's muscle springs uptight – *'What in Hell's name are you inferring? Eh?'*

'I'm not inferring. I'm implying. You're inferring from what I'm implying…'

'THAT'S IT! YOU'VE FUCKED ANY FUCKING CHANCE I HAD OF FUCKING WRITING ANYTHING FUCKING WORTHWHILE TODAY! I'M FUCKING GOING OUT!– FUCKING LOCUST! FUCKING HUMAN STAIN! FUCKING SUFFOCATOR OF THE FUCKING CREATIVE FUCKING PROCESS…'

And with that, he was gone.

For a while Chlamydia continues her chores in calm protest, appreciating the tranquillity of Helmut's furious wake. She wonders where the Hell on diminutive Morass Helmut will take his tsunami. She is acutely aware of Helmut's precious manuscript placed on the desk all latent and self-important. It pleads for an audience with Chlamydia's shell-like and so she obliges. She rights Helmut's chair and settles at Helmut's desk, begins at the beginning, studying each beautiful passage without fear of interruption.

The story was tragic yet beautiful – right up Chlamydia's beaten track.

'Come Hell or High Water.'

by Helmut Mandragorass

Chapter one.

'An island?' Celia's blue eyes widen wide.

Anton nodded and smiled indulgently-

'Butb it will cost the earth!'

I can afford it ,' he replied arogantly.

She twisted thering on her finger and gazed at him with something approaching awe. 'You would spend a fortune on me me?!-

!For the woman of my dreams money doesn't enter into it. But I XXX want you to go and see it, give ityour approval before I finsih the deal.'

'oh Anton XXXX I love you!' Celia flung herself into his arms. 'Its the mostkw wonderful present a girl could ever recieve. You'll come with me of course you will?'

He xkixssed her hard before holding her away at arms lenght. 'Afraid not, darling.' His clear grey eyes met hers almost apologeticallly. 'not unless you want to ~~cancel~~ postpone the honeymoon?'

'Not on you life!' Celia tossed her head in anger, long black hair swinging all ~~silky~~- lushous forward across her face. With gentle f-ingers he tucked it behind her ears and cupped her lovely chin in his selfish hands. 'Well then you'llhave to travel alone - arrangements hav e been made - you fly in the morning.'

'So soon?' Celia was astonished, but because she loved him and because he was offering her the most amazing weding present a girl could exxxh ever recieve, she did not argue. 'well, in that case you'd bettergo so I can pack.' But even after he had gone she did n not begin. Everything happened so quickly she could not believe it was true. Her engagement to Anton Merriwether had been like a dream in the first place. She worshipped him froma distancae ever since joi-ning Merriweather Holdings straight from secretarial school, but he had never ever even noticed her. Not even until she was promoted to his personal secretary earlier that year when his father was ill and poor Anton had been forced to take x more interest in the ~~buisi~~- firm. Now his father had ~~actually~~ died and Anton was in compLete comtrol.- and she, Celia, was to become his wife!

It took getting used to for sure. the thought that in a few weeks she would be MRS Merrriweather with all the prexxix- importance that being the wife of the owner of the whole company would bring.

She sighed a bit and reaching down her travel case from on top of the wardrobe she began to pile into it the few bitsa nad pieces she thought she would need for a few days in the sun. She really did wish Anton was going with her to the island but also knew that the pressures of buisnesswould not allow it. Celia was up bright and early, ready for the most exciting journey of her life. Anton called for her at eight and drove her to the airport and very soon she was on her way.

The first leg of the journey was to the SeYhcelles, staying overnight before taking a boat to the island of Morasss which is about a hundred miles of the Seychelles. When the plane landed on [redacted] Celia was enchanted. It was a far cry from London;s grey strreets. Lush tropical vegetation, coral white beaches and the deep blue Indian Ocean took her breathe away. Her Hotel wascomfy and friendlly and exotic and she felt ~~a heady anticipn~~ looked forwardto what was in store. If Morass wqs anything like this she would not hesitate to accept it as a wedding presnnet from Anton ~~kask~~. ~~She just wished he was xherextaxsharexherxhappx xixxxxxx~~ sx she was getting used to the ideato such an expensive present she ~~xxx~~ couldn' wait to get there to see what it was like. But anton had mysteriously told her thatshe must make up her own mind and not be influenced by anyhting that he had said. She never felt so ecited when she climbed aboard the boat the next morn ing her heart was pounding in her mo uth, painfully. All she wished was for Anton to be with her, so they could share her excitement, herx appreciation of his magnificant gift. Their journey took almost nearly two hours. All the time Celisa was on the lookout for ssmxom. The cruiser boat was owned bya freind of Antons who told her she was lucky to have caught his bachelor mate.

'IKnow I Am.X' she said, smiling delightfully, jer dimples in evidence ,her dark hair streaming back from her face by the cooling breezes. Her eyes were as blue as the sea is blue. Anda healthy pink coloured her e cheeks.

'oR i should say that Anton is the lucky one?; ~~xaid~~ He said - his eyes lingering like they liked ~~xxxx~~ whatbtney saw.

'WE both are = lucky' dimpled Celia graciously. 'How much longer before we get to Morass?' She was ~~accoustoume~~dus used to flattery. Realisng modestly that she was an attractive girl with ore than her fair share of good looks. The saying that gentelmen preffer blondes was certainlyx not true in her case. Her thick Raven ~~hair~~- black hair attracted men like bees around honey, butbshe was used to dealing with them and had little qualms about handling the man at her side should he try it on.

The man did little more than llook. A few minutes later he told her theY were- were there. Any second now the island will come into sight. Celia was on the edge of her seat with exitement, shading her eyes against tye sun so she nmight see the horizon. Morass pax appeardas a small mound on the horizon. Purple and distant, but soon showed true colour, lovely green plants and brilliant white shores, hills and valleys and the odd sparkle as the sun reflected off glass. Soon she was steeping a shore and saying goodbye to Anton's sea faring freind.

'I will Pick you up in two days Time, he said'have fun'.'

anton had been thoruough. No detail overlooked. She paused until the boat had dissappeared before looking about her surroundings. She was thinking 'If I say 'yes' THEn all of this will be mine...'

Morass was not as she had imagined exactly. Her mind's eye had imagine d something smaller, the desert islands of postcards almost. Instead it stretched into the distance, as far as the eye could see-green and fertile, soVERYutiful. lovely.

The old rotten wooden landing stage was repaired and and impresive and a sandy road led away though a smaLl forest of palms and takamaka trees. A white house gleamed at the top of the hill, the only indication that the island was inhabited. Asshe stood hesitating an ox-drawn cart appearded along the sandy road. The dusty-skinned driver stopped and jumped down smiling braodly, 'Miss Fete?'

She nodded and smiled back.

'W elcome to Morass. I;m from Hotle Krauss. Sorry I am late but Samson's been playing up.'

Samson was presumably the OX. Hewas so tiny that Celia could not help smiling at his poor choice of name. 'OH I didn't expect to be met,' she said, so don't apologise. I am admiring your beautiful island.' He looked pleased. He swung her case on to the wooden seat, helping her up and makijng sure she was settled before coaxing the animal to make the return journey. Celia felt like she had been transported back into ano--ther age when time stoood still. They swept silently along lanes shaded by palms and ~~casuarı~~ flowers and a peace stole over her that she never felt anywhere else especially not London, and she knew that there was no way that she was going to evre refuse Anton's offer to give her the lovely beautiful island in paradise.

This was utopia!

They drove for a mile through forest before arriving at hotel Krauss. It was easy to see ~~from~~ where it got its name from. Orange trees surro-

surrounded the complex and greww betweenthe individual chalets, their branches loaded with ripening fruit. The idea of picking fruit with her ownn bare hands instead of going to the supermarket appealed to Celia. On he journey she also noticed banannas and other fruits she could not name. The main building was low and sprawling. Chalets spread around the gradens their roofs thateched walls whitewashed., snow white. It was a t taSte of paradise indeed!

She signed the register and was shown to her chalet. People were friendly and she felt at home but also in a hotel. There was A serenity here - as though everyone moved around on tiptoe and spoke in hushed voices. The bungalow was light and airy, cool after the heat of the sun, and more spacious than it appeared from the outside of it. The main room had sliding glass doors so that she could step right outsid e on to the terrace with its array of flaminf poinsettias and other tropical flowers. A bedroom led of one side with adjoining bathroom, and a kitchen from the other - a nice touch, she thought. Everything xxxxxxxxxxx was so nice she wished she was spending her honeymoon here instead of ta the white water rafting anton had organized.

She longed for him all of a sudden. Sadness tinged her euphoria. But once unpacked and changed into shorts and a halter top and eaten a delightful lunch she felt much better and felt eager to begin her expoit explorations. Wisely she decided to wait for the eveneing. It wasd too hot to walk - instead she took a leisurely swim in the pool and rested int eh tx shade in the terrace. There lots of people about, but Celia p reffered to be alone, daydreaming about the day she would own the island She realised the island was oval shaped, three miles long and two miles wide, fringed with white sandy beaches, and with a central mountain whi ch was easy to climb from one side but dropped away vertically on the other. Celia decided this was the best way to survey her island. She began when the heat had gone out of th4 sun. Even so, she was sweating a lot. She wished she had brought a drink of water with her. Perhaps whoever lived at the top might ~~offer~~ give her a drink of water? She ~~hope~~ hoped so. ~~The path-x-x~~

The path zig zagged constantly and Celia was usre the journey was more like two hundred miles than the half she had been told at the hoetl. But the magnificent views she saw at the summit were really worth the effort.

From up here she could see the whole of Samora - the white fringing shoe shoreline, forests, vegetation, and plants - the sprawling ~~hotle~~ hotel complex and on the other side, more or less imediately below the steep side of the mountain, more bungalows, which she presumed were private. Ther wxxx were no vehicles- motor vehickes on morass, oxcarts wxx were the only means of transport and she could see several now making their way along the networkm of snady roads which criss-crossed the island. The house, set into the side of the mountain, and which had looked tiny from the shore was surprisingly large, reached by a flight of steps flanked by fancy stone balustrade its severe whitenessrelievd by potted exotic plants. The balcony was wide, whith white iron furniture and immense red umbrellas, furled at the moment, pointing upwards towards the sky like minature rockets waithing to take off. Even though the place looked deserted windows were flung open wide, implying someone wa s home.

Celia mounted the steps, feeling aPrehensive. She scolded herself savagy svagely. For goodness sake, all she wanted was a drink, for heaven's sa sake! Why be so silly?

She tapped on the door timidly. When their was no answer she knocked louder. Still no repy. She turned the handle. The door opened to her touch, and inside she saw a black and white tiled hallway, a gilt chair upholndt- covered in red velvet, and a pyramid of potted plants casc-cading gracefully in one corner. 'Hello! IS there anywone there?' she called, quietly ath first . but repeating the question loudly.

In london she would never dared enter anyones house withouta permission. Here she moved inside. Her motuh- mouth was sod dry that she must have a drink before making her way back down the mountain. She could not ima-gine anyone objecting - especially when they realised thay had not heard her innocent arrival.

Each oF the rooms she looked into were empty, expensively furnished, but unnocupied and wen she found the kitchen Celia decided to help herself to a glass of water. It was taking a liberty, but there was evry chnaceh every chance that the house was empty, and even so, suerly the owner would not begrudge her a single measily glass of water? She would leave a note in case they realised someone had been in there house and won-dered who and when and why? She found glasses stacked haphazardly one on top of another, but to her horror, as she reached for one, the whole pile collapsed and shatterd on the rloor at HEr feet. She was so appalled BY what she had done that she did not hear footsteps approac-ing

, heard nothing until a rocky voice demanded seriously, 'What the hell's going on!' Who the devil are you and what are you doing?'
C elia span and wqs confronted by the hardest, unfrendliest face on earth She couldnt have spoken had she wanted too. She merely stared, rooted to the spot wishing the ground would open and swallow her up. Normally she was not intimidated but there was something about this man that would qe quell even the toughest of characters. She felt herself withering benath etehh his gaze, but for s few ~~minutes~~- moments, no more. She asked her= self why she was afraid. She had a good excuse. If hex had answered thes door none of this would have happended.
'Sorry about the glasses,8 she said quickly. 8 'I'll pay for them of con se. All I wanted wasa glass of water but-'
'So why didn8t you leave when I didn8t answer the ddoor?'
The voice was soft, but Celia was not deceived, and when cold tawney eye s regarded her with mean?minded nastyness she looked away. She bent and began picking up pieces of glass. 'I was thristy... Its a long way up..'
8Then you should have come prepared,' he said, 'Instead of intruding'.
'Well that's a very unChristian view view, Mr...?8 And are you ~~saying~~ begruding me some water?'
'Yes I jolly-well do! You're not welcome here - now leave '.'
'Before I've cleaned up this mess?' She siad sweetly. He disturbed her i this man with dark tousled hair and harsh face. He was goo-looking in a rugged sort of way and there was something vaguely familiar about him. That she could not explain. She had certainly never met him before, it would not be easy to forget suchxx a man.Perhaps x he reminded her of s someone? Who? His eyes narrowed dangerously. ' I don;t find that amusing of course you must clean up before you go'.
'What about a drink of water?'
He noded. 'Hurry. I have work to do. You're wasting valuable time.'
Celia;s blue eyes glittered. 'Oh if you expect me to say sorry I'm not.W have you a dustpanand brush?'
'somenwhere -' He sounded disinterested in petty things like dustpans a nd brushes. 'You've cut your finger! did you know?'
No she didn't. She looked at spots of blood on the tiled floor. and then at xk her finger. There wqs a sliver of glass sticking out from it. Sheu pulled it out and more blood pumped out more quickly than before.
She put it over the sink and looked at him. Wondering whether he might give her a plaster or something.

'Are you accident prone or something?8 he asked abruptly, opening a cupboard and taKing down a tin box.

'Not usually.' She said indifferently.

'only when you;re in someone else's house?' he turned on the tap and dam dampened a piece of cotton wool. Celia wanted to tell him she could mang age. that she could do her wound herself, but somehow found herselfi incapable of speech when he had Her wrist between strong brown fingers and wipped the cutb clean. He was not gentle. She didn;t protest. She held her breath until he wrapped a plaster around her finger, letting it gaxh go when finished. He returned the tin box to the cupboard and resumed scrutinisng her. Celia became extremely conscious of her shorts and the green spotted halter top which revealed more than she wanted this man to see at this moment in time. Her hair, earlier on, had been tied back, bt but the ribbon had slipped off and it now hung in a silken black cascade across her cheeks, her fringe, thick and heavy, hiding her fine brows.

'if it wasnt for the costume,' he said, 'I would think it was Cleopatra herself who had come to visit me!' It was not the first time Celia had been payed this compliment, yet she did not feel at all flatttered today of all days. She tossed her head xxxx scornfully. 'Icretainly don't think you re T Anthony! No tell me wher the dustpan and brush is.' His insolense unsettled her. Her heart pounded in a unusual manner, and all she could think of was that the sooner She was away from this inhospitable house the better. She had felt his aggression when he had tended her finger, his desire to be rid of her, barely controlled, yet now he was doing little to speed herv depatture. He opend a tall cupboard innt the corner with an assortment of brushes and cleaning materials 'Take your pick!' and stood back, leaning indolently agaisnt the wall muscularva arms folded across a powerfull chest, hard eyes still staring. He wore faded denim jeans, a patchy blue tshirt even more faded than his jeans. He claimed to be the owner of the house, but doubt entered her mind. 'Exactly who on earth are you?' She said. 'Exactly what right do you have to order me out of this house?t How do I know you're not a burgler yourself?' His golden eyes blazed with sudden fury furry. 'I'm not sure I need to answer any questions in my own house!' He jerked a broom from the cupboard and thrust it at her so violently she stumbled backwards, saving herself from falling by grasping hold of the door. It creeked beneath her weight and the hose from the cleaner sprung out onto the floor with a noise. The man swore. He left the room in anger. Celia picked up a tin of boot polish and chucked it at him.

He turned at the door to tell her off again and received the polish righ in the face! Celia clapped hand to mouth, gazing in horror. She didn't no wether to laugh or to cry - but when she saw he was not hurt she began to giggle at firts. The more angry he became the funnier it was. She did not stop until he stormed across the room and took her by the sholders and shook her so much her teeth rattled. 'Im soxxxxxyx sorry she gasped, 'Her wide blue eyes looking up at him with unconscious appeal.

'You deserve punishment!' he said, 'Not content with breaking in you even try to injure me. Get the hell out of here before I do something I'll regret! He thrust her from him and turned his back. In these seconds-whi while his hands rested on her shoulders Celia had been aware of his imme imense strenght - off of dynammMaiishdTEgggk SEXUAL shhhfgex dynamic attraction and instead of runing away she stood staring at his broad back, tempted to try and offer another apology.

For a few mokmenst- moments all was silent. Then slowly he pivoted rouno to face her. His tawney eyes flecked with gold she noticed at close rang range were enigmatic, resting colly upon her face. She felt hypnotysed. Could not move if she wanted to. She wanted to no if he was immune to her charm. Most men wernt, especially When they found themselves alone wiht her. Unconsciously her lips parted aNXNDKKKKKKKXXand she moistenede the tip of her tongue, her pulse rate increas,hghhhhi- ing dremi- drammmatically. His eyes narrowed dangerously again and took a step cloeser. She REalised that he though she was invignt- inviting his advan ces, but then all of a sudden Anton came into mind!

But it was ttoo late, tremendously powerful arms pulled her roughly aginst iron hard muscubar hardness of him, fullcool lips closed on hers in a brutally punishing kiss sending her all over the place, one powerful hand slipped inside her top cupping HEr breast. She dhhhfgggg strugg;ed almost angrily, this was not what she wanted! How dare he! Beneath the urgent pressure of his mouth her own lips parted. Breathing became ragged, throat ached, and unable to hhpo help herself she responded to his kissses. All thoughts of Anton fled and time stood still. Anton

With unexpected exasperation, he thrust her from him. 'Ha!.Hust as I expected!' he said 'You cam e here for one reason only - i should have kown You8re not the fistgirl whos tried to force themself upon me. Is it money or publicity you're after?'

Celia was outraged. Euphoriax was replaced with anger. 'My GOd! Are you serious? You ~~fancy yourself~~- have ea a high opinion of yourself! ~~I we~~-

I wouldönt sleep with you if you were the last man alive !' She held out her hand with its brillliant solitaire diamond. 'I already have a man, thank you, and I'm more than satisfied.'

He looked at her with disbekief. 'The poor fool has my sympathies. So what are you after?'

'A drink of water!'

'Well you can have one' he said, 'ILL get get it for you!

She watched as he filled a glass at the sink, thinking hehad suffered a change of heart, when unexpectedly he threw the water over her face.

'There!' he saidin a satisfied voice, looking at her with a cool contemplation. 'Clean the mess up and leave!'

'ANd if I refuse?'

8Don't tempt me' He said. She decided not to risk his anger. She got on her knees and began sweeping up the fragments of glass, emptying the pan into a pedal bin in the corner of the room. She checked for pieces then checked his face for approval. He had watched her every move. She felt colour in her cheeks, and she was more thirsty than she ever was evre before. 'Done.' she said, trying to keep er voice steady. 'If I can leave now I promise I will never disteurb you agagin.'

'You expect me to believ that!' Well, since my work has been well and truely interrupted why don't you stay for that drink you claimed you wrere after? I would like to hear a little bit about yourself.'

Celia regarded him with suspicion, was tempted to hurl his offer in his face, but her thirst won.It was miles home and she would survive the journey if she were properly ref-reshed. She nodded.

'Good. We'll sit on the terrace. I presume you know you're way?'

Celia went outside and waited while he got drinks. She sta on a white chair and considered events. She had never dreamt of meeting anyone like him. He was unlike anyone she had ever known, and she hated and begrudgingly admired him. He had an air of power combined with raw masculinity that so few real men really actually have. Even Anton with his millions and thriving buisiness could not meet up to this unknown persona. Who was he? Puzzled by his vague familarity. A celebrtiy? A TV personality? Could he be a an athelete? He had an athelet's build: poweflu, dynamic, muscular.

In her mind's eye she saw hsi dark curly hair and striking chiselled features, his direputable clothes and square big tanned strong hands. She trembled at the thought of them touching her skin and her own hand involuntarily touched her own breasts where his hand had been. An unfamiliar ache set in her stomach and she closed here yes. She asked herself - why should she feel so imotionally disturbed? She was engaged toJohn after all. She had no right to think about this man in this particular way. She told herslef that she only met him by chance, that it was not her fault. She told herself their paths would nevert cross again but what happended when Anton bought the island? What then? It was stupid to think they would not meet. The chink of glasses brought her out of her reverie and she looked up at her host as he settled thetray on the table.

He wore sunglasses, hiding his expressive eyes. Shethought she should be grateful that she could not see his undoubted hostility, could pretend they were friends, but she wasn't.It wqs as if he were hiding behind a msak. She felt uneasy. Inquisitive. He unfurled the umbrella over the table and sat down.

'Shall I pour the drinks?' she said.

He nodded and settled back in his seat, watyching her fill each glass with crushed ice bfore adding lime. Celia handed his to him. His fingers touched hers in the exchange. What's wrong with me? She thought.

Why do I let this man disturb me when I have a loving finace waiting at home? She could not answer. She took a long cooling drink, unaware that he was still observing her.

'You needed that. I should apologise for making you wait.'

'I would enjoy an apology, but I know for a fact that you will not make one...'

His mouth twitched. 'How do you know?'

'Because you don't strike me as a man who would say sorry to anyone.'

His thick brows rose above the glasses, furrowed-lines furrowing his forehead. 'Go on then, tell mewhat sort of man do you think I am.'

'You won't like it.'

'I've broad enough shoulders to take it. Come on. Give you verdict.'

He was goading her now. She wished she ahdn' attempted to get the bettre of him. But she shrugged and said; 'In my opinion you're a person to be avoided at all costs. As a matter of fact I'm not sure you actually own this house - - your clothes don't entirely match

She paused to ~~elliet~~ get a reaction. But he just watched from behind hi glasses. 'on top of that' she continued,' I would say you have a high opinion of yourself, youx like to be in command of every situation, your aggressive rude, uncaring about other people's feelings - is that enough? Ox Or shall I continue?'

'And you? Shall I tell you about you?' Celia had not expected this. Her blue eyes widened. 'Not really, But I'think you're going to tell men anyway.'

In the distance the sea murmured and the faint rustling of leaves distud -urbed by an early evening breexe. The sun was pleasantly warm and it might have been perfect had she been here with instead of this stranger whose identity she did not yet know. Anoton -

'First,' he said abrupty, 'you're engaged to ax man youdon't love.'

'That;s a lie! How dare youxx insinuate such a thing!'

'Then account to your reaction to my kiss.' He said,'if you love this man as you say, you'd be indifferent to all others.'He wasited a moment before continuing. 'Second, you are out for a good time. Otherwise you would never have entertained the idea of coming to this island without him.'

'Well how do you know he's not here on the island as well.'

'because You'd be together like young lovers.'

'Right!' she said with a huff.

'Anyway, you're not going to get what you want from me!'

8'Oh that again!' said Celia. She finished her lime and stood. 'If you're only going to insult me then I'M going. Thank you for th& drink and goodbye.'

He caught her wrist in a crushing grip and yanked her back down. 'no one walks out on me in the middle of a conversation. I8ve not finished x with you!'

Celia refused to answer. Seconds passed and he began; 'So why are youxhe here on Morass A last-minute fling before you hook some mug for life? Or had you decided he's not the one and you've come here to escape or x make up your mind?'.

'Neither!' said Celia stubbornly. 'if you must know, I'm here because Anton's going to buy it for me for a wedding present.'She assumed that this would impress him, but she was not prepared for the reaction she got.

'Anotin?' He swiped his glasses off. 'Not Anton Merriweather by any chance?'

His face was harsh again. eyes cruelly intent.

'You know him?' Siad Celia suprised.

He nodded. 'A dvious move. Sned in the the fairer sex. Was that what he suggested? Tell him he's wasting time and money.'

Now celia was perplexed. 'What are youtaliking about?'

'Don8t pretend to be innnnconet with me!' he hissed. ' I know what his i little game is. He was taking a chance sending you - or he doesn't care what happens to you so lang as he gets his hands on MORASS?'

His face was now creased into an ugly scowl. Jowl taut. Hands clenched.

'Whate do you know about Anton buying Morass 'said Celia.

'That he's been trying to get me to sell for years. I don8t appreaciate this new tactic - no disrespect to you, of course.'

'YOU own Morass ?'It was the last thing on earth she had expected.

[illegible]

[illegible]

[illegible]

Chapter Two.

'Merriwether

'It's a geat act!' He said. ' was right to send you. You're very good. But he's underestimated me. Would have saved you this journey.'

'I'M not acting.' said Celia hurt. 'I came here becuase Anton sent me because he wanted me to see if I like the island.'

'he doesn't care about you. He'll drop you when this attempt fails. How long ahve you known him?'

Years' Celia Lied.

8Liar. Anton had a differ nt girl here last year. He even brought her here.' His confidence allowed doubt to creeep in.

'SO? We weren't Engaged then.'It wastrue. Celia had been suprised when she was sent alone. 'but if Anton wnated me to get round you he would hve mentioned you so that I would have introduced myself. I had no idea who this island belonged to.'

He shook his head. Anton wants MoraSS . He thinks money can buy anyhting. Surely you know that? That's how he gets his girls.'

He was lavish with money. But she would have loved him wherether he he was poor or rich. 'Money had made no diffenec to our relationship. Anmton loves me and I love Anton That's all there is to it. You are being despicable.'

He laughed mirthlessly. 'Oh Anton is far more divious than you give him credit for. He knew what he was doing sending you here.' His eyes flickered over her body rudely. 'You see, he knows the type of woman I like. He couldn't have c hosen better. He assumed I'd fall for you -

soon I8d bcome compliant with the plan - God he was mistaken!'

'You mean I'm not your type?' Said Celia., hurt.

He looked her up and down. 'oh yes your my type all right. But he seemst to have overlooked the fact that mykxx desire to hang on to Samora is stronger than my desire for another woman. Living alone suits me well. I have no desire to change my lifestyle.'

'And you can afford to turn down Antons offer' Celia looked at his shabby clothes.

'Dont' be decieved', he said. 'I dress this way because I prefer it. Morasss is my retreat - where I can be myself and not give a damn what anyone else thinks.'

Without being invited Celiarfilled her glass. She was thirsty again. 'I can't see where this converstaion haxs got us', she said primly. 'I dont see any reason to stay here any longer.'

A hint of a smile lifted the corners of his mouth. 'Anyway,' she said 'Ithought I was holding up your work Mr...?'

'Gilbert. Marcus Gilbert. And no - I shall not work again today. Let's say my thoughts have been inturrupted far too much - Cleaopatra.' Someth thing suggestive lurkee behind his golden eyes. ~~how to~~ spell it right?

She ought xto refuse. She knew, but the offer was tempting.The idea of eating alone at the hotel was uninviting.

'I'll accept if you don't mind my improper dress - my name is Celia.'

'I don8t give a damn what you wear. I think Iprefer Ceopatra to celia - It suits you better. Celia suggests someone sweet and innocent, not the seductress I see before me!'

'I'M no such thing!' Said celia. 'You've got me wrong.'

'Really' He said, eyebrows rose disbelieving. Golden eyes held hers.

'Well I'll go and see about dinner. It'll be cold. My housekeeper had x left it for me already.'

'Do you want any help?'

'I thought you'd never ask' he said.

'Don't be insulting Mr Gilbert, or I might change my mind and go.'

'Feel free.' He said imprassively.

'I get the impression you don't like peaople. I think you shut yourself away to get away from women.'

'No,' he said, 'To get away from all mankind.' He sad.

'Why?' she said. 'Do you hate the human race so much?'

He shook his head. 'no. Not really...' He stood over her. Towering and powefful, smiling sensuosly, Celia felt a physical awareness tingling in her extremities. Whoever he was, he had an imesnse magnatism - a xixi a virility sure to be felt by all who come into contact withh him. She felt ceratin he wqxx was deliberately setting out to attract her, no d doubt to prove himself right. He was an expect she was sure.

'I don't live here all the time,' he said 'For the periods I do, peace and quiet is my aim.'

'Where do you live the rest of the time?' She said.

'I travel a great deal. Do many things - but I',m sure you're not really interested.'

Celia tossed her head scornfully., her black hair swinging across her face. She looked at him from behind its protective sheild. 'Shall wexdxp we drop the subject.'

'Yes.' he bent down and took her chin and planted an unexpected kiss on her lips. 'Good idea.'

She was trembling and haterd herslef for it. She was engaged to [illegible] Anton and she must remeber that. The feeling she felt was noghting more than revulsion. It had to be. There was no way that she could possibly i like Marcus Gilbert.

They ate on the terrace - avocado filled with mouthwatering prawns ina creamy sauce, followed by a salad with a whole baby chicken, washed down with plenty of wine, and a basket of fresh fruit.

She felt deliciously replete afterwards. Marcus Gilbert setk himself out to be charming company. All his earlier belligerance had gone. MK It had been such a long time since she had spent such a very pleasant evening.

When Celia tried to tidy the plates when they had finished eating he waved her away. 'Leave them. My houskeeper will see to it in the morning'

'But I'd like to she said. 'its the xxxxxxxxxxxxxxxxxxxxxxx least I can do after you've been so generousx in sharing your food.'

'Payment? For supper?' He mocked. 'Ican think of a better way.'

'I've no doubt you can.' she said.'But if you don't mind, I8ll chose this one.'

'Suit yourself. But don't expect me to help. '

She didn8t. besides, those big firm hands would proberlydamagex the delicatechinaware. 'I wouldn't dream of asking you. Why don8t you go an relax.'

It was a relief to be alone, away from the stifling atmosphere of his p presence. She was conscious of nothing eles. Thoughts of anton fled and she felt guilty. She was being disloyal, but she couldn't help hersl£. The doubt Marcus had planted in her head were growing by the minute. Little things to which she attatched little significance now reared ugly heads. Anton s unexplained interest in her, a mere secretary - their brief courtship. The honeymoon, thexxedxing this trip - both of which he had arranged himself instead of asking her - she was his secretary after all. John must have known what would happen. He was relying on her startling good looks to clinch the deal where all other plans had failed. In fairness, she would to hear Antons side of the story when she returned. It was nonethelless disturbing.

She returned from the kithhen to the tearrace, but it was empty and shee felt lost. Should she leave now? Should she seek him out in the house? What did he expect of her? Would he be angry if she looked for him in t the house and found him?

The he appeared. He smiled warmly, hearstoppinngly.

'I have music playing inside - come and join me.'

XWhat happened to his desire for solitude? Celia did not refuse. He had a power that was undeniable. And while she was feeling depressed about Anton she was warmed by Marcus's intrest. He took her to a long airy room at the rear of the house. It was carpeted in green and one hole wal was filled with sliding doors which xxx were open, revealing breathtakig sights ofthex outside. Plants overflowed into the room. It was like ant extension of the outside. Cathy immediately thought of it as the 'garden room'.

Soft sweet music came from one corner where there was all sorts of xpxx specialist expensive music equipment. One half of the room was clear of furniture, perfect for dancing and the remainder held deep armchairs covered in xxmchair jungle print.

It was a restful room where one would find it easy to relax, but somehow Marcus Gilbert did not strike her as a restful person. She could imagine himpacing the room like a caged tiger, changing one record for another, never still, never xt satisfied for one single moment.

His physique suggested.an active lief life, she guessed he thrived on it - why then had he told her that he came here for peace and quiete? He also said he worked here! What work could one do in such a sleepy place? He intrigued her, that was for sure.

She sat in a chair that seemed to ~~mt~~ eat her up, eyeing him up as he lounged in another. Niether spoke for a while. He studied her. She growed warm. The more she looked at him the more liked what she looked at. In a way he struck her as an honest man. She could imageine that he would lie about Anton had no reason too, and she became more sad about her predicament with being engaged to such a shabby person.

'How did you meet Anton' She said.

'We ~~mxe~~ were at Oxford together. We met infrequently after - the less t the better. Anton uses people too much for my liking.'

'He's not using me,' Celia declared.

'He is' he mocked. 'I think your8e beginning to realise it.'

'You think you know everything about me. What makes you so sure?'

'I study people. Its part of my job.'

'What is your job'. She said.

He smiled mysteriously. 'I am suprised you don't no. I'm usually recognized onn sight.'

'Are you annoyed I didn't?' Although he was familiar! Hqd she seen his picture somewhere? on television? in the papers?

Not in the slightestx Its a nice change to meet someone who doesn't know me, or of me.XX It saves the usual questions.'

'You don't like the usual questions?' she said.

'They can be irritating.' The record finished and he rose to change it. He was a forceful charcter. Even Anton withall his money was weak compared to this man, and although she resisted she became more attmacted by the second.

It was time to go. He was an exciting, stimulating male animal who could set any woman's ~~hrart~~ pulses racing.

'I'm going. You have wo rk to do. I'll let you get on.'

He took her in his hands. ' Afraid? Think you've bitten off more than you can chew?'

She was aware of his virility there and then.There was a tangible aura emanating from him. 'Nothing of the kind MR Gilbert. Its just time I went. Thank you for dinner.'

She tugged her hands but he held them tight.

'Call me Marcus,' he daid softly. 'the night is young, What's the hurry?

'I happen to be engaged to another man, MR Gilbert, that's what!'

8 Have I made any improper advances? Anyhting that Anton might object?'

Where is page 17? (18.)

before giving her a chance to react he continued; Its all innyour mind. Stay and see what happens. Prove to me you're not what I first thought.'

The cahllenge could not be ignored, Celia stared defiantly. 'Very well, Marcus.What shall we do know?'

'The choice is yours. We can sit, drink a little, dance a little, whatever you wish.'

'I'd like a drink.'She said.

'Of course'. he said.

When he let go of her hands she felt bereft. Angry with herself for entertaining such high emotions, hen it was Anton she loved. This was pure animal attraction. Any woman would be attracted.

He handed her a glass of amber-coloured liquid that matched his eyes. 'to a pleasant evening'. There was mockery inn his voice. And Celia retorted; ' But one begrudingly given?'

An eyebrow raised. ' No. I don't think so. No one but a fool would turn away something like you away.'

Celia felt degraded, insulted and her eyes flashed hostilely. 'Marcus Gilbert, my motive for coming here were genuine. I don't like your insinuations.If you think I'm of easy virtue you're mistaken. I know what the soft music, drink and fine words lead up to.'

' I think you like it' His fingers touched her bare shoulders, moving beneath her hair, sending shivers of delight through her hole body. She was paralysed, wanting him to continue but knowing he ought to stop. Anton never affected her like this. Anton had never been very romantic. He had showered her with gifts, declared his love, but that was it. There was nothing very intimate bewteen them. He never touched her like this made her fell so deliciously femminimne.

His head lowered and followed the contours of her ~~neck~~ throat.

'Why don't you try stopping me?' henwhisperered.

Celia tried to speak but couldn't. Throat ached with quelled passion, now awakened. She closed [illegible]ck her eyes he took her drink from her hand, his big long arms wrap around her slim loevly ~~waistx~~ wai st, her body pressed tightly against his, his own vibrant response to her slim compliant form. She felt DrugGed, lightheaded, and had absolutely no control over herself. He knew what hewas doing

'Youre proving me right!' he said.

'You're the most loathesome man I've ever=had= met!'

'You wanted me to make love to you!'

'Go to hel l'. she said.

He picked up her glass and said; 'Oh drink up, this situation is of your own own making.'

'Ha!' she laughed, ' All I came here for was a glass of water, not to be xrpx raped!'

'Don8t fretn_ that would never happen!'

'Well, if that's that, I would like to go. Goodbye.' With that she left, leaving the house quickly, almost running down the hilldside without once looking back. She was breathless by the time she reached her room and the first thing she did when she got in her room was to turn on the shower in an attempt to wash away any lingering impression of Marcus Gilbert's hands over her body. She did not suceed. As she lay in her bed a little later she could still feel his hardness alll over her, and the pressure of his lips, and she was ceratin that when she went to sleep that ~~should~~- she would dream of him.

All she wished was that she would not cross his path, Two more days! She wished she knew how to contact the boatman. It had all seemed so idyllic in the begining, it would still be if Marcus Gilbert kept out out of her way. She had no intention of ever going up there again - ever,

She soon fell asleep, the evnets of the day taking their toll, and surp-risingly she did not dream a thing at all. She slept deeply and peacfefl peacfeully and woke the next mornig completely refreshed, able to laugh at her fears of the night before.

She spent a few hours after breakfast lazing p outised her chalet, ~~occa occasison~~- sometimes swiming, not once ~~peeri-ng~~- looking up the hill which o~~verlooke~~ddominated Samora, with its white house on the top ~~of th~~ occupied by that ~~fatal dangerous- letyal~~ lethal combination of good looks and ~~arrr~~- magneticxx sex appeal.

It was ~~difficult~~- hard to ~~gethi~~ getx him out of her mind, but she was determined to get him out of her mind, and after a [illegible] lone brxxkfxxtx lunch in the hotel Celia picked up a book left behind by a former occupant of the chalet that she was in, and, sitting in the shade on the terrace, began to read.

It was her type of book, although she knew it was an international best-

-seller - as were all Gilbert Marcus's books. He was a houshole name - reknowned for his real-life research as for the original style of his writing. It was not until Celia saw the fotograph on the back cover did Celia realise exactly who it was. She should have recognized him immediately - he had been on TV enough times, and in newspapers. Eve his name Marcus Gilbert should have told her. Yet the simple inversion had d done the trick. No wonder he had been so cross when she had disturbed him. He must do his writing here, Presumably everyone else on the island knew. No=one had told her. Anton had known and had not told her -

For a very- long time she looked-at studied the photograph. His wild curly hair was taMed here. He wore a collar and a tie but the expression in those light eyes might have been just for her. He looked as though he had recently made love. They were alive vibrant and tormented her as they loooked out from the page.

'Now you no'.

She did not have to look up to see ho the throaty voice belonged.

'Why didn't yountell me- me?! she asked at lenght.

'It suited me not too. Mind in-f- if I join you?'

'Yes I do.' she snapped irritably. 'Iwant tot be on my won.'

'WHy?'

It was a resonable question. Looking at his photograph had disturbed her. To have his physical presence here as well was too much.

'No particular reason.' She said. 'I just want to read.'

'You're a fan of my writing?'

She looked up. ' Sorry to say, but no. I'm not a fan.'

' Then why my book?'

'Because I found it in the chalet. It was left behijd.'

He smiled wrlyly. 'A few more like you and I'Ll be ruined!'

' I don;t think so', she said. ' Your books sell by the millions. Everyone knows that.'

'What do you know about me'.

'You8r A best-selling-auther the best selligng auther Gilbert Marcus. is that your real name?'

'Marcus Gilbert. the inversion is in fact my real name. Its amazing how many people don't realise.'

'You must be constantly amused' She said sarcastically.

'No. Its not much fun being in the LIme light all the time.'

'Do the islanders no who you are?'

'Most of them - they respect my privacy.' He said.

'I didn't know.' She daid.

'I'm begining to believe you. What I can't understand is how you let yourself be fooled by Merriweather?'

'I love him.' She said plainly.

'I don't believe you. I think ~~money turned your head.~~you are in love wih with the idewa of being in love, especially to a rich buisiisnness man.'

'Anyway,' she said, 'Why aren't you writing?'

'Because a young lady had disturbed my thoughts.'

In the Dominating prescence of Marcus Gilbert all thoughts of her fiance faded and ~~began-~~ she began to wonder why this man had souught her out when he made no bonesk yetserday about insisting on privacy.

Why had he come here today?. Was she FlatTered? She felt anger mixed with ~~hatred~~ glowing awareness. What was his game he was playing?

'Aren't you writing today?8 she said testily.

'Like I said, you disturb my thoughts...'

'Why come ~~hE-re-~~ here? Why seek me out?' she said.

'I feel sorry for you. Poor gullible little you taken in by smooth-talking Anton. I thought you might like to see something of the island before you go backhome'.

'Listen. I love him, despite your tactics, you might think it funny to try to take me from him, but it won't work. I love him despite your tactics. despite what you've told me. I know when i get home it will all be a lie.'

He lifted his huge broad shoulders. 'You8re a funny creature. Smart. self-asssured onnthe out=Side, but on the inside nothing but a crazy mixed up kid.'

'I'm no child! I understand the ways of men like you.'

'Like me?' His mocking smile. ~~I'm willing-~~ [illegible].

~~She-~~ Marcus Gilbert was a man set apart from all others. And he knew it. That was the worst part of it. If ~~she-~~ he set ~~otu-~~ out to seduce her there was little she coulfd do about it.No woman i her right mind could urn him down. He was a senuaous alpha male whose tawny eyes could laugh or be serious, go light or dark in a fraction of a second. They ~~wr lau-~~ were laughing at her now, teasing, mocking, laughing. Shivers ran down her spine and she turned her head away quickly. He knew what he was doing. He knew she knew to.

'I think it's time you left, Marcus.'

'So you don't want to see the island?XX A few hours by oxcart? Its beautiful Celia, beutiful. Its the most beuatiful island in the whole wide wworld.'

'And it belongs to you!' she snapped savagelynastily.

'Is it because its me asking? If it were someone else would you go?' Hei he said. She picked up the tray of empty things and took them to the kitchen. Back out on the terrace he continued.

'Why don't you want to come with me?'

'Because,' she said slowly, 'I would feel guilty knowing that I was keppign keeping you away from your precious work.'

'I stopped writing of myx own free will.' He said.

'But you said I disturbed you.' The moment the words were out she wished she could reel thmm back in because it sounded like she was flattered by his admission.

'Writers get mental blocks sometimes. I have a mental block. Will you come or not?'

Suddenly he caught her wrist and pulled her down onto his lap. Contact felt explosive. Celia knew she was going to say yes.

'Yes.' Said Celia.

Celia felt like knocking the smile from his face but knew it would get her exactly nowhere. Marcus wore jeans, well worn but clean. His vets - vest moulded his superbly muscular chest, hiding none of his manly strea strengWWth. His tan was deep makm mahogany and he looked more at home weilding a pick axe or shovel than tapping the kejs of a typewriter.

He rose. Smiled down into her yearning eyes.

The oxcart was waiting outside. Marcus pulled her up effortlessly onto the oxcart. She sat down, their bodies dangerously close. The oxcat moved away. They began their trip.

Celia was entrn enchanted by it all - by the old planter's houses built on pillars above the ground, by the myri different species of birds with their colourfull tropical jungle plumage, the exotic vegetation, the-wd the wide coraline roads, and the sweeping beaches on the other side of h the island. She had her bikini on under her dress and they swam in the clear warm blue clear waters, laughing and shouting, splasinging each other and playing as though they were young lovers.

Lying on the sand afterwards Celia was intensely awArE of Marcus at her side and the fact hg that his XXXXXXXXXXXX+hdtd- thigh ~~tou-hed-hersbrh~~ brushed hers. An electric current ran through her and it was all wrong. Wrong becquse this man was an enemy. He had told her stories about her finanace that she did not reallyt want to hera let alone believe.

She sprang to her feeet. 'I think the man in the oxcart must be fed up waiting for us, we should head back.'

'Lie down, he's uded to it.' ~~drawl~~ said Marcus lazily.

Celia shook her head adamant. 'NO. I want to go bak to the hotel. I've had enough for today.'

'Enough of me for today?'

More than was good for her, she thought. She neededtto escape before she gave away her true feelings. She knew that Marcus was trying to lurek hr her away from anotin was trying to make her fall in love with HIM.

And it would be so easy. He was far more attractivex than Anton, in a di fferent kind of way. He was handsome, in a different kind of way - he h had charisma, an all-powerfull projection of his persona that noone could deny.

As they approached the Hotel he said to her. 'How would you like to come have dinner with me again tonight?'

Celia feigned disinteterst. ' Nothanks... I8m busy'.

'Rubbish, You're coming and that's that. I want your company. Iwant you!

Celia stared. Noone had ever spoken to her like that. He wanted her? Ixt In what way? She wanted him, her wh le body and soul ached for him, did he mean it like tha? It was difficult to believe what was happening, did people really fall in love like this?.

She loved Anton, didn't she? How could she love Marcus too? Anton paled io to insignificance. SxXXX Marcus dominated her thoughts wether she liked it or not.

'Why?' She shouted. 'why, when you made it very clear yesterday that you wanted to be on your won? You turn up today and now you want dinner?

He smiled a ~~mysterious~~mischevous smile. 'Cleopatra, you're irressistable

Her face said okay.her decision reflected on her face.

'Good.' he said. 'I've been without company for so long, I'm begining to feel uncivilized.'

She went inside the ~~eah~~ chalet to change. She chose a simple short eyen-ing dress. It was soft baby pink which suited her dark complxion. Marcus looked but said nothing. Together they climbed the hill. Whenn they got inside the house he turned to Celia and said. ' My housekeper ~~cou~~ did not come todday, so I wondered wheteher you'd like to cook instead?'

CHAPTER THREE.

'Of all the devious underhanded things - I hate you! How could you?'
He laughed at her anger, as though itnwere some kind of teasing court-ship.
'I'm going back to the Hotel.' shouted Celia, but he blocked her way.
'Come on, I'm hopeless at cooking. Please stay. I dont mind sanwiches.'
'And you accusedAnmtonof using People?'
Marcus stood his ground and smiled a mocking ~~smile~~ and sinister smile. ~~S She-k~~ She knew she could not escape untilshe had done what he had asked.
'I'm not exactly dressed for the occaison.' she said.
'Look in the Kitchen. Maman Terre's got a apron around somehwhere.
The kitchen was beautiful, fitted with every modern convenience. It would be a pleasure cooking here as long as he kept his word and stayed out. Celai found an apron which was a ~~vbx~~ voluminous affair. She was glad there wasnt a mirror because she looked a sight. She considered something exotic but plumbed for something simple that would not go wrong. An hour later theybwere sitting eating.
Marcus had changed out of his denims into a pair of white slacks. and a black shirt, the sleeves rolled up to reaveal powerful long arms. His dary tawny curly hair was still wet from the shower, brushed neatly into place. A few grey hairs showed but added something distinguished to his appearance.He looked more like the image she had seen on the back of th e book. Only his great big hands belied the fact that he was a wrighter. They didnt fit the part. She could not ~~imagexi~~ imagine him pounding away at a typerighter. They looked too big. Yet when they had touched her her that first time, when they had slipp~~phkhhs~~ slipp~~xdx~~ed inside her tp ins~~XXXXX~~ inside her top they had been incredibly tender and gentle, he had know what he was doing. Those hand might be big but they were not clumsy. For starters they had melon and after thatbthey had steak with chipped potatoes, mushrooms and fried tomatoes. Celia also made a flan filled up with fresh fruit. Marcus opened a bottle of red wine , a heady w sweet mixture~~k wit~~ which teased her palate and made her head fell like cotton wool. ~~She wondered~~
Marcus complimented her on her lovely vooking. After clearing the dirtyt table they returned tot the garden room. Marcus opened the windows and

walked out onto the terrace andnwhen he took her in his arms she was not very surprised.

'Thank you for a lovely meal,' he said again, and kissed her.

Celia thought her herat was going to stop beating. For ever she seemed poised in infinity and then her heart began pumping again, painfully inside her ~~breats~~ breast.She wound her arms around the back of his head pulling his head closer to hers, meeting his lips. She was breathing deeply and wndered where all this might end. She was ~~lis-hj~~ living for the moment. Suddenly she realised she might have fallen out of love for Anton and fallen in love for Marcus, It occured to her that the feelings she had for Anton the ones she thaught were LOve, had been mere ingatuation for a man with lots of money, infatuation for the boss. It was not true love. They wouldn't be happpy, she could ss that now. It had taken this man here on this island to make her rewlize it. But did she now Love Marcus? Or was this merely infatuation to?'

Marcus was holding her and now she was holding ~~Marcus~~ him back more tightly than she realized. His kisssses became possive threatening to swamp her ~~drown~~ her but she did not care. She coult not bretathe, bu she wnated him and whatever he did she had not intention of stoppping h him. Yet it was Marcus who drew back, drew the line.

'Ithink that's enough.'

he said quietly,

and there was atremor in his voice, as though something had happened to him as well as her.

Celia returned to the room and sat down. Her legs were weak and her heat heart was fluttering.

She looked up at Marcus and her face was pale.

'I'm sorry', she said. 'I didn't mean to -'

'No Its I who should apologize. I had no intention of that happening.'

'Shall we have another drink?' He added?.

He walked across the room.

Celai was able to breathe agian.

He did ~~thigs~~ things to her that should never be allowed.

She looked at his broad back his ~~poer~~ powerful thighs, at the dark curly hair falling over the collar of his shirt. He was the most virile man she had ever met in her whole life, ever.

He handed her a drink. Then sat down across the room. He had placed sme music on. It was not soft romantic music but h rd rock, something Celia had no sympathy for but all the same it might break the spell that had built up between them.

Mardus excused himself leaving Celia alone in the room. She was restles and ~~began pacing the room.~~ drawn to the row of books on the bookshelf written by him. He was some specimen. Himx It wqs no wonder that it took him so long to write each book, his research had taken him to all corner of the world, below ground level, to the botomx bottom of the ocean and out into space. It was no wonder it took him several years to reseach each book, she thought.

She took one of his earlier books from the shelf, flicking through the pages noticing his peculiar way of writing, able to identify it with the man she was now with. There was another photograph on the back cover, a much younger Marcus this time, but still with the arrogant profile. Her heart began to race at the sight of the picture. She held i it agianst her breast. She was being foolish, but could'nt help it. She studied the likeness again, examining every detail of his face, his s sensuaous lips to the deep eyes, the determined chin and the irrepresi-ble curly hair. There was a caption beneath.

XXXXXXX XXXXXXXXXXXXXXX Gilbert Marcus lives on the island ofxXXXXX morass with his wife and child'

It was enough to tell her she was wasting her time here. She replaced th the book and walked out of the house. Back in her chalet she took offxher her dress and stood beneath a freezing cold shower, but felt no differen The shock was still there. She felt numb, ashamed, angry. ~~miserable.~~

In bed she lay staring at the ceiling. She wanted to scry but tears would not come.

'Oh Marcus, why?Please tell me why, oh why, oh why!'

She had one more day to endure before the boat came to take her back. If there was only some way of contacting the boatman. This love she felt was like nothing ever she had felt before. It was like a seed growing inside her. If she never saw him again it would still cintinue t o grow inside her. She was determined not to see him again.

The next morning she set off on foot for the other side of the island. She was desperately exhaustaed aftera sleepless night, but she drove but she drove ~~herslef~~ herself on, only allowing herself to sit and rest when aching legs would carry her ~~nomore~~- no further. There weren't many people on this side of the island and Celia was able to relax, ~~reli~~ relieved that she did not have to pretend everything was alright, when really she thought the world had come to an end.

As morning dragged past she bagan to feel hungry. S Hunger pains were adding to her misery. She did not want to ask at any of the private ~~hou~~ houses for fear of having to explain herself. So she went into the foret t and pulled down a bunch of ~~banabanaba-a~~- bananas. They were tiny, but delicious. Then she found a mountain stream with clear tricki ling waters and she cupped her hands and drank from it. It was like liquid nectar. Replete, she lay down. She was asleep.

Se Hours later she was aware of someone standing over her. Her eyes fluttered open and she saw an elderly ~~gentelman~~ man with steely hair and piercing blue eyes. He looked worried but smiled also.

'I'm afraid you've got sunburn.' He said nicely. 'Come with me, mx my wife has cream.'

'Its alright, I've got oil back at the hotel.' Said Celia bewildered. The man would not take no for an answer. 'i insist he said, and ledx took her hand and lead her along like a child. Celia followed. He seemed kind. He introduced himself as ~~Albert Fran~~ Francois. He was retired. His wife, Emily was a plump woman, took Celia under her wing, smoothing a a cool white lotion over her sunburnt face and arms.

She tuuted'You poor silly child! What made you go to sleep in the sun?' Celia smiled intenally. 'I didn't sleep well last night.'Ixxxxxxxxxe Emilly clucked. 'A young girl like you no ot sleeping? What's wrong by boy trouble?'

Celia shooke her head. Emily did not believe her. She was grateful for the glass of ice cold milk she was given.

'Stay for supper.' said Francois.SI 'if you've nothing better to do. Its not often we have company. We'd love [redacted] you to stay.'

Celia looked at their happy smiling unc omplicated faces, and nodded. 'I'D like that.' she said.

She helped Emily in the kitchen with sandwiches and soon forgot her t troubles. She had lost her own parents when she was small and so took an instant liking to Francois q and Emily, felt like she could confide in them. She need someone to talk to. But not just yet.

Long after their meal was finished they sat talking and it was dark when Celia said she should return. She told them she was staying at the Hotel but lead them to believe she was on holiday, shy of the real reason. Francois offered to walk her but she refused, although she did promise o to visit them before she left the island.

Long before reaching the hotel her happiness dried up. It was apleasant walk but she was soon accompanyied by Marcus. She knew she would be haunted by him in London to. Only time could heal her.

Where was his wife, she wondered? Perhaps they were sep rated? And his child? How old was it? Did Marcus ever see them? Was he divorced? These were questions she was desperate to xxix ask but knew she could not.

Bak at the hotel she went to bed and fell asleep easily. But it was not long before she was dreamingxf of Marcus. terter terutureous bad dreams - each time he rejected her. She woke feeling more tired than when she went to sleep.

She packed her case and placed it on the porch ? in readiness to leave. A ferry called at the island that morning, taking away tourists and brix bringing new ones in. She watched and wondered if she should just leave on the ferry. But she thought of the arrangement with the boatman, realised he would have a wasted journey if she left with the fery insted She also had time to xixt visit Franseis Franscois and Emilly.

twerex 'We're so happy you came to say goodbye' said Emilly welcoming herxinto the house. 'We thought you might forget. How is the sunburn?'

'I'd forgotten all about it!' Said Celia gaily. ?

'You don't look too happy. Are you sad to be leaving?'

'Yes' ~~'In a way'~~ said Celia.

'Are you missing your boyfreind?' Asked the old woman sagely, lifting u up her= Celia's hand to inspect the diamond. 'Cant think why he'd let a pretty thing like you come ~~on your own~~ here on your own. He must trust you.'

Axxxxxxxxx----- after luch Celia walked down to the shore. She daren't look back up at the house. It occured to her there that Anton would want to know what had happened. He wolud wonder if she had met Marcus. If he was guilty like Marcus said he was then he would have expected something to have happened and would quizz her closely. Oh how she wished they ~~hadva-~~ had all never met!

She waited and waited for the boat.
She wiated all afternoon and half the evening. It slowly dawned upon her that the boat was not goijg to come. She could have sat down and ~~cried~~ ~~wept~~ sobbed.
There were no other boats on the island. It was an isolated island shy of traffic. There were no telephones. Mail was picked up by the three-weekly ferry which she had just seen leave.
She returned from the shore to her chalet to find it occupied by a couple with a baby. The couple broke out in an angry foreign languge an d Celia gleaned that this was now their chalet ~~xx~~ since she was no longer supposed to be staying there.
Reception was equally unhelpful. They Pointed out that she was only ~~xt~~ booked to stay a limited time and now the chalet was re-allocated. Worse still they had no more rooms available.
In desperation she thought of Francois and Emillly. They were the only nice people she knew on the island.
It was dark by the ~~ttimx~~ time she arrived. ~~Theyxxwerexinxtheirxnightclo~~ ~~they-were-a-lo~~ She tapped on the door and they were a long timE answeing . Theywere in their nightclothes and looked worried. But worried looks became beaming with welcome when they saw who their visitor was.
'Come in, come in! ' said Franscois. 'What's happened? We thought you were leaving?'
'The boat didn't come'. said Celia wearily, close to tears. 'there's not another ferry for three weeks. I don't know what to do - the hotel is full. I8ve got nowhere to go -'
'We only have one bedroom, but you can stay the night. In the morning we'll sort something out.'
Celia fell asleep easily. In the morning her troubles flooded back.
At breakfst Emilly announced; ' We have an idea. We'll ask our son if you can stay with him,'
'YOUr son?' Said Celia surprised. 'He lievs here - on Morass ?'
'Oh yes' said Enily. 'Francois will go see him when he's finished his breakfast.'
Her husband nodded until finishing his breakfast and then disappeared as the two women set to clear up.
'Your son - do you see much of him?' said Celia.
'not really. He' busy. He bought us this bungalow. He makes sure we

want for nothing.'

Soon Franscois ~~returned~~ returned..

'Absolutely fine', he said cheerily. 'He's happy to help - on one condition.'

'Trust him!' exclaimed Emilly. 'What does he want?'

'Can you type?' Asked Francois.

Celia nodded., 'What does he do, this son of yours?'

Suddenly the door burst open and Marcus Gilbert stepped inside.

'You!' he said.

CHAPTER FOUR

His parents frowned. 'have you two met?' Theybsaid.

'She came into my house un-invited for a glass of water and smashed some glasses.' Said Marcus seething.

'Is that it?' Said Emilly astonished by the ~~degree~~ level of animosity.

'It wasn'nt that ', said Celia tensley. ' It was because I disturbed his work. Geniuses dont like their work being disturbed.'

Marcus8s face hardened. 'Celia,' said Emilly, 'why didn't you tell me you knew my Son?'

'I had no idea he was your son. You didn't ever mention his name.'

Celia wondered if Emilly and Francois would side with their son. She was desperate and realised that now she even needed Marcus to let her stay at his house.

'Well I8m glad you've met. It will make things easier. Don't work her to death Marcus, she's fragile'.

'You know my terms ' said Marcus with stony indifference.

Francois and emilly shrugged at each other.

'Dont worry MR Gilbert. I8m an efficient secretary and a very tidy typist. I will not let you down.'

Celia climbed into the oxcart unaided. Marcus's father placed her case in the back. She waved at Francois and Emilly gaily as though she ~~wrexx~~ were going somewhere nice.

During the ~~torturourue- torturepu~~ painful ride up to the hosue Marcus remained silent. No doubt if she had asked for his help he would have refused.

He looked nothing like his parents. His mother was round cuddly and soft and his father was old and weak and frail, nothing like his son. Marcus was ann individual, an immensly strong character who had developed ed in his own unique way. ThEY must be proud of him, she thought, proud of his success, proud of the statusx it had given him.

At the house Marcus dissappeeard, leaving Celia standing in the hall. She waited not knowing what to do. Footsteps sounded and a thin gxexy grEy haired old woman appeared with long sharp nose and beady eyes and beady eyes and a forbidding expression on her mean old lady's face. The housekeeper. For somee reason she already didn't approve of Celia.

'Miss Cielia, come with me.' Celia followed her up the marble staircase and along the red carpeted corridor. Celia was introduced into her room. Compared with the palacial splendour of the rest of the house it was SParton.

A bed with white cotton throwover in one corner. The bare boards were not ~~relieeve~~ relieved by even the tinest of carpets, the white walllsxLS white and simplE and unadorned. A ~~small~~ tiny window looked out at the mountainSIDEe rising steeply above them and she almost expected to see iron bars at the tiny window. But she thought she should be thankfull at leats she had a roof over her head. the housekeeper vanished and Celá was x left wondering whether it was Marcus's idead to put her here oR wheter the mean housekeeper had done it herself.

Manam Maman Terre he had called her. Mrs'Terrible'Celia thoughtdisre-spectfully. Why wAs she so protective of Marcus? She had no need of for concern concerning Celia. She was here to doxaxjob work and work she xx would. She had no further wish for further entanglement with Marcus. There could be no satisfying end to such a relationship, only more heart heartache. The wisest coyrse would be to remain alooof, do as HE asked and keep herself to herslef toxhersel Three weeks wait for the ferry was not so long was it? Two days had ~~almost killed her~~ seemd and age , three weeks was a lifetime. And then there was Anton to consider . He wonder what had happened to her. Perhaps he had found out the boatman didn't turn up and he'd have sent another. Perhaps she should leave a no note at the hotel. But when she thought how he had decieved her she chnaged her mind. Let him worry! it would serve him right for getting her out here under false pretenses.

~~She sighed and began emptying her case. Once her lovely dresses were hung behind a curtain in one corner and her underwear all neatly putt away in the drawers,~~ she made her way back downstairs. She did not no which rroom was Marcus's study. She walked along the corridor listen-ing at each door. She thought she heardopapassmsmd the sound of a type writer

and pressed her ear to the door.
Suddenly the door was ~~x~~ flung wide open and Marcus stood there, a thunderous frown creasing his forehead. 'WHTa the HEll are you doing??' he demanded.
'I was trying to find your study. I'm here to work.' she said.
'You should knock, not listen at keyholes,' the biting reply.
Oh what had happened to the Marcus she had learned to love? she asked herself painfully. This was Marcus, the man she hated. He had two sides to his character and it seemed this was the one she was destined to ~~suff~~ suffer most. Yet it was preferable. If he was nice to her she would not be able to work in such close proximity without ~~expe-~~ giving away her true emotions.
'Come in.' he said with reluctance. Inside all~~x~~ was chaoSS. At complete variation with the rest of the house. Celia's horrified eyes surveyed the littered desk and open books, a tape recorder with tape spilling out onto the floor like a ~~cat's~~ kitten's ball of wool toy. He had difficulties keeping order. Celia could not help smiling inside h herself at the plight of this bestselling author's mess.
There was enough work to keep someone bust for a lifetime. The filing kabinet had piles of papers on the top, drawers half open, files pulled out. It needed organising. He might be a ~~great~~ brilliant writer, ~~gifted?~~ she ~~theguth~~ thought, but he was out of control.
'So I'm not the tidiest person in the world. Is it too much for you? Is that what you're thinking??'
'No, no,' said Celia. 'I was just wondering how someone could work in such a mess.'
He frowned. 'Actually I know where everything is. I've had busybodies like you here before tidying up ~~after me~~ around me, and when they leaveI I can't find a thing.'
'You need a system.' She said polietly 'If things were file properly it would be easier for you to find things.'
'Can you do it?'
'Yes.'
'Fine. But I must tell you, this manuscript over here on my desk is taboo. You must not touch it. I Don't allow anyone to see my work before it is published. Okay? I'm serious.'
'Where shal I start.' She said. Love bubbling over inside her, but resigned to be proffessional with the Marcus she didn't care for.

'Start there'. He said pointing at a cabinet. He turned hisback on her sitting down at his desk and begining to type, For a moment Celia watched as his braod fingers touched the typewriter keys lightly. He typed faster than any woman, faster than herself. She could not help admiring him.

he was in a world of his own. Had forgotteN she was there. She felt she could walk up to him , touch him, k kiss his nape, and he would not have noticed, so immersed was he in his typing.

She was tok to be a filing clark not a secretary after all. It was quite clear that he would be doing all of the typing. She hope that if things turned out well he might let her do some typing as well; it would give her and insight into hsi charcter, told her a little about himself, the way he ticked. She was sure it would be impossible to write a book without a little of the author creeping into it.

Lo0king theough the files she was able to see exactly what was wrong. The whole sysy system was A-Z. Anyhting beginning with the letter A was filed under A, anything from antelope to aeroplane. The files were-bulging obviously need sub-- sub-indexes.

It was a Mammoth task.

Very painstakingly and methodically she began the mammoth task. She began to sort into groups. She found a box contian new unused files and set out her subject headings, slipping each paper into the approprate file as she came to it. It took x her the whole moring just to do the letter a. But she was determing ed to succeed. Had it not been for the housekeeper announcing lxxx lunch she would have been prepared to work through until whatever time Marcus suggested they stop.

He frowned at the interuption. Nodded to Maman Terre but continued to type letter after letteru word afet word. Celia was at odds. She didn't know whether to take a break or stay with Marcus, immersed in his relentless typing. In the end she got up and went to the dinning room. The table was set for two. She ate slald and smoked salmon. She ate with rxxxx relish, but even when she felt-replet- replete Marcus did not xxx come. She decided to take lunch to him on a tray.

He did not appear to hear her enter, but when she put the tray on his dk desk, moving a few papers to clear a space he stopped typing to look at her.

'What are you doing? Leave me alone!'

'Your lunch.' Said Celia. 'You'll work better if you eat.'

'You sound like my mother.' He scowled. 'Go away!'

Celia returned to her filing scorned.

In the filing cabinets there were lots of ~~letters~~ poisonous letters sent to officious civil xxxxx servants and court officials. Also there was a lot of his genuine research. She knew that she could at least make an impact upon his memory of her by making sure she left him with a fool-proof filing system. Looking behind her she saw he was eating and drinking the coffee she had made for him.She smiled inside. He poured a second cup of cofee. The day passed quickly after that. Celia became so immersed in her work she even forgot Marcus. It was not until his rapid typing skillfull typing drew to a close and Marcus declared he was finished for the day did Celia realise it was almost seven o clock.

'Your time is your own. Do what you will with it. I'm going out.' He said Celia wanted so to ask where he was going but knew better than to ask. He was a strange man and the more time she spent with him the less she understood him.

Once again she ate alone. Then, unable to bear the lonliness of the ~~his~~ house she walked down the hill and made her way to his parent's house. They were pleased to see her. They asked how her first day at work had gon.

'Marcus came by an our ago', said Emilly. 'We asked him how today went but he was not interested in wnswering. Are you getting on?x '

Celia was aware of there encouragement, ~~but wondered why~~ she was confused because somewhere or other he had a wife and a child? ??

Celia tried to appear happy. ' Time flew by. Must mean I was enjoying myself. Marcus is a very busy man.'

'Bust? Yes!' sighed Emily ~~resig-~~ with resignation. 'We think he works to hard. We tell him, but he doesn't take any notice of us. 8

'I can't image him taking notice of anyone. He's very determined.' said Celia.

'Oh so you've found that out?' said Francois, wryley.

'The first day I met him.' said Celia ruefully.

'I can't imagine him appreciating you going up to his housen for a glass of water unnanounced and then breaking some glasses.' Said his mother laughing. ha ha ha?

'It wasn't the best moment of my life' said Celia laughing too.

'Marcus likes his privacy,' said Francois, 'Especially since -'

'Francois!' Shouted Emilly. 'Celia. Have you eaten?You must be famished?'

What was he about to say? Thought Celia. ~~thoughtxthenxthoughtxbetterx~~

'No, but I8d love a cup of tea.'

After the two women had talked Francois was good enough to xmkk walk cCelia to the botttom of the hill. He would have goNE all of the way, kt but Celia insisted it was too much for him and sent him back.

'Francois, there's nothing to woory about - no poisenous snakes, no wild anmals. No ha m will come to me!'

At the house she found Marcus waiting for her.

' Where the hell have you been?.'

tx She looked at him with disbelievef. 'Itk I've been to see your parents. If that's okay?'

'Next time you go out,' he said angriley - 'leave a note.'

'Oh don't tell me you were worrie concerned. 'I imagine you'd have been pleased if I hadn't returned. I Know you're only putting me up for the sake of your parents. I know you're toying with my emotions. I know the other night didn't mean anything. It didnt mean anything to me nietr either. I forgot it before you turned up this emoring- xmx this morning'

'So why did you run away this morning?'

'I just wanted to go out.' Said Celia holding his gaze to prove she was telling the truth.

'So if it meant nothing you don't mind if I test again?' His eyes stormed over. Celiaxxxk He- Before Celia could anticipate HIS his xxxms arms long strong arms slid behind her back, pullling herxxxxxxxxxxxx against him, his mouth taking hers fully. She fought for a bit, but suckumbed to the pleasure of the moment. She began to kiss bakk back but them suddenly he thrust her from him with a gesture of disgust.

'Yxxxxxxxxxxxxxxxxxxxxxxxxxxxxxxxxxxxxx 'Why didn't you fight?' he spat.

'Becuase your kisses leave me cold. You're wasting your time.' She wiped his kisses from her mouth with herxhandy a gesture of distaste. Marcus frowned and dissapeared fromthe corridor into his study and slammed the door. Celia wondered if he was going to work a ll all night. Why should she care? Letb- Let him work himself into an early grave if he wanted too.

Celia went to bed. She couldn't relax though. She listened to the s sound of his fluent typing, and waited to hear the sound of his feet steps on the stairs. She knew she could not rest until he too was in bed

It was about three before she heard his feet climbing the stairs slowly like he was tired or soemtthing. ~~She knew how draining writi~~ She now understood how exhausting writing was - especially writing on that old manual Tab-o-matic typewriter. She wanted to go and comfort him but daren't invite a writer's wrath. Soon sge fel asleep. She woke with a sh shock the next morning to find it was past nine.

Celia jumped out of bed, disapointed that she was late for work. She ran into the bathroom, washed and dressed quickly and hurried downstairs, missing breakfast and going straight to the study.

Marcus was already at work at his typewriter, which was a suprise given his late night writing. He did not look up from the manual keys nor answer her polite 'Morning!'

Celia made her way to her pile of paers and began work, silently, but aware of the man writing just a few yar feet from her.

By mid-mormid mid -morning Celia was very hungrey. She could not do any concentrate until she had eaten. She wondered if she was to the houskeeper had made anything, or if it was alright to go to the kitchen herself and make something to eat for herself and perhaps Marcus if he wanted anything to eat.

She stood next to thex his desk. 'would you like anything from the kitchen? A drink? Some food?' she said.

Without stopping his skillfull work he said 'No thanks.' and continued typing at breakneack speed.

In the corridor Celia bumped into the housekeeper bring a tray of two cups of tea and some sandwiches. Celia offered to take it. 'Ah! Just what we need!' she said friendly. But the housekeeper would not smile nor give the tray. 'Ix can manage.' she said. She went past Celia into the study, placed the tray on the side and left without a single word.

Celia took a cup of coffee to Marcus and a sandwiCH. 'Stop for a minute to replenish.' she said sweetly. 'You must need rest after working so hard and so late into the night.'

He sighed and his dextrus fingers stopped typing. 'When will you learn that I cannot abide interuptions? And how do you know what time I worked until? '

'I couldn't sleep.' she said pleasnatly. ' strange surroundings I suppose.'

'Or maybe you you were hoping I was going to come into your room? Was that it? Afterx telling me my kisses meant nothing? You wanted me to share your bed - is that why you twisted your way into my house?'

'Had I know Francois and Emilly were your parents I would have declined their kind offer to helpxmex ask their son to help me. Mothing would have persuaded me to xxxx share this hellish place with you. I came here because I didn't want to hurt you praxxxx parents.' She said angriy 'You like them, don' you?'

'Yes I do. They're warm and friendly, unlike their son.' she said. ~~sharp~~ She was amazedx that he simply nodded xxxxxxxxxxx ~~nicely~~ friendlily finished his coffee and carried on typing swiftly without another word. Yet he was till the most anti-social person Celia had ever met in her life.

Over the next few days Celia became used to this ~~pattern~~ work patter. They would work all day, rarely speaking - when they did they argued. In the evenings Marcus would go out. Where Celia had no idea. ~~He-ca~~ came back late. By then Celia would have gone to bed, bored with her own company.

She had taken to reading his books. Had almost become a M~~arcus Gilbert~~ xxxxxxxxxxxxxxx Gilbert Marcus fan. It was not difficult to imagine him living the part of some of his chracters, especially the one who became an undercover pimp so that he could save his xxxxxxxxxx ~~from the sex slave industry.~~ childhood sweetheart from the international sex slave industry. He would be good undercover.

The filing was going well but Celia was sad that Marcus never once asked how is it goiNG? In truth her love for him was growing with each day. A desperate love that she tried to ignore. But working so close , watching him at work on his typewriter, feeding him, watching him, aching for his attention was hell.

Nights were worst. Long lonely nights lying alone in her single bed, listening to his typing, and knowing when he came to bed that he was so near but so far. She imagined his room was luxurius. She wondered why her's was so barren. ~~But she would never complain.~~ *[delete]*

Sometimes she would escape to see his parents. She k~~ept silent about~~ did not tell them how difficult things were for fear of them asking Marcus questions and then he would think she had been telling tales behind his xxx broad strong back.

It was wensday or thursday when Celia found Marcus standing over the filing cabinet. Waiting for her. All her papers were scattered across the floor. He was furious.

'Where's thMYe notes on xxxxxxxxxxxxxx volcanic islands?' He snapped.

'I've split eac file into subheadings. Would it be under V for volcanoes or G for geology? What dou you think?' she said provocativeley.

'How the hell should I know?' he said.'Isn't your system supposed to be foolproof?'

Celia picked up the Ge file and found Geology. He snatched it from her and found his notes on the subductive power of volcanic magma chambers, but threw the other papers onto the floor.

'Ee There's no need for that. I've only just sorted those. I8m doing the work as thouroughly as I can and you've not once said thank you.'

'You8re in the wrong place for such absurd niceties. You8re here to work. This serious work not some kind of My writing is serious. Its torn from my soul. Its not a hobby. You're here to make it a little less painful for me, so that I can creatx continue. What do you exPECT expect from me?'

'A little civility?' she snapped.

He shrugged indifferently. 'Would you prefer I leave?' She said.

What a loathsome man. How could she possibly love him so?

'He lifted one eyebrow mockingley. 'Do whatever you want.' he said, knowing full well there was no way she could get off the island until the next ferry came. She was a prisoner on his island.

She wondered how practical things like illness were dealt with.

She knew there was a doctor on the island and some sort of hospital clinic, but what if anyone got seriously ill?

And what of Gilbert Marcus's international fame and his need to travel around the world soaking up accolayed? Selia wouldn't be surprised if he had a helicopter hidden away somehwhere so that he could woosh off to p celebrity parties and premiers.

She looked at the mess he had made of her files and anger welled up and she picked up a file and threw it mith all her might at the back of his head. Her aim was not whatxshe good. The file landed on the pile of papers next to his manual typewriter and the manuscript flew onto the floor.

'Sorry!' she cried. 'I didn't mean to do that!'

'What in hell's name have you done?' He shouted.

'I'll pick them up for you and I promise not to read any of it.' she implored, remebering his insistance that she never look at it.

She expected him to explode with anger but instead they both knealt and he let her pick up the papers. Being so close to him made her heart quicken. Her pulse sounded like a drum in her ears. She wondered if he could hear. Or whether he had noticed the redcolour flooding into her hot cheeks. When the papers were all gatherered up she went tO take them from him.

'Pleas let me put them back in oredr for you. Please.' She said ernesTly

He paused. And then to her surprise agreed.

At her impromptu desk she put the pages into numeric order, but it was impossible not to read a few lines. She tried not too. But words and phrases simply lept out at her. The manuscript was wmtx worked with crossingsxout crossings out and scribbles and notes made by hand with a pen. It was ~~the most~~ an ~~indictment~~ d xxindictment of human struggle - the most coragoous and honest thing she had ever read.

It From what she read, she it was a gushes with pathos - it howls inta deep into an ocean of profligate introspection, all-in-all it is a love-death triangle that juxtposes the Sissyphssswith Sis-syheian Sissyphean with the Herculean - and now Celia far better apreciates the author's sensitivity to his desx destined magnum opx opus being read before the auther achieves emotional closure.

She returned the pages to his desk in good and proper order. He nodded with his head absent mindedley. Thatvwas all the thanks she would get. Celia felt close to tears.It was becoming so pianful working for this man. It hurt.

So it came as a sincere shock when hex Marcus announced that that eve=ning he was not going out andxx she would have ~~thepleaseyure~~- the pleasure of his own company, during dinner.

as she went upsters to change CeLI-ia fonun found herself huMming softl y . ~~It bro ut back pa nful memories, b~~ - It was the happy est she ha d felTt since c omming here. It was silly re ally, they were onl iy eating , nothing morxE. It was not un thinkabl e to thingk that he mite not even speek to her. She changed into the pink she wore on that fatefull night it brought back xx bad memories, but it was the only apropriate thing she had with her on this trip.

Downstair s Marcus was wearing a creamy suit jacket which complimented his mahogany tan tax perfectly well. He never looked so attractiive to x a woman's eye. His dark lovely lushoud hair was combed neatly and he set himself out to be the most perfect host a girl could wiSH for. During dinnerd , conversation turned to writing. Celia discussed the several books she had now read all the way through to the end, and without thinking, made the mistayke in asking hixmabout the one he wasworking on as we speak. It was trueley the worng thing to say, a fous pas.

'I've told you in no uncirtaine terms! My writing and my book are private! I really cant abide anyone ~~interupting~~ poking their nose into it before it is finished.'

'I'm sorry.' said Celia. 'I was making conversation. I did not mean to pry.'

W 'Welll the topic is ferbidden, okay?8

'Suit yourself' said Celia, hurt.

'You think I8-- I'm being unreasonable?'

'Yes I do.' she said. Her lovely pretty blue eyes now wide and hostile and yet aslo strageley inviting. 'I~~ly~~ I think you've been ~~atsershu~~-- ~~atreshus~~ foul over ~~my-hol~~ the whole affair of my being here in your house

'As I never wanted you here I don't no how you can say that?' he said, ~~xxxxxxx~~ swallowing a mouthfull of wine indolently and stared at her coldy.

~~Ix~~ 'I'm doing a fair days work for the privelege of your charity and a roof over my head. and food inn my stomach. You are the most ~~ungrayte~~ mean minded person I've ever come across I wish I did.nt have to stay here!'

Marcus8s nostrils flared widly and Celia could see his nuckles gleam ed-x white as he clenched his knife and fork tight. ~~Right~~- She had the feeling that he would like nothging betre than to stab her with the knife or fork. He had a crazy look in hiseyes, a wild crazy look, She could not understand why his book could not be discussed. ~~She-had-~~ It was a very very moving story and from the little she had read she knew it had been writtne with great felling - almost as though it were something he was going through himself. Why guard it so ~~sealousix~~ jealously.?'

'Perhaps we should work eperately in seperate rooms.' He said.

'Celia felt like weeping. He was shutting her out of his study and his life.

'WHy she said. ' I haven't stopped you from hammering away at your ~~xpecial~~ typEwriter for hours on end. I don't know how you keep it up. Y You don't even pause for thought. The words flow.'

'Are~~aye~~-- you an authority on writing now?' He said impatinetly. ' you don't no the first thing about writing. Anyway, I'm not happy with anything I've written since you came here. You disturb me.'

Disturb him? Not in the way she snould lik. Not in the way a woman a man enough to incite him to ravage her. This was waht she wanted. She wanted for nothing less than for him to share the same feelings for

her.
Each time she thought of how creul and cold he was she felt sad and cut off. He had only let himself go once, and she suspected that he was not as immune to her as hex made out. But she wondered why he ~~now~~ was being all aloof. why he was rejecting her so spitefully. But she musth go on wondering. Ther was nox no ~~whay~~ way of asking , no ~~wahyx~~ way that her own pride would let her admit to herself thqt she loved him. When the time was up to go and leave she would go and leave and that would be that, a bitter end to this bitterf-sweetx interlude. She pushedher food away hardley touched and then she ~~sto~~ stood up.
'where now brown cow?' He said savagely.
'I cant't eat any more she said', 'Imsuddendly not hungry.'
'Conversation to much?' he snnneered. and then he to rose, to her ~~xxxxx~~ suprise, his face changing dramaticallly. 'Damn the foed,' he said, thickly, and pulled her into his arms. 'is this the sort of fooed you want?' his mouth ~~dangerously~~ dangerously ~~xlxs~~ close t0 hers. 'you look at me with love starved eyes all evening, is ~~th~~ this waht youre after?'
oh had she really been so obvious? Her breathing deepeneed and emotion threatened to choke her. She was afraid to look into his eyes. and did not even cry out when he he caught a handfull of her hair ~~roughly~~ and roughly jerked her head back ~~roughly~~. ~~Hxxxx~~ He covered her face with kissses, hot searing kisses, long lingering hot searing kisses, and Celia clenched her eyes against the passion she glimpsed breefly on hiS face . When hsi ~~motuh~~- moUth covered hers in a harsh demandingh hot searing lingering kiss she was carried away on a tide of humah ~~emoti~~ emotion. She pressed herself against him. feeling the hardness ofx~~hixxxx~~ of his ~~thf+gxxxx~~++ thighs against her own soft thighs, her breasts cruh ~~cru~~- crushed against the cast iron muscle of his ~~steel~~ stainless steel chest.
when he lifted herx into his arms and carried her out of the rooom she thought for a ~~moment~~- one brief ~~exsetaitex~~- ecstatiC moment that he was takIng her to bed. She began to struggle in a half-~~xxxxxx~~hearted manner but ~~hwn~~ when his steel arms tighten in an iron clasp she knew she had little chance. But it was not to the bedroom that she was taken, it was to the garden room, he p laid her down on the deep piled carpet and she moaned softly, holding up her own arms, lips parted, blue eyes shing

shining like a jewel.

chapter five. ([illegible])

Marcus towered over her like a giant, physically exciting, emotionally exhausting - the only person she ever wanted in her whole life to posses her fully. It was strange at this moment that she should think about Anton, and unconsciously her finger sought the place where his ring had been. She had in fact taken it off while handling the files and had forgotten to replace it on her ring finger.

Marcus noticed what she did and his face changed sudenly, darkening around the edges with deep hue of suspicion.

' Whxx where's your ring?' He said. And when he did not get an answer : ' Does it mean your engagemnet is over? Do you intend telling Merriweather when you get back that its all off? I cant believe at last you-ve come to your senses.'

His con demning-tone shatttered Celia's warmth and she struggled, ashamed that she had been lying there, openinly inviting him inside.

'I was afraid of losing it'she said.

'But not of losing Anton,' he said, scathingly.

She did not no what to say. She was not sure of her emotions for Anton were. She knew it was impossible to love ixxx two men at the same time and in the xxxxxx exact same way. She looked at Marcus and knew in her heart of hearts that she would never marry Anoton He paled into insignificance beside this strong virile man who excited her.

She ached to be owned by him. But she knew it was more than a temporary possession she wanted. At first she only considred being his lover, but now she wanted to be his best friend, his closest companion she wanted to spend every day ofxherxlifexwithxhim, and every night ofxh her life, to share his sorrows and his joys alike, his ups and downs, to bear his children and share in his pleasuRE. It was true love she felt. The down side was that she did not think there was any chance that he might return her feelings. His attraction was physical. He was a perfectly healthy male animal who wanted a woman, and she was ready and willing.

'I didn't encourage you,' she said.

'Youxwerexas But it was what you wanted, aiit There's no denying that.Xu You were as ready to recieve me as I was - ' he stopped. Without xxx another word crossed to the drinks cabinet and poured himself a glass of whiskey. He downed it in one and re-filled the glass before coming overx to where Celia was still stanfi- standing still.

Celia felt tears prick the back of her eyes. She was tempted to run from the room while he downed the whiskey, yet she reacted as any would any other girl when a man as attractive as Marcus attempted to makexitxexxtxn seduce her.

'I'd like a drink too,' she said, eyeing his glass.

'the get yourself one,' he snapped.

She was happy for the excuse to move and went over and poured herself a Napolean Brandy.

'What do you suggest we do know?' asked Marcus with ill intent. 'I shou ld have gone out.'

'I wa wish you had, Life's nicer when you're not around.'

'I couLD say the same about you,' he replieD. 'Anyway. You're not my tye type. And what are you going to tell Anton when you get back home?'

'the truth!' she said.

'Well you've managed to find yourself into my home, what's next?8

Celai saterd at him angry. 'You know damn well that I don't want your island, or anything teedee connected to you!'

His lips curl derisively. 'You still believe that Anton was going to buy it for you? My God your more naive than I thought! He wants it for himsf himself, can't you see that? He'd drop you like a red-hot brick if you managed to clinch the deel. What's the matter - don't you carexxx enough for him to do it? Doens't even the thought that he might offer you a has handsome settlement tempt you to try and persuade me to sell?'

His taunting angered Celia but yet she was determined not to lose her t temper. 'The Day I try and get round you for anything MR Gilbert wil beh be the day I'm certified insane!'

He took her glass away, then holding her by the shoulders drew her howna twxxdyfxxftxyxdx- towards him. HE Her heart fluttered like the wings of a xgxxdxbird caged bird.

'Don't you find the challlegge exciting?' He said. 'Wouldn't it give you as sense of power if you thought you could twist me round your little finger? Go on, let me see how you work, flutter those long lashes, part those inviting lips, rub your delicious body next to mine. you were ready and willing a few momments ago. what happened? did you chicken out or did thoughts of Anton prevent you? Perhaps itxwas your conscience pricked you?'

His vitility reached out to her like a magnet, her breathing grew ragged and sge stared at him with wide blue eyes.

'You're horrible!' she jerked. 'I'm not the ~~type~~ kind of woman who uses men to further her own ends. If Anton wants the island he can do his own dirty work!'

Marcus laughed. 'I almost believe you! But I know how women with limpid blue eyes can beguile and appeal, hiding the truthe depth of their feelings.' A harsh light came in his eyes as though he was remembering something painfull.

'What do I have to do to make ~~me~~- you believe me?' she cried.

'Try being yourself!' he said. His fingers tightened andx digging inx painfully into the thin flesh on her shoulders. She raised her hands and pushed against himbut to no avail. He laughed and his face drew nearer. She felt the pressure of his lips on hers, but there was know tenderness It was meants as punishment, was harsh and ~~brutal~~brutal, pressing her li lips back against her teeth. He ~~ed~~ explored her soft moistness with savage intensity and she knew that he must be aware of the shivers of delight he was causing her. She felt that if hem let go she would fall into a crumpled heap on the floor. Hexxxxxxxxxxx Even though his kisses were a mockery, she could not help herself from responding. Thmx

When his lips lifted she cried 'Oh Marcus!' and it was a cry from thexhx heart.

He pushed her away forcefully and she fell back against a chair losing her balance and crashing to the floor. She expected an immediate apology thought he would rush to pick her up, but no, for the seconds she lay he gazed down at her laying there with dispassionate eyes.

'you 8ve got no more than you desreve.' he said harshly. 'I hate women who throw themselves at me.'

'I didn't' cried Celia. 'It was -'

'I did nothing ~~more~~ that any full-blooded male wouldnt do when he has it handed to him sfm on a plate. Youre very atttractive, but Ism don't pxst

'Goodnight Marcus, I8m sorry I can't say thanks for a pleasnt evening because it has not been pleasant at all.' ~~sha~~ said Celia as she slammed the door and exited to go to her bedroom. Marcus didn't answer. As ~~xxx~~ ~~shegg~~climbe~~d~~ the stairs her heavy legs became lead. by the time she she reached her room tearRs were rolling down her cheecks.

For the first time she wished there was a bolt or a lock on the door so she could vent her emotions in private. She was afraid to cry ~~ineade~~ in case Marcus heard her sobbbing and came up to gloat all over her. But tears flowed and she buried her head in the pilllow, sobbing silently u~~un-y--~~ until she became calmer.

It was clear Marcus had intended to taunt her. She must learn not to take any notice of his taunts if he was to taunt her again. There were t still two more weeks until the ferry, so she must do her best to ignore any further fur~~hetrhrte~~ ~~futt-~~ more taunst. She only hopee that Marcus would sugg est no more intimate evenings. If he stayed in then she would go out. It was ~~the-~~ as simple as that. It was the only~~+wy~~ way.

Had this scene affected him as much as it had her, she~~xx~~ wondered, or was he laughing, perhaps he was planning this all ~~the-way~~ along?

It was as if he was trying to seduce her but was frustarated, and so was being nasty to her instead. She had no idea where he spent his evenings, wether there was another woman or wether he went for a lonely drink at the hotel. All she~~x~~ knew for a fact was that he kept clear of her. This was the first time they had got together socially and it was a disaster.

Celia picked up Anton's ring from the little jug on the dressing table and slippped it back on her finger. She felt safe with it their. It was a barrier between her and Marcus and even though she had every intention of giving it back to Anton when she returned to ENgland for the time ~~be~~ being it woulf never be off of her finger.

She spen a restless night and was down in the study before Marcus the next morning. It was unusual for her to be first and so she wondered wether the events last night had anything to do with his lateness. She doubted it. Men Like Marcus Were immune to scuh upsets. It would have paissed over him like ~~x~~ water on a duck's back. No doubting he~~x~~ slept ~~x~~ deeply and soundly, so deeply and soundly that he had overslept this morning.

~~It was about ninethirty befo[illegible] was suprised to se~~
~~[illegible]~~
~~She almost expected an apollogy, and was even di sapointed when noth-~~
~~ing was forthcoming. He sat at his desk, ignoring her as was usual, but~~

It was about ninethirty before he came in and Celia was surpised to see shadows beneath his eyes. She almost expected an apology, and was disapa disapointed whenn nothing was forthcoming. He sat at his desk, ignoring her as usual, but his typing did not seem xx to be going so well this m morning. he had intemittent bursts when he would go at great msufge- spe speed but then he would rip xxx the paper out of his machine and tear it into shreds. tatters?

When Maman Terre brought food he pounded on the cofee gratefullly but still did not speak to Celia. She took her own cup and returned to her corner, sipping it slowly, studying the bac of his head.

As though aware of xxxx her scrutiny Marcus swivelled and saterd at her coldly, eyes resting xxxxx for a second on the diamond ring.

'Is anything rong? Is there something you wanted?' he said tersley.

'No. Iwas just thinking how tired you lokked when you walked in.' She said.

'I could say the same thing about you.' He retunned tersely. 'Your face is fxx hardley a picture of health. Didn't you sleep well?' He said.

'Not really.' she said.

'because of what happened last night?' he said.

'No.' she said.

'Then why couldn't you sleep?' he said.

'No reason. What about you - why couln(t you sleep?' she said.

'I didn't say that I didn'T' he said.

'Are you having trouble with your writing?' she said.

That made him mad. He finished his cofee and stood up. ttxkxxtx

'Take the rest of the day off. I'm going out.' he said.

This was so out of character Cleia was worried. He lived for his work. Never once had she experienced him not complete a full days work. And Mo Morass was so small, where was there for him to go? She knew better than to question him, merely watching sadly as he laft the room.

For a while she continued her work, she was near to finishing all of the filing, but know her heart was not in it. Things were getting worse instead of much better. Left alone inside the house Celia felt disinclined to work. She wandered about the room and found herself being drawn towards Marcus's desk. Almost without realising it she sat down and began to read. The story was tragic but beuatifxull - right up Celia's street.

Chapter Six

With a glass bead readying to hurl itself from its trembling mantle, Chlamydia Love replaces the sacred manuscript on Helmut Mandragorass's holy writing altar, hoping the author rewards this magnificent creation with the happy ending his characters deserve – she loathes dragging herself to the conclusion of a book only to find death lingering on the final page. So far this wonderfully uplifting story has done nothing but prompt real heartfelt feelings from its first ever reader – and maybe, one day soon, in the near future, when it is published in its millions, Chlamydia can purchase her very own copy and find out what happens in the end.

Gaping optimism sighs back into the present and unable to face even the thought of feasting and purging alone, she decides to give Helmut's mother and father, Mr and Mrs Mandragorass, or Günter and Brunhilde as she now knows them, an impromptu visit – it seems aeons since she saw them and finds them more than pleased when they discover her hammering at the front door.

Mummy Mandragorass no sooner has the hot chocolate on than not.

'We've been wondering how you've been getting on with *our little one…*' says mummy. Daddy nods. 'He was here the other day,' she continues. 'I scolded the little pig. Gave him a piece of my mind. Castigated the little brat. Reproached him…'

'*Little brat…*' adds daddy shaking his mottled old pate.

Chlamydia shakes hers wryly. 'I guessed you might have said something. We endeavoured to share dinner together last night – an attempted war reparation. But no cigar. We ended up fighting rather badly. I'm afraid to say your son hit me again.' She shows them the pretty collection of yellow, green, purple and blue bruises on the fleshy wing of her translucent arm. 'Helmut and I don't see eye to eye – only an *eye for an eye*. It's total war up there on the volcano, scorched earth, year zero…'

Daddy interrupts her genocidal flow before he's irreversibly implicated:

'Poor child, and do you argue in the cold light of day?'

'Oh no, no, no not at all – we don't ever speak.'

Mummy and daddy exchange eyeballs. 'I was hoping you might have drawn him out from his shell,' says mummy. 'He has so much on his mind – he's troubled,' she winks and nods.

'Y' know – *busy* – upstairs.'

'Oh I can very well see he's busy,' says Chlamydia with kiss and tell concern. 'His writing must take its toll – especially Helmut's hands-on method.'

'Mmmm,' mummy hums. 'I'm afraid it's more than that. He wouldn't thank me for exposing his private affairs – but you might treat him with kid gloves, he's emotionally damaged, sore – been through a rough, rough time. An emotional ghost train.'

Chlamydia assumes Helmut's mummy is alluding to Helmut's marital status – perhaps an acrimonious divorce possibly giving rise to a latent and unresolved hatred of women. She wonders how the child has faired in the trade-off – probably wrenched asunder, poor little stray. She imagines a pile of bloody arms and legs. Mummy clears her throat loudly.

'Heavens!' says Chlamydia. 'I was a million miles away.'

'Daydreaming about your man-friend back home?' says mummy pointedly. 'I imagine you miss him? *Do you miss him?*'

'Miss him? Well I imagine he's wondering where the Hell I am – why I haven't returned.'

'It's beyond your control. He'll have made inquiries, found out why you're still here.' Says daddy winking at mummy.

After breaking bread and chewing the fat Chlamydia declares

it is time to vamoose. She forges her excuses and embarks on the long journey to haul her fat arse back home.

At the foot of the volcano Chlamydia's daydream is accosted by a miniature voice calling out and pleading with her to slow. She recognises the all too familiar frame of Helmut in the distance struggling in her direction petitioning her to wait up. So she waits for the toddler to catch up, sitting down on the sand, but he is nearer than he appears and oddly enough, seems to have mislaid his ill humour:

'Isn't it a nice day?' he says, all cheery-pops. 'Where have you been today?'

'To visit your mother and father,' Chlamydia replies with studied caution.

'Oh, that's nice. And how are they?' he says with only a forensic inflection of guilt.

'Fine, fine… they're both very well. And what have you been doing today?' she says.

'Oh a walkin' 'n' a talkin' 'n' a thinkin' to myself…'

Suspicion presumes Helmut's walking, talking and thinking are dedicated to solving his present creative crisis, but Chlamydia declines being drawn into a naked enquiry. Instead the odd couple climb the volcano urging each other on with uninspired pleasantries. At the door Chlamydia offers to make dinner but Helmut no sooner settles for a simple sandwich, 'I'd hate to put you to any trouble,' he says opening the door for the female of the species to enter.

In the foul kitchen Chlamydia drums up two chicken legs, an omelette, and a boiled egg. She finds Helmut in the study blinking at his typewriter as though it is a booby trap set to snare his fingers. She places the laden tray on the desk in front of his wincing fear. He regards the edibles, compelled to read the riddle staring up at him from the plate.

He squawks at the chicken omelette: 'Oh I get it! *Which came first – the chicken or the egg? DON'T YOU THINK I'VE GOT ENOUGH ON MY PLATE WITHOUT ADDING YOUR LITTLE CONUNDRUMS...!'*

'Oh you self-centred buffoon!' says Chlamydia, expelling herself from the study in disgust to her own poxy room where she meditates upon her dim circumstance, paying especial attention to her next move. She decides to take mother's advice and treat mummy's son with kid gloves – take a softly-softly approach to the hardened soul she thinks she knows she loves. She sashays back to the study, slides though the swing in the door, tiptoes onwards to arrest her softly-softly flesh upon Helmut's hardwood table top.

'Are you really going to tap, tap, tap all night?' she says, fluttering her tarantulas.

'*W-h-y-?*'

'I thought we could listen to some music... a little chat... a little *cha-cha-cha*... who knows?'

'What are you after?' And in a miniature voice mimicking a browbeaten child: 'Perhaps we could arrange for Algae to come by for a play day – I'm sure he'd love to listen to some music... have a little chat, chat, chat and dance a lickle...'

'Algernon? Come here to your island? That's a laugh! Golly-gosh, you're a prickly pear! I was only trying to be nice. I thought you could do with a little light entertainment to alleviate all that heavyweight enlightenment. I thought you'd enjoy a little company... but no, you only see the negative in things. Mark my words – you'll get your comeuppance some day soon...'

'Who's been gossiping? mummy spill the beans? Took her long enough! Well you can tell that unwholesome bitch she can go to Hell the next time she sees fit to blab about my private life to an absolute stranger... and you can go to Hell too – the two of you... together – and my father! All three of you... To Hell with all three of you! – and Algernon… all f-f-four of you…'

'You shouldn't speak ill of your parents!' Chlamydia fists the tray causing it to flip over and catapult its fowl load over Helmut. 'You're just lucky they're still in the land of the living!' She exits stage left without pausing for his response. Upstairs, she positions herself on the edge of her bed, listening to the sound of thunder bolting up the stairs. The door flies open and Helmut scrambles in with egg all over his griddled face. Chlamydia moons up at him all faux coquettish – but Helmut jabs at her, his tight little fist almost propelling her backwards onto the bed. As though spring loaded, Chlamydia bounces back, bolt upright – her rubberised motion releases the hidden rag doll from beneath the mattress onto the floor with a soft thud, drawing attention away from Chlamydia's new hurt.

'What's this?' Helmut snatches the cloth doll from the floor. 'It's… *Fru-fru… Maman Terreblanche's Fru-fru!* Why, she's been looking for *Fru-fru* everywhere. What's *Fru-Fru* doing here – in *your* room – under *your* bed?'

'Oh it's Maman Terreblanche's all right! It's her doll for sure – a *voodoo doll* – a votive impression of me – look at it, the *likeness* – it's uncanny! I found it with pins sticking in it. Covered in nasty rusty pins!'

'Pins? Of course it's covered in pins – it's Maman's pin cushion! Look…' he tugs at his ill-fitting trousers and shirt. 'Maman Terreblanche sews all of my garments – she always has – since I was so high… *Fru-fru's* older than I am!'

'But I saw her in the church cemetery, doing evil voodoo – they buried poor Isaiah. I saw it. They buried him and now the wretched soul's walking around with the humanity sapped from him like he's living *and* dead!'

'I told you not to go out at night!'

'Why? – because of Maman Terreblanche's evil goons? And what of your *invisible wife and child* – what did Maman

Terreblanche do to them? *Did your housekeeper transform them into zombies?'*

'Zombies?' Anger shatters into irreconcilable shards – just like the glass tumblers that precipitated the whole sordid affair. With an unfamiliar, sonorous tone: *'What did mother tell you... about my wife and child? Tell me before I rip the stinking giblets out of your filthy guts and feed them to your tactless mouth...'*

'Nothing –' Chlamydia confesses – for the first time truly terrified. *'Honestly,'* she adds, 'your mother gave nothing away. I read about your wife and child on the back of one of your books...'

Helmut stumbles from the room clutching *Fru-fru,* clipping the door frame as he exits – visibly beside himself...

Chapter Seven

Chlamydia retches awake sick as a dog and heaves along the corridor to yelp into porcelain. Good manners slips a cursory note under Helmut's door to excuse herself from the morning's toil. Her paw ring finger throbs in complaint of the corruption that spreads virulently enough now to seek proper medical attention. Maman Terreblanche's watchful eye peers from the socket of the vile volcano as Chlamydia zigzags down the slope to unearth Isaiah, embedded in his ramshackle mud hut. Isaiah's slumber is captive to a dogmatic coma – bulging eyes balloon in thin air above shallow breath, and strings of veins acting like delicate crimson nets moor the swollen orbs to lifeless sockets. His stolen body shudders, haunted by fizzing nerves and effervescent hallucinations. Beads of sweat shake from Isaiah's sodden corpse as the visitor drags him into an exotic tongue screaming blue murder.

'Isaiah! Isaiah! Calm yourself! It's me, Lydia. I need you to take me to the infirmary. I desperately need your help. Isaiah, look at my poor finger – the infection is making me feel ill… unwell… I need antibiotics…'

Isaiah cowers. '*But Miss Love, de infirmary id a wicked place – an unholy place indeed!*'

'Why *wicked?* Look at my finger – it's bursting with unholy green pus! I don't need God – I need proper medical attention.'

'*Oh, yo' get attention fo' sure – but id ain't medical – no sir!*'

Chlamydia's inelegant threats move Isaiah to harness ox to cart albeit reticently. Perching next to her begrudging driver, she is duly touched by his superstitious fear of hospital and medicine in general. A pang of guilt compels Chlamydia to console her punctual twinge by drawing attention to Isaiah's skillful command of the ox – hence, subtly patronising the slave's relative mastery over Nature. Isaiah lashes the dozy beast forward with irrigated resentment. Even in fresh air, the driver's soiled hue pollutes the senses, and Chlamydia respires with shallow sips, much as a whale siphons microscopic plankton from the immense ocean. Isaiah reeks and Chlamydia's vain sensibility contorts her face appropriately in face of the decay that forms its disgust. And yet Chlamydia's revulsion merely emulates the withering expressions of those guardians who patiently indulged her own infantile olfactory journey when her own loving smell was, in fact, a stench.

Isaiah beholds the road delivering him to fear, laden with tears clinging impossibly to his pitiful rock face. Poised behind the ox's methane wake, rein in hand and bereft of words – petrified beyond Chlamydia's unerring capacity for timeless chitchat.

So the ambulance hangs a left from the sea road into the glowing green aperture of an overgrown dirt track. The track long surrendered to neglect – perhaps a marker of indigenous human fitness, nonetheless Isaiah assures Chlamydia that the old passage leads all the way to Morass's well hidden medical facility. Chlamydia clings to her finger, squeezing it intermittently to check whether *in all honesty* pain merits such a tortuous journey. Isaiah's skin shrivels with every forward stride – the ox bellows deep into the infinite hopelessness of its existence while strings of spittle foam from its dehydrated jaw to seek a less tormented state of being. As time stands still they draw near to an old wooden tongue-and-groove structure lost in the emerald tangle and being equal in dilapidation to the path that serves it. Before her, the grotesquely distempered hospital barely assembles into solid substance for the avid jungle that claws at it with withering vines hellbent on reclaiming the tamed whitewashed timber back into the indilute chaos of the forest. Vacant windows billow with gasping mosquito nets and a broken porch belches a limp access ramp that serves a lightless void that is the infirmary's sombre portal. Isaiah teases the nervous beast close enough for his passenger to set eyes upon the formless shadow seething inside the black hole and twinkling with an uncanny host of pale blue eyes. An abrupt cough betrays the owner of a fevered mouth, now differentiated from the coagulated black mass. A dull limb moves to cover up the incriminating symptom that ushers the attention of the Grim Reaper to its ill-fated owner. From the hospital door, a blinding white angel emerges, escaping the composite of lethargic black flesh collapsed against wall, floor, bedpost or column.

Chlamydia's relief greets Dr Günter Mandragorass dressed in a reassuring white coat – yet his stethoscope hangs limp and noose-like around his withered craw in impotent tribute to the alleged hegemony of western medicine. He is forlorn, head askew, as though hung by the very same neck.

'Dearest Chlamydia! What in Heaven's sake brings you here?'

'*My finger is sore…*' she confesses flatly, perplexed by the doctor's burdened posture, '*it's hurting enough even to make me vomit…*'

Midway up the buckled ramp, horror well appreciates how Heaven's good name has been invoked to query her arrival in such a hellish location. From her prying elevation she witnesses bodies littered about the place, openly abandoned of hope. As if incriminated by the quivering chaos the doctor confesses:

'The infirmary is little more than an ancillary morgue – the virus ravages their tissue without the slightest impedance…' and casting his arms in a helpless arc, 'it's little more than a hive of infection – a disease within a disease… they queue to expire with the least pain. There's nothing more I can do other than facilitate the passage between misery and death…' And with a civilised pause: 'I'm sorry to hear your finger's got worse. Come… come to my surgery – let's see if I can alleviate someone's pain today without need of the last rites…'

Dr Mandragorass leads through the dingy ward, stepping carefully over languishing flesh weeping and squirming like open sewers on both sides of their passage, both fearful of slipping sideways into the soft necrosis that festers in gaping ulcers. Likewise, patients cower on either side performing clumsy gestures of genital shame, withdrawing slowly like snail antennae flinching from an invasion of their agony. Chlamydia casts a glimpse outside to check on Isaiah to witness the poor fool genuflecting vigorously in the dust like a madman teased by the sun.

The doctor opens the portal to a haphazard surgery and Chlamydia enters at his gentle request. Inside, a dim lightbulb flares according to the sudden physical exertion of the man manning the exercise bicycle moored to the floor and connected by simple jump leads to a fizzing dynamo.

'That there's Ormond – my right-hand man. Faster! Ormond! Faster! Let's shed some light on Miss Love's complaint!' Ormond peddles hard and struggles uphill for a smile. His courageous sprint illuminates the doctor's inner sanctum. It is an elaborate description of medical panic, a stochastic flow cascading from failure to temporary solution. Catastrophe is stabilised long enough for the good doctor's absent mind to receive the next calamity with earnest surprise and a consequently novel solution. He catches Chlamydia squirming at the tarry dull blood shrieking in oxidised gouts up wall and ceiling – he notices her wince at the sharps bin overflowing with inky swabs and bloody handwritten notes – he sees her jaw fall loose at the sagging shelves stacked with jars of immortal biopsy tissue sprouting sinewy root into murky fluid and the odd pickled baby mooning down with cheerless washed-out eyes.

'*The blood on the walls –*' he gasps, gesturing all around the room helpless '– is cardiovascular pressure. At the end, their poor hearts explode…'

On the good doctor's desk, company to a worn microscope, Dr Eduard Pernkopf's *Topographische Anatomie des Menschen* lies spread-eagled and well-pored. The surgery's workbench is solid armature to an odd assemblage of medical tackle recombined in modified purpose. Dissecting forceps are tightly clamped to the bench to hold fast a well-numbed mouth gag – pierced with stainless nerve hooks pulled taught by clip curettes to an eager set of dilator forceps with lung spatula wedged between ear polypus forceps and a shock-absorbing sponge, all held by a set of salad tongs to allow a dripping syringe held laterally by tissue forceps, towel clamps and tongue depressor nailed to the wall with a percussion hammer from which a vascular dilator serves a gall duct dilator, a haemorrhoidal ligator, a bristling manifold of aneurysm needles by way of lengths of rubber suction tube that drape to the floor where radiating tube has been snipped by super-cut scissors, nipped by laryngeal forceps, compressed by speculum vasectomy forceps, fastened by dissecting forceps, crimped by haemostatic clamps, clamped by tubing and intestinal clamps to regulate the flow of fluid into the score of plastic test-tubes which bulge like infected teats on the business end of the rubber lengths; all around rendered spent, pliers, power cutters, ligature forceps, tissue forceps, a bone hook, hand-held retractors, self-retaining retractors, bone & rib shears, barbecue tongs, choleystectomy forceps, trocars, bone files, a monkey wrench, chisels, elevators, gouges, osteotomes, raspatories, a ring cutter, vaginal bone ronguers, a Gigli saw, ice-cream scoops, a mallet and a pair of rib spreaders all arranged in helpless disarray like spare parts at a pathologist's funeral.

During the good doctor's hushed examination, disease seeps below the door. Agonised moans escape bodies seeking respite like a sleeping child turns a burning pillow to cool a nightmare. Chlamydia can hear the undead struggling with the great leap of faith between last breath and everlasting life. She can hear the faithful call out for mercy as they shamble towards the beckoning light – only to falter at the precipice of their conviction, back away from the metaphysical edge to steal one last gulp of mortal air.

'Is it contagious? The disease? *Am I at risk of contracting it? This disease within a disease?'*

The old man is too engrossed in his craft to fashion a reply – and without so much as a please or thank you descends upon Chlamydia's finger to suckle at her wound – applying as much suction as old gums can muster. Before Chlamydia can raise a scream, he empties out into a kidney dish and wipes his mouth clean with a filthy swab.

'Crude but effective...' Without a pause he orders his gobsmacked patient onto her front and spikes her buttock with a staple antibiotic. When he is done he washes and dries his hands, shuffles to the surgery door, it dressed with an emaciated Venetian blind. A bony finger dents a rib and Mandragorass's fear gazes through into the heart of Hell.

'Listen! – They're calling out for God. All they have is me. But what comfort can I give? They come, each morning, through the jungle – abandoned at my door by those who no longer recognise their own loved ones for the delirium that possesses their souls... I treat them as best I can... nothing more than decide the order in which unimaginable pain is allowed to surrender to inconceivable peace.'

'But why are their eyes so very blue?'

'A side-effect... of the drugs... *quite beautiful!'* His frail shoulders shrugging in a gesture of precocious despondency. He takes Chlamydia's pulse, examines her eyes, ears, nose and tongue – presses firmly on Chlamydia's abdomen and inadvertently forces his own contemplations to exhale: '*It tints their eyes...*' he says in a daze, '*exquisite...*' Lost in the reflex methodology of his professional examination, Chlamydia prompts the doctor back into the present.

'And there's no cure? Günter? *Doctor?*'

'No... No... Not a single soul saved – to my knowledge. Any specimen we send is generationally obsolete before it reaches the lab, so all countermeasures are doomed... the strain adjusts its own evolution transversally... *like us...*' Abruptly the doctor's searching hands withdraw from Chlamydia's body as though dignity has returned and her body is her own.

'So! Chlamydia you've come to see us because you're not feeling well? Nauseous? Physically sick?'

'Yes! Yes! Nauseous! Physically sick!' says Chlamydia, ill at ease with the proximity of her physical sickness to the dead and dying. Furthermore, the wise old doctor nods deliberately in protection of the authority of his diagnosis.

'Well,' he says, nodding. 'I'm relieved to tell you that the infection in your hand isn't a matter of life or death... However, *your sickness is...*'

'*My sickness?*' Chlamydia gasps.

'Yes, sickness,' he smiles. 'A matter of life *not* death...'

Chlamydia frowns.

'I take it you're unaware that you're expectant...?'

Chlamydia gasps.

'Dearest Chlamydia – *you're suffering morning sickness!*'

'*But it's impossible! It can't be so! Pregnant? How long?*'

'Can't say. Not without tests.'

The sea is room temperature and Chlamydia lazes amphibiously in the shallows, allowing kindly waves to flip her dorsal to ventral axis like a fishburger. Eventually she wades up the gradient to indent the hot sand and contemplate the sun's full attention horizontally. She squeezes sun screen onto her palm, shovels it over her corpse, allowing the greasy liquid to melt on simmering human leather – especially her face, neck and breasts; and working the warm white cream into her tender tum-tum, Chlamydia Love reflects upon the human parasite clinging for dreary life within.

Just audible above the sound of Chlamydia Love clenched in foetal position and wailing like the Amazon, the drone of an outboard motor homes in to shore. Chlamydia shoots to her feet, shading her eyesight to scour the horizon for a boat bobbing in the near distance – the very same vessel responsible for delivering her to Hades. She shrieks, cartwheels and waves like a madwoman and scuttles along the water's edge to greet and meet the craft as it eventually breaks surf. Woe betide Captain Oceanic when she gets her hands on him! He'd better have a watertight excuse for not returning when he said he would! Better have a rainproof excuse as to why he left her in exile on this God-forsaken penal colony – *bloody bastard!* She curses, in private.

A cheery voice disembarks. 'Ahoy there – matey!' – intuitively grating on Chlamydia's nerves. Hope of an immediate escape fades at the radiantly gauche apparition of Consultant Surgeon Algernon Hertz dropping anchor – the diabolical affront second only to Captain Oceanic's appearance on the port bow, and having the audacity to pitch into the mêlée:

'Vell, didn't I say you'd never vant to leave Morass... Ja?'

Algernon wades ashore cackling like an old woman, trousers rolled to the knee, holding his pumps like a girl's blouse, he stops to wave adieu to his ex-patient now leaping up and down on the aft deck.

'Thanks for the ride!' howls Algernon to his friend.

'*Zuper-good! I return to Morass in ze few days – if ze weather-bitch permits! Chow Algae-baby!*' yells the rabid skipper above the clenched roar of the diesel engine.

'Algernon! *Algernon!* I've got something very important to tell you –' says Chlamydia, now a flower wilting in poisonous salt water.

'I'm…' *Splosh.*

• • • • •

'*One Mississippi, two Mississippi, three Mississippi, four Mississippi…*' Daylight comes-to with Hertz's hands-on pulmonary resuscitation purging a pretty water feature from Chlamydia's gaping groan – she half expects to see her unborn foetus flapping around like a newt next to her on the wet sand.

'Poor Chlamydia! You've been out in the sun too long – I warned you! Look at your face! Scar tissue's cockled in the heat! Look like a patchwork quilt! Silly girl!'

Algernon is exactly as she remembered – tall, dark and horrendous – and fails to provoke any tingling in her special place. 'I've been waiting for the boat for ever – and now it's gone!' she says, coming round, matter-of-fact, all metallic like a robot.

'Well I've been pretty damn worried too!' says Algernon. 'Captain Oceanic's boat sank in the storm – he barely escaped with his life!'

'*Liar!* Look see! There's *The Amorous Peacock*! Exactly as before!'

'Well praise the Lord! They dredged her up from the dreaded sea bed! Hallelujah!'

Algernon's perjury confirms Helmut's character assassination, and in her heart of hearts Chlamydia is secretly glad Helmut is right because she is so very angry with

Algernon and will elect to play him at his own game. 'Oh *Algae! You came all the way to find me!*' she cries, laced with sarin. 'Oh *Algae!* It's such a wondrous place – *sublime!* I almost died when I set eyes upon it! – What a wondrous wedding present! *Thank you! Thank you for ALL OF THIS…*' – her outstretched arms referring to everything in sight; Algernon shimmers with a momentary inkling.

'But you deserve it, sweetpea!' he says with skillful poise. 'Let's go to the hotel, freshen up, and you can tell me all about it! And what's with *Algae?*'

'*Algae?* Isn't it your nickname – *from university?* Oh Algae, I'm not staying at Hotel Krauss. When the storm came I was forced elsewhere. A wonderful man took pity on me and let me share his house on the top of the volcano – you know *Helmut Mandragorass, don't you?*'

'Gosh, yes! Helmut Mandragorass – my old pal from Oxford – it'll be wonderful to see the old soul again.'

'How wonderful, you'll be able to reminisce about old times.'

'Yes, yes… *Oh happy, happy days…*'

• • • • •

Chlamydia leads Algernon up the volcanic garden path, drawing relentless attention to the fauna and flora – to each and every detail of her fictitious domain with pitiless glee. By the time they reach Helmut's house Algernon's jovial countenance has distorted such that his painful grimace threatens to give birth to his own bloody skull through his own widely dilated lips. Bubbly Chlamydia urges her fiancé forward up the steps and through the front door, along the corridor, pointing out the weathered Eames and the immodest oil painting of naked Adam and filthy Eve spread-eagled across a jagged surface of broken crockery.

'Here we are,' says cheerful Chlamydia at the study door, well aware of the sado-mechanistic typing inside. Chlamydia shoves the door open hard and stands framed with infanticidal indolence.

'We have a visitor!' she announces with lopsided glee and without an ounce of concern for Helmut's creative flow. Helmut arrests his frenetic tap, tap, tap with a spastic frown swiftly corrected by an expression of mild indifference. Algernon steps into Helmut's literary lair with the visible expectation of being verbally savaged and then metaphorically eaten alive.

'We meet again,' says the sweaty typist rising to his tiny feet without disclosing a splinter of surprise or hostility. 'Come to reclaim your rent-a-chattel? She's all yours! – *However, no deal on Morass!*'

'*You mentioned our "special business" – to her? To Chlamydia?*'

Algernon casts an anxious glance at his fiancée.

'Oh I see, we're keeping up the pretence,' says Helmut blithely, with gimlet squint needling Chlamydia, while a tiny hand lashes out to snatch the present page from the tired old typewriter and place it atop the sacred pile with arrogant purpose. 'You imagined that her frigid anatomy could possibly succeed where all your persistent bids and offers have failed. That's a tremendously tall order for a vagina. Nice try, but no cigar!'

'Is he telling the truth *Algae-baby?*' sneers Chlamydia. 'Is that why you sent me? Tell me he's lying? Defend my honour!'

'Sadly, it's *all* shades of falsehood and fabrication... It's true I made an offer to help Helmut, but it was dignified and humanitarian. It's important you understand that the wretched half-life you see before you is a clinically pathological liar. He forms compensatory delusions like you or I have hot dinners, and fantasises his way out of despair – he achieves temporary respite in megalomania, but collapses back into paranoia. In his deluded little big head he believes we are intimate friends and categorically denies that *he is the patient and I the doctor*. Helmut is in dire straits, mentally and now financially. Isolation is his ruin. I offered to take charge of the island, hold it in trust and return it when he is of sound mind. This solution, dear Chlamydia, is the most expedient for my patient's financial and psychological health…'

Algernon plants a reassuring palm on Helmut's hunch.

'*Liar! Liar! Pants are on fire!*' spits Helmut at his detractor. '*I'm not mad and you're not a shrink – not even a doctor let alone a sodding consultant! You know full well I'd never sell my island to you. I'd poison Morass with anthrax, cement it over, raise it to the ground, sink it, tear it apart with my bare hands before I ever let you spoil Morass – not even your fiancée's charming persuasion can change my m-m-m-mind.*'

'Charming persuasion? What does he mean Chlamydia – *charming persuasion?*' Algernon casts a comical angry eye at Chlamydia, designed to offset her legitimate rage with his sham anger. 'Darling Chlamydia, I trusted you… *What have you done?*'

'Trust?' she shrieks. 'You sold me down the river! Up shit creek without a paddle! I've been marooned here without any way of getting off!' She wrenches her ring over the swollen knuckle and throws it full pelt and pus at her ex-fiancé.

'Oh, I like that. I buy you a tropical island, and you throw it back in my face!'

'*It's not for sale!*' screams Helmut, stamping his foot.

'Helmut dearest, may we have a moment's privacy?' says Chlamydia with momentary repose.

'Be my guests…' says Helmut, and exits with an almighty slam.

In Helmut's absence Algernon pulls Chlamydia into his bosom

to kiss her and confuse the issue. But Chlamydia is repulsed by the spoilt orifice puckering towards her and repels his saturated weight with holistic inner strength.

'*Go fuck yourself!*' she snaps.

'Lord! Your language is awful! Is this how they speak in paradise? Be honest Chlamydia – you're conducting a sordid affair with this deranged scribbler, aren't you?'

'To think, I journeyed halfway around the world to weigh up a non-existent wedding present!'

'I don't deny I've made the odd offer over the years – each refused until Mandragorass came crawling to me because he's bankrupt – *and mad!* I made a generous offer, and the solicitors are in conversation with the psychiatrists as we speak…'

'So I wasn't a *sweetener?*'

'No, no, no! You're my *sweetness* and love!'

'And you're not using me to persuade him to sell?'

'No! I love you more than words can say!'

'So why is Helmut even more determined than ever to keep his island?'

'*Trust a woman to balls it up!*'

'What did you expect? He hates us! He's convinced I was in on your absurd caper from the start!'

'You sound concerned. Worried about what he thinks of you…' he says. 'Are you? – concerned? Worried? – or *lovesick?*'

She absorbs his salacious spite without complaint, but Algernon continues nonetheless – rubbing salt in the wound, adding insult to injury and even flogging a dead horse: 'He's not your type,' he says.

'*My type?*' she says. '*Well neither are you!*' She squeezes her eyelids tight before despair betrays her. In answer to unsaid prayers in the dark, the door sounds shut while Algernon is optically no more. Not a second later, the door swings open, and tenacious like a bad penny, Helmut rolls in to witness

Chlamydia's dependable tears.

'What now?' says Helmut.

'Please Helmut! Please let me stay until Captain Oceanic returns! I'll stay out of your way, and when the captain comes, I'll go! Never to return! Ever!'

'I've got a better idea! How about you stay on and work for me full-time – *I'll pay you handsomely – take dictation – words straight from the horse's mouth! Can you type half as fast as me? You've filed my files to perfection! – In fact, I think I've found the personal secretary I've been looking for – what's more, I know I can trust you because your Aunt Shigella works in publishing and she's a senior editor and you grew up in publishing…*'

–

Chapter Eight

'You're joking, of course – or you're simply insane! I've earned my keep! I've filed myself under *E* for exhaustion! Now I just want to go *H* for home…' Wishing beyond her resigned whisper that she might stay here with Helmut for ever – and yet with persistent thoughts of Helmut's wife and child shrieking vehemently in her abattoir mind; *she wanted to ask but didn't dare.*

'Files?' says Helmut. 'What about the files… Fuck the files! There are things here I need doing that make filing look like child's play! But if I can't ignite your sense of danger, I'll assume you've surrendered to vapid mediocrity and the wedding vows simpering away on the horizon of your dreams… So please yourself, remain *in situ* with your custodian Algernon until Captain Oceanic returns. *But I warn you… Keep out of my way! Both of you! I have work to do! Now run along and d-d-degrade yourself…*'

Naturally Chlamydia's exit finds Algernon loitering outside with ear hard-pressed to door.

'What's up with him now?' says Algernon, fingering his air-locked lobe. 'What did he say? What does he want? What did he say about *me* – about why I'm here?'

'Mind your bee's wax – it's none of your business.'

'Oh but it *is* my business. *Big business!* I've got plans for Morass. *Big plans!* I intend to liberate it from Helmut's egotistical clutches. I've got nest-eggs to crack, piggy banks to plunder, assets to grab, filthy lucre to mop up and then I'll transform this retarded atoll into something to write home about! They'll flock for the attention of these miraculous hands! Sun, Sea and Sand – *unhippocratic surgery is grand!*'

'You'd flood paradise with cellulite and vanity? What about the islanders? What about their traditional way of life? It'll be lost for ever! And what about Helmut? How will he write?'

'*How will he write?* Good God! Wake up to the sound of r-e-a-l-i-t-y! Helmut doesn't give a jot for you – he only cares about *verbs and nouns!* Funny though – his gobbledygook is about as vital to culture as pentapetides!'

'That's not fair! His latest book is a masterpiece!'

'*Masterpiece?*' scoffs Algernon, 'another compulsory burden upon the British Library bookshelves…'

'Be that as it may!' wails Chlamydia. 'When Oceanic returns I'll leave Morass and never see Helmut again!'

'*So my heart bleeds!*' snarls Algernon, thundering down the corridor.

• • • • •

In the kitchen's hectic ferment, Maman Terreblanche's enlarged capitulum nods leisurely without bothering to heave attention from the barely edibles she is kneading into compliance.

'*He bin here before, dat man – many a time. I don't like dat man, not one single bit. I tell Massa Mandragorass – I curse 'im an' hope he never come back…!*' She sucks her teeth and gestures to spit on the floor.

'Actually, he was once my fiancé – but I saw sense –' says Chlamydia, sucking her teeth while gesturing to soil the filthy floor. 'Maman Terreblanche, maybe you'd prefer it if I make up a room for Algernon and save you the trouble?' says Chlamydia, sweetly.

'*Back off motherfucker – fo' I busta cap in yo' ass! Anyways, yo' better take it easy girl, in yo' condition an' all…*' She winks and sucks her ivories once more leaving Chlamydia to sway on the spot, felled by the cutting remark.

How on earth does the housekeeper know about

Chlamydia's *condition?*

Doctor Mandragorass's professional discretion is beyond speculation.

Helmut Mandragorass is none the wiser – evidenced by the simple fact that he has failed to vent malice upon the defenceless contents of her busy womb.

Algernon is also oblivious – for the reasons given above.

Goaded into realisation by the arresting grimace, it dawns upon Chlamydia that she is no longer in the company of *Maman Terreblanche* but face to face with the *High Priestess of local voodoo*. And the grotesque spectre is plainly relishing her victim's glacial seizure – brittle Chlamydia fumbles for the door, splinters along the corridor pursued by the cavernous laughter chomping after her like a relentless Pac-Man.

Chlamydia is even relieved to unearth Algernon planted on the terrace outside, slouched beneath a sunshade, topless, stripped of his sodden linen shirt and sitting uncomfortably. Chlamydia observes the ill-fitting birthday suit – cannot help but draw salutary comparisons between *his* and *Helmut's* physique. Although full size, Algernon's torso is pale and prone to infernal gravity, harsh cellulite webs ripple in frilly pleat, nipple and tuck. Despite the many attempts to shed pounds for charity, his physique reflects little success in shedding fat – and by extension – little success in feeding the Third World. As Algernon gobbles up Chlamydia's admiration, Chlamydia wonders anew what she ever saw in him, perhaps an attractive man waiting to burst free – a lithe prince held captive inside a bulging pink toad. Admittedly, Chlamydia was once upon a time flattered by his attention, had allowed Algernon's affluence to giddy her head and weaken her dignity. His kindness flowed into Chlamydia's hollowness – filling up the piteous shallowness worn out by a lifetime's low self-esteemness.

'*Want a drink?*' says Algernon, gesturing to the flask and glasses twinkling on the table.

'Anything to take the *con* out of consciousness...' She pours a large G and T to quench her fright. So Algernon and Chlamydia sit, condemned to each other's company, while the clatter of Helmut's manual typewriter ekes out its merciless mechanical revenge inside. Caught between volcano and portable Tab-O-Matic, Chlamydia sighs deep into the upper canopy.

'*I'm sorry things didn't turn out –*' Algernon consoles, lazily.

'Sorry for who?' Chlamydia pounces. 'Sorry for yourself – sorry because your plan turned tits up?'

Algernon manages to smile and feign hurt simultaneously. 'Oh but surely you can't blame me for trying... Morass will change – like it or not – it's as inevitable as *Abacus, Bible, Computer.* You can't stall the momentum of momentum once kinesis is stimulated from slumber. Anyway, I've been supplying Morass's tourist trade with indigenous tribal junk for years – *all of it imported from the Chinks.* Tourists never doubt the authenticity of the garbage they haggle over 'cos they're too busy ripping off the savages – penny pinching from the poor – *that's* free-market enterprise. If the nouveau riche don't give a toss for *noblesse oblige,* why should I?'

'I feel sorry for you...'

'Sorry? Why? Because I choose to despise the pathetic idealism that permits this place to survive the concrete...'

Chlamydia's astonishment is silenced by Maman Terreblanche arriving to escort Algernon to the room she has made nice and comfy for him. Algernon leers past Chlamydia as she hurls daggers from her eyes. Chlamydia retires to her own room to steal forty winks with the distant clack of Helmut's qwerty keys tampering with her slumber.

• • • • •

A tender stroke of Chlamydia's derelict temple brings her awake feeling warmed by the lightness of touch. She discovers Helmut looming, satisfied by his superior elevation. 'It's nearly time for din-dins,' he says. 'Chlamydia, Helmut and Algernon too – sounds like a whodunit. Think you're up to the challenge?'

'Why not?' she replies in a metallic voice, hollow like a robot being goaded to emote.

'See you downstairs…'

Chlamydia chooses a cool green cotton bikini intended for beach wear. Her diminutive wardrobe is repeating itself, but she is loathe to replicate her outfit on this particular evening when all is at stake. In the dining room she finds Algernon and Helmut already present and poised in amicable conversation. Chlamydia adopts a smile for the approach. Helmut intercepts with a drink. She receives it graciously.

'What a treat!' says Algernon.

'Lucky us!' says Helmut.

'Oh but the pleasure's all mine!' says Chlamydia.

'I've just been telling Algernon what an incredible job you've made of my filing system,' says Helmut all cheery.

'Yes, I've been hearing all about the chores you've been undertaking in return for your humble board and lodging,' says Algernon, proud of his well-crafted insinuation. 'The conditions of lodging sound anything but boring…'

'Is it to be a chimps' tea party or shall we play grown-ups?' says Chlamydia, light and airy.

Algernon shakes his head impressed. 'Really Helmut, I thought you'd find Chlamydia's razor wit irresistible.'

'And you thought *witless sarcasm* would work?' says Helmut.

'Oh yes,' says Algernon. 'I imagined sarcasm would bring you close together – a meeting of minds – I imagined I'd find you joined at the hip.'

'Jack 'n' Jill fall head over heels. Then you blackmail her into pressurising me by threatening to say she was in on your plan? Then what?'

Algernon shrugs.

'But you lose Chlamydia *and* Morass. You're not bothered about her in the slightest – she's not the first wallflower planted in my soil to do your filthy work. But what about Morass and your big-time business plans?'

'I'll get it in the end – you know I will. *Remember university?'* He smiles, all arrogant.

'I'm bored,' says Chlamydia. 'Why don't you boys cut to the chase and have an arm wrestle? I might like that.'

'Yummy! Let's eat!' says Helmut.

They sit. Helmut rings a tiny brass bell to draw the gargantuan spectre of Maman Terreblanche into view laden with mouth-watering starters. Chlamydia's pet anorexia picks at the avocado and tiger prawns drowned in clotted cream – she nibbles at the mixed salad, plucks at the high priestess's chicken hearts and sluices it all down with bone-dry Rhodesian Chablis. Chlamydia picks and Algernon and Helmut both devour. Conversation is cursory, light and uncomplicated. Helmut and Algernon manage to lock away any pejorative thoughts from the proven articulation of two foul mouths, and when Chlamydia returns from the little room to announce she is replete, Algernon and Helmut concur, being equally swollen downstairs – and governed by indelible good manners, Chlamydia begins to tidy.

'Oh do leave it fussy-pants. Maman Terreblanche will see to it,' Helmut chides.

'But I can do it,' says Chlamydia gaily, 'it's the least I can do after this evening's *ménagerie à trois*.'

'In lieu of payment for emotional damage?' Helmut mocks,

'Oh I'm sure I can think of a more sympathetic way.'

'I'm sure you're sure Mr Mandragorass, but if it's all right with you, I prefer to tidy.'

'Careful,' says Algernon, 'I'm not completely out of the picture yet…'

'Let's put some music on, relax – have some fun – join me,' says Helmut.

They adjourn to the beautiful room with sumptuous crimson carpet, lush pink walls decorated with pretty watercolours and drawings. Algernon says he especially likes the images of vulnerable human forms decapitated and crowned with ambivalent clown heads, loves the stick figures haunted by evanescent dreams, adores the depictions of Hell conjured into existence by a rampaging paranoia – the allegorical apparitions fuelled by fevered imagination – the walls irreparably distempered with compassion fatigue. 'Oh Heavens!' he says, 'I just adore the Pinocchio sculpture skulking in the corner!'

'Au contraire – 'tis not Pinocchio, 'tis Fuckface,' says Helmut, matter-of-fact.

'Fuckface…' echoes Chlamydia all nonchalant and au fait.

'I just love what you've done with this room – it's a veritable chamber of curiosities. I love the ambiance. Helmut, pray tell – where on earth do all these exquisite ethnographic sculptures and statuettes come from?' And picking up a small wooden carving, checking underneath, Algernon catches Chlamydia's eye, winks, then replaces the sculpture while pulling the corners of his eyes into a sinister slant.

'As a matter of fact, most of the carvings you see are indigenous to Morass.'

'*Indigenous.* Is that so?'

Helmut mans the Ferguson high-fidelity, guiding the stylus to a sad ballad drumming-in hopelessness and human insignificance.

I spy free 'n' easy dol-phins
Breakin' surf in the settin' sun
I'd maim for such meek sim-plicity
Cos' I really dig friendly fun

'I'm addicted to this tune,' says Helmut, singing along as the melody wafts out into the asphyxiating twilight. As if in sarcastic exchange, exquisite wild flowers with perfumed scents blossom from the balcony into the room. Mindful of Helmut's languor, Chlamydia and Algernon traverse the small area corralled by deep-set armchairs upholstered in extinct fur and set aside for wild dancing. Chlamydia and Algernon settle, swallowed hole by hungry armchairs. Helmut joins them loaded with a wicker tray of drinks that he hands to Algernon in exchange for Chlamydia's paw.

'You'll excuse us, Algernon?'

'Be my guest!' says Algernon, making compensation with a heavy slug of whisky.

Helmut gyrates around Chlamydia's gravitational pole, presses hard against her feminine resistance – forcing his cheeks up against her cheeks, his bosom next to her breasts, his happiness next to her hips. If it is true to say that the act of dirty dancing gives promiscuous sexual contact a permissible social form, Helmut's physical expression alone denudes dirty dancing such that his present rhythmic contortions appear nothing less than unadulterated coitus. And so Algernon snorts like a pig, slams his empty glass on the table and trots from the room. Chlamydia disengages from the primal act and the lament continues alone.

'What's eating Algae?' says Helmut, out of breath, leering like a villain hankering after crime.

'You know very well,' says Chlamydia.

'Oh it was just a *little* lesson… how to let a beautiful thing slip between your fingers…'

'Well it was unnecessary and unfair,' says Chlamydia, furtively flattered.

'Unfair? He tried to take all of everything I own!' he says.

'Possessions, yes! But I'm not an object to be bartered or exchanged or stolen or swapped – I'm flesh 'n' blood! I have a heart! *I feel!* You're only sniffing me out because a rival male has stirred something deep inside you – it's latent homosexuality, nothing more = nothing less! *Textbook!* Psychic angst finds *symptomatic* expression – in this particular case – the female form – *my* female form,' she says.

'You sound like some two-bit shrink! You wanted me to want you as much as I wanted you to want me! Am I right or am I right?' he says. 'Anyway, how d'you think you ended up here? D'you really believe Hotel Krauss had *no room at the inn? Not even a lowly stable? I OWN HOTEL K-K-KRAUSS!* I instructed the manager to invent a reason to turn you away! *Ha, ha!* – So you had no choice but to throw yourself on the mercy of my parents – *tweedle-dumb and twaddle-idiot* – they were guaranteed to seek the charity of their golden boy upstairs on the big, bad volcano!'

'And you call *Algernon devious!* You're *insane!* – And I know what I'm talking about – I'm in therapy as we speak!' states Chlamydia defiantly.

'*Therapy? – Ha! Internal cosmetic surgery for the inferiority complex!*'

'Symptomatic claptrap! Denial upon denial!' barks Chlamydia.

'*Denial? Oh let me guess! You'd happily pay good money for some hapless shrink to crane over your p-p-porous corpse watching it leak like a rusty bucket, and the more you leak, the more she trills like a pet parakeet on a day perch. So you tell her you've been feeling "a little m-m-maudlin, a little s-s-suicidal, a little under the w-w-weather" and she's listening and nodding and urging you on and on, and the nodding is a sure sign that she empathises – that she understands it's not your fault, that others are to blame – and soon she transforms you from a wretched narcissist into an innocent victim... et voilà! You're cured!'*

'Tut tut! You Tutankhamun of denial! I'd keep a tight lid on all that unresolved stuff! *Phew!'* says Chlamydia, mopping her brow of unresolved stuff. 'Anyway, my Dr Heimlich would eat you up and spit you out like chicken gristle – you *crybaby!'*

'*Oh, I'm the crybaby?* – And dear old Algernon really, really, really only wanted us to *be best of fwends, pen pals, goons, cronies...* Wake up Rumplestiltskin! There's nothing platonic about Hertz's desire for companionship.' Chlamydia's eyes salivate – Helmut wades in. 'Maybe poor little Cinders still loves Algae! Well of course! I should say so! You were going to make an honest man out of the liar.'

'I've had enough. I'm going to find Algernon.'

'Why so?' says Helmut, leering, distorted through Chlamydia's tears.

'I'm going to apologise to him on your behalf,' she says.

'*P-p-p-p-pwease don't leave me all by my own!'* he says, with insinuating sinew and ligament threatening to catapult him beyond his present near-repose. He reaches out as far as the two plainly ridiculous arms and wrists and handy-pandies can-can, taking her firmly by the barefaced shoulders, pulling her ample torso into his pint-sized chest, his clammy hands against her sticky flesh, her bleeding heart pumping with feelings unduly hurt. Chlamydia's heavy doll eyes roll back in porcelain sockets. Not one for missing his emotional cue – Helmut sets into motion, smoothing his hands about

Chlamydia's neck and shoulders in the manner of a caring and selfless massage, the kind of caring and asexual caress that is really a premeditated prelude to fully-blown genital penetration or soapy-soapy fucky-wucky. Anyway, he works his way around, smoothing around her back, cooing like a plumped-up wood pigeon. He smoothes and coos – allows his hand to fumble blindly across Chlamydia's bikini tie, to peck, peck, peck it loose, allowing the bright green bikini top to drop to the floor and reveal two naked breasts upstairs. Helmut withdraws a step, absorbing the optical illusion with an unmitigated sigh. Adding a childish grimace, he cups her in his clammy hands, strokes and teases until the two nipple areas are sound awake, and only then does he reach up to Chlamydia's face already bending down, beneficently forces parted lips open with his exploratory glossa, before relaxing back from tiptoe to head height to kiss, lick and suck her breasts one by one in sequence, being mindful to pay equal percentage to each. 'Mmmmmmmmm...' he says, 'don't go back home with Algernonnnnnnmmmmmmm... stay here on Mmmmmmmorass with mmmmmmmmeeeeeeeeeeeeeeee...'

Chlamydia peeps at the absurd suggestion sucking on her left and right and left and right teat. She is quiescent in his arms, but deems to struggle free – and does so easily – knowing too well, that further acquiescence will be in danger of melting into pure blissfulnesslessmess. After all, there *is* wifey to consider (and the child – *at a push*). But Helmut's hungry kisses threaten to suffocate. His hands manhandle in their ambidextrous assault, but Chlamydia manages to unplug her succulent maw from Helmut's penetrative tongue.

'*Cool your jets Mr Mandragorass!*' she mouths emphatically, '*Let me go!*' So then he does and Chlamydia gathers up her emerald bikini top and hoists it to its rightful place on the upper canopy.

'Why?' he says.

'I just can't,' she says.

'Why? Guilty? – *For Algernon?'* he says. *'You're off your rocker!'*

She shakes her head sincerely hard. 'There's nothing between us. Not now. *Rien. Nada – not a sausage*. But it doesn't mean I can stay here with you. I can't.'

'W-w-why not –' he rasps, sinews tightening '– w-w-why the Hell not?'

'I can't!'

'Why not? *WHY NOT?'*

'Because… I'm pre-pre-*pregnable*… I'm too *pregnabl*,' she says, and disappearing from his sight last heard muttering: '– I need to be more… *impregnable*…'

• • • • •

Chlamydia wishes for nothing more than a comfy bed to lie on and a plump pillow to dam her waterworks. For her sins, she finds Algernon hogging the top of the stairs eager like the swine he is. He catches Chlamydia's arm roughly and swings her into his own room. Chlamydia cannot fail but instantly appreciate how Algernon's abode is nicer than hers – nicer four-poster bed, nicer carpet, nicer wallpaper, nicer curtains, nicer bedside table, nicer table lamp, nicer dresser, nicer wardrobe, nicer en suite – *all in all* nicer furnishings all round. But mindful of Algernon's grave demeanour she pays the decor little more than a cursory glance, however, she can't help feeling a little hurt.

'Algernon,' she sighs, 'I'm tired. And you're really not my favourite person right now. I'm going to bed. We've nothing more to discuss *[especially the fact that I'm pregnant with your child and I can't bear the thought of having anything of you in me],' she thinks to herself.*

'*Au contraire*!' says Algernon. 'There's much to speak of!'

'Like what?'

'For instance, why did you lie to me? The evidence is self-evident – *you two dancing together like that* – cheek to cheek – cheeky beggars…' he says.

'Oh Lord…' says Chlamydia. 'Helmut was putting it on for you – a little act – tailored for your benefit.'

'And you were clearly enjoying it,' he says.

'He's playing with you Algernon,' she says. 'The flirting ceased the moment you left. Anyway, *you've* got a cheek! You planned for us to get *intimate* – even sank so low as to use our wedding as a pretext to get me here so I could let you in the back door. Creep!'

'I love you as dearly as I ever did! I just worry you're selling yourself cheap!' he says.

'*Dearly? – Cheap?* It's all about value with you…'

'*Did you know he's married?*' Algernon casts a sidelong glance to impress upon Chlamydia the *gravitas* of Helmut's ineffable marital vows.

'So what? It makes little difference now. The first opportunity I get, I'm going home. I want to be on my own. *Independent.*'

'How decent! But I wonder what Helmut would say if I told him how desperate you are – how desperately you *love* him!'

'*You dare!*' Chlamydia hisses.

'Oh the next few days are going to prove a lot of fun. I'll enjoy studying you two love-birds. But be careful Tweetie-pie, I swear he'll pluck 'n' stuff you 'n' pick you clean to the very bone…'

• • • • •

Slingshot into next morning by the entire gamut of unpleasant nightmares including bludgeoning, garrotting, raping, stamping, hanging, gouging, slicing, knifing, flaying, gutting, piercing and burning, Chlamydia slips from the cruel white house unnoticed, saunters down the volcanic slope to find the beach and sea lapping each other like juvenile lovers. The shore is deserted. A band of damp sand records the tidal reach before turning tail to retreat back into the seething swell. Not a solitary footstep tarnishes the horizon and kooky Chlamydia slings her slingbacks over her shoulders and skips along the sand without a care in the world. She pirouettes and leaps like a ballerina, sings and dances with the sham innocence of a child. She only arrests her flouncy jaunt to inscribe her kooky name in the kooky sand with her kooky big toe – but the mean-minded sea is having none of it and launches an abnormally powerful wave to erase the existential scar from mortal existence.

Chlamydia is rendered speechless, watching her precious moniker cruelly dragged out to sea. Nonetheless, kooky is as kooky does, Chlamydia shakes off nasty thoughts and prances on her kooky way.

Further along, a small peninsula purges into sight where Chlamydia discovers an isolated cove and decides it safe to undress and wade naked into the sea. She swims a little making sure she stays within her depth before relaxing on her back, floating aimlessly, enjoying the sensual caress of the current on her naked hull. The sun looms affectionately in a cloudless sky, pure blue like the azure sea all around her. It is all so perfectly serene that Chlamydia's petulant troubles soon dissolve and wash away.

Back-lit by the burning sun, a carbon-black vulture appears wheeling overhead and is soon joined by two more. Chlamydia calls out to them gaily but they continue circling unimpressed. Like this she floats until the scowling kites become disinterested and flock off. Checking she is within her depth once more with a sedentary foot, Chlamydia finds she has wandered beyond her safe midriff measure. She cranes her head upwards to see the shoreline already drifting away on the horizon. Mild panic flips her onto her belly and engages front crawl. Groping out for land, head swaying to and fro, blow hole gagging for air, our swimmer catches sight of a grey shadow rippling beneath. She continues her desperate trawl with counterfeit aplomb hoping the shadow will sink from sight. Instead it turns, slides past in the opposite direction, this time a telltale fin announces its genus, cutting the surface as it slices by. Now the marauding killer dips to make its deadly assault from below, but fortunately Chlamydia's aquatic technique favours aggression over grace, and in her desperate quarrel with the water the attacker receives an inadvertent volley of doggy-paddle blows to its endolymphatic pores, the very sensitive ducts that lead to the macula neglecta and a series of semicircular canals with which the poor beast endeavours to hear. Nonetheless, during the fleeting skirmish, Chlamydia's leg receives a nasty scratch due to contact with the fish's uncouth skin – the poor soul swims away to lick her wounds while Chlamydia continues her desperate struggle for land – ha, ha, get it? Eventually a charitable tide thrusts Chlamydia's exhausted husk through bloody surf into gentle shallows, where she is able to scrabble the final distance onto the beach on all fours, only to find – to her horror – that someone or *something* has stolen her clothes.

In a terribly naked panic Chlamydia scours the vicinity for her errant attire, running up and down the beach as though searching for amphibious remnants discarded in an earlier morphological manifestation. Up and down she runs, all the while making a vain gesture in covering her naked breasts and nude genitals in an absurd permutational hand sequence that ultimately renders her own erotogenic parts even more fascinating to anyone captivated by the unmitigated libidinal economics of sexual prudence. Eventually, immodesty calms, and plants its hands on hips in visible defiance.

'*Right!*' she says calmly. Then: '*GIVE ME BACK MY CLOTHES RIGHT THIS INSTANT!*' she crosses both arms over doe-eyed breasts and stamps a foot into the soft, hot, damp sand.

A churlish giggle untangles from the dense knot of unkempt jungle growth curbed into compliance by the toxic arrest of Morass's barren beach. From the very same shadows, the diminutive spectre of Mr Helmut Mandragorass steps into full human view, sporting an indelicate swimsuit, stylishly offset by a plentiful towel jauntily draped over his under-inflated pectoral girdle. He strives to contain the vain giggles that sincerely haunt his unfortunate physiognomy, but misbehaving eyeballs rudely extend on withering stalks, plainly transgressing the threshold of courteous restraint. He enjoys the sight of Chlamydia caught red-handed in all her glory – is thriving on being the cause of Chlamydia's present need to bend and buckle in defence of her birthday suit – twisting on the spot to counter the weaving gaze keen to exploit any spatial gaps in her scant privacy.

'I want my clothes,' she says, reasonably.

'Come and get them!' hurls Helmut indolently.

Chlamydia stands her ground.

Without warning Helmut attacks the beach from the jungle, shedding his own ample cotton towel to the sand and snatching Chlamydia into his little arms to drag her up the beach roughly like a sideways crab. The sensation of cockled male skin drives all other complicated thoughts out of Chlamydia's cautious mind.

'*Oooooo little mermaid! My little mermaid!*' snips the sarcastic crab, entwining his fishy claws into Chlamydia's salty sodden hair, pulling her lovely head back, wistful of her compliance, challenging Chlamydia's reliably beady eye to seek out his soul, or plaice, or cod. Chlamydia studies Helmut's face and recognises the same compound arrangement from the night before when he pleaded with her to stay with him for ever and ever, amen. But today Chlamydia recognises the unmistakable mark of male abstract desire – the solitary expression of an entire species, the compulsive drive that unconsciously obliges men to give subjective substance to an idiotic supersensible urge. At a pinch, Chlamydia shakes off sentiments of a vengeful female anti-logic while Helmut clings on for dear life.

'Let go Helmut, I want to get dressed in a black uniform then whip you up into clotted cream,' says Chlamydia, all delirious, naked and cold.

'I'll keep you warm,' says eager Helmut, without a hope in Hell, but indulging a cosy somatic fantasy nonetheless. Now Helmut notices the red blood streaming from Chlamydia's shark infested leg and drops to his own knees, weakened by the abrupt dilapidation of his transcendent libidinal urge.

'Chlamydia! What in Hell's name have you done?' he says in a fearful tone.

'It's a shark graze...' says Chlamydia, all matter-of-fact, shallow and hollow, familiar with the harrowing sight of blood on account of her own luscious menstrual cycle.

'I've been attacked by a small great white...' says Chlamydia, euphoric that she didn't drown before being eaten.

'It's damn deep,' says Helmut. 'It'll need forty to fifty stitches – maybe more.'

'Nonsense,' says Chlamydia, 'a plaster will suffice...'

Helmut wrestles Chlamydia into his miniature arms, and with her kind assistance manhandles his patient all the way up the volcano without dropping her once. He drags her directly to the kitchen, sits her on a chair, drags the screeching stepladder across the floor to the chipped lip of the enamel sink, climbs to the top, fetches the tin box from the cupboard clenched beneath his arm, descends and levers the lid open with jagged teeth, takes out a piece of dusty cotton gauze and a loose plaster, leans over to reach the tap, moistens the mildew, descends back to the ground, passes the tin box to Chlamydia to hold while he kneels next to her leg. He attends to the wound. Chlamydia wants to halt this abrupt display of concern, wishes him to stop, to tell him forcefully, in no uncertain terms that, in point of fact, the injury did not give permission for him to enter into pleasantries. But Chlamydia's tongue is tied up bound and gagged – especially manacled when his jaundiced grip tightens upon her calf, him dabbing the gash in her feminine leg. And his touch is anything but gentle. Chlamydia refuses to protest, maintains mute composure until pink elastic waterproof stretches around her circumference and the adhesive is firmly stuck one end to the other. She snatches her plastered leg from his lingering grip, casting a look of abject disgust, it cracking into a *trompe-l'œil* smile and a fake –

'*Thank you.*'

He delivers the tin box upstairs where it lives, drags shrieking steps back to their home on the concentrated scribble. Attracted by human commotion, Algernon staggers in, unshaven, green around the gills, his face is pasty, pale, pallid, ashen, washed-out, sickly, white as a sheet, waxen, drawn, ill, lacklustre, drained, wan, his eyes are reddened, he is visibly under the weather…

'I feel like death warmed up –' he says, 'I've eaten something – food poisoning for sure!' he says, invoking a staple alcoholic excuse, listing sideways as the room tips and sinks into the corner. 'Don't understand it! Didn't drink *that* much... What's up with her?' Pointing at Chlamydia.

'She's only been bitten by a small great white!' snaps Helmut, rabid. 'Anyway, *what's up with you?* Are you drunk? Have you got a drug problem?'

Algernon takes a moment for his maw to ferment a bilious reply, then pops with the alcoholic mirth of a champagne cork.

'No Helmut. Actually I don't have a drug problem – *I don't have any drugs, and it's a problem!*' He laughs without reserve, mirth edging towards self-ruin – he slides diagonally across the kitchen, motivated by the coffee pot lightly simmering with roasted grit; he decants brown sludge into teacup and steals bitter sips in between verbal outbursts tangled with curdling delirium: '*Ha, ha, ha! Helmut's little fins! He's a seal! Ha, ha, ha, oink, oink! Hey Helmut, I've got a joke for you: why is going to the toilet like going to the cemetery? Because when you gotta go – you gotta go! Ha, ha, ha!*'

Helmut ignores his polluted rival: 'I shall be in my study – *studying.*'

'*Oink!* I'm off to Hotel Krauss to find someone normal to talk to...' says Algernon.

Chlamydia limps to her room where she peels her clothes off and replaces them with a fresh outfit. She limps undetected to the library, and savouring her solitude, selects Helmut's notorious book, *Explaining Christians to Dinosaurs,* smuggles it out onto the *plein air* terrace, selects a well shaded recliner and sets about delving into Helmut's concrete genius with the ambition of reading word for word and with every bit of feminine focus she can summon:

It is common knowledge that a time of chaos existed on planet Earth before law and order was established by Mankind, and that a time *of primeval pandemonium occurred in order to allow Nature fully to flex itself in the dynamic manner of a newborn egg, growing in readiness for Adam's rib to create Eve and the ensuing reproduction cycle of human life to begin in earnest. And yet, during this period of terrible turmoil the whole world was inhabited by monstrous beings, vindictive creatures appearing to contradict the very image of paradise depicted in the Lord's Holy Bible. Evidence of these ungodly creatures can be witnessed in any natural history museum around the world, and relying on paleobiochemical carbon dating that has suggested the last of these monsters – or 'dinosaurs' as we now know them – died at least 65 million years ago. It is fossil evidence that betrays their presence upon the planet since fossils represent the flesh and bone of dinosaurs once compressed under the articulated weight of metamorphic rock. In death, an organism's hydrocarbon atoms undergo a process of mineral redeployment, and under extreme pneumatic pressure, H_2O seeps down through sedimentary rock, permeating the interred fibre of bone, leeching out the marrow and depositing silicon and calcium atoms, replacing organic hydrogen, nitrogen and carbon. The schematic substitution of organic by pseudomorphic material occurs extremely slowly, atom by atom – a meticulous replacement process that causes little or no disturbance to the integrity of the whole. Eventually, only the structure of the skeletal organic material is retained while its chemical content is entirely transformed. Organic bone is flushed away and replaced by inert stonezzzzzzzzzzzzzzzzzzzzzzzzzzzzz…*

Chlamydia wakes with a start as a nearby woodpecker rattles her cranium.

'Jesus Christ!' she exclaims. '*Explaining Christianity to Dinosaurs* has given me a bloody migraine…! She places the book face down, out of sight, wipes her clammy brow free of salty hard labour.

'I apologise for your headache…'

'*Helmut!* How long have you been standing there?'

'Long enough,' he says, stony-faced as a petroglyph. 'Did you buy that book?'

'No. I got it from your library,' she says. 'I hope you don't mind.'

'No, no. Not at all,' he says, tainted with disappointment. 'How's the leg?' he says, compensating *his* minor injury with *hers*.

'Oh fine, luckily its bark was worse than its bite...'

'Would you like a drink?' he says, and despite the oasis of civility being offered, Chlamydia assumes citing mention of *Explaining Christians* would be gauche, but nonetheless braves reference to his present literary toil:

'I'd love a lime cordial please – if you have any. But don't worry if you don't – *I'm sure you'd prefer to get on with your writing...*'

Helmut shrugs. 'No. Not today... Words aren't flowing – at least not in the right order. Too many interferences – *physical and mental.*'

'I apologise for Algernon. I'm appalled he had the audacity to show up.'

'It was to be expected. His ego was bound to make a dazzling appearance sometime or other. He was compelled to show concern – just in case you'd achieved what he wanted you to do...'

'You mean becoming *special friends* – with you?'

Helmut nods. 'It was essential to his plan. But he's unhappy now it's happened.'

'But I wouldn't say we're *special friends*...' says Chlamydia, seeking.

'But we're not enemies...' says Helmut, hiding.

'We are most of the time –' says Chlamydia, seeking. 'You wouldn't likely describe ours as the best relationship in the whole wide world... would you?'

Helmut observes Chlamydia with something approaching awe and time crystallises perfectly still.

'Will you be glad to go?' he says, voice vertiginous – balanced on the edge of Chlamydia's abysmal answer.

'*Yes*,' she says, matter-of-fact. 'It will be *good* to return home… but… on the other handy-pandy, *no*… it'll be *bad* to return home. I've grown affectionate for dear Morass, even after I thought it was going to be *mine – all mine*…'

Helmut shrugs and evaporates away into the house to reappear soon after with pleasant liquids. He sits with Chlamydia. Chlamydia and Helmut drink together undisturbed. Chlamydia finds breathing a strain in Helmut's vicinity. Her lungs dither and heart dawdles – autonomic functions weaken and nerve signals are overwhelmed by Helmut's sentience. Chlamydia wants to be crushed to death in Helmut's incapable arms – wishes she could get the awful truth about her womb off her chest, but knows the one she secretly adores is not free to marry – or doesn't love her – merely finds her body physically stirring and wants to use her hole but not in a wholesome manner.

'How's the leg?' The loop in his chatter showing through.

'Oh fine… fine… It seems that its bark was worse than its bite…' A little perplexed at the repetition.

'If you like I can change the dressing later. You can't be too careful in this climate,' he says mooning up at the sun.

'That's very generous. I appreciate your concern. If it gets septic I can always go to the infirmary,' she says.

'*The infirmary?*'

'Oh yes. I went on account of my finger – Isaiah took me. Your father Dr Mandragorass was very kind to me… very kind… *So he didn't mention anything – to you – about me – being there?*'

'No. Nothing at all… *Why would he?*' he says, nervously.

'Anyway. I was cross-referencing some old notes in the study late last night and I was able to retrieve them immediately – your filing system truly works wonderfully. I'll miss you. You've been very useful.'

'*Useful?* Considering you didn't want me here in the first place,' she says, 'I'll take that as a compliment.'

'You should. I don't hand out compliments willy-nilly,' he says, all cheery-pops.

'Why thank you!' she says, cautiously coquettish.

'My pleasure!' he smiles without reserve.

'I feel guilty sitting here on my useless rump while you work like a nigger-bitch inside. Are you sure there's nothing I can do to help, work-wise?'

Helmut rises and holds out his flipper graciously. 'You can keep me company while I prepare your lunch. Maman Terreblanche has taken unwell. I think Algernon makes her stomach turn... *Although I think it's more mutual than Algae might imagine*... I thought I'd get lunch ready and then we can eat when we feel like it. I doubt if Hertz'll be back until very late, so we have the whole day together. It'll make a nice change – you and me, alone.'

Chlamydia takes his hand and rises to her feet and with Helmut's aid, limps to the kitchen.

Helmut takes food from the fridge and begins to butter bread and create sandwich fillings.

'You know,' he says, buttering, 'the offer still stands. I would love you to stay here and work with me.'

'I can't,' she says, leaning precariously against the sink watching him.

'It would be fun. You and me – anyway, *all work and no play makes Helmut a dull boy*...' he says, buttering.

'Really, I can't,' says Chlamydia, welling up with the desire to tell the one and only she adores that her womb is occupied with the progeny of the one she hates, and is terrified that the one she adores will hate her and will refuse to adore her…

'Don't go back with Algernon,' he says, buttering, 'stay here on Morass with me.'

'I can't,' she says, wanting so much to say yes…

'Why? Guilty – *about Algernon?*' he says, stiffening.

She shakes her head sincerely hard. 'There's nothing between me and Algernon. Not now. *Rien. Nada – not a bean.* But it doesn't mean I can stay here with you. I can't.'

'Why not?' he rasps, sinews tightening. 'Why in Hell's name not?'

'*I can't!*'

'Why not? Tell me! *TELL ME C-C-CHLAMYDIA!*'

'Because… I'm pre-pre-*pregnant!* There. It's done. It's out. I've told you. I can't bear the thought of carrying Algernon's *thing!* I don't ever want to see him again… my life's all cocked up now…' she weeps.

Helmut stops buttering. Arrested faciality dissolves within the ordinal outline that is his vaguely human head; facial form shears along a vertical axis, undone like a pink zip – a dog snarl now twisting and shearing simultaneous with insectoid bug eyes that bulge unfeasibly until they too drip from dull sockets. It is as though a volatile inhuman force within humpbacked Helmut is exotherming violently beneath the epidermis, *nose out of joint* being *rubbed up the wrong way* simultaneously. Helmut gapes like the mouth of a plastic bag caught on barbed wire:

'*PREGNANT?*' it flaps: '*PREGNANT? – PREGNANT? PREGNAAAAAAAAAAAANT! HA, HA, HA! PREGNANT! OF COURSE! WHY NOT? ANYTHING ELSE? ANYTHING MORE TO TEASE MY EXISTENCE FROM THE FACE OF THE F-F-FUCKING PLANET?*' Helmut's laughter twists past the wellspring of consciousness, deep into prebiotic dementia. There, he contorts his facial mess away from Chlamydia's sight to hide his Jekyll, hunched into the fearful and grotesque rapture of a morphological regression. Added to the transformation, a sinister musical accompaniment escapes the bottles of fetid milk deposited over every work surface in the kitchen, belching in time – a chorus of emphysemic tracheotomies enjoying the infectious excitement. Rising above the entropic bedlam, webs of rotting vegetation can be heard loudly rasping in the manner of human vocal chords:

'LEAVE ME! BEGONE! SHOO!' it says, *'GET OUT OF MY SIGHT!'* it says, *'BEGONE! WHORE OF B-B-BABY-LON!'*

Banished by the sound of frantic buttering and volatile male anguish, Chlamydia escapes to her room, emotionally distraught by Helmut's negative reaction to her happy news. For a while she listens to Helmut's rage softened by the peaceful feathers of her pillow, and no sooner or later sleep arrives to soothe Chlamydia's torment away and deliver her into the land of nod, where she can suffer nightmarish violence to herself without actual harm.

Later, Chlamydia wakes to the sound of unexpected visitors hankering at the front door of the Mandragorass abode all timid like a mouse so as not to disturb anyone. Chlamydia finds Helmut's mother and father making a casual visit, dropping by to say *bonjour*...

Brunhilde is immediately vexed by the sight of Chlamydia's chewed leg and insists on a peek inside. The bleeding has stopped but when mother peels Helmut's lint away it begins again prompting mummy to re-dress the wound.

Chlamydia offers explanation as to why the apple of their eye is not to hand:

'Helmut is in his study *writing, writing, writing.* Unfortunately, my fiancé Algernon – *Consultant Surgeon* Algernon Hertz has made an unannounced appearance – has come all the way to Morass to find me. However, a change in circumstances has dictated that I call our engagement off. Hence the atmosphere in the house is tense, and so I must apologise if my being here or Hertz's presence here causes any inconvenience to you or your son.'

'Good! He's in his study! It's about time he finished his book,' cackles Brunhilde.

'He's been at it long enough. This one's taking longer than they normally do,' gloats Günter.

'He normally rattles them off bish-bosh! What's it about? Is it good? Is it a bestseller? *Will it make Hollywood?*' urges Brunhilde.

Chlamydia shakes her head, not for anything in the world would she admit to having even glimpsed the manuscript. 'Absolutely forbidden!' she yelps. 'Are you crazy? No one is allowed to read his precious work before it's committed to print!'

'Baloney! Twaddle! Gobbledygook! What utter claptrap! I often read his work – check his spelling and his grammar – he's quite insecure about his scribble and he relishes mummy's advice – doesn't he Günter?' says Brunhilde, vigorously supported by Günter's archaic endorsement.

'Apparently this one's *different...*' says Günter, leadingly.

'I made the slightest enquiry and he almost bit my head clean off. So much for a son's need of a mother's advice...'

'*Or daddy's...*' adds hubby, all hollow.

So Chlamydia and Brunhilde and Günter eat alone, and fail to catch Hyde nor hair of the tormented author Helmut, who remains locked away in the laboratory of his inner thoughts.

Eventually Chlamydia feigns tiredness, excuses herself so she can evacuate the edibles before they dare to become digestibles, and Helmut's parents recoil down the volcano by way of local ox cart. Even before Chlamydia can imagine escaping to the good old-fashioned comfortable comfort of a comfy chair and a nail-biting book, Algernon turns up in possession of a facial expression to soften a gargoyle.

'I think I've eaten something…' he winces. *'Urrggh! I'm dying…'*

'You're drunk!' reproaches Chlamydia coldly.

'I wish I was… *urrggh!*' he winces.

Chlamydia manhandles the poor soul to the foot of the stairs in time for Helmut to appear at the study door and witness his house guests in a tangled embrace. Agony renders Algernon all too oblivious to notice the bystander, but Chlamydia catches Helmut's naked jealousy as mutilating claws drag him back into his torture chamber.

That night the typewriter raged, haunting the house with belligerent industry. Twilight crept up like an embalmer's shroud and Chlamydia found herself knee-deep in a morbid dream.

In Chlamydia's morbid dream she is wading downstairs in Helmut's house. At the bottom of the endless stairway swamp she finds Helmut standing like a statuette in the infinite corridor holding silent vigil outside his own study. Although Helmut is standing on two feet, his eyelids are glued shut plus he is asleep plus presumably lost in his own nightmare. The persistent harbinger of doom booms from inside the writer's study:

'An Island?' Celia's blue eyes widen wide…

Oh, no, no, no Massa Mandragorass! Dat no good at all! Dat should be:

'A whole island?' an appetite for pathos twinkles in Celia's eye *like* fossilised light flickering in a distant galaxy…

Now dat much, much better… Oh no! Dis is terrible:

'Not on your life!' Celia tossed her head in anger, long black hair swinging all luscious forward across her face. With gentle fingers he tucked it behind her ears and cupped her lovely chin in his selfish hands…

No, no, no, Massa Mandragorass! Dis mus' change to dis:

'Over my dead carcass!' Her expression contorted with incendiary rage, lengthy black mane flaring across the contours of a warped grimace. Only the most delicate surgical caress can tease static whiskers back behind fleshy lobes while Algernon's free hand locks her masticating trap shut…

Now dat much better! Now let me see… No, no, no! Massa Mandragorass! Dis bad, very bad!:

'Everything happened so quickly she could not believe it was true…

Dis id hopeless!'

Outside the closed study Chlamydia gasps open wide: '*Maman Terreblanche* is editing Helmut Mandragorass's manuscript! Of all people he chose that common housemaid!

Oh Helmut why didn't you trust me? *My Aunt Shigella works in publishing – she's a senior editor at...'*

Sheer disappointment wakes into the sonic void left by the absence of Helmut's typing. Chlamydia lies still, supine inertia gasping in the vacuum for a sound. Downstairs, a champagne cork squeezes from a bottle neck and chinks on a lone glass. Cigar odour suffused with the drone of a broken man creeps upstairs. Chlamydia heeds the tormented celebration until the bubbly dries up, hesitating long enough before tiptoeing downstairs to confront the obese spectre pawing all over Helmut's manuscript – *instead*, she finds Helmut curled asleep outside his study. Chlamydia fetches her bed cover and draws it over the foetal pile. Bending to kiss Helmut's forehead tenderly, she is made aware of a strange incandescent light strobing in the crack beneath the study door. Curiosity enters to find the *High Priestess of Xerox* presiding over a classic *5028* – the obese spectre looms over the shuddering altar, her face rendered luminous by some such demonic light now summoned into attendance. The spectre does nothing to acknowledge Chlamydia's interruption and continues to insert page after page into the photocopier. Escaping emerald beams scan the contours of Maman Terreblanche's unholy countenance and without disruption to her rhythm lifts her monumental face to pin a menacing stare at the disturbance.

'Sorry Maman Terreblanche... I was sleepwalking...'

• • • • •

Chlamydia wakes to the lurid tics and spasms of the dawn chorus – to Mother Nature's florid Tourette's syndrome swearing in the day. Morning is eerily absent of the alphabet being put to task, so she dresses urgently, dispatches her compliment of morning sickness into bedside bucket and limps downstairs to find an empty puddle of cloth in the hallway. Like a Victorian child, Helmut is nowhere to be seen nor heard.

Thinly veiled inquisitiveness risks its beady eye to stalk through the merest gap in Helmut's study door. It sees no Helmut, no Maman Terreblanche and eerily still, *no Xerox 5028*… Chlamydia follows her nose into the kitchen where coffee simmers in the percolator. She pours a cup, allows a smile and sips.

Just then, Maman Terreblanche eclipses the doorway. Her eyes are as alive as tumbleweed. Her mouth arid as the desert. In wrestler's arms she grips a considerable stack of big brown envelopes in haphazard balance, such that Chlamydia can see they are liberally stamped and internationally addressed. It is clear that Helmut has concluded his epic and Maman Terreblanche is tasked with posting the completed manuscript to the publisher – *although why there are so many copies Chlamydia cannot explain. More to the point, the sight of Helmut's packages raises Chlamydia's hopes in the assumption that it must also mean that Captain Oceanic's next visit is imminent…*

• • • • •

So she sits and sips in tremulous apprehension of the pendular mood of Algernon and Helmut, certain that Helmut will have drawn dire conclusions from Chlamydia's midnight grapple with Algernon at the foot of the stairs – Helmut's reasoning is as twisted as Algernon's bellyache, but the boat will come soon, she thinks – soon she will be free of twists and turns.

– Slowly time nibbles by.

– Chlamydia's leg is a peg less painful today.

– It is a beautiful day outside and the typewriter is silent…

Maman Terreblanche reappears in the kitchen portal empty-handed to stare at Chlamydia's limb, causing it to flinch with phantom pain. So moved, she limps to the volcanic terrace, hobbles down into the garden basin – pausing here and there to probe the draping blossom. How enchanting it would be to reside in paradise, she thinks – how wonderful to learn all the names of the flowers and birds and bees off by heart and back to front. Behind a listing wisteria she unearths the drab specimen of Algernon who effuses an atmosphere of pollution.

'I'm not very well!' he fumes in wake of the unhealthy stench that contages his air space.

'You poor thing!' admits Chlamydia. 'But I'm afraid you'll get no sympathy from me Mr Hertz! *Agony is the wage of ecstasy!*' she scolds. 'It's self-induced after all!' she adds, wagging a puritanical finger with earnest disdain.

'It's not *just* a hangover! I should know – I'm a doctor! I'm telling you I'm *seriously ill!*'

In escape of the outrageous sun, poor Algernon shambles into the next swathe of shade. As he winces by, Chlamydia clocks an angry red rash protesting on his neck. Diverted to the exotic bloom that draws her nose further down the pretty path, Chlamydia discovers Helmut perched on a lovers' bench out-weeping the willow that cranes over him in sympathy. He is beside himself – so Chlamydia's compassion sees fit to sit next to him.

'I haven't set foot in your enchanting garden before – it's a garden of earthly delights!' she says, hoping to lighten Helmut's earthy burden. 'Do you come here to contemplate your woes?'

Helmut lifts his head with the pneumatic aid of a single solemn sob.

'Sometimes…' he sobs.

'Like now?' she says.

'Yes... yes... Like now,' he sobs.

'Sad because you've finished your book?' she probes.

'Finished my book? FINISHED? WHO SAYS I'VE FINISHED MY BOOK?' Helmut's emotional exposure is promptly cloaked in lurid rage. *'Finished?'* he yelps. *'WHO SAID IT'S F-F-FUCKING FINISHED?'*

Chlamydia shrinks on the lovers' bench like a sea anemone flinching on a brow beaten groyne.

'...but I swear I saw Maman Terreblanche with your manuscript...' she whimpers, 'I heard champagne being opened last night... smelled cigar... heard you weep with the bittersweet taste of creative closure! I just put two and two together and *assumed*...'

'*Assumed?* Yes you *did* assume! And what should I assume about you, eh? *EH?* What should I assume about Algernon carrying you to bed last night – up the stairs *two by two* like animals... What should I assume about *that!*' He prods Chlamydia's hectic womb.

'Well, since you put it like that, I'll leave you to your *unfinished* masterpiece and take my own biological work of art from your unappreciative sight!'

Chapter Nine

Exiled to the terrace Chlamydia is confronted by Maman Terreblanche looming over the garden with obese inquisitiveness.

'*Where id Massa Mandragorass? Where id his guest? Where dey gone to?*'

'Oh, didn't they tell you? – *It's hide and seek and you're it…*'

• • • • •

For lunch Chlamydia picks at edibles all on her lonesome and expels the few distasteful mouthfuls before they dare to break down into digestibles. She adjourns to the vacant terrace for a *plein air* nap, sequestering Helmut's *Explaining Christians to Dinosaurs* to urge her on her way. But sleep evades her and obstinate consciousness manages to lurch to the turgid neo-Darwinian conclusion. Returning to the library she finds Helmut perched on a log, leaning idly against the fireplace mantle with whisky in hand.

He regards her blankly.

'Helmut. I've something to say. I'll be leaving Morass soon… Never to return,' she announces. 'Never, ever… Does that bother you? – In the slightest?'

Helmut swigs the wee dram and slams the glass onto the marble defiantly while struggling for his balance.

So the day elapsed with indolent reluctance – seconds scraped across the diurnal cycle and hours threatened to distend into fully blown days. Algernon and Helmut were nowhere to be seen, both nursing their public injuries in private. That evening Chlamydia waived dinner and put herself to bed where she toyed with the idea of seeking out Helmut's novel – but thought better of it. Instead she waded in and out of shallow sleep before heeding the late tide deliver Algernon to his own crib. But no sooner had calm settled upon the house than a lurid thud told of his fall from slumber. The drunken sop – the revolting pig – never before had Chlamydia experienced her fiancé like this, an unashamed drunk in the company of others. An hour later, Helmut entered the house to make his way neatly up the stairs to his bedroom where his door closed with a pedestrian *click*.

In the morning Chlamydia woke to Algernon's acute cough spluttering above the sound of Helmut descending the stairs. Good Samaritan Chlamydia finds Algernon sunk in his bed saturated with bodily humours and barely disgestibles. He is ashen, save for the rash of vivid yellow pustules that grip his throat and now plague one half of his ugly mug.

'I feel... numb – *numb and stingy*...' He peels his desiccated cheek from vomit-sodden bedclothes to moon up at nurse Chlamydia.

'Mercy!' she says. 'You're in a terrible state! What's happened to you? What *have* you been doing?' She has a stab at turning him over but he slips away delirious. She administers a medicinal slap to the unblemished side of his face, which forces two eccentric orbs to spin into precarious focus.

'*Who are you?* Oh! Chlamydia? Dearest Chlamydia! The bloat! The bloat is coming! It's coming today! The bloat! This very morning! Oceanic is coming *now!*'

'Fool! You're delirious! And don't dare tease me Algernon – you know how desperate I am to leave Morass!'

'No! *Honest to God!* Oceanic is on his way – coming, here, now – even as we speak! Coming! I beg of you, don't leave me here to die!'.

Chlamydia tumbles downstairs to find Helmut munching

toast.

'Is Oceanic coming today? Is Algernon telling the truth? Helmut, tell me! TELL ME!'

Helmut interrupts his vegetable spread reluctantly.

'Yes… I believe so… I think Algernon might have said something to that effect…'

'But we have to take him to the infirmary before the boat comes – urgently! It's serious! He's sincerely worried about his own health – and he's a doctor so he knows best! We can take him to your father – leave him at the infirmary and then I can take the boat and he can come home when he's fit to travel!'

'We? We? "WE" have to take him?'

'*Please* Helmut! *PLEASE!* I can't bear your mockery!'

Helmut snaps the scorched crust without so much as a blink.

• • • • •

So Helmut's watchful eye peers from the socket of the vile volcano as Chlamydia manhandles Algernon down the slope to unearth Isaiah, embedded in his ramshackle mud hut.

'Isaiah! Isaiah! It's me, Chlamydia Love! Your friend Lydia! You must take us to the infirmary. We need your help. Algernon is sick, sick, sick…'

Isaiah cowers. *'But Miss Love, de infirmary is a wicked place – an unholy place indeed!'*

Chlamydia's inelegant threats move Isaiah to harness ox to cart. She perches Algernon next to the begrudging driver, takes the whip from Isaiah and personally lashes the dozy beast forward with Captain Oceanic's boat in mind. Even in fresh air, Algernon's soiled hue pollutes the senses, and Chlamydia respires with shallow sips. So the wooden ambulance hangs a left into the glowing green aperture of the overgrown dirt track leading to the infirmary. The ox bellows deep into the infinite hopelessness of its existence as they draw near to the grotesque hospital being clawed by withering vines hellbent on reclaiming it back into the indilute chaos of the forest. The vacant windows still billow with gasping mosquito nets and the broken porch faithfully belches with the handicapped ramp that serves the lightless void that is the infirmary's sombre portal. Chlamydia teases the nervous beast closer.

'Chlamydia! What in Heaven's sake brings you here?' The ancient voice of Dr Mandragorass.

'It's Algernon... He's been vomiting...'

'But the infirmary is little more than an ancillary morgue...' And casting his arms in a helpless arc, 'Bring the poor soul to my surgery – let's see if I can alleviate someone's pain today without need of the last rites...'

Dr Mandragorass leads through the ward, Chlamydia and the doctor manhandling poorly Algernon through the languishing flesh that weeps and squirms like open sewers on both sides of their passage. Outside Isaiah genuflects vigorously in the dust like a madman teased by the sun. In the doctor's surgery the bulb flares and Ormond is peddling like a lunatic.

'Doctor Mandragorass, I must leave my ex-fiancé in your capable hands! I'm determined to catch Captain Oceanic's boat back to the mainland, and from there continue home. Algernon is too unwell to make the journey today and so he must stay here in your charge until he's fit enough to return!' And with that, kooky Chlamydia turns and tiptoes at breakneck speed through the flinching nerves of the undead back out into the dying sun. 'Forgive me doctor! Kisses to Brunhilde! Isaiah – giddy up! To the beach! *Au revoir*! Until we meet again!'

Chlamydia beats the living daylights out of Isaiah's ox with

Isaiah's whip until the vehicle is purged from the green capillary track out onto the beach to trundle along the coralline road towards Hotel Krauss – alas, merely in time to witness the profile of *The Amorous Peacock* dissolve into the hopeless horizon – prematurely despatched from the shore by the solitary figure of Maman Terreblanche who decants from the small jetty with gimlet eyes and a mouth grinning wide open to greet Chlamydia's expression of sheer, utter, hopeless despair.

The poor girl even buckles to her knees.

'*WHAT IN HELL'S NAME AM I GOING TO DO NOW?*' she shrieks.

'*Swim?*' quips the obese spectre before splintering into a mocking cackle.

• • • • •

For the next three days Chlamydia incarcerates herself in a dreamless suspension, only condescending to remove the physical barricade of her emotional protest to slop out and retrieve the paltry offering of food left at her door each lunch time.

On the fourth day of somnolent reckoning Chlamydia emerges to find Algernon returned from the infirmary only in slightly better health and Helmut horrified by the sudden curvature of Chlamydia's stomach…

Algernon greets her with a green tinted grin tinging the gills. 'You thought I had the pink-eyed lurgy didn't you? That's why you abandoned me in that godforsaken place with those other saps… Well I'm feeling a lot better, no thanks to you!'

'No thanks to me? It was *me* that took you to the infirmary – I didn't abandon you!'

'No, it was your conscience that took *you* to the infirmary and abandoned *me* there –'

'Oh why don't you just kiss and make up?' says Helmut,

intent upon Chlamydia's churning womb. '*You have so much more in common than you think…*'

Chlamydia glares at Helmut in reinforcement of their little secret.

Days pass by with a tedious uniformity only cheered by Maman Terreblanche's intermittent provisions. Helmut loiters impatiently, ill at ease, as though waiting for something to happen – *or to arrive*. Algernon languishes from shadow to shadow in hypersensitive maintenance of his hurt. Chlamydia entertains herself as best she can. She takes to the beach, sunbathes and swims. She reads, listens to music and walks in the emerald forest – all the while making mental notes on the configuration of her new life plan, post-Morass.

One night, after yet another busy day full of nothing at all, Chlamydia's dream dreams up the sound of an angry squall caught in the trees, and imagines the night air being choppered into tiny little pieces by an ominous black shadow hovering above Maman Terreblanche with a bright sunbeam aiming down at the obese spectre's mooning eyeballs. She shields herself from the swirling night dust as the ancient machine comes to land and the pilot delivers a mail sack to Helmut's dutiful housekeeper.

At dawn, the house wakes to the unambiguous tones of Helmut going postal in his study – him wailing like a banshee while a cosmology of inanimate objects suffer the full force of his rage. Algernon, for his sins, is drawn to the top of the stairs where Chlamydia's tympanic membrane is already stationed to pick up titbits of superheated monologue. In silent recognition of their mutual curiosity they acknowledge each other's shameless nosiness with a symmetrical nod and resume their patient eavesdropping. Downstairs, Helmut's highland fling is nearing its thermospasmic crescendo.

'THE BASTARDS! THE F-F-FUCKING ROTTEN BASTARDS! WHAT DO THEY KNOW ABOUT TOIL AND TORMENT? LACKEYS! MENIALS! PEN-PUSHERS! BECAUSE EACH FAILED TO ACCEDE TO THE TASK OF GREAT LITERATURE THEY'D HAPPILY STIFLE A WORK OF GENIUS SIMPLY FOR FEAR OF IT SPOILING THE CONSOLATIONS OF MEDIOCRITY! DESPITE THEIR BEST ATTEMPTS I'LL REACH MY PUBLIC – COME HELL OR HIGH WATER!'

The fireworks seek fresh air and so Helmut evacuates the house with sparks flying.

Algernon, duly entertained, skulks back into his room content to nurse his bad guts while Chlamydia makes a beeline for the ravaged hive downstairs. Inside, the full-scale destruction of a diminutive rage bares itself to Chlamydia's eye – his precious Tab-O-Matic spilt on the floor gobsmacked, his special chair cast adrift with back broken and Chlamydia's own alphabetical filing cruelly undone – pens and pencils ruthlessly snapped and mangled paperclips strewn everywhere – even the patron saint of writing hangs on the wall at a jaunty angle with glass and decorative frame wrecked. The one-man maelstrom has flung everything into sickening disarray and yet the eye of the storm has left Helmut's desk eerily undisturbed. There Chlamydia uncovers a paper trail of disaster, which begins its destructive spiral with a letter yet to be dispatched:

Faber and Faber
3 Queens square
London WC1N 3AU
United Kingdom
England.

dear Faber and Faber,

I enclose COME HELL OR HIGH WATER for the purpose of your scrutiny in the hope that you might be grateful for the triumph of my efforts. Since this is my first work of fiction I thought it best to begin withx romance since I know much about love and loss.
I can do no more than await your response.
sincerely
HELMUT MANDRAGORASS, author.

HARLEQUIN MILLS & BOON
LIMITED

Mr H Mandragorass
PO Box 52688
London

N7 8TZ

06 December 2007

Dear Mr Mandragorass

Thank you for submitting Come Hell or High Water for our consideration.

Whilst we appreciate the care and attention that has gone into the preparation of your submission, regrettably we feel that your story and characters are not sufficiently developed for publication in any of our publishing programmes.

Here are our top tips to bear in mind for your next submission:

1. Ensure that your story and conflict are character-driven.
2. Focus on the internal emotional conflict of your characters.
3. Use secondary characters to add richness and depth to your central romance but don't let them take over!
4. Target your work to a particular series – this means you need to read current books in the series you are aiming for and understand what that series delivers to the reader.

We are pleased to have had the opportunity to see your work, and thank you for thinking of Harlequin Mills & Boon.

Yours sincerely

Editorial Department

Find more writing tips at www.eharlequin.com and www.millsandboon.co.uk

Eton House, 18-24 Paradise Road, Richmond, Surrey, TW9 1SR, England. Tel: 020-8288 2800 Fax: 020-8288 2899
Registered Office: Eton House, 18-24 Paradise Road, Richmond, Surrey TW9 1SR. Registered in England No.100449 VAT Regn. Nos. GB 232433496.
www.millsandboon.co.uk

[redacted]

[redacted]

[redacted]

Helmut Mandragorass
PO Box 52688
London N7 8TZ

6th August 2007

Dear Mr Mandragorass,

We appreciate you sending us your manuscript for *Come Hell or High Water*, it looks a very exiting read.

Unfortunately we cannot entertain unsolicited manuscripts as we simply do not have the resources to deal with them. All of our books come through agents, and you would be best served following this route. You might consider purchasing a copy of *Writers Market* (available on amazon.co.uk) which contains vital information on getting your work published as well as a list of agents.

We wish you luck with your project and every success in the future.

Yours sincerely,

[redacted] Editorial Department

[redacted]

[redacted]

PICADOR
Pan Macmillan
20 New Wharf Road
London
N1 9RR
T +44 (0)20 7014 6000
F +44 (0)20 7014 6001
www.panmacmillan.com

Helmut Mandragorass
PO Box 52688
London
N7 8TZ

21 August 2007

Dear Helmut Mandragorass

Thank you for sending me your interesting manuscript, *Come Hell or High Water*. It is certainly original and engaging but, I'm sorry to say, I just can't quite see where it would fit on the Picador list.

I wish you luck with finding it a safe home.

Yours sincerely

Charlotte Greig
Editor, Picador
Pan Macmillan
20 New Wharf Road
London N1 9RR

Helmut Mandragorass
PO Box 52688
London N7 8TZ

Dear Mr Mandragorass,

Thank you for submitting Come Hell Or High Water for my consideration and apologies for the time it has taken to get back to you.

I'm afraid to say that your manuscript really didn't do it for me. I can't explain exactly what "it" is - only that I know it when I read it. And this most certainly is not it.

Please don't be too downhearted though as this is only my opinion. More a matter of taste than a reflection on the quality of your work.

With every good wish for the future.

Michael McCoy

Michael McCoy

IN
DE
PEN
DENT

INDEPENDENT TALENT GROUP LTD
Formerly ICM London
OXFORD HOUSE 76 OXFORD STREET LONDON W1D 1BS
TEL: + 44 (0)20 7636 6565 FAX: + 44 (0)20 7323 0101

There are other letters of rejection skulking beneath those that Chlamydia sets eye upon… each missive as pitiless as the next. Their reckless composition would unfairly tip anyone foolish enough to have placed their creative worth in such a precarious balance. It dawns upon Chlamydia that Helmut's earnest yearning for publication has lead him voluntarily to degrade his own reputation by submitting his work willy-nilly to the cold scrutiny of strangers. She comprehends the magnitude of Helmut's fruitless meltdown while sifting the bitter evidence with trembling empathy. But before Chlamydia can set eyes upon the next damning document, a monoxide whisper hisses from a fissured maw.

'*There's no need to skulk about like a common thief!*' It quietly fumes. 'It's all there before you, on my desk, plain for the eye to see – an *open book* unfit for publication. Feel free – be my guest, rake over the evidence of my worthlessness… witness how they saw fit to rubbish me! Assassins! Butchers! I should've taken heed of your wise words – remember? *You said I was unreadable… you had no idea why I bothered to write? Well, well – evidently you share an opinion with those that seem to matter…*'

Helmut's bloody hue deepens to the ruddy blush of a looming muscular rage. His sinews braid around the trunk of his bulging neck, wiring head to shoulders as though a cork ready to pop. Chlamydia interposes herself into the volatile calm.

'No Helmut! It's not true! Your writing is magnificent!' she soothes. '*Yes* – the earlier stuff is pontificating claptrap – jammed so far up your own arse only a medical publisher would give it light of day! But *Come Hell or High Water* is different. It's a different voice. I know what I'm talking about – my Aunt Shigella is senior editor at a major publishing house – I grew up in publishing! Your work comes right from the heart. I admit I did read your manuscript when you were out one day – it moved me to tears. I ask you – *who has the guts to write real life romantic fiction nowadays?* Nobody! These days it's all about navel-gazing queers shambling around in the remains of the conventional novel – stories about stories about stories, on and on, anon. No one has the balls for good old-fashioned —'

'Oh bravo! Splendid! I'm sorely touched!' Helmut's little hands clap with intimidating vigour. 'There's nothing more diplomatic than adding *sympathy* to injury… I'll wager you waded through Audrey Turner's critique… No? Well when you do you'll concur with me that I got what I paid for! *YES! PAID FOR!* I found the Authors' Workshop on the internet – they offer an honest service for the crestfallen writer seeking professional advice.' Helmut snatches pages from the table then reads aloud. '*Thank you for allowing me to read your novel,* she says… *do make up your own mind whether you want to take these suggestions on board or not… it is your work, your voice,* she says… *the decision is yours…* £250 for the sterling advice of a Good Samaritan fearful of inadvertently precipitating the hangman's noose around the neck of a despairing author. Her critical elegance saved my feelings but murdered my soul! Less judicious was the remark that I confuse clichés for characters – and downright rude was the assertion that the title of my *ill-fated* novel is… yet another c-c-cliché.'

'No Helmut… it's not true!'

'True? Read it! *IT'S TRUE ALL RIGHT! Read the death sentence – penned by the hands of the suffocators of talent! Chokers of fate! Destroyers of destiny!*' Helmut froths as little fists screw page after page of Audrey Turner's critique into tight balls.

'I'll show them!' he howls, retreating from the seat of his creative sovereignty, out into the corridor and up to his little bedroom. *'I'LL SHOW YOU ALL! JUST YOU WAIT AND S-S-SEE!'*

In the wake of Helmut's fury and under the beneficent gaze of Jeffrey Archer, Chlamydia unclenches Helmut's tightly clenched balls and settles down to read them aloud:

Come Hell or High Water

Dear Helmut,

First of all thank you for allowing me to read your novel, and secondly do understand that although I can direct you to specific processes that might help your work in general, my points regarding *Come Hell or High Water* can be taken as subjective.

Therefore what I prefer to do is highlight areas of the work that may not work to its full advantage and ask you questions. I obviously give my opinion but I can't 'tell' you how I would write a scene as this simply wouldn't be your voice, your vision, or indeed successful. Therefore what this report is intended to do is to get you thinking and perhaps editing/altering your text via points/questions, if you feel this is needed.

Again, do make up your own mind whether you want to take these suggestions on board or not. It is your work, your voice, so ultimately the decision is yours.

Firstly to respond to your letter, you say this is your first fiction project and that is good to know, you also say you thought it might be good to begin with 'romance fiction'. My only question here is, why? Is it something you read? Is it something that you think has a large market? It's just good to know where your impulses come from. Because writers almost always pour what they read into what they write, it's unavoidable and actually healthy practice: you really should know what you're getting yourself into! So if you haven't read much 'romance fiction' (the contemporary stuff) and you want to be specifically on genre (your letter seems to indicate this, I'm not saying this is something I personally do as a writer) then go out there and see what is on the market in the popular 'romance genre'. This is just a suggestion if this genre is the one you wish to stick to.

Also you ask if the editor has any ideas re: possible endings. I'm afraid I can't point you in that direction! I'm sure as a reader I have loads of ideas, that's what we do as readers. Do they go off into the sunset Daphne Du Maurier style (because there's lots of *Jane Eyre/Rebecca* stuff going on here), or does the first wife really come back? These plot decisions really have to be up to you, I can't fill in these gaps, because in fact they aren't gaps there's a whole absence of a ending here! So again, all I can do is ask you questions that might get you thinking about your own conclusions. Writing can't be by numbers (in my opinion) it has to first of all come from you, and then via feedback, that's when you might 'fill in the gaps', alter certain aspects, or indeed stick to your guns.

The novel and the genre

Okay. The overall impression is that you have a particular place and plot here that on the whole work. I like the way you dive straight in with 'An island?' so there's no prologue-preamble, you are straight at the heart of it. This pattern is repeated with the chapter breaks too. The way one chapter moves to the next, it simply follows on and probably for this genre this is a good thing to stick to.

The island itself is intriguing. The smallness of it, the isolation of Morass does work (though I'm not sure about the name, too obvious?). The geography of it is pleasing, the fact that Celia is trapped (she can only get off on a pre-arranged boat) and her abandonment as a plot move (the hotel room taken by the French couple, her wandering off and sleep in the sun) does work. And here the fact that the entire piece does settle on Celia is good. You don't swerve off. We are with her all the way. And those Jane-Rochester type conversations she and Marcus have are compellingly over-the-top. On the whole I enjoyed them as Marcus touched the bases of both Heathcliff and Rochester. There is also the interesting line of a novel about a writer writing: it's a 'romance' novel with the 'romantic hero' as a writer of those thrillers you find in airports.

These are all foundations that you can work on, I think. You have the focus and it's simply about getting back into it and considering these following points:

a) Can you execute this in a less clichéd and so finer way?

b) Can you really say you know who Celia and Marcus are?

c) Hence do you know what pattern each of their 'conversations' needs to be? What point they have to get to, to move *on* to the next 'act' and (probable) resolution?

d) Can you come up with an 'ending' or at least a decision as to what your story is?

e) Do you think you know what a scene is?

These are the questions I think you need to address, you've got your setting but these elements are rather unbalanced. Basically the set up, the place is interesting but you really do need to work hard on the way it is *told*.

Overall View and Specifics

What I will say at this stage is that this does really read like a first draft, hot of the press, not just because of the number of spelling errors and lay out problems (don't do that to an agent!) but also because of the dialogue, as Celia and Marcus do actually go around in circles in their dialogue sections. Hence it doesn't read like you've gone back to it and honed it in any way. Unfortunately this is something you just have to do, many times (not just you, all writers!) so hopefully this time has given you breathing space to do this, and don't worry, it will come; it's just part of the writing process. In fact I hope you haven't edited this since you sent this in, so now is the time to go back to it and examine these conversations in this way:

1) Their first meeting and the drinking water. This has the Marcus in the 'Heathcliff' role (vicious, unpredictable, sexy). But in this section you need, when you edit, to hone Celia's reaction to him.

Yes, his whole point is his unpredictability, but Celia often contradicts herself from one thought to the next (pgs 8 onwards). He's vile, then she's attracted, then he's vile again (which sounds OK but it doesn't read 'OK' on the page, it reads like the writer isn't in control). Also, the language falls apart rather and again I do think this is down to the text being unedited (not read through either?) For example, on p. 11 she cries 'You deserve to be castigated!' and this just doesn't sound like Celia, it sounds like a strange Regency throwback (the same could be said of the prose here, 'abruptly she remembered Anton!'). Just calm it down a little, this may be romantic fiction but these are contemporary people. They speak like contemporary people no matter what genre they are in. Also at this stage you begin what I've called 'the questions.'

2) 'The questions'.

I want you to go through the text and put a line through every question that stands outside of the dialogue. The question in prose is what happens in a first draft. It's what the writer does to find their own way into the narrative, to find out what the characters are thinking and what might happen. These questions move from ones grounded in 'the real':

'What was he? She thought, again, puzzled by his vague familiarity. A celebrity perhaps? Someone she had seen on the televisions? Could be he a sportsman or an athlete? Or an actor?' (p. 13)

To the general ones that really do go on:

'Why? She asked herself once again. Why had he come? What was he trying to do?' (p.30). See page 38, page 40, etc, too.

To the ones that go on and on, p. 33 (it's too long to repeat, but begins 'but how, in what way?')

Cut literally ALL of these- then see what you've got, then put back a few, but just a few – one a chapter if you must!

I hope this enables you to see how you simply don't need these narrative nudges, these questions that just read as writer finding their way in a first draft.

3) Another thing to pay attention to in the dialogue is the basic 'she said', 'he said' – you really don't need them so much.

Another exercise is to take page 18 and 27 and put a line through all the 'she said', 'he said' – does it make any difference? Is it cleaner? I think you'll find it is. Also it's 'she said' lower case after dialogue with a comma. In general you have a lot of copy editing here but that isn't the purpose of this report and I think you need to address some of these basics first.

4) Another dialogue point is not just to have a drafting handle on where your characters are going in a conversation but a) what they say and b) how they say it. There's a lot of loaded stuff in Celia and Marcus's 'conversations' – verging on a fear of rape and indeed talk of rape later.

The way we truly hone dialogue is to try and grasp what dialogue is there for, for writer as well as reader. Is it solely there to impart information? Or is it rather there to gradually build up a character so firmly that we as readers know what their voice would sound like, where they would pause, and how they would stand or look away as they spoke? What works about your dialogue is that you don't have big blocks of prose, Celia and Marcus really do ping-pong back and forth, but sometimes, quite often actually, their dialogue seems random and rather non-naturalistic (even too 'staged' for romantic fiction). It also goes the other way, and suddenly Marcus sounds like a different Marcus on p.17

'Don't be daft,' he said, almost menacingly. 'I dress like this way (*sic*) because I prefer being casual. Morass is my retreat, where I can be myself and not give a toss what anyone else thinks.'

Compare this with p. 48, 'the normal practice is to knock not listen at keyholes,' he said.

Is this difference clear?

It is not that your characters don't speak, they certainly do. This is good; too many blocks of prose can utterly kill a text, particularly one that lies within a commercial genre. So keep up the talking, and keep up the observations like p.20 'She was dithering when he appeared. But he smiled warmly for a change.' These work. But I want you to examine not what your characters say, but how what they are saying or indeed not saying reveals them.

I think that all these points about dialogue are linked to a basic problem to do with telling, and this is a problem that is linked to the phrase 'show don't tell'. This leads right back to your character problem mentioned earlier.

'Show don't tell' is a mantra of writers (annoying as it is). What it means is that in any kind of prose what you need to do is create an impression, a scene and how a character interacts with this place/situation – you need to show it- using all the senses.

And to build up character is not simply to tell the reader everything about this person – this is purely superficial- what we need is to be allowed to observe this character, to see how he/she interacts with the world. We need scenes that tell us something implicitly rather than explicitly. You are getting there in these scenes as the details (the spectre of the glass of water in the first dialogue scene, and the tin of varnish) are really important, but you need to focus in (as an exercise on the characters' senses).

The phrase (show don't tell) also means avoid the over-explanatory, and trust the reader: we'll get it in the end. So in terms of character and plot try and avoid summarising the past or even the present, and you have a lot of summary going on here (see p. 3 which should really be two scenes, at least!)

The phrase 'show don't tell' also means don't 'translate' what your characters are feeling/thinking by directly telling us; let what they do/say and what they intuit from their surroundings do this work. This allows the reader to make up their own minds. If someone 'looks away' or 'folds her napkin, tight edged' etc, etc, it gives a clearer picture than 'she was upset.'

It's simply that the reader wants to come upon things sensually- we want to hear, taste, smell, etc, these things, we don't simply want a list of facts, whether this is in blocks of prose, or in dialogue. What we want is an attempt at naturalism, a 'scene' where we witness things happening. But you must be wary of what I call the 'translation aspect'. If something happens, just let it happen and let the reader deduce: we are the detectives, and we want at least the illusion of being in control of this information, or these 'clues' the writer leaves. Don't tell us everything and try this exercise with each of your characters (just Celia and Marcus if you wish):

Make a list of 3 random objects

Make a list of 3 small objects that might fit into her, then his pockets.

Make a list of 3 smells they might remember from childhood and 3 noises (each character).

Make a list of 3 actions they may have done as children.

Now what I want you to do is connect one of each.

For e.g. 'pink ribbons', 'sponge cake' and 'fingers drumming on a tin lid'

Just try it and see what happens, experiment. Some may not work, but try and get into the living memories of your characters. This may or may not work for you, but what it may do is allow you to discover new things about your characters.

Conclusions on Character

The final thing to say about character here is to be wary of cliché, even within this genre. You say you are going for 'romance fiction' and when you do this consciously I think you then allow yourself to let the clichés run and run. I'm not saying you can't use cliché at all (because a character can TALK in clichés after all, I'm always hearing people say 'At the end of the day,' and *Come Hell or High Water* is a cliché in itself!) But perhaps at the very beginning of the novel, because you have the nice and interesting island, something unusual happening, I think you can spend a little more time veering away from cliché in the description.

Does Celia have to have 'raven-black hair (that) attracted men like bears to honey.' I just think she can have black hair but transform the cliché a bit, put a bit more backbone into it.

Scenes

This is the final 'big' thing, I think. You need to understand what a 'scene' is and it's simply done, all you need to do is put in line spaces to donate passages of time and don't skim over time 'telling' us everything (see page 32 for e.g. and p.3).

This skimming is reflected in the fact that you have almost an entire novel in 4 chapters.

I think what you need to do is locate the end, write it, then go back and organise the scenes. These scenes then become chapters. So think, is the first chapter all the way to Marcus saying 'You're a very good actress' or is it Celia arriving on the island, the reader getting to know her and her isolation? Then the walk and the thirst as chapter 2? Do you see what I mean by the pacing? Just think about each chapter that you currently have and count up the 'scenes' in them. Divide these scenes then with one of the spaces

that denote passage of time.

Pick up any novel. Over 80 pages there will be more than four chapters, in this genre at least.

Specific Problems

This is just a list of phrases/words that were problematic or simply didn't make sense. Use this list after you dealt with above. This is the second editing stage.

1) Spelling! At times maddeningly bad.
2) Layout, again use any novel as an exemplar. Either indent or leave spaces. Use spaces to denote time has past since the last sentence.
3) You must be careful of phrases like 'the dusky-skinned driver' p. 5
4) By the end of this extract Celia must have bruised shoulders, Marcus is always pressing them.

5) Some of your phrases seem either a bit lazy or don't make sense so watch this, i.e. 'his hands felt electric on hers as through an electric charge was passing between them – as though the two of them formed an electrical circuit.' (see p.23- also – how can 'he play her like a fish'?)

6) Watch the adjectives- use one. Watch the adverbs, try not to use them.

7) The almost-sex scene seems uncovered. 'Romance her'? 'descend?' 'possess her roughly'? 'be plundered by him' ? p.63-64.

8) Surely Celia would ask something about the wife? It seems a little strained this sort of silence.

9) Finally I think you've just run out of steam at the 'end' – you need to go back and simply think, 'what happens next?' It's hard writing a novel. It's harder editing.

Thanks and I hope this helps,

Days passed before Helmut resurfaced from his inner dementia to rekindle his acquaintance with his unsolicited house guests. His first able-bodied formality was to advise Chlamydia and Algernon of an all-important announcement to be made at dinner that evening.

That evening Algernon and Chlamydia attend the lounge in tremulous expectation of their precarious host. At nine o'clock the obese spectre of Maman Terreblanche enters, eclipsing Algernon and Chlamydia's diffident eye to eye contact to serve drinks and canapés before Helmut makes his entrance full stride – launched towards the mantelpiece with muscles co-opted into transient cooperation. There, he turns awkwardly to connive an officious profile and deliver his urgent proclamation. First, he attends to the tangle in his knotted throat.

'As you b-b-both well know, I could never part with my b-b-beloved Morass – however, it is t-t-time for a change. I've thought long and hard and come to the decision that I shall c-c-commercially develop Morass to its f-f-full potential. Hence, I propose that you, Algernon, join me in this exciting v-v-venture.'

'Good God!' gasps Algernon.

'*NO! YOU CAN'T!*' exhales Chlamydia. 'You can't mean it!'

Algernon leaps up leaving his agony remaining seated.

'Well, since I won't be getting hitched that'd be hugely convenient!'

'*You're only doing this because I'm pregnant!*' yelps Chlamydia.

'*Pregnant?*' says Algernon, lightly nonplussed.

Helmut addresses Chlamydia purposively. 'Chlamydia, you've made your own bed – now you must lie in it. Captain Oceanic will come tomorrow at precisely one o'clock to return you to the m-m-mainland.' And to Algernon: 'You will stay so that we can flesh out the finer details of the new alliance.'

And to both Chlamydia and Algernon: 'Maman Terreblanche has surpassed herself with a f-f-farewell feast. *Enjoy!*'

'You're a malicious pig!' hisses Chlamydia as she sets off for the exit.

Algernon's excitement evaporates into a raking cough, prompting Maman Terreblanche to reappear with a modest tumbler of amber liquid.

'Oh Maman to the rescue!' splutters Algernon. 'My *remedy!*' he says, swigging the preparation down in one in the firm belief it has zero active ingredients.

'Don't drink that, Algernon – it's poison!' says Chlamydia, paused in the doorway. '*It's not bellyache – they've been poisoning you all along!*'

Algernon grins wide at Chlamydia's melodramatic outburst but no sooner grimaces enough for the obese spectre to manhandle him from the scene. Chlamydia rounds on Helmut ferociously – but her hot-headed glare is deflected from his burnished indifference as the mirror cracks a smile deserving of seven years' bad luck.

• • • • •

The next morning Chlamydia wakes, packs her few belongings and waits like an evacuee desperate to flee the domestic blitz. When morning reluctantly yields to the prearranged hour, Chlamydia decants her Samsonite bag and amniotic sac from her chamber. She makes a success of avoiding Algernon like the plague but is contaged by backward glances from Isaiah's rickety cart as they escape the house, hoping for a last minute sign of romantic salvation. But nothing. Not even the spasmodic twitch of a lace curtain.

Isaiah makes cursory conversation in lieu of Chlamydia's morbidly absent chitchat and soon they reach the wooden jetty where the driver offers his sincere regrets for having to abandon his charge for the gain of another job. Nevertheless, Chlamydia waits alone, mesmerised by the cosmic swell of the ocean, imagining Captain Oceanic's vessel crystallising in the distance – aware of nothing other than the wistful glimmering between her lucid imagination and the vacant horizon. Time stands still.

And then from nowhere *The Amorous Peacock* appears in all its maritime glory – but so do Algernon and Helmut, loitering behind her. Algernon is grinning from ear to there while Helmut's tics are subdued by jiggling from one foot to the other. Chlamydia naturally assumes they have descended to mock her departure – but when she clocks their sleeveless hunting jackets riddled with utility pockets, their matching hats and rods, she comprehends that her ungracious evacuation is to double as a fishing trip.

No sooner are they on their way than playmates Algernon and Helmut are gripped by stern visions of swordfish, barracuda and marlin. Chlamydia solemnly contemplates the circumstances of her prodigal return, all aloof on the fore deck. Captain Oceanic eventually sees fit to slow to half speed and bark a command to bait their lines while Chlamydia resigns herself to the masculine abduction of her more prosaic desire to return home.

Helmut and Algernon fiddle with hooks and worms under the scornful seaman's eye of Captain Oceanic, and when they are finally good and ready they dangle their tackle into the frothing spume, lounge back in their deck chairs, drink beer and wait for a bite.

So time passes by with the timeless wastefulness and the eternal exaggerations that transform fish into killer whales. So Chlamydia clenches her gills to the fishermen's prattle, allows the nautical defamations to wash over her and sinks into *The Amorous Peacock*'s pitching motion.

Soon enough the peace is disturbed. Algernon yelps with unbridled excitement as his nylon line tightens almost as taut as the steel sinews in Helmut's jealous neck.

'I've got one!' he shouts. 'I've got a fish!'

'Reel it in man!' Helmut snaps. 'What's wrong with you? Wind your s-s-spool! Reel it in! *REEL IT!*'

'Aren't I supposed to "play" it – let it out and pull it back in? Y' know, wear it out?' shouts Algernon in a happy-go-lucky panic.

'No! Just reel the thing in b-b-before you lose it!' shouts Helmut furious at the injustice. Algernon rises to his feet to reel like a madwoman. Helmut shouts invidious commands before the specimen is wrenched from the water, reeled to an inch of its tiny life –

'It's... *an anchovy!*' shouts Helmut. 'You've caught a bloody anchovy!'

'It's piddling!' laughs Algernon. 'You'd lose it in a sandwich!'

Algernon is wracked with laughter, but no sooner is his amusement kidnapped by the cough that plagues his physiology than the tiny fish flaps about on the deck, pursued by epileptic Helmut. Algernon, now bent double at the sight, loses his footing and disappears over the rail into the frothing wake of the vessel's screw. Chlamydia leaps to her feet.

'*Man overboard!*' she yells. '*Man overboard! Help! Captain Oceanic! Algernon's fallen into the sea! He's ill! He can't possibly swim in his state!*'

Helmut abandons the anchovy hunt, and to Chlamydia's utter amazement, hurls himself gracelessly into the sea like a human depth charge. As he sinks like a pebble, a dark triangular fin can be seen to cut the surface of the water near Algernon. It circles around effortlessly, its malicious orbit passing close enough to *The Amorous Peacock* for Chlamydia to notice that the shark's endolymphatic pores, the very sensitive ducts that lead to the macula neglecta and a series of semicircular canals with which the poor beast endeavours to hear, are damaged.

'*My God!* It's the same brute that attacked me!' screams Chlamydia.

Captain Oceanic locks the rudder in the tightest circle possible, but not before the shark commits to the kill. As it closes, speeding up, an upward force lifts it from the water with an expression of earnest surprise plus little Helmut attached to its cheek with t-t-teeth embedded in its sorry hide. Helmut shakes the beast like a rag doll. The shark flees with its fin between its legs, and as the boat slows alongside the two men, Algernon's salty salutation can be heard.

'*You risked your life to save mine!*' he splutters as his carcass is hauled onto the deck. '*Dearest friend, I owe you everything! EVERYTHING! How can I ever repay you?*'

'Oh don't worry!' says Helmut – and under his breath – '*You will...*'

'*I get ze rum from ze cabin, ja?*' adds Captain Oceanic loudly, and casts Helmut a sly wink.

'Well done Helmut for saving Algernon!' chirps Chlamydia. And inside her head – '*Something smells very fishy – and it's not the anchovy's cunt...*'

• • • • •

London was so very pleased to see Chlamydia it wept tears of rain. Her sorry womb swelled up like the balloons that neglected to muster a welcome, and at night she was swept to sleep by floods of tears as her love for Helmut bloated instead of drained away. To escape the malevolent hustle-bustle of South Kensington and an answer machine clogged with Heimlich's relentless petitions, Chlamydia begged Aunt Shigella to come rescue her from her metropolitan meltdown. Dutiful Aunt Shigella appeared before dawn with open arms harbouring an anxious frown for Chlamydia's sunken complexion.

'My dear, you look positively awful!' she announced, docking with her niece in an emphatic hug. 'Fresh air! Plenty of sleep and the unconditional affection of our farm animals is all you need! Come with me to the country!'

Thus flung headlong into dread, they drove into the dawn as though convected into motion by some morbid vortex. Chlamydia observes Aunt Shigella's sentient jowl, her craggy rock-face bathed in the crimson brake light that stabs deep into the broken dawn. As the yawning sun begins its omnipotent deluge a helicopter scythes between silhouetted skyscrapers, grim rotor blades slicing the bilious air and tears of acid rain weeping from Heaven's underbelly. The city street lamps crane to a fluorescent shut down, the odd one adorned by clutches of withered flowers in a spontaneous memento mori to the unjustly mown down. Onwards they weave, passing kerb-crawlers inching along the choked asphalt scouring for affection from tenderised prostitutes who advertise their goods aided by miniature red lights, smoking like factories while soliciting for business on the periphery of the financial district. Where the road thickens to aid escape, the swarm congeals in lava rivulets to flee the city's hideous social intimacy as it rages inside the hardened arteries – the crazy paved crossings, the treacherous mosaic underpasses, pedestrian escape routes, bleached bolt holes and rat runs. Chlamydia and Aunt Shigella haemorrhage past landfill breeding labs, witness the unmitigated overspill that yawns with the mass grave of compound organic trash self-organising from nascent slime to living mucous, the seething tenement hives and colonies of agar estates erupting with sour culture, the cabbage patch kids flowering up through weedkiller hallucinogens, the playgrounds patrolled by packs of rabid dogs ridden by orphan mongoloids riddled with surplus love. Aunt Shigella and Chlamydia squeeze out from the suburb sprawl into no-man's-land where satellite cemeteries and prisons play host to the dead and defunct, where stigmatised flesh is exiled off-world. As the traffic verges upon escape, space stretches out, and metrically placed along the route lonely motels and lowly transit hostels wink with come-to-bed neon. But then the unimaginable compresses into an invertebrate tailback, compelling the mile-long queue of absorbent stares to rubberneck this morning's metallic mutilation – today, a Citroën Xsara Picasso overturned, crumpled, dented and cubist-faceted, thrown from the wreck a weeping woman distraught at the sight of her own ugly creation. Only when *tragedy* has reiterated its forgotten potential in the apparition of disaster, can Chlamydia and Aunt Shigella and the host of unblinking eyeballs continue onwards into the spoilt lattice patchwork of green, yellow and slurry-brown countryside.

• • • • •

In Aunt Shigella's lavishly converted Cotswold farm, Chlamydia's foreboding finally bursts its banks.

'*The engagement is kaput!*' she weeps as Uncle Kaposi shambles into view. '*I'll be alone for ever!*'

'My dear, you look wonderful!' says Kaposi, tipping forward to embrace his niece. 'Fresh as a daisy! I don't know how you girls do it!'

Time, the great healer, dragged by tooth and nail. Chlamydia's anaclitic affection for Aunt Shigella duly fermented, while her inner-biology nurtured the fateful fetus in preparation for the first turbulent breath of air to rattle its untarnished lung.

Lovesick Chlamydia took to the countryside, marched up and down bridlepath, footpath and warpath, pacing the wracked rural pastures of her inner-psyche in a desperate attempt to disentangle the events knotting her mind. She indulged the capricious affection of her aunt's horses and returned their warmth by mucking out. She petted the rescue donkeys, stroked the cats, walked the dogs and shot the rabbits. Aunt Shigella fussed like an old hen, while sly old farmer Kaposi ducked Chlamydia's watery tragedy by militating serf against vermin in the timeless feudal tradition of creating senseless labour. Hell bent on shaking Chlamydia from her spiralling stasis, her kindly aunt distributed pamphlets, brochures, booklets, festival guides, biennales and galas. But Chlamydia was wholly preoccupied by backward reminiscences such that forward motion seemed unfeasible. She did endeavour to contact Algernon (in a vain attempt to glean news of Helmut), only to be told by his PA – *a repulsive blonde going by the pet name of Trixiebellend* – that her boss had relocated to Morass, and severed contact with all that knew him. Derelict of shame, Chlamydia insisted on leaving her chlamydia.love@googlemail.com address, but was no-sooner rewarded with a deluge of messages alluding to the sexual malfunction of the male partner she yearned for. Hence premature hibernation set in, and Chlamydia surrendered to languor, dividing her ennui between daytime TV and night-time torment.

• • • • •

To gain an afternoon's peace from Aunt Shigella's tireless harassment, Chlamydia feigned humble pie, allowing her lifeless husk to be delivered to the pretty village of Carterton where she is duly enrolled into a life-painting class before Aunt Shigella casts an inspired *chow, chow,* and discards her moribund niece into the capable hands of Ruben Threadwell – the vivacious village artist.

Carterton village hall is creativity unbound. The zealous perjuries of the Carterton Dramatic Society haunt the air, and Montessori uric acid sours the nose. Beyond the busy preliminary animations of the art class the far wall hosts a congregation of disreputable youth club furniture with vinyl ritually slashed. Luminous with invidious attempts at self-promotion, the parish notice board is a nested pool of human endeavour, bemoaning lost cats 'n' dogs, oddjobbers, gardeners, babysitters, epiphanic mid-life mystics, damaged reflexologists, patent healers and plain cobblers. Each appeal is drawing-pinned into shallow cork with conviction to crush a skull. Everywhere polite notices nag at waning imperatives:

REMEMBER! RECYCLERS DO IT
AGAIN AND AGAIN!

REMEMBER! SWITCH OFF A LIGHT –
TURN ON THE PLANET!

REMEMBER! NOT ALL ALIENS ARE FROM
OUTER-SPACE – ILLEGAL DOMESTICS ARE
CLEANING US ALL OUT!

Cast adrift from the destitute spiritual aspirations of the adjacent church, the village hall is now the epicentre of a tenacious secular resistance against the violent disaggregation of the universe. Yet the microcosmic chaos Chlamydia sees before her is much like the intensive myopic disorder of her inner-city therapy group. The particles of matter are much the same – odds and sods, damaged in one way or another – brimming with a tendentious energy too eager for healthy release.

Circled by tired old easels, young Joshua, the swarthy life

model, is set upon a sturdy stool, poised nude *or naked* – most likely a local farm hand that urbane Ruben Threadwell has bent towards the arts – is now corralled by elderly glaucoma, a tasteful celebration of his Apollonian physique and Dionysian prowess for the inspiration of those with a creative sensibility. Ruben orbits Joshua's maypole, weaving braids of aesthetic wisdom for the practical benefit of the class.

'Remember... Quickly sketch the basic shapes using a colour that will not overpower the final colours... use pure colour... put it down onto the paper... be decisive... when you work intuitively a painting will paint itself... an artist often exaggerates for effect, he experiments with brushes, texture and technique... remember: be alert and trust your eye, eyes are not always level, noses are not always in the centre of a face... flesh is not always pink – look for colour in the shadows! Think shapes, not mouths – never smiles! Think shapes not eyes... shapes not noses... shapes, shapes, SHAPES!'

Posted to a vacant easel, Chlamydia takes an eyeful of Joshua's sculptural form and dips paintbrush into paint and then plants paint onto paper. She works vigorously from left to right and right to wrong. Presented with the task of painterly verisimilitude, Chlamydia's kooky mind wanders off all on its own. She wonders about Morass – wanders amongst the pretty fauna and flora, the swelling ocean that laps its golden-grey beach. She recalls the proud volcano, and Hotel Krauss set in the leaf-green cavern of the jungle, she journeys back along the endless dusty lanes shaded by giant palms, and breathes the heavy saccharine atmosphere – the purest surgical air that only comas are made of. She visits Isaiah with his sooty face sweeping long and equine like an ass, and his faithful ox. She conjures a mental image of old friends Günter and Brunhilde...

'My word, Chlamydia! You've been a busy-bee! A very busy-bee indeed!' Ruben's counterfeit enthusiasm wrenches

Chlamydia from the stagnant shallows of introspection. All artistic eyes turn to the virtuoso declaimer. 'Well it's plain to see our Joshua failed to move you in the least!' he says. 'You've ignored the poor soul altogether! Joshua, darling, Chlamydia finds you wretchedly uninspiring!' And to Chlamydia: 'What is there to be gained by enrolling on my life class if you insist on indulging your own petty scribblings – one after another?'

Mealy-mouth titters tease at Chlamydia's petrified gape. Nevertheless, her picture is speaking volumes to Ruben, and so he draws closer into its merciless turmoil. His taunting falsetto shears in pitch, as though adolescent – now a manifestly sombre tone betrays the archaic resentment of an unrequited artist buried deep within... 'And yet there is something unusual about this petty scribble... some rare quality... mature beyond its years! Chlamydia – where does this picture come from? It smoulders with seditious expression... so naked, so nude, so bare! Pray tell Chlamydia – how did such a picture come about? What knowledge of sublime torment guides such a young hand?'

Chlamydia's idle mind slops back into the vacant mental void of her skull and is not pleased with what it sees.

'*...Come Hell or High Water...*' a murmur escapes.

Gushing Ruben ushers the other paint-stained hobbyists gather around, and complimentary cooing begins in Pavlo-Heimlichean earnest. Deaf to Ruben's earnest praise, Chlamydia sees how everything that was once hidden inside is now outside – and appalled by her witless descent into earnest catharsis, snatches up her naked symptoms and flees the primal scene. From the godforsaken car park of Carterton's own village hall, a Messianic wail blubbers into Chlamydia's wake:

'*Chlamydia! Dearest Chlamydia! Come back! I want to put you in a group show!*'

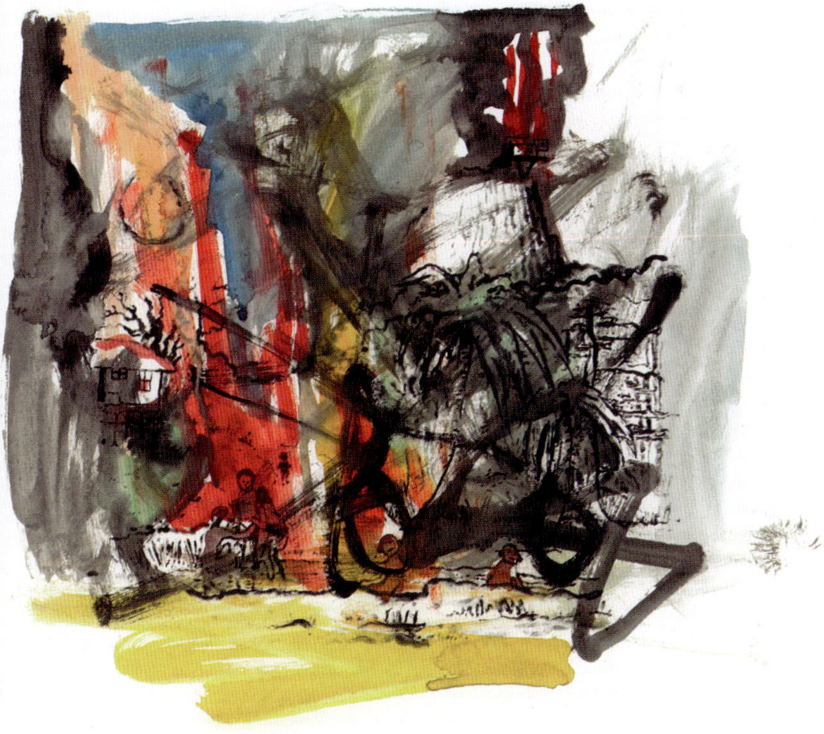

Visions of Morass

Part II

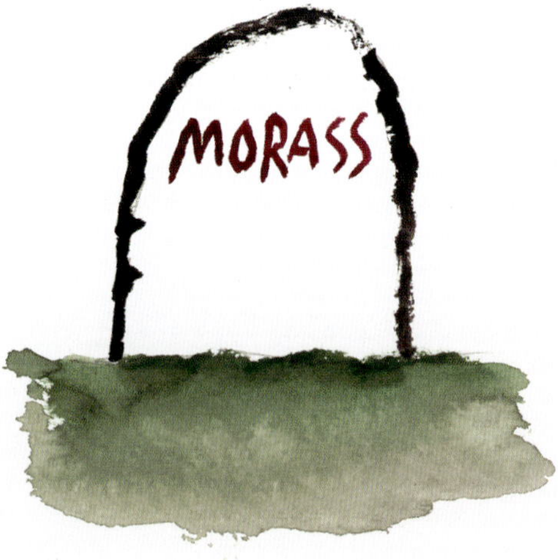
MORASS

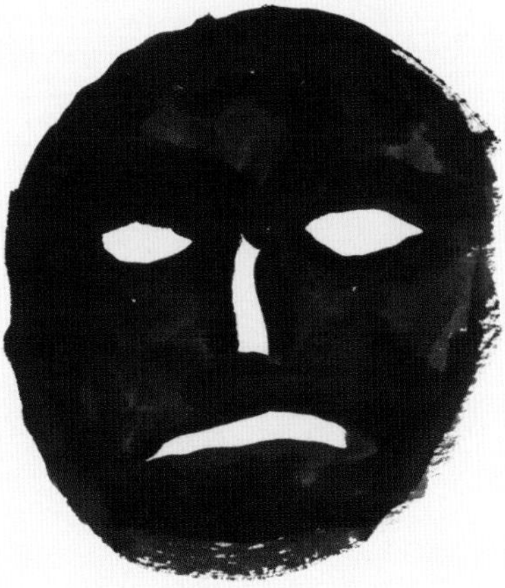

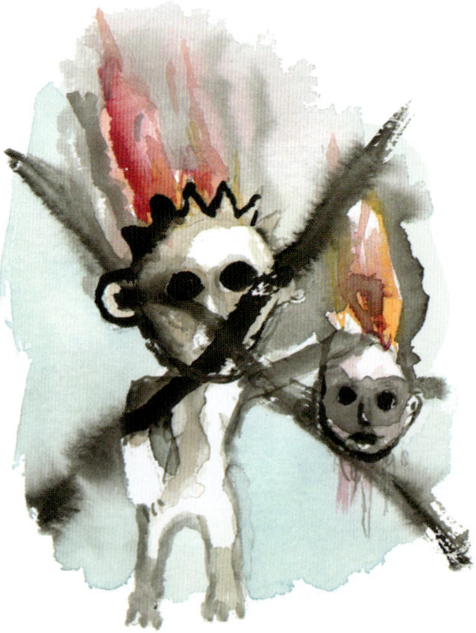

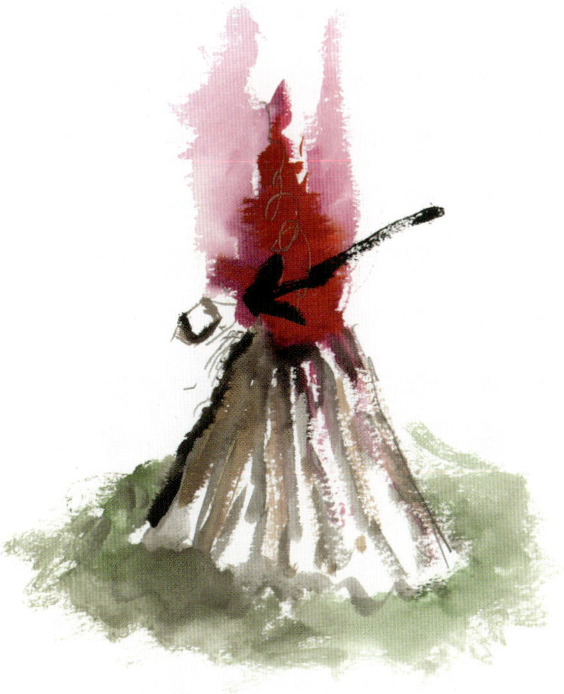

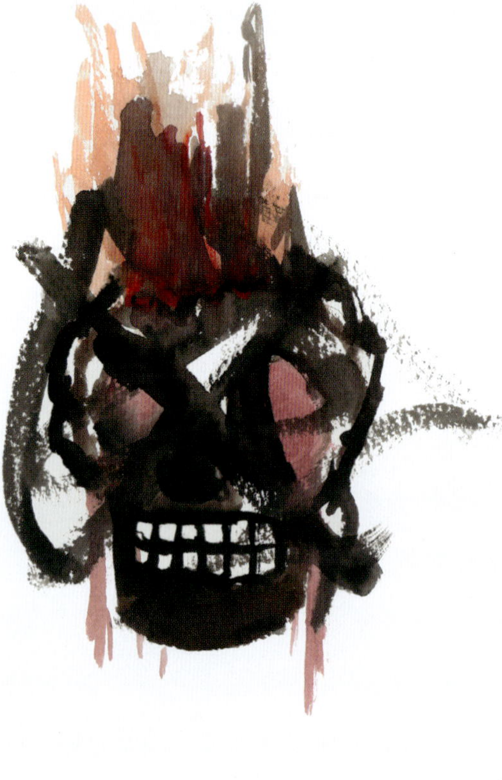

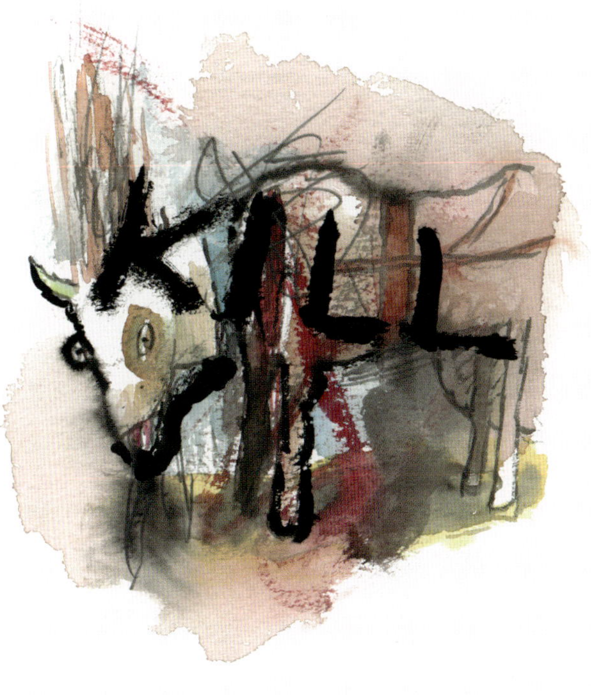
KILL

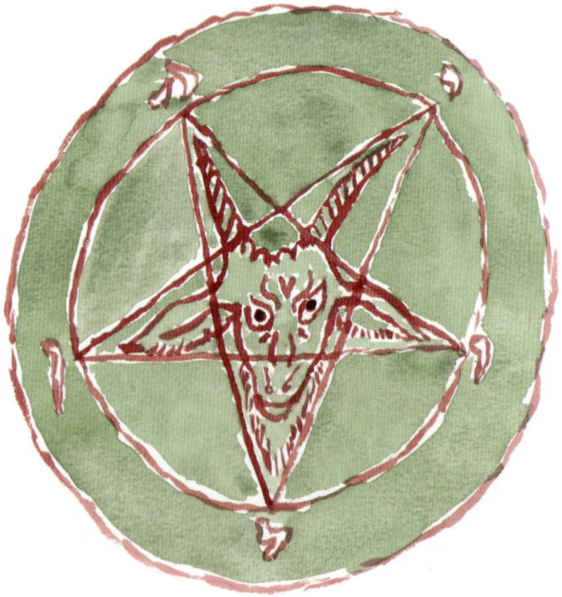

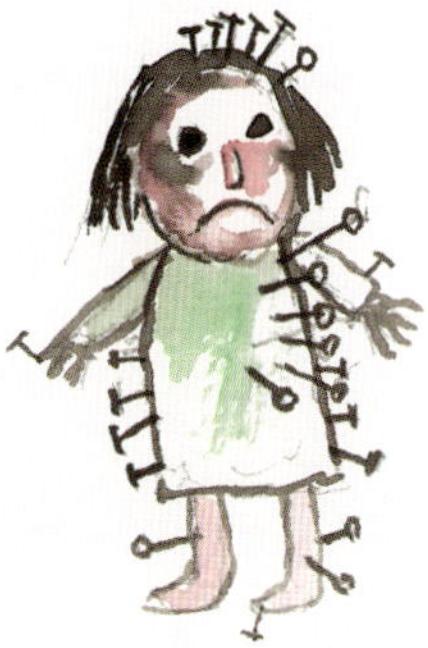

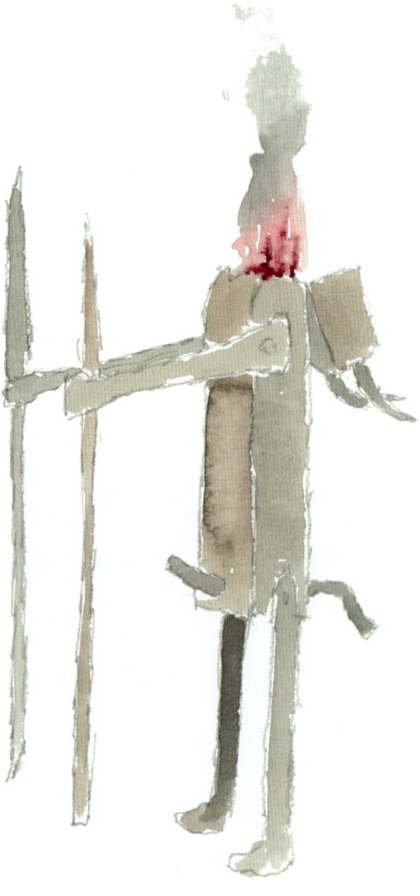

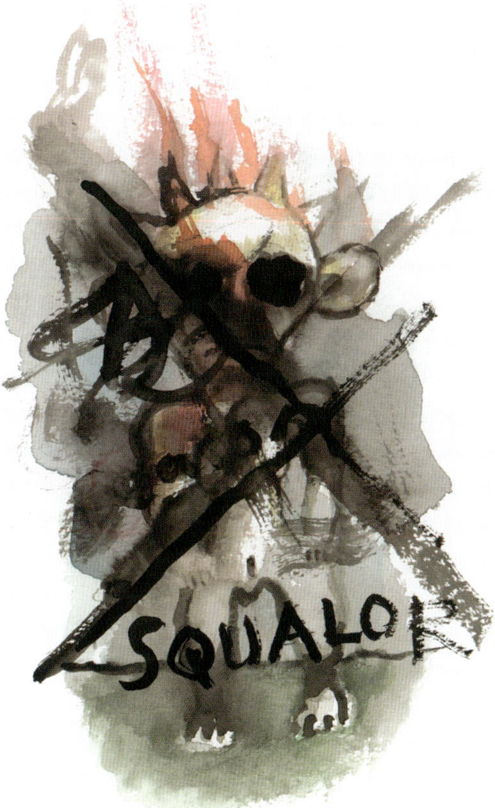
SQUALOR

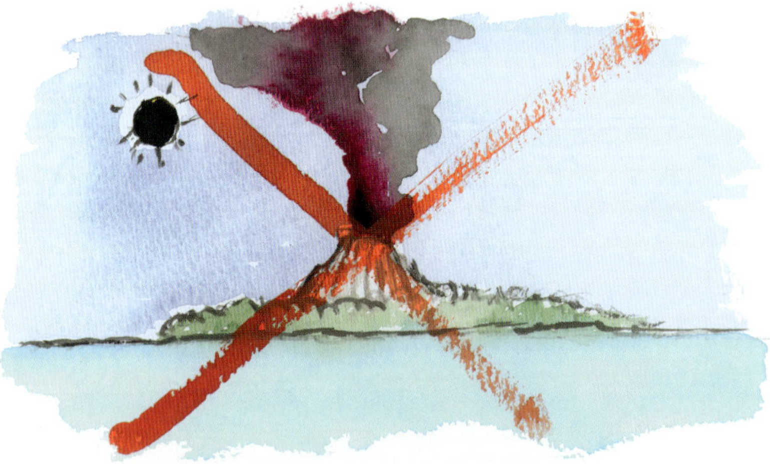

The following evening Aunt Shigella enters Chlamydia's limp periphery to switch channel.

'You don't mind do you? Do you? No? Good! Because the *Culture Show* is on the other side,' she says. 'They're featuring a writer – the real deal...' she says. 'Apparently he single-handedly rescued his best friend from the jaws of a great white! He's rumoured to be quite a formidable character – larger than life. Strange name – *Helmut Mandragorass*. They're spitting blood at the office – livid we missed the opportunity to publish him. Apparently we had the manuscript, but that imbecile Meredith passed on it...'

Chlamydia is suffocating in silence at the vision of Helmut stuttering all hammer and tongs on TV. He endeavours to summarise *Come Hell or High Water* but his physiology is all at odds with his doomed exegesis. The interviewer disguises the author's media malfunction with an exciting announcement of an especially rare appearance at the forthcoming *Guardian* Hay literature festival, and with that – the item caves in to lesbian potholers hellbent on challenging the unabashed phallic tyranny of *Homo erectus* with hard evidence of a neglected antecedent, *Femme domus*.

'Would you like to come – to Hay?' says Aunt Shigella, searching in a nearby drawer for the corresponding brochure. 'Jobwise, I'm obliged to go. But I swear it's a blast! It's not all vindictive northern poets and rejoining southerners. Everyone does book bollocks all day and in the evening we all piss off to the pub and it's bollocks to books and all-out bloody gobbledegook! For God's sake, even Bill Clinton reckons it's the "Woodstock of the mind". Mind you, how would he know – he didn't inhale... I mean, for Christ's sake! He side-stepped drug allegations by saying he only pretended to get stoned! Fuck me Chlamydia! I mean, he even lied to the fucking hippies!'

'Thank you Aunty – but it's not really my cup of tea...'

• • • • •

Aunty Shigella wades back from the glorious sixties, through festival mire, swearing like a trooper, and fending off the truncheon blows of anxious fathers. Chlamydia would surely prefer the company of maggots to the idle chitchat of bookworms, but a chance sighting of the unmentionable is enough to bring her out of her shell. Suffice to say, she knew right there and then that she would attend the literary festival in disguise – a wig, obstructive spectacles, unpresumptuous garb and humble ergonomics to ensure anonymity from the two people she knew to be there – Aunt Shigella and *Helmut Mandragorass*...

• • • • •

As if to mock the bone-dry intellectual pretensions of the gathered literati, black clouds are massed overhead the small market town of Hay-on-Wye with the maleficent threat of returning paper back to pulp. Despite the overhead intimidation, the Braille tent loudly hums with the deaf, dumb and hard of hearing in raucous oblivion – the poetry tent ruminates with metaphysical squalls as the wind tangles with its dainty guyropes. Outside, the evil meteorology even promises to uproot Kafka's bouncy castle and cull a nascent generation of storytellers.

Nevertheless, a kindly mime battling the wind directs Chlamydia to the *Guardian* reading tent where a portentous blackboard mounted on a painter's easel tells the running order of recitations and Booker Prize book signings. Inside, a polite thread of apologies humbles its way through the milling throng to join the main queue leading to a bowing trestle table laden with fresh copies of *Come Hell or High Water*. Sheltering behind, the diminutive spectre of Helmut Mandragorass defaces his own work with scribbled signature.

'Who is it for?' he says wearily and without lifting his eyes. 'What would you like me to write?' he says, now looking up in encouragement of the awkward mute craning over the table. 'Usually people ask me to dedicate it to someone,' he says, *'or they just give me a name…'* But the tongue-tied, bespectacled blonde merely sees his eyes are filled with sadness.

'– For C-C-Cytherea…' she whispers.

Mandragorass's brow gathers into its inertial glitch, before a kinetic shudder frees his cranium of the frozen thought that grips him. He closes the book and hands it *to Cytherea, with love, Helmut Mandragorass…*

Behind Helmut, Aunt Shigella mingles with the upper echelons of the British publishing world. Chlamydia wilts back into the tangle as Helmut is rescued from the queue of rasping corduroy and canvas shoulder bag by a festival official, only to be drawn into an inexorable orgy of shaking hands. So he freely nods and smiles but resists the latent winks and tics – nervously strained in defiance of the next imminent epileptic spasm haunting his nerve-wrenched mass. In the mêlée, Helmut's tiny paw is permutationally destined to meet Aunt Shigella's, and when it does, a breathless niece observes aunt and ex-lover swap professional pleasantries like flower and bee. Then, *Helmut Mandragorass* is announced to rapturous applause, and the chitter-chatter settles. The author effects his composure, and commences thus into the microphone:

'Th-th-thank you for your kind reception… I would like to r-r-read from *C-C-Come Hell or High Water*.' He pauses… clears his throat… catches his breath… pauses once more… 'huh-hmmm… S-s-she opened the d-d-door and s-s-stared into the indelible face. Her heart pounded violently and she stood b-b-back for him to enter.

"Please come in," she said f-f-faintly.

Anton s-s-stepped past her, then waited while she closed the door. He had f-f-flowers. He was much t-t-taller than she remembered, so very handsome, and she could only manage a weakish smile as she led the way into the sitting room. He wore a smart dark suit with a beautiful black shirt and yet looked familiar and yet unfamiliar all at the same time.

"My aunt said you might come..." she said.

"Dear Celia, you're exactly as I remember you were – a bit ashen in the face, perhaps, but I expect that's because of your illness," he said.

"Yes. The flu," she said. "Would you like a cup of tea?"

"Tea. Yes of course. That would be very nice. A nice cup of tea would be nice." He followed her into the kitchen where he watched her movements closely as she reached up to get the best teacups and saucers from the cupboard high above the sink.

"Why did you leave London?" he said.

"I wanted to get away from anything that reminded me of my past," she said.

"It was quite difficult finding you," he said. "If it hadn't been for your aunt I'd still be scouring all over the Earth," he said.

Celia's mouth fell open at Anton's vulnerability. "But why did you want to find me?"

"Don't you know?" he laughed. "Isn't it completely obvious to you?"

She shook her head and her lovely shiny hair flicked between her shoulder blades like a horse's tail. "No. I have no idea," she said.

"Well I'll show you then if you don't know." He came towards her with a gleam in his eyes.

Although she felt as if she wanted to back away and save

herself it felt as if she was hypnotised and was rooted to the very spot she stood on. His eyes held her eyes and her breathing became constricted. His hands were sliding up her back as he pulled her into his chest with great strength. She felt as though she might have the life squeezed out of her, but really didn't mind dying here and now in his powerful arms –

"Oh Celia," he said. "I've missed you so much I could have died a thousand times over and over again."

"I've missed you too," she said.

"Come back to Morass with me. I can't live without you – it's too unpleasant for my heart," he said.

But Celia is plagued by thoughts of Anton's wife and child and so the idea of being his mistress goes against everything she believed in. "I can't," she said.

Anton fell limp. "But I've pursued you halfway across the world! Isn't that enough for you?"

"But you're here to promote *Come Hell or High Water*."

"That too. But it was the only way I could justify to myself coming back to England to look for you. I scoured London."

"I'm sorry Anton, but I will not return to your island," she said.

'Why the hell not?' he replied.

Because I love you too much, she wanted to say out loud for him to hear. She wanted to tell him, but when she sensed her aunt's perfume waft from the front door she realised she had never been so thankful in all her life. Aunty came straight into the kitchen.

'Oh you came!' she said cheerily. 'I'm so glad.'

Anton greeted Aunt Shigella's cheeks, and smiling warmly said: 'You're just in time for tea.'

Once the tea was made they took their cups and the teapot on a tray into the living room and Aunt Shigella began:

'So, dear boy, tell me – why has Chlamydia been so secretive about your liaison?' she said.

'Aunt Shigella!' said Chlamydia as if she'd given away a secret.

'Chlamydia darling, it would have remained a mystery if I hadn't come across the charming dedication in his book!'

Helmut looked amused at Chlamydia's discomfort and Aunt Shigella continued:

'I've read *Come Hell or High Water* – it was a very good read. You have a unique voice.'

'Thank you, but you really don't have to say anything like that,' he said politely.

Aunt Shigella rose to her feet. 'No, I meant it – really – I should know, I'm a senior editor at a major publishing house. Anyway, enough of my chitchat – I'll go and put dinner on and leave you two love-birds alone. Helmut you must stay for dinner.'

Left alone, Chlamydia was resigned to an uncomfortable silence.

'Is something wrong? Would you prefer it if I were to leave?' he said.

'No. I'm just overwhelmed by the sight of you,' she said.

'But why don't you come back to Morass, Chlamydia? Please come!' he pleaded.

'Because... Because I can't *just* be your mistress,' she blurted out loud.

Helmut was astonished. He slid to his knees in front of her. 'My dearest Chlamydia. Isn't it clear? It's a wife I want. I love you with all of my heart. Life has been Hell since you left. Please – I love you desperately!'

Tears welled in her eyes as he spoke. She could hardly believe what her ears were hearing.

'Be your wife,' she said. 'How? What about *her?*'

'*Her?* My wife? My wife is dead, God rest her soul,' he said quietly. 'I thought you knew. Didn't my mother tell you?'

'No.' Chlamydia was sincerely horrified. 'I had no idea – I'm so sorry.'

'Don't be,' he said, leaning forward to hold her tightly. 'It happened a long time ago. But the death of my son was so unbearable.'

Chlamydia was aghast. 'Both of them dead?'

He nodded. 'Both dead. Drowned – a terrible boating accident.'

'It must have destroyed you!' she cried.

'Things were difficult between me and my wife at the time – she was trying to take little Joseph away from me, never let me see him. I grew to despise her.'

Chlamydia's tears spilled over, soaking his shirt as she buried her face in his chest. 'Helmut,' she whimpered, 'I am so sorry they both drowned!'

'There's no need,' he said. 'It's all water under the bridge.'

'Is that why you resented me when you first met me, why I had to stay in that horrible little room?' she said.

He nodded. 'I thought you'd turn out like her. I wanted to love you, but was afraid. It was only after you'd gone did I realise just how much in love I was and that I wasn't afraid.'

'I wish you'd said,' she said. 'It would have made such a difference. I was quite convinced that you still had a wife somewhere and only wanted to see me as your mistress. I do love you Helmut, I've loved you since the first day we met – even before. I've loved you all my life.'

'I know,' he said. 'Algernon told me when you left. It drove me out of my mind. I had to find you.'

Chlamydia frowned. 'I left word that I had come to the country – in the vain hope that you might try to seek me out here. I didn't want to disappear off the face of the planet without trace, just in case.'

'I tried to find you – I was beside myself. You were the only reason I agreed to do the *Guardian* Hay literary festival because I made a point of asking them to mention it on television – hoping you'd find out and come and find me there.'

'Oh Helmut I did! I came in disguise! I saw you – oh Helmut!'

'Darling Chlamydia, you have no idea! If you refuse to marry me now I don't think I could go on living.'

'I'll marry you, Helmut!' she cried joyfully. 'But I have a confession to make first...'

'Nothing you say will make the slightest difference.' Helmut holding her close so that she felt absolutely safe and secure – like the most wanted woman in the whole wide world.

'I read your book, I read most of *Come Hell or High Water* when I was on Morass. But I didn't realise it was about you and me...'

She expected anger, but he smiled with the warmth of the Morassean sun.

'I don't mind. It was a difficult book to write but now it's done and dusted. With you as my wife I shall be able to forget the past and move on.'

'I promise to make you happy,' she said softly.

'I know,' he said and pressed his lips upon her lips, and for a while time stood perfectly still.

From the couch, an apathetic blink spies a mischievous twinkle in Aunt Shigella's beady eye. Shigella is bent over her sleepy niece, keen to wake her and give the bestseller she has just purchased from Carterton village book store.

Chlamydia reads: '*Come Hell or High Water*,' she shrugs: 'By Helmut Mandragorass... *so?*'

'Open it... read the dedication printed inside.'

The beautifully illustrated cover creaks open to the first crisp page.

'*For Chlamydia Love... so what?*'

Chapter Ten

'Well, you tell me…'

'It's true. I had the fortune of meeting the mysterious Helmut Mandragorass on the island of Morass. He owns it. He offered me lodgings in return for taking dictation, editorial – *that sort of thing*. Algernon sent me there because he said he was to buy the island as a wedding gift. Naturally, Algernon's generosity turned out to be as *priceless* as my engagement ring. Marooned in paradise, it dawned upon me that I didn't love Algernon at all – I just thought I did. I terminated relations and fled home. Regarding the dedication, I can only assume Mandragorass is belatedly expressing gratitude for my help with his novel… Dear Aunt – that's it in a nutshell – *now leave me be!*'

'Well it sounds like you did the right thing – *I only hope I did…*'

'Did what?' Chlamydia's attention sits up to beg.

'*You'll see* –'

• • • • •

Later that very day, Richard and Judy are rudely disturbed by an unexpected knock at the front door. For once, the omnipresent Aunt Shigella is nowhere to be seen and so her lethargic niece must tear nerve endings away from her afternoon lobotomy to answer it.

She stares into the indelible countenance as a stinging heart leaps up through hiatus hernia into bilious mouth.

'*Come in.*'

Helmut steps past, waits gingerly, wilting into the florid Laura Ashley, while Chlamydia bolts the stable door. He has flowers – offers them out from the tangled wallpaper. She says thank you, cold like a robot. He is much smaller than memory recalls. She affords a weak smile before Aunt Shigella's scent miraculously fills the interstitial void.

'Oh you came by!' she says all cheery-pops. 'I'm so glad. Chlamydia, why don't you take your guest into the living room – I'll put the kettle on. Is Darjeeling to your taste, Mr Mandragorass?'

Aunt Shigella takes Chlamydia's pretty wreath into the kitchen. She bounces back with a tray of tea, which she sets upon the occasional coffee table.

'There!' she says. 'Isn't that nice? I've got to jolly-well pop off to the butchers to buy some yummy tripe. It was very nice meeting you Mr Mandragorass. Maybe Chlamydia will invite you to stay for din-dins. Oh, and I shan't expect you to eat the dog's dinner! *Chow! Chow!*'

Aunt Shigella exits with Chlamydia hot on her heels.

'*You can't leave me here on my own with him!*' she hisses.

'Why? You managed quite well all that time on the island…'

Helmut perches on the edge of his seat, balances on the edge of sanity, casting an abnormal smile, a facial contortion emblematic of strained containment rather than social mutuality. Chlamydia can plainly see he has effectively passed the point of no return, and even the popular success of his new novel has failed to temper his volcanic state of mind. Why is he here? After rejecting her so emphatically on Morass? Why is Chlamydia being drawn back into the labyrinths of Helmut's inner-pandemonium?

'– I imagine you're over the moon about the success of *Come Hell or High Water…*' risks Chlamydia, sitting down, breaking the ice.

'*Ecstatic*… It's a perverse twist of fate to be sure.' His eyes defer attention to the table, 'I hope you don't mind – in your absence I took the liberty of being mother…'

'Thank you…' says Chlamydia, taking her cup, smiling and sipping.

The Darjeeling tastes oddly familiar and familiarly odd.

'*Oh no…*'

'*OH YES!*' snorts Helmut, leaping to his trotters. '*Maman Terreblanche s-s-sends her love! You h-h-humiliated me! Broke my h-h-heart! You let Algernon in through the back door so he could turn Morass into a surgical haven to ugly rich hags! You think I'd let that fucking imbecile steal my island for the purpose of his superficial butchery? Never!*'

'But you invited him to stay! I was there! You asked him to stay so you could discuss his plans!' cries Chlamydia. 'And what have you done to Algernon? Not a squeak from him since I left Morass!'

'*Still your precious Algernon? – I gave him just what he wanted! I gave him my island! GAVE HIM MORASS!*'

'What do you mean? *Where is he?*'

'On his beloved Morass… *for ever!*'

'*Why… you killed him?*'

'Not quite…'

Chlamydia tries to evade the gluttonous comfy armchair now swallowing her hole but slumps back, all light-headed.

'*You even got rid of your wife and child – didn't you?*' she gasps. '*Admit it you monster! You murdering pig! You filthy murdering monster-pig!*'

Helmut kneels down before Chlamydia. He is scrutinising her very closely. Pure malice leans forward to pinch her limp arm, which fails in turn to react with even a hint of a withdrawal reflex. Chlamydia is now wholeheartedly inert – save for the passive obscenity of her eyes – watching as a bespoke canvas pouch unrolls in front of her feet, presenting a family of stainless tools as sharp as the light that grazes along their edges. From an inside pocket Helmut conjures a textbook, flattens it with his palm and follows its direction with a studious finger:

'To begin… *a straight transverse incision below the line joining the anterior… superior… iliac spines…* Hey ho! – A transverse incision it shall be!'

'Helmut!' the patient slurs. 'What on earth are you doing?'

Helmut returns his attention from textbook to Chlamydia like a consultant condescending to the lay symptoms of his patient. But this patient has already conceded to pitilessness, numbness has slipped into paralysis, torpor sliding into coma.

'How rude of me! – Please excuse my appalling bedside manner!' Helmut hurries to his feet, snatches one of Aunt Shigella's lacy throws from the couch to toss over Chlamydia's anaesthetised head.

'There! Avert your eyes! Chlamydia – I presume such a sensitive flower to be squeamish!' And then: 'Now, if you're sitting comfortably,' he says, 'I'll begin. But remember children! – The first cut is the deepest… *subcutaneous tissue bulges upward after the skin is cut and floods with blood…* there… so it does!'

Beneath the censorious Victorian veil the patient is aware of forceful pressure being applied to the lower half of her body – in fact, she is now a dense lump of blubber being manhandled without consideration for her modesty.

'*Cut beneath the subcutaneous tissue… to the layer of fibrous tissue holding the muscles and abdominal organs of the abdominal wall in place… incise this layer and using the index… and third fingers… s-t-r-e-t-c-h the abdominal wall layers in a caudal-cranial direction…* caudal-cranial? *…thereby enabling the separation of layers… The p-p-parietal p-p-peritoneum is also opened transversely to avoid damage to the bladder…* damage to the bladder? I don't think we need concern ourselves with that…'

Alone in the lacy gloom, Chlamydia considers the blatant discontinuity between the painstaking surgical instructions being diligently read out aloud and the gouging, scraping and cack-handed mutilation she knows is occurring by the sheer brute force and sound of Helmut's personal industry downstairs.

'*Peel bladder away from uterus*...' he grunts, '...*make incision in uterus underneath, through the thin segment so as not to harm the baby*...' he groans, '...*further manual lateral stretching of the uterine incision*...' he heaves, '...*with exteriorisation of the uterus, place two index fingers into small incision to first allow fluid to spill*...' he moans, '...*then place hand inside the uterus*...' he labours onwards, '...*feel for the head*... Yuk! Got it! Ha! Now for the moment of truth! Yes! Here it is! *Algernon's love-child – from his mother's womb untimely ripp'd!*'

Wrenched from Chlamydia's body the gelatinous squelch of human brawn being purged into the world devoid of any corresponding maternal sensation downstairs. Numb-nuts can do nothing more but eavesdrop the inharmonious sounds and gauge Helmut's reaction to the arrival of her newborn.

'*It's*................. *A BOY! IT'S A LITTLE BOY!*' he mocks – 'AAAAAA! HOW CUTE!' Adding – 'My oh my! What little *hands* you have... What little *arms* you have... What little *legs* you have... *My-oh-my-oh-my! – WHAT AN ENORMOUS FUCKING HEAD YOU HAVE! Mummy's surely thankful you left home by the window and not the catflap! And what rusty-red hair you have!*'

From the anaesthetic depths of Maman Terreblanche's blowfish venom, Chlamydia's sanity struggles to release the dreadful truth permeating the doily darkness – a frail whisper barely escaping Chlamydia's autonomic shutdown:

'*Look at him Helmut! Look at him! I can't even see my baby – but I know he's yours!' she gasps. 'He's your child Helmut! Your own flesh and blood – it's the truth! HE'S YOUR SON!*'

To this obscenity the infant's *black hole* vents a primordial utterance, the violent *breath of chaos* unleashed in the first shriek of the *big bang*:

'WAAAAAAAAAAAAAAAAAAAAH!'

Helmut's own engorged *red dwarf* shrieks its bloodcurdling return:

'LIAR! LIAR! P-P-PANTS ARE ON FIRE! THIS HERE VILE CLOT WRIGGLING FOR DEAR LIFE IS ALGERNON'S BUNDLE OF JOY, NOT MINE! I WON'T BE DUPED BY YOUR MENDACIOUS LIES! I WON'T PERMIT YOU TO JILT MY FEELINGS AGAIN! AND YOU WON'T DEPRIVE ME OF MY RIGHTEOUS R-R-REVENGE!'

'Oh Helmut! You've surely lost the plot! What are you saying?'

Evil calms its ugly head:

'Well let me jog your memory…' he says. 'You made an unmitigated mockery of Morass and Nature in general, turned mother and father against their beloved son! Maman Terreblanche has nothing but disdain for my emotional frailty and Isaiah and Isaiah's ox refuse my c-c-custom. You even scuppered my writing – stole my happy ending! Come Hell or High Water *is nothing but a parody! A charade! A sham! Little more than a romantic novel, legitimately despised by anyone with an iota of judiciousness – you've reduced me to a caricature, belittled by my own shadow! A two-bit clown, a buffoon! – A village idiot suckling on a sow's teat for the entertainment of scorners! You came to Morass, infected me with yearning – then cured the infection and left me with nothing – not even pain – abysmal emptiness. I've subsisted with the misfortune of being born! My daily death wish only underscores a cowardly reluctance to relinquish a life that was from the outset a matter of sublime bad luck!'*

'But Helmut! – Everything is different now! *It's just you – me – and our son!* He was yours all along! Not Algernon's! But I didn't know… How could I? It must have been some kind of freak immaculate conception? Please Helmut, *DADDY… lift the veil from my head, let me set eyes upon our child!'*

'OVER YOUR DEAD B-B-BODY!'

Chlamydia's mortal transience is seeping into Aunt Shigella's pretty Afghan war rug. She nonetheless conjures a comforting image of Helmut swaddling the helpless infant in his smart dark suit jacket. But a lifetime's contempt is beating down on her wilting corpse like the profligate beams of the Morrasean sun. And then Helmut's voice, this time gentle and tender –

'Hush now! There, there! Be calm, oddity! Be calm little one – be calm Hans Mandragorass.'

And as the worms and maggots somewhere stir, Chlamydia summons a dying rapprochement: *'But how does it end Helmut? How does it all end? You know I can't bear reaching the end of a book only to find death lingering on the final page!'*

'I'm leaving it wide open Chlamydia,' says Helmut, *'wide open for the sequel… But don't fret Chlamydia, only in death does a being become larger than life…'*

And with that, the lights are killed and hope extinguished. The door clicks shut and daddy wails from the scene with *little Hans* cradled in teeny arms. And in the darkness, a lone voice:

'I am the turd that is ready and the world is the wide open anus…'

Epilogue

The silver shore unfolds a cool sea breeze sweeping inland. Earth is scorched black for nightmares to rage and all seems well with the dying world. Supernatural beams deflected from sun to moon illuminate the dazzling piety of the white church. Freshly laid daisies shiver in the cemetery as the hallowed soil stirs with a lifeless hand, clawing up through loose dirt – *Consultant Surgeon Algernon Hertz wakes to a posthumous inheritance of the paradise island of Morass…*